Praise for Scott Frank's
Shaker

"A gripping, strikingly original debut novel. . . . Every one of the characters, in particular the teenage gangbangers, springs to vivid and tragic life." —*Booklist*

"I never give quotes. But I love thrillers. And *Shaker* is the best thriller I've read in years. Someone needed to say that." —William Goldman, author of *Marathon Man*

"Frank captures the underbelly of Los Angeles's streets to perfection with sharply written prose and biting dialogue. . . . A richly layered crime story." —*BookPage*

"Screenwriter Frank's well-plotted first novel will remind readers of Tom Wolfe's novel *The Bonfire of the Vanities*. . . . Impressive psychological detail." —*Publishers Weekly*

"Scott Frank's *Shaker* is brilliant and dazzling and everything good. Reading it, it's not hard to believe the author wrote two perfect-pitch adaptations of Elmore Leonard novels. . . . This is one hell of a good book, and I can't stop myself from saying so." —Lawrence Block, author of the Matthew Scudder series

"*Shaker* is very, very, very good. Hard-core and real in every moment. Crazy pure characters, instantly alive and unique. Platinum dialogue—although that was a gimme with Scott Frank—but still. It's sick and funny and perfectly detailed. I was even fooled by the end—never saw it coming until I was supposed to. And yeah, it's a page-turner."

—Tony Gilroy, writer and director
of *The Bourne Legacy* and *Michael Clayton*

"'Thriller' is the perfect way to describe *Shaker* because it's a rush to read. It's smart, funny, compelling, and complex. It's kick-ass entertainment."   —Janet Evanovich,
author of the Stephanie Plum series

"*Shaker* is a stunning debut novel—a smart thriller that grabs you by the throat from the opening scene and keeps you on edge as it races to the end. Scott Frank brings an exciting new literary voice to the crime genre—totally unique, with a hint of homage to the great Elmore Leonard."

—Linda Fairstein, author of *Devil's Bridge*

Scott Frank

Shaker

Scott Frank began his career writing such films as *Little Man Tate* and *Dead Again*. His screenplay adaptation for *Get Shorty* was nominated for a Golden Globe Award and a Writers Guild Award for adapted screenplay. Frank's adaptation for *Out of Sight* received an Academy Award nomination and won a Writers Guild Award. Frank also wrote the screenplays for *Heaven's Prisoners, Minority Report, The Interpreter, Marley & Me,* and *The Wolverine.* He wrote and made his directorial debut in 2007 with *The Lookout,* which won the Independent Spirit Award for Best First Feature. Most recently, Frank adapted and directed *A Walk Among the Tombstones. Shaker* is his first novel.

Shaker

Shaker

Scott Frank

VINTAGE CRIME/BLACK LIZARD
Vintage Books
A Division of Penguin Random House LLC
New York

FIRST VINTAGE CRIME/BLACK LIZARD EDITION, JANUARY 2017

The Library of Congress has cataloged the Knopf edition as follows:
Frank, Scott.
Shaker : a novel / Scott Frank.
pages cm
1. Murder for hire—Fiction.   2. Assassins—Fiction.   I. Title.
PS3606.R3845S63 2016   813'.6—dc23   2015025230

Vintage Books Trade Paperback ISBN: 978-0-345-80570-6
eBook ISBN: 978-0-385-35004-4

Book design by Iris Weinstein

www.weeklylizard.com

Printed in the United States of America
10 9 8 7 6 5 4 3 2 1

For Jennifer, who knows why

Part I

Prologue

A swarm of nearly seven hundred small earthquakes—most in the 2.0 to 3.0 range—rattled the Mojave Desert between June and September. The Little Shakers, as geologists began referring to them, were centered mainly in and around the area of Joshua Tree National Park, about 130 miles to the southeast of Los Angeles. There were few injuries, all minor, and the only reported fatality happened when a twenty-six-year-old rock climber named Erik Comeau, bivouacked for the night a few hundred feet up the face of a granite formation known as "G-String," fell out of his mummy bag. There was, however, some question as to whether it was one of the tiny quakes that caused Comeau's fall or the handful of Granddaddy Purple gummies he'd ingested a few hours earlier, the residual amount of cannabis in his system being well over the 1.5 number that ultimately pinged the Richter scale.

The explanation for the sudden seismic frenzy was sourced to the long California drought, by then in its sixth year. Groundwater, having seeped deeper and deeper into the parched and panting earth, was steadily building up pressure while at the same time lubricating the myriad underground plates that made up the Pinto Mountain Fault, thereby making it a lot easier for the ground to move.

And move it did.

By the first week of September, the Pinto Mountain quakes had grown stronger. Eventually, one of them tipped the Ricky at 4.2 and gave a hard shove to the bigger Rialto-Colton Fault in Riverside, provoking a 5.0 "roller" that did little more than set off car alarms, knock a few soccer trophies off shelves, and, most damagingly, send shards of broken glass into the salad bar at an Olive Garden in San Dimas.

Less than twenty-four hours later, the still settling fault under the Rialto-Colton basin gave what amounted to a gentle pat on the back to a northward section of the much larger San Andreas Fault, which, in turn, delivered a more vigorous jolt to the Hollywood Fault to the west. These last two handoffs were made possible by a grant from ExxonMobil, whose extensive fracking around the Los Angeles basin allowed for what might have remained a local event to now expand some fifty miles through newly created fractures in the bedrock.

So it was on September 2, at four minutes after ten p.m., a shaker with what would later be determined as a moment magnitude of 7.1, a Modified Mercalli intensity of IX ("Violent"), and ground accelerations that went a full 2Gs, grabbed the city of Los Angeles by the throat, and throttled it like a wolf on a weasel for a full twenty-two seconds.

The worst damage was in Hollywood, where portions of over a dozen large structures, including the Chinese Theatre and the Roosevelt Hotel, collapsed. A mile-long stretch of Sunset Boulevard kicked up and started rolling along in a two-foot wave of twisting asphalt that knocked Priuses onto sidewalks and ruptured water and gas mains, creating the unusual circumstance of fires and floods at the same time.

A mixed-use development, including two residential high rises still under construction at the corner of Argyle Avenue and Yucca Street, suffered major fire damage when a sinkhole some eighty feet in diameter opened up between the structures, causing a gas explosion so big it could be seen from downtown. A dozen more sinkholes, one over a city block long, opened up all along Hollywood Boulevard. The parking garage below a new condominium building on Western Avenue collapsed into yet another crater, taking four of the twelve units with it.

Inside the Body Shop, a strip club on Sunset, performers and patrons alike found themselves inside a warping and rippling house of mirrors before the lights went out and the panicked horde began crashing into the glass and each other in an effort to get the fuck out. A bouncer and several dancers made it to the street, the latter clad only in the velvet curtains they managed to yank down in the midst of their escape.

In Griffith Park to the east, eighty-foot-tall pines were cracked like bullwhips, snapping off at the top and leaving the ground throughout the park strewn with what looked like miniature Christmas trees.

One of the weirdest Act of Godliest events had to be when eleven members in good standing of the Rollin' 30s Crips were killed as the marquee and part of the exterior of the El Capitan movie theater came down on top of them. Only moments before, the R30Cs were in the middle of what would later be described by law enforcement as a "mass mugging," running up and down the sidewalks, knocking tourists on their asses, grabbing cell phones and handbags as they went. Most of the homies were piling into four cars when the ground opened up and swallowed two of the vehicles whole, while the toppling building buried the rest.

Many of the collapses along the boulevard were facades, turning some of the older structures into giant dollhouses, the rooms visible from the street once the shaking stopped and the dust settled. The image of a seventy-nine-year-old ex–background player named Della Kress hanging on to the side of a clawfoot bathtub, legs dangling from the now exposed eighth floor of the Montecito Apartments, would be all over YouTube by the morning.

A few blocks away, the American Cinematheque was just wrapping up an event at the Egyptian Theatre when a good portion of the ceiling in the auditorium came down. Luckily, the evening's program had been a Henry Jaglom retrospective and the theater was only a quarter full. The collapse of the Egyptian would ultimately claim six lives and send eleven to the hospital, all the result of cardiac arrest, save one ruptured bladder.

The people in the parking structure behind the undamaged ArcLight theater a mile away weren't so lucky. While the crowd exited the cushy multiplex in relative calm, there was mass panic inside the swaying cement parking lot behind it; people running over and into each other trying to get the hell out of there. The Heyman family of Los Feliz, five in all, had just safely escaped the structure and were pulling out onto De Longpre Avenue when, above them, a panicked driver in a Chevy Tahoe accidentally launched himself off the roof of the structure and came crashing down onto their Subaru Forester, instantly killing everyone in both cars.

At Hollywood Presbyterian Medical Center on Vermont several surgeries, including one open heart, were aborted as patients were thrown from their beds, while next door a sewer main at Children's Hospital burst and flooded the basement cafeteria and the first floor with a four-foot-deep mix of human and medical waste.

Outside of Hollywood, the impact was significantly less, though, in Pasadena, the Fuller Seminary suffered enough damage it had to be shut down and relocated to a former roller skating palace along the L.A. River in Glendale. And while downtown L.A. was left, for the most part, unscathed, an entire wall collapsed at the Sumner Redstone Building at the USC Film School. There was some damage—mostly cracks and buckles—to many roadways, including the partial collapse of the elevated carpool lane connecting the 110 and the 105 freeways—that one taking out some twenty-seven vehicles including one city bus and a catering truck.

Up in Beachwood Canyon, every letter except the "H" and the "Y" in the iconic Hollywood sign was either knocked down or damaged in the shaking. A dozen drunken tourists who'd hiked up in the dark to take a group selfie while sitting in the crossbar of the letter "H" were sent to the hospital with injuries varying from broken bones to impalements.

L.A.'s main communication tower on nearby Mount Lee went down while over on Mount Wilson two microwave towers and three TV towers toppled onto one another like dominoes. Throughout the city, cell phone towers—many of them disguised as fake palm trees and all of them top-heavy—hit the ground in neighborhoods even where the shaking wasn't as strong.

This last bit of damage would take the city back to the pre-cell-phone stone age of the early nineties. For weeks following the quake, people would gather at a few hot spots throughout the county in order to make calls. Places like the parking lot at Dodger Stadium were full of antsy folks sitting in their cars, talking on their phones. MacArthur Park and the Griffith Observatory became prime hot spots to hang out and make a few calls. Certain minimalls put up signs saying that their parking lots were "up zones." Security guards would monitor the lots, the stores charging by the minute for spaces where one could stay a full five minutes for free, but only after patronizing one of the stores.

Somehow, Brentwood, Beverly Hills, and Bel Air were all untouched. Residents in Pacific Palisades and Malibu found themselves with little damage beyond the occasional toppled chimney. A month earlier there had been a fire in the hills along the Pacific Coast Highway and, afterward, all anyone saw when driving through parts of Malibu were chimneys without houses. After the Hollywood Quake, on the Westside, there were now hundreds of houses without chimneys.

It was as if the quake had broken the city's neck, twisting its head around to some grotesque angle while leaving everything above and below looking relatively normal.

In the end, some eleven thousand people would be sent to hospitals all over Southern California while a mere 137 would be sent to the morgue.

Was this "The Big One"? It was hard to say. Some thought it was. The folks on the Westside sure hoped it was, *believed* it was, heaving a big sigh of relief when they realized they had gotten through it relatively unscathed.

Until two weeks later, when an aftershock of almost equal force would hit a wider part of the city, and the message would be clear: for all its mild weather and laid-back vibe, Los Angeles was, is, and probably always would be, a city out of control.

one

Five days after the quake, Roy Cooper boarded USAir flight 626, LGA to LAX, to pay a visit to a man named Martin Shine who had been, according to Harvey's brief message earlier that morning, "hiding out with his Armenian whore somewhere in North Hollywood." Roy packed a bag, unsure as to whether or not his kit would make it through security, and took a bus to the airport. At LaGuardia, he watched the ground crew out the window and, for a second, pictured his dad down there on the tarmac, leaning against a trailer full of luggage. The man in his thick glasses with the black frames, all the time grinning, pointing his index finger like a gun as he said hello to anybody who happened by. Roy stared until they called his flight over the PA and the image vanished.

When he checked in, the tall gentleman behind the counter with what Roy was sure had to be dyed red hair and wearing what Roy felt equally sure was eye shadow, somehow got Roy to admit that he'd never flown before.

"Never?" the guy asked, one hand on his chest. "Never ever?"

"No, sir," Roy said in his usual polite tone. He'd been inside lots of planes, but never up in the air.

"Well, then, let's see if we can't find you the best seat in the house," the counter agent said as he began typing away at the terminal in front of him.

The guy was smiling at Roy the way everyone smiled at Roy. Like he was a child or mildly retarded.

Once they were in the air, Roy, bumped up to First Class, watched a flight attendant with real red hair and a nametag that said her name was MEG work her ass off, passing out first drinks, then trays of some bright yellow cat vomit that, according to the little menu they gave him, was supposed to be some kind of curried chicken.

Roy sipped his Sprite and was trying to figure out exactly where to plug in his free headphones, the opening credits of some superhero movie now up on his personal screen, when the guy sitting across the aisle from him, a lean and tan gentleman in his forties wearing jeans that looked pressed, tasseled loafers, and a striped dress shirt, flagged down Meg. The guy launched into a loud harangue about how his meal wasn't what he ordered. How last week when Gail, his assistant, booked the flight for him, he had her ask specifically for a special meal.

Meg asked, "And what was it, sir, you *specifically* asked for?" Hitting the word the way he did. Giving him something back.

Roy liked her immediately.

"The gluten-free."

Meg said, "I'll go back and check my list, but I didn't see your name on there the last time I looked."

"This chicken is breaded," the man said. "I can't eat it."

"We have one vegetarian meal."

The man closed his eyes partway, trying to stay calm. "I need protein."

"Let me see if maybe there's a boxed meal in the back that you might like."

"From the back? That's gonna be awful." But talking to her ass, as she was already walking away.

The man turned and saw that Roy was looking at him.

"There a problem, bro?"

"No," Roy said. "I'm sorry." And turned back to his movie.

When the plane landed, the pilot announcing the temperature in L.A. at near eighty, in early September, Roy couldn't believe that just that morning, he was in Queens, feeling the new fall chill as he walked to the Mail Boxes Etc. on College Point Boulevard and 14th Avenue and picked up a legal-size envelope containing the plane ticket, Martin Shine's address out in California, and thirty-five hundred dollars in crumpled twenties that looked like they'd been buried the last few years under Harvey's prize-winning azaleas.

Roy rented a Ford Fusion from Payless Car Rental, a white one with a good radio according to the tiny black woman behind the counter who looked like she was still in high school. Roy thought if he hurried, he could make it out to Martin Shine's place by dark and still be back in New York City, asleep in his own bed, by morning. He didn't like new places. And the warm weather was already making him feel strange. Exposed.

The rental car smelled like a mixture of popcorn and stale cigarette smoke. Roy rolled down the windows. It was loud on the 405, but it didn't matter, the radio was busted, so there was nothing to listen to. Instead, Roy thought about North Hollywood and wondered if it was part of regular Hollywood, where all the movies were made. That got him wondering, what was he rushing for? Maybe he would take a tour of one of the movie studios while he was here. Roy wasn't much of a movie fan. In fact, he rarely went. He preferred sports, especially baseball. But he thought since he was already out this way, what the hell? Maybe he should go have a look at a movie studio, too.

The traffic on the freeway was barely moving, half the lanes shut down for repair, so Roy took the opportunity to glance at the map the lady at the Payless counter had given him. She'd taken a bright green pen and highlighted the route out to North Hollywood. There was a GPS on his phone, but Roy didn't like to use them. He had a terrible sense of direction and, no matter how specific the voice was, telling him to turn right in one thousand feet, Roy would just get confused. He preferred to study a map beforehand, commit the directions to memory, do it that way.

It appeared as if he would have to take every freeway in L.A. The 405 to the 101 to the 170. All these numbers. No names. He had just merged onto the 101 South and was moving through some place called Sherman Oaks, but without an oak tree in sight. This stretch of the 101 near Studio City was down to one lane, road crews out repairing the cracks and holes that had turned the freeway into an obstacle course. Roy passed what looked like a bombed-out tanker truck that had been dragged off to the shoulder. The truck was lying on its side and charred completely black. It struck Roy as odd that no one had yet towed it, things being still pretty fucked up even five days after the quake.

He was glad he wasn't there for the big event. He found the idea of the earth moving underneath him truly frightening. He imagined himself standing there while buildings fell all around him. Thousands of people rushing into the streets in a wild panic. He'd lived through a couple of tornadoes as a kid. But all he could remember was the family sitting in the cellar playing board games and binging on junk food while they waited for the wind to die down.

Roy got off in North Hollywood at Laurel Canyon and looked out the window at the dark warehouses and thought there's no way they make movies around here, the place is way too ugly. Hell, Queens was nicer than this. But then he thought, it was getting dark, and the shadow of the big quake hung over everything, so maybe he wasn't being fair.

He followed Laurel Canyon north and gradually the warehouses became apartment buildings. There were palm trees in front of each complex, but they were so tall you didn't really see them, just the long trunks, the bushy heads way up high, out of sight. It seemed to Roy like every building had a FOR RENT or a VACANCY sign out front. Some looked like they were falling down. Roy stopped at a red light, checked out the building on the corner and saw that it actually *was* falling down. The gate was boarded up with plywood, but he could see chunks of concrete on the ground inside the courtyard. Several windows across the front were broken. A balcony had partially collapsed, but still clung to the building at a slight angle, a black Weber barbecue lay on its side, ready to fall onto the patio directly below.

As the light changed, Roy remembered his neighbor, Rosa, telling him about how the quake was a seven something on the earthquake scale, and about the aftershocks—how some of them were like small quakes themselves.

Forget about the studio tour.

Just get this done, and go straight back home.

two

Martin Shine lived on the corner of Laurel Canyon and Kittridge in a two-story building called the Luna Terrace Apartments. It was a small complex with the units upstairs opening onto an open walkway. To Roy's mind, the place looked a lot like a boat, one of those old steamships with an upper and lower deck. He pulled over and leaned across the seat and had a look out the passenger window. Shine's unit was upstairs on the far side.

Roy continued on past, made a right onto Dehougne, and took a drive through the neighborhood.

Other than a few collapsed chimneys, there wasn't a lot of damage that he could see. A redwood fence had fallen over onto a driveway and someone had parked a minivan on top of it. Just drove right up onto the planked wood, not bothering to move it. Roy decided it was that kind of neighborhood, so he had to be careful where he parked the car.

Just past the mouth of an alley he stopped at an intersection marked at the corners by four low-slung bungalows. The windows were dark in three of them, Roy just able to make out the peeling paint and brown lawns.

There was a party going on in the fourth. A crowd of people stood out on the lawn and the front porch of the little house. Speakers were set up in the open windows and Nicky Jam blasted the neighborhood.

The lights were bright in the bungalow and Roy could see dark bodies bobbing in the windows to the music. Behind the house was a row of taller apartment buildings and Roy recognized Martin Shine's boatlike building among them.

The party would be a bright, noisy landmark when it came time to find his car, a quick walk back around the corner, while, at the same time, no one would notice the plain white rental car.

A light was on in Martin Shine's apartment by the time Roy climbed the stairs to the second floor, Roy relieved that he wouldn't have to hang around downstairs hiding behind some tree waiting for the man to come home. He figured, even with the walk to the car, he would be on his way back to the airport in fifteen minutes.

But then Roy heard a woman's voice inside the apartment and his heart sank, thinking he'd now have to wait around after all, but then he recognized the voice. It belonged to Phoebe, the blonde in *Friends*. She had always been Roy's favorite. He couldn't really tell the others apart, even though he watched the show almost every night. Once, for an episode or two, he thought the brother and sister were fucking each other, but then he remembered that was just something he'd read had happened in real life.

Anyway, Martin didn't have company. He was watching TV.

Roy reached back and pulled the ancient Walther PPK from his waistband. He opened the folded Ziploc taped to the barrel and took out eight of Harvey's homemade hollowpoints—smokers or reamers or whatever Harvey called them these days—and carefully loaded the gun.

Roy had decided to wait until the last minute, because the gun, like all of Harvey's guns, was an antique with a fussy trigger and Roy hadn't wanted to risk blowing his own ass off three thousand miles from home.

He reached into his windbreaker and removed a pair of black leather gloves. He pulled them on, stood on his toes as he reached up above his head to unscrew the porch light, and then knocked on the door.

three

"Would it be all right if I smoke?"

"Sure."

Roy had caught Shine coming out of the john, a section of newspaper in his hand, the TV up loud so he could still hear it while he was in there, oblivious to the fact that a lot of people on the other side of the country wanted him dead. Roy walked right on in—the door was unlocked—the Walther down at his side, Roy knowing immediately he wouldn't have to point it at the guy. Something in Martin Shine's eyes saying, *Shit. You got me.*

Roy nodded to him, "Why don't you stand over here, Mr. Shine." Roy wanted him in the middle of the room, away from potential trouble.

Shine nodded back and took a step into the center of the room. He grabbed a cigarette from the pack on the coffee table and shakily thumbed a pink Bic a half dozen times before he got it lit. He stood there a moment with his eyes closed, trying to steady himself. Though, Roy thought, he'd be steady soon enough.

Martin Shine had a round look to him, like everything was inflated below the waist. He wasn't tall, only about five-five, with a little bit of hair capping a fleshy face, two tiny eyes magnified behind thick, rimless glasses. He wore an orange terrycloth bathrobe with wide rainbow stripes a little too cheerful for his current situation, the accountant's belly crowning through an opening in the fake satin that ran down the middle.

It occurred to Roy that this wasn't Martin Shine's bathrobe.

"Anyone else here?"

Shine shook his head. "She's in Armenia. Visiting her sister."

Roy looked down the hall, could see a bedroom, but knew he wouldn't find anyone who went with the bathrobe or the pink lighter back there.

"I feel stupid just standing here," Shine said. "Why don't you just shoot me already, get it over with."

"This won't take long." Roy went around the room, closing the curtains, turning off all the lights, all except one. A lamp. Giving the room some mood while eliminating any shadows someone might see down on the street.

The dim light certainly made the old furniture look better. The couch was some kind of burgundy fabric with wood arms, the kind you couldn't ever sleep on. Looked nice, but was useless. Something Roy's mother would have had. There was a television sitting atop a table covered with a sheet. A bowl of soup and a napkin sat there watching the sitcom. A wooden, straight-backed chair that looked about as comfortable as the couch stood a few feet back from the table.

As he pulled shut the limp curtains alongside the kitchen table, Roy could see a pot on the stove, a wooden spoon sticking out of it. Roy could see the handle was broken and thought, this guy's already gone.

Martin Shine, watching his every move, said, "I feel like praying."

"Go ahead."

"I'm not even religious."

"Then don't." Roy reached into his coat and took out the silencer Harvey had given him.

"What do guys usually do in these circumstances?"

Roy gave the guy a look. He didn't want to know.

"They beg?"

Roy had some trouble screwing the silencer onto the end of the gun. It wouldn't thread right. Martin Shine watched him with those magnified eyes.

"Think it's too late for me to talk to them?"

"You're asking the wrong guy."

Harvey gave him the wrong silencer. Awesome. Roy looked around the room.

Shine said, "Maybe we should call them right now."

"I don't think they'd listen to you."

"How do you know?"

"They never do." Roy walked over and grabbed a pillow from the couch, a little satiny orange square that would cave in, you ever actually laid your head on it, but fine for Roy's purposes.

"You know why they want this done?"

"You're gonna tell on them or something."

"That the reason they gave you?"

"They don't give me their reasons," Roy said, staring at the pillow. "They don't have to."

"They gotta tell you something."

"They tell me where to find you," was all Roy said.

"It's because I used to work for Johnny DiMarzio."

"Who?"

"Come on. You never heard of Johnny D?"

"No. I don't think so."

"Well, take my word for it, he was big. I started out as his book-keeper, worked my way up."

His way up to what? Roy wondered, looking around the shitty little apartment, thinking about the broken spoon.

Roy may not have known this Johnny D, but he could picture him and a bunch of other guys posing for pictures in front of trucks, or standing around on golf courses leaning on their putters or sitting in red leather booths smoking cigars, drinking wine out of short glasses. These tough guys, their whole lives, they've never even been out of whatever neighborhood they grew up in. Eating at the same table at the same dark restaurant every day, then later wondering how the fuck the FBI was able to wiretap them so easily.

They were all the same.

Roy never understood them.

"Mr. Shine," he said. "Why don't you come on over here, kneel down on the floor for me." Roy looking right at him now, the man standing there, shaking all over in his brightly colored robe.

"It's as good as done, right? Nothing I can do?"

Roy shook his head. "Come on."

"Where you gonna do it? The mouth?"

"Back of the head," Roy said, keeping his voice low, calm like

a doctor with a nice bedside manner. "You won't even see it coming. Won't even feel it. It'll all be over in a second." Roy thought he
would have made a good doctor.

"Just one?"

Roy didn't want to say "That's all it's gonna take," wig the guy
out any more than he already was. He thought about telling him
about the old days, not so long ago, they'd do six shots: one to each
ear, one to the mouth, one under the chin, two to wherever else they
could fit a bullet. Maybe tell him how these days, with the stuff Harvey made in his basement, you don't have to shoot a guy so many
times. One does the trick just fine. But all Roy said was "That's all."

Martin Shine nodded, came over to him now, looked Roy in the
eye.

"I'm not gonna beg you."

"I appreciate that."

Shine got down on his knees, looked back and watched as Roy
wrapped the orange pillow around the gun.

"But you should know I got a safe, right here in the apartment."

"Turn around, Mr. Shine."

"There's over two million in there. Money I skimmed from Johnny
D. It's all yours."

"Turn around."

"What I'm thinking, I give you the money and you walk out of
here, forget what you came here for."

"I do that," Roy said, "and someone's going to come looking for
me next time." He gestured with the gun. "Now turn around or I'll
shoot you in the face."

"I'll tell you the combination."

Roy lowered the gun an inch and asked, "What's to prevent me
from shooting you and then taking the money anyway?"

"You don't know where the safe is." And now Shine turned
slightly, talking to Roy's legs as he said, "It's fuckin' ingenious where
I hid it. You'll never find it."

"Mr. Shine—"

"The combination is nine-twelve-fifty-two, same as my birthday."

"You were born in 1952?"

"Yeah, I know, I don't look that old."

"I was thinking you've lived a good life."

Shine looked all the way up at Roy now, all hope drained from his face.

Roy told him once more to turn around. Then added, "Please."

"It's all right with you, I remember this prayer from when I was a kid. I'm just gonna say it."

Roy waited, one hand holding the gun while the other held the orange pillow tightly around the barrel as Shine turned, closed his eyes, and began reciting in a whisper: *Oh my God, I am heartily sorry for having offended thee . . .*

That was about as far as he got when Roy shot him, a split second before he was ready. Harvey's fucking heirloom with its old pins and springs. It didn't matter, though. Roy watched as Shine fell forward onto his elbows and then waited, expecting him to crumple the rest of the way, but Shine remained in this bent position, looking like those men in Iraq or Iran Roy had seen on TV, rocking back and forth, praying. Except those guys weren't dripping blood and whatever else all over the carpet.

Roy looked up. The soup actually smelled good. And he was tired. Part of him wanted to lie on that bony couch and sleep for an hour or two. That's the way it always was, once Roy finished one of his errands he wanted to go right home, have some dinner, go to bed.

He'd been running errands going on twelve years now. Harvey and his wife, Rita, taking phone calls, sending Roy out to work for people he didn't know, though some he'd heard of. In that time, Roy's errands had consisted of everything from moving furniture to bouncing at a club to bill collecting, bartending at a christening to, once in a while, shooting people in the head.

Not at all like the days when Albert ran it, they would be killing people all of the time, hardly ever moving furniture or pouring drinks. Back then, Roy sometimes wondered if they were even getting paid for it.

Roy once saw this famous actor play a "hitman" on a TV show. He was this stone killer who wore nice clothes, had all this electronic shit, and was paid in gold bricks or something. Roy had never seen a guy like that in all his life. Not even Albert, who was as stone cold a killer as he'd known. There was a time Albert would have killed someone for a steak dinner and a slice of pie. Roy and Albert killed a lot of people back then. They did a lot of things back then. Most of it, in and around Kansas City in the eighties and early nineties. The town, mobwise, even then, was already finished, ceding control to places like Chicago, New York, and Miami.

Roy and the old couple, Harvey and Rita, were the only ones left. They brought Roy to New York when he was barely twenty-five and set him up running "errands" now and again for some heavy people in Brooklyn. As a rule, they didn't trust him with anything too complicated, on account of they didn't think Roy was all that bright. Outside of Albert, not many people did.

As another rule, Roy never left New York. He didn't like to be far from home. Especially at night. He wanted to be in his chair, watching TV, preferably baseball. Martin Shine was an unusual gig for him. Traveling all that way. But the Cardinals, Roy's favorite team, were coming to town to play the Dodgers in a week, and Roy figured that maybe he would stick around, go see The Kid, his favorite player, pitch in person.

Roy spent the bulk of his time installing alarms for Harvey's security company. Roy enjoyed the work and, for a while, thought he might one day even be a full-time electrician until one afternoon in the backyard, over Arnold Palmers, Harvey told him the union was run by fuckers and that Roy didn't want to deal with that.

"Stay with me," he said. "I'll take care of you. You don't need a union. You don't need anybody but me."

Same bullshit Albert used to say.

It was too late now anyway, make that kind of change, so why even think about it?

Roy picked up the spent shell casing from the carpet, then opened the breech on the gun and ejected the round inside. Safety or no safety, Roy was taking no chances.

He put the gun, the casing, and the round in his jacket pocket and then walked down the hall into the back bedroom. Shine's clothes from the day were laid out on the black silk bedspread. Roy looked at them, the beiges and browns giving off a vibe as sad as the man who wore them, and went into the closet. He studied Shine's wardrobe, then stepped to the pole and slid the hangers all to one side so that he could get a look at Martin Shine's safe, ingeniously hidden in the closet behind the Hawaiian shirts.

Shine hadn't lied about the combination. Roy got it open on the first try. Inside he found a nickel-plated .45 in a holster duct-taped to the inside wall, placed there so that Shine could easily pull it, should someone happen to be standing behind him holding a gun to his head. An extra clip sat atop a passport and a coffee-stained insurance policy.

As Roy expected, there was no cash.

He left the door to the safe open, just to make the cops think burglary if they were lazy, and then walked back into the living room, where he turned off the light, started for the front door, then paused beside the dead man, who was somehow still kneeling in the dark.

Roy heard a soft knocking sound from the kitchen and saw the wooden spoon rattling on its own in the pot. Roy felt a sudden lightness in his balls the way he did every time he rode a fast elevator and realized that the whole room was shaking. He stood there, panicked, as now the pictures of the old guys on the wall all began to sway on their hooks. Roy thought about diving under the coffee table or getting into a closet, but before he could make any kind of decision one way or the other, he felt his legs carrying him out the door just as Martin Shine crumpled to the carpet behind him.

four

Roy couldn't find the rental car.

He had been walking around the neighborhood, the ground no longer shaking but his heart still racing, for nearly half an hour when he came to the conclusion that someone must have stolen it. Maybe someone from the party. Or maybe someone walking by had their eye out for a white Ford Fusion they could part out for a few bucks somewhere. It couldn't be worth that much. The radio didn't even work.

That is, if someone stole it in the first place. He wasn't even sure that he'd been up the right street yet. He had already walked up and down several streets behind Martin Shine's place and, for some reason, still hadn't been able to find the little house with all the people dancing on the lawn. If he could find the house, he could find the car.

He stopped and stood there listening for the music, get a sense of which direction to head in. But all he heard was a dog bark one time and a voice—a woman's—yelling something that sounded like *Get off the fence Jojo!*

Then footsteps. Behind him. Roy turned around.

"On your left," the man said as he jogged past. Roy couldn't see his face. He was dressed in a gray sweat suit, the hood pulled tight over his head.

Roy called to him, "Excuse me. Sir?"

The man turned back, but kept jogging in place.

"You wouldn't happen to know where the party is?"

"Party?" He was breathing hard, looking at Roy with a look that said he was annoyed he had to stop. He made a big show out of holding up his wrist, pressing a button on the digital runner's watch he wore so as not to ruin whatever personal record he was probably just about to break before some asshole stopped him to ask a stupid question.

"There was a party around here a while ago. I can't find it now."

"I don't know of any party."

Roy could see the guy was in his sixties. And tall. Over six feet. With a gray beard that almost got lost in the hood. His running shoes glowed in the dark. He was already turning to go.

"Sorry to bother you."

"No bother." And the man was off, pushing the button on his watch as he ran off into the dark.

Roy knew that even if he could find the party house, he couldn't just walk in and ask, "Any of you stoners see who jacked my car?" They would certainly remember him once the stink in the apartment a few blocks away got reported.

Roy caught sight of the jogger again at the next corner as he crossed to the other side of the street and then started back the other way, Roy impressed how the old guy moved along, making up time no doubt.

Roy came to the end of a cul-de-sac and reversed his direction.

At one point, what looked like a patrol car drove past. On the side was stenciled VALLEY WEST SECURITY. The driver gave Roy a long once-over, then pulled to the curb, shone his beam into the windows of a dark apartment house on the opposite side of the street. The place had been fenced off with signs that said CONDEMNED STRUCTURE, KEEP OUT and WEITZMAN & SONS SEISMIC ENGINEERS hooked to the chain link.

Roy looked back as he heard the car door open, and then watched as the officer got out, crossed to a house next door to the earthquake-damaged building, and started gathering up what looked to be at least a dozen newspapers scattered about the driveway. The people who lived there, Roy thought, might as well have left a big sign that said, Hey, we're not home! He was thinking about how once upon a time, Albert would have seen those newspapers and gone in, not looking to take anything necessarily, but just to do it, leave some kind of sign that he'd been inside—like hanging one or two pictures upside down or turning on the television—freak out whoever lived there and was dumb enough to let the world know they were out of town. Roy was thinking about one house in particular when he heard the music.

It was coming from the next street over. He turned left at the corner and quickened his pace. The houses and apartment buildings now all looked familiar, yet this time he noticed that there were a few metal-roofed industrial buildings mixed in. Company names like MAYFIELD MARBLE and CABINETWORX jumped out from signs next to more run-down homes that Roy hadn't seen the first time through.

The music got louder and Roy could feel the heavy bass down to the sidewalk. He recognized the music as that rap crap he sometimes heard the kids listening to beneath his window, usually when he was trying to watch TV.

He approached the mouth of an alley, wondering what made the people at the party switch to this shit, when he heard a voice shout, *Down on your hands and knees, son!* Roy looked around, but didn't see a soul.

I said, get on the motherfuckin' floor!

Roy kept himself back from the mouth of the alley, but peered inside and saw the jogger he'd passed earlier now down on all fours. The man was in his socks, Roy couldn't see what happened to his fancy running shoes.

There were three of them, black, none older than fourteen, fifteen tops. One of them waved a little .25 auto at the jogger.

"You do like we say or you gonna get fuckin' worked, you feel me, Herb?"

The kid was heavyset, wore a down vest over a Dallas Cowboys jersey, and new, white, Nike high tops. A blue baseball cap was perched off angle on his head, the name of some malt liquor stitched across the front.

A tiny speaker hooked up to somebody's iPhone and a brown grocery sack sat up against the wall directly below the dark windows of an upstairs apartment. Leaning against the wall next to the sack sat another kid, legs folded up under his chin, a bored expression on his face. As he took a drink from a bottle of something tucked inside a bag, Roy noticed this one was wearing the jogger's shoes.

Drops of blood specked the ground all around the old man's sagging head. His hood was off and Roy could see now that the man was totally bald, a wide gash opened just behind his ear.

"Yo, homes, check out my man."

A new voice. Roy saw that this one belonged to a smaller kid in baggy jeans, mustard-colored work boots, and a giant T-shirt with a couple of wide blue stripes. He had his head cocked to one side and was staring down at the jogger.

The small kid said, "Dude look like one a them fuckin' dogs, got the hot chocolate on their neck."

The bored kid sitting on the ground said, "C'mon, Science. Fuck that fool. Let's go turn out that fuckin' party 'round the corner."

But the smaller one, the one called Science, ignored him, nudged the jogger with his boot, bent down and said in the man's ear, "Yo, doggie, where your motherfuckin' Swiss Miss at?"

He then tugged at the jogger's sweatshirt and said, "That is a mad hoodie, Herb." Roy watched as he then pulled the hooded sweatshirt off of the jogger and said, "Thank you very much."

He pulled it on over his head and turned to the fat kid. "Check me out, Shake. Stupid, right?"

Shake, the fat kid, laughed. "It's fuckin' double XL, cuz. You look like a fuckin' Tiny in that shit."

Science said, "Yeah?" and then turned to the bored kid on the ground. "How I look, L?"

L barely looked at him before he said, "Real stupid, Sci." Nothing in his voice, the kid pretty well baked. He reached over and turned up the music.

The jogger was shivering. Roy saw that the man was in pain, his knees and palms bleeding. He tried to sit back to relieve the pain and the small kid, Science, kicked him in the ribs. "Don't you fuckin move, less I tell you to." He then took the jogger's watch from his wrist and examined it. "It stopped," he said and threw it at the jogger. "It busted."

Science crouched down in front of him now.

"What's your name, son?"

"My name—"

"Yeah," Science said, "the legend they give you at birth?"

The jogger raised his head. Started to get up. "Good Christ," he said. "You're just a boy. This is wrong—"

Science hammered the man on the head with the butt of his clenched fist. "What's your name?"

"Please." The jogger looked at the kid. "I have a family."

"I didn't ask you had no family, motherfucker. I ast your name."

The jogger said, "Frank Peres," and Roy got the feeling that he expected the kid to recognize it.

But the kid, Science, just said, "Stand up, Herb. I think I might want them hoodie pants."

"No. Enough. Stop now and you won't get in any more trouble."

"I ain't the one in no trouble."

The fat kid came over and poked the gun in the man's eye. "Take them pants off."

The jogger pushed off with his hands, slowly got to his feet and rocked back and forth, unsteady from the blows. Science looked at the man's sweatpants and burst out laughing. He took out his phone and shined the flashlight on a dark stain that had spread across the front and down one leg.

"Yo, son, don't you got no home trainin'?" He looked over at the kid sitting by the boom box, "L, check it out. This motherfucker done pissed hisself." He then looked up at the jogger and the smile went away. "You ain't all that no more, Senior Peres." He stepped up to the jogger. "You just like me."

And then he pulled down the jogger's pants and laughed even harder and said, "Check out the Herb standin' in his jockstrap."

Roy's first thought was to shoot all three of them, go back to looking for his car. He didn't give a fuck how old they were, they were making way too much noise talking some made-up, bullshit street language, all the while playing music he hated. But more than that, he didn't like the rush they were getting from the jogger's fear. The more the man appeared afraid, the more they seemed to get off on it. Roy was never into that. Drawing it out. Punishment hits where you cut up a guy a little piece at a time. Torturing people, all the while giving them some dumb message from this or that grease-ball. Roy thought that even Albert, who was into that sort of thing, would have been disgusted at this situation. At least Albert liked things to be fair, always saying he was like the cat, wanted the mouse to respect him. Not these kids. This was more like pulling the wings off flies. This was out of control.

Albert would have shot them each once in the elbow or the kneecap and left them there to think about the error of their ways. Roy had enough left in the Walther to do that. Hell, he didn't even need the gun to make his point. These kids probably only used to hitting, but not getting hit.

But then Roy remembered Martin Shine, on all fours, bleeding from the head all over the floor of his apartment.

No, this wasn't Roy's problem. The jogger got pulled through a door he didn't open, but it was up to God to decide just how far it would go. Roy didn't think they would kill him. They'd have fun until they all looked as bored as the kid sitting by the speaker and then move on.

They would walk away pumped, reenergized from the older man's fear, confident that no one could touch them. And the man himself would certainly have learned his own lesson. Roy could see him lying in his bed, playing it all over and over in his mind, his wife asleep beside him while he experienced the adrenaline and the fear all over again until after a few months of this, anger gradually replaced humiliation and the moment became embedded in his memory like a knife in the head.

Whatever he felt a month from now, Roy knew the man would keep on running the next time he saw three li'l homies step out of an alley in front of him.

Roy had started to turn away, was thinking fuck the rental car, he'll go find a cab to take him back to the airport, when he felt something cold against his neck, the muzzle of a gun.

And now a new voice: "Yo, Science, check my man out."

Roy moved his eyes slightly so that he could see the new kid, one he hadn't seen before, now standing beside and slightly behind him, holding what looked like a big pistol but was really a small machine gun to Roy's neck, Roy wondering where he got hold of a weapon like that. This kid was tall and lean, Roy's height, with a jet-black face and one sleepy eye on the left side above a small, maybe a square inch, of wrinkled skin. A burn of some kind.

"Motherfucker was watching the show."

He shoved Roy into the alley. The small one, Science, came walking over to Roy now, forgetting about the jogger for the moment, and instead put his hands on his hips and stared up at Roy.

"Dude, what you think this is, motherfuckin' HBO?"

The fat kid eyeballed Roy and pounded it out with the newcomer. "S'up, Truck."

The one sitting on the ground, L, was now staring up at Roy, no longer looking so bored. He slowly got himself to his feet as Truck, the newcomer, shoved Roy over to where the jogger sat up shaking.

They were all giving Roy their best wolf, but the one Roy couldn't take his eyes off of was Science. Up close, the kid was good-looking with smooth skin and clear eyes that bespoke of more going on inside than was Roy's initial impression. These were dark, intelligent eyes set amidst a fine-boned, near angelic face. The kid looked out of place here in this litter-laden alley with a man bleeding on the ground. He looked too innocent, too clean to be hanging out with these loud assholes who kept kicking the old man on the ground and then punching each other's fists.

But Roy had seen that look before. The innocent face. The easy smile. Here the kid was, standing in the middle of some heavy shit and he didn't seem to give much of a fuck. If anything, the jogger's pain put him at ease. There were lots of words to describe someone like this. Over the years, Roy had certainly heard them all. His entire childhood had been organized around and by such words. There was always someone trying to figure out what made people like Roy and Science tick.

Roy realized, then, that he'd made a mistake.

This kid with the face of an angel was a real killer. Roy just hoped that the kid didn't know that yet.

Truck poked his gun into the jogger's ribs and said to no one in particular, "Like, who the fuck's this Herb?"

The jogger nodded to indicate Roy and said, "Let this man go," he said. "Before you get in any more trouble."

Roy looked down at the older man shivering in his jockstrap, bleeding from the head, and yet still trying to help Roy. Still thinking he could get these kids to walk away.

Science ignored the man, said to Roy, "Turn your ass around, motherfucker."

Roy summoned Albert from some place deep in his memory and looked at the kid. Looked into his eyes and let him look back into his. Knowing that something there now would make the boy step back.

He did. But he smiled. "You trying to wolf me, motherfucker?"

Truck raised the machine gun, pointed it at Roy's face, and said, "Turn 'round."

All of them were standing too far away to grab. No way to make it back out of the alley either as the one called Truck now stood behind him.

Science said, "You deaf, motherfucker?"

So Roy turned around, gave Truck the same look he gave Science. If it bothered the kid, Roy couldn't tell.

Science said to Truck, "He moves, like at *all*, fuckin' splash his ass." And then to the fat kid. "You two, Shake."

The fat kid, Shake, pointed his gun at Roy's head and Roy felt Science start to pat him down. He pulled Roy's wallet out of his left front pocket; the rental car keys out of the right.

Science held up the rental fob and asked, "Where's your ride?"

"I don't know."

"You don't know? The fuck you mean, you don't know?"

"What I said, I can't find it." Roy looked over his shoulder. "Maybe you wanna go look for it."

Truck asked, "What is it?"

"Ford Fusion."

"The hybrid or the regular?"

Then Shake's voice, to the jogger: "Hey, Herb, you know how to throw down?" Shake poked the jogger with the gun. "Break off a little sumpin, Herb, dance for us."

"I'll do no such thing."

Roy could hear the man trying to get some control back into his voice. He sounded a little like Martin Shine telling Roy about his safe; like a man who thinks for a brief second that there might be a way out after all. And then Truck walked over and hit the jogger across the face with the machine gun. Then again on the back of the neck as the man bent over and covered his face.

Shake laughed. "Yeah, do that work, son. Work that motherfucker."

The jogger stood there, stooped over, both hands on his mouth. Blood roaring between his fingers. Truck stared at him a moment, then put his gun back on Roy.

Shake, meanwhile, waved his gun at the other man's wet crotch. "C'mon, dude, bust some moves 'fore I blow your motherfuckin' dick off."

Only one gun on Roy now.

He felt Science's hand in his back pockets. From the left, he felt the kid pull out the directions the lady behind the Avis counter had given him, now folded up into a square. From the right, Science pulled the piece of paper on which Roy had written down Martin Shine's address. Science looked at it for maybe a second, then tossed it aside.

"That's it, Herb. Keep dancin'."

Roy looked back to see the jogger moving slightly to the music. Shake and Truck both laughing at him. The jogger looked up at Roy. His mouth was full of blood, one of his upper teeth was dangling. Throughout all of this L stood there, stoned, staring at Roy. No weapon in his hand.

Grab that MAC 10 from Truck and kill them all.

Now, Roy thought. *Do it now.*

Then Science found Roy's gun.

The Walther in his jacket pocket, loaded with Harvey's home-made hollowpoints. Rippers. That's what Harvey called them. Roy just now remembering this at the same time he heard Science let out a soft whistle.

"Check it," he said.

Shake and Truck turned to Science as he held up the gun. The jogger stopped moving, stared at the gun in the boy's hand, then at Roy with a new look on his face. Truck stared at the gun with that one good eye, and then at Roy. Circumstances had suddenly changed and Roy got the feeling that Truck wouldn't let the game go on much longer. He was the one Roy worried about.

Science reached once more into Roy's jacket pocket and came up with the live round Roy had ejected and then the spent shell casing. Science barely looked at the shells before handing them to Shake, who dutifully stared at them sitting there on his palm, then tossed them over his shoulder.

Science poked the muzzle into Roy's kidney. "What you doin' with this gat, cuz?" Roy turned around as Science held it up and clicked off the safety. "And like who the fuck are you?"

Shake said, "Yeah, son, like who are you? I don't see no badge, so I know you no po-po. Not with that piece."

Roy didn't answer. He looked at the jogger, the man now asking the same question with his eyes. Behind him, up in a second-story window, Roy thought he saw the curtain move, as if maybe someone had been there a minute ago.

Science smiled that beautiful smile at Roy. "He's like Mr. Freeze, you feel me? Look at him. He's like so fuckin *icy*."

L, no longer looking so baked, took out his own gun, a scratched, taped-up nine-millimeter, and walked up to Roy, put the gun to his head, and said, "I'm a blow this dude up."

Shake said, "Yeah, splash the motherfucker."

But it was now Science who couldn't take his eyes off Roy. Something was making him uncomfortable. "My boys, they wanna do you."

Roy watched the jogger, the man on the ground and once again on all fours, looking a lot like Martin Shine did half an hour ago.

"I heard."

Science smiled. "You the real truth, motherfucker?"

"I don't know what that means."

Science laughed, was waving the gun no more than a foot from Roy. His finger was on the trigger and Roy wondered if it would go off. It would be no problem to take it away from the kid. If he did it now. L had that old automatic at his temple, but Roy wasn't worried about L.

Truck stood apart from the group, his leg shaking like he couldn't control it, the one wide eye glued to Roy.

Science waved Roy's gun, said, "You a fuckin' badass?"

"No," Roy said. "I'm not a badass."

"Maybe you just sprung?"

"I don't know what that means either."

"Fuckin' crazy."

Roy said nothing to that one.

"On your knees, like this other Herb."

Roy didn't move.

Science smiled at the others. "He's so fuckin' icy, am I right?" And then he walked to where the jogger was on all fours and said, "Eyes up, doggie." And when the jogger looked up, Science put the gun to the man's forehead, looked back at Roy, and said, "You icy enough to watch me do *him*?"

The jogger said, "Please."

Science said, "You don't get down, and I'm sayin' like right the fuck now, I'm gonna blank this old Herb, you feel me?"

The jogger looked up at Roy. Please.

Roy said, "Take my money and go."

Science stared at Roy. "What you say?"

"You heard me."

Science looked at the other three, then burst out laughing. Shake joined him.

L and Truck didn't move.

Science said, "You think I'm like stressin' for loot, motherfucker?" He walked back to Roy, reaching into his own pocket with his free hand. "You think this poor nigga needs your help?" He pulled out a thick wad of cash and threw it at Roy's face, let the bills flutter to the ground without looking at them. "I got the fat bankroll, son.

"I'm not here for your money," he said, once more pointing the gun at Roy's face. "I'm here cuz I'm here. That's all. You feel me?"

"I feel you." Roy said, then slapped the kid on the side of the head, popped him hard on the ear, and said, "You feel *that*?"

For a moment, none of them did a thing. They were all in a kind of shock they'd never experienced before. Truck, he could see, wanted to do something, but was right now staring at Science as the smaller kid shook his head, tried to get the ring out of it. Even the jogger stared up at Roy, having, for the moment, forgotten about his own sad predicament.

Science held the old gun on Roy, looked like he might cry now.

"C'mon, motherfucker," Roy said. "Let's get this done. Shoot me. *Blow me up* or whatever the fuck you wanna do."

Roy watched Science, the kid feeling the others waiting on him to do something.

And he did.

Science looked up at Roy and pulled the trigger.

Roy listened to the hammer fall on the empty chamber with a flat click, was reaching for the old Walther, but Truck was already ahead of him, had that machine gun up on Roy and Roy realized that his moment had passed, thought *And down I go* when Science shouted, "Wait!" and once more everybody froze, though Truck kept Roy locked down.

Science looked up at Roy and said, "I'm a do this motherfucker, not none a you." He then carefully racked the slide back on the Walther, chambering a new round but instead of pointing it at Roy, he once more put the gun to the jogger's head, looked at Roy and smiled.

"But first, you need to know, this dude here's on *you*. I was gonna let him pass, but now, he's fuckin' *got*, you feel me? It's all *you*."

Roy said, "Wait—"

The gun went off loud in that little alley. L was the only one who didn't jump at the sound. Science's arm jerked slightly from the recoil as the jogger's head snapped back ahead of the rest of his body, which was knocked backward into a sitting position. Roy turned his head as a thin red spray hit him in the eyes.

For a moment, nobody moved. There was just the sound of the music and the smell of burning hair.

And then Shake, realizing his down vest was covered with blood and brain matter, started backing up like he could somehow get away from it. "I got fuckin' Herb all over me!" He started ripping the vest off in a panic.

Science stared at the small, black hole on the front of the jogger's face, saw the back of the man's head was entirely gone. Science then nudged the body with the gun and watched it fall over.

Roy cleared his eyes, focused, and saw Truck staring at him down the barrel of the little MAC 10. Roy was waiting for the shot to come when they were all bathed in light.

They all fell back against the walls as the Valley West patrol car pulled deep into the alley, nearly running down Shake, scattering the rest of them. L spun around and shot off rounds in every direction as Truck fired the machine gun through the car's windshield and then took off running after the others.

The security guard bailed out of the car, hitting the door against a wall, his own black automatic already clear of his holster and squeezed off half a dozen rounds at the four dark shapes now just beyond his headlights.

Roy came off the wall and started moving, got maybe a foot before he felt a red hot wasp sting him in his left side, then another in his left thigh and fell to the ground beside the jogger. He could feel the slick warmth of the other man's blood under his cheek and tried to sit up, but felt another, hotter, pain this time in his chest. His hands felt warm with his own blood while the rest of him seemed to be shivering from cold.

Roy was vaguely aware of the security guard screaming into his radio, but couldn't make out what he was saying, his ears still ringing from the gunshots and a new sound, a roar that came from above. Roy rolled over onto his back and was immediately blinded by sunshine. He squinted, registered the shape of a helicopter now floating overhead. He closed his eyes as the tips of his fingers went numb, his whole body shivering as if cold. He had to get up and get out of there.

He rolled onto his other side as the chopper now played its spotlight over the area around the alley, illuminating for a split second what looked to Roy a lot like a white Ford Fusion parked just across the street. He was thinking that he would have to tell the little black lady behind the counter about the broken radio when he passed out.

five

Kelly Maguire had just sat down to some sushi from Vons, eating healthy tonight as part of the "New Kelly" routine, when Randall, the watch officer, called her from downstairs.

"I got a walk-in down here, I don't know what to do with."

"I'm code seven."

"You're in the building."

She looked across the room at another detective, a few years younger, bent over in his chair, head on the blotter, sound asleep, the only other body up here right now.

"Ronnie's up next."

There was a pause. "I don't think he can handle this one."

"I'm eating." She put a piece of fish in her mouth and said, "Hear that? That's me chewing."

"Don't be that way."

The woman stood barely five feet tall. Walking over, Kelly had put her age somewhere in her fifties, but as she reached out to shake her hand, Kelly realized she was much younger, somewhere closer to her late thirties. She wore blue jeans that were too big, belted at the top, a gray sweatshirt, and dirty white Keds. Shelter clothes. Kelly had seen lots of women like this, their lives stamped on their ruined faces. This lady had dark black skin, covered with acne scars. Her eyes had the yellow burn of an animal and she couldn't seem to figure out what to do with her hands, one of which held a rolled-up manila envelope.

Kelly figured her to be a junkie once, maybe still.

She said her name was Ruth Ann Carver and then asked, "Are you a real detective?"

"Wanna see my shield?"

"I only ask because I been here two hours, they keep passing me around to fools in uniform. I need a detective, somebody can do some digging for me."

"After midnight," Kelly said, looking at Randall, the cop all of a sudden super-busy at his computer, "it's slim pickings around here."

"I couldn't get here sooner. My shift goes to eleven, and the bus went a different way on account of that hole in the middle of Vanowen, took me nearly a mile the wrong way before I could get off."

"You want some coffee?"

"I've had plenty coffee, no thank you."

"Why don't we sit down over here and talk."

Kelly led Ruth Ann Carver to a couple of plastic chairs that sat outside the watch commander's office. It was quiet here, everybody at a 7-Eleven on Lankershim on what had begun as a robbery before quickly progressing into a kidnapping and, finally, a double murder. Everybody but Kelly anyway. Still curbed after her little outburst a month earlier, Kelly got to deal with the walk-ins and other assorted and sundry late night bullshit.

She smiled the best she could at Ruth Ann Carver and said, "What is it I can help you with?"

"You dye your hair."

"Excuse me?"

"I know hair and I can see you ain't really that black, or that straight."

"Ma'am—"

"But them green eyes are real. They pretty."

"Thank you."

"And that's a real smart blazer you have on."

"Thank you."

"It looks good, you wear it with jeans and the white blouse like that. Simple. I used to work in a office, the ladies all dressed like that."

Kelly nodded, let the woman fidget with the envelope some more before she finally said, "I need you to find my son."

"He's missing?"

"He was stolen from me."

"When?"

"Eighteen years ago."

"Ma'am—"

"But I saw him on the street two days ago."

"You saw your son?"

"I saw my husband."

Kelly's stomach growled. "Mrs. Carver—"

"Miss. Jared's father is dead. Got kilt in Soledad twelve years ago."

"Jared is your son then."

"Don't know what he's called now. You have a cigarette?"

"No ma'am."

Ruth Ann Carver just nodded, didn't seem disappointed.

"Two days ago," she said, "I'm walking up Vermont, near Eighth. You know it?"

"You live in Koreatown?"

"There's a hair salon there, does weaves, I go over there sometimes, they give me work sweeping up or helping the girls out. I told you, I'm good with hair. Used to work in a salon myself, a good place on Hoover, but . . ." She shrugged. "That was a while ago."

Like with the cigarette a moment earlier, she didn't seem disappointed. Just a fact.

Kelly wanted to ask Ruth Ann Carver if Koreans were getting weaves now, but didn't want to distract the woman from getting to the end of whatever it was she needed to say, so that Kelly could get back to her shitty dinner and, more importantly, feeling sorry for herself.

"The other day, I'm about to walk into the salon, I look across the street and I see my husband waiting on a bus."

Ruth Ann Carver then opened the envelope she'd been twisting and took out a wrinkled photo of a black man, barely a man really, he was eighteen or nineteen with a shaved head and held a baby.

"You say this was this man you saw?"

"I don't *say* shit. I know it was."

"You saw your dead husband? The same dead husband who was killed in prison?"

She shook her head at Kelly. "You just as thick as them others."

She jabbed the photo with her index finger and she said, "Wasn't my husband I was looking at. Was my *son*. Eighteen years later."

Kelly looked once more at the photo. The boy holding a baby. An image she'd seen too many times. But this boy was familiar to her somehow. She tried to place him as Ruth Ann Carver went on.

"I couldn't move. I just stood there, watched him get on the bus and that was that, the boy was gone. *But it was him,* I know it was. Was a dead ringer for his daddy. Could only be my son."

Kelly studied the photograph a moment longer while she collected her thoughts. Maybe she didn't know him. Maybe the guy just looked to her like every other thug with a baby.

"You said your son was stolen from you?"

Ruth Ann Carver took another breath. "You sure you don't have a cigarette?"

"Someone might," Kelly said. "I could ask."

"It's all right." The tiny woman looked around, worked her palms into her jeans, back and forth, as if she was trying to rub something off.

Kelly crossed her legs and waited her out. She could feel the little .22 inside her black boots pressing against her ankle. A Beretta nine sat upstairs. The Glock she usually carried on her hip was at home. Too big for the purse. And she wanted to wear the suit for the meeting she had earlier in the day with her union rep. She was wondering, given all that had happened, the kind of trouble she was in, why she even bothered to carry a gun anymore, let alone two, when Ruth Ann Carver started talking.

"Was a Monday morning, eighteen years ago. I went to this bodega used to be off Florence a few blocks from our apartment. I was working at the salon and going to night classes at LACC to be a paralegal. I had a job waiting for me when I got my certificate. My husband was working a lathe at this machine shop in Torrance. They made radiator caps I think. And other parts. For old cars. You know, classic cars. Rich people can afford that kinda thing. We were making good money. The apartment wasn't so bad even after the baby was born. Anyway, on that Monday, I'd run out to get some fruit. I was gonna start making his own food. I'd been reading about that."

She saw the way Kelly was looking at her and knew what she was thinking.

"I wasn't always like this. We had a life. I could see me working for a firm downtown, my husband with his own shop. It was all good. Until I got distracted by the damn apples."

"The apples?"

"I needed McIntosh, they the best for applesauce, but I couldn't find any. That's what I was asking the man owned the place, Manny I think his name was, where he kept 'em at. I had Jay in the stroller, so I walked to the end of the row to ask that one little question. When I turned back, maybe a second later, the stroller was empty. Was right there where I'd left it, but my baby was gone.

"First I thought he'd fallen out and was crawling around the store somewheres. I wasn't even panicked. The place wasn't that big. So I started looking around. You know, calling his name. But he wasn't there. I'm looking under counters and even in the beer and soda cases. But he was gone. Then I look in the back, could see daylight coming from a open door and I just knew. I ran out into the alley, and then I ran out into the street and started screaming."

She turned to Kelly.

"You have babies?"

"No ma'am."

"Then you might not understand how it was my life ended that day. Everything just died. My husband lost his job. Then he reconnected with some old friends and got busted. My job, my school—that shit was done. All of it went away with that baby. It was like another version of me was born right then. And that's what I been since. That other version. My son was my life, and then he was gone. For eighteen years. Until I saw him the other day. And all a sudden I remembered who I was before."

She sat there, still no emotion in her voice. Kelly wondered if maybe she had none left.

Kelly asked, "How did he look?"

"Look?"

"When you saw him that day. Did he look healthy? What were his clothes like?"

"Oh." She thought about that for a moment and then said to the floor, "Someone's taking good care of him."

Ruth Ann Carver replaced the picture of the boy's father in the envelope and handed it to Kelly.

"You keep this."

Kelly took it and asked, "You remember the number of the bus he got on?"

"No. But it was one of the Wilshire lines. And it was a Saturday."

They both stood.

"How do I contact you?"

"You can leave a message for me at the Good Shepherd Shelter, it's on Beaumont."

"I know it."

"But most of the time I just sleep down at the rail yards, near Union Station."

"That's not safe."

"It's better than some places."

She stood there another moment, then nodded and walked back up the corridor.

Kelly watched her, knowing this whole thing was a loser. If Ruth Ann Carver really saw her kid, the best thing in the world for her, for both of them, would be for it to just fade away. The lady was right, she was born that day into another person with another life. And her son, too. If it even was her son.

A loser to be sure. Kelly wanted nothing to do with it.

She was turning for the stairs when she saw Randall nudge past Ruth Ann Carver and frantically wave at Kelly.

"You gotta go, like right the fuck now."

"Go where?"

"Shooting on Dehougne. Two down."

"I'm not supposed to leave the building."

"Everybody's still at Cahuenga. The sergeant over there said you gotta go help secure the new scene until they get there."

Kelly couldn't move. The last place she wanted to be was outside. Even at this hour. And the *very* last place she wanted to be was at a crime scene.

She hoped to Christ that, at least, given the late hour, there wouldn't be a crowd.

six

Kelly knew it was bad the moment she turned onto Dehougne and saw the chaos half a block away. She pulled in behind a red and white ambulance and sat there a moment, watching a rookie uniform whose name she thought was Oscar something—Quincy maybe—as he tried to move a crowd of two dozen neighborhood people back across the street, away from the alley. She didn't see any detectives. Nobody here yet. Just her.

Kelly grabbed the clipboard off the seat and got out of the car. She walked up to the uniform, the nametag said QUINTANA, and asked him what was going on.

He nodded to the alley where Kelly now saw a man without a shirt leaning against the wall a few feet away from where two paramedics worked on another man, this one flat on his back.

"We roll up, two guys are down, we see the rent-a-cop over there, he's all hyped up, going on about how he broke up some gang shooting, but we don't see anybody around but him."

Kelly looked into the alley and saw Quintana's partner listening to a slight but animated guy in a security guard uniform. Right above their heads, two stories up, was a dark window.

Dark, but Kelly could see a face up there.

The face looked at her, then moved away. She turned, glanced at the growing crowd across the street, then spoke into her rover and requested more bodies. There was a lot of shit on the ground, she knew the night guys would want all of it.

She felt strange walking the scene without Rudy, but they were short. The only way they would ever let Kelly show her face in public.

She pointed to the window and said, "Go upstairs to the apartment, the one overlooks the alley, see if anybody up there saw anything."

"What about all these people?"

"Go," she said. "Right now."

Quintana nodded, moved off around the building.

As Kelly walked further into the alley, she realized that the shirtless man was dead. A good portion of his head had been blown off, most of it baked onto the stucco wall he was now leaning against. A small black hole leaked blood a few inches below his left eye. He was barefoot and Kelly automatically glanced around to see if his shoes were lying about somewhere, but knew that she wouldn't find them.

She turned her attention to the man on the ground, watching as the paramedics cut away his bloody shirt and trousers, and saw at least two gunshot wounds.

But when the man looked up at her, met Kelly's gaze, he seemed utterly at peace. He seemed to be in no pain at all. He watched Kelly with calm eyes as she came over and crouched down beside him.

"Who shot you?"

The man just looked at her a moment, then closed his eyes.

Kelly watched as one of the paramedics inserted an IV into the man's arm and asked, "He tell you his name?"

The paramedic shook his head. "Guy hasn't made a sound since we got here." He patted the man on the cheek and the man's eyes came open again.

"Try and stay awake, okay, buddy?"

The guy looked once more at Kelly. She said, "What's your name?"

He didn't answer. He looked to be near forty with sandy brown hair and pale blue eyes. Maybe it was the way he was looking at her, or the small features and smooth skin, whatever it was, Kelly felt like she was looking at a child. More than that, she felt something she hadn't felt at a crime scene in a long time: she felt sorry for him.

"Sir, can you tell me your name?"

The man opened his mouth, but made no sound.

The paramedic said, "We gotta load him."

Kelly said, "Someone needs to go with you." She then squeezed the man's hand and stood back as they lifted him onto a gurney.

She walked, taking care not to step on any of the dozen or so shell casings that littered the ground, to where Quintana's partner, a black cop with a shaved head and huge forearms, was listening to the security guard.

She said, "Officer," and Quintana's partner turned and looked at her. His nametag said FRY. Kelly nodded to the paramedics who were loading the gurney into the back of the ambulance. "I need you to ride with the guy, get a Dying Declaration."

Fry considered her a moment, gave her a look like he was in a bar, just saw her walk in, wasn't sure yet how he felt about her. Kelly had been getting a lot of these looks from the black officers lately.

"There a problem, Officer Fry?"

"No, ma'am." Fry nodded to the guard. "This is Mr. Dooley," he said. "He's the one called it in."

Kelly said, "Thanks," then extended her hand to the security guard, Kelly putting him somewhere in his early forties.

"I'm Sergeant Maguire."

The guard shook her hand and said in a breathy rush, "Man, it was hairy."

She watched as the guard walked about in place, still all amped up on adrenaline. "They just started shooting," he said. "Like that. No hesitation, no thinking about it. We all just started shooting. I must've emptied my whole fucking clip."

Kelly said, "I'm going to need your gun."

He stopped moving and turned to her.

"And your holster."

"What for?"

"Techs need it. Find out who shot who."

"I can tell you that."

"I understand, but I'm still going to need you to surrender your weapon, please."

He looked at her, not so hyper now, and took off his holster and handed it to her. "It's a Glock," he said, "case you're wondering."

"Thank you."

"Same as you, I bet."

She took the holster, looked to where a long-haired detective she knew worked auto had just now arrived, was crouching down marking shell casings. Rick something. Or was it Ron?

Jesus, no wonder they all hated her.

"Hey." She took a chance: "Rick."

The auto guy looked her way, took out a cigarette, and looked off at the dead man, now covered with a blanket, and said, "He looks familiar to me. Anybody ID him yet?"

"I just got here."

Dooley said, "He looked familiar to me, too."

Rick looked at him. Then at Kelly.

"This is Mr. Dooley," she said. "He's one of the shooters."

Rick eyeballed the guard and said, "Looks like there was a lot of shooting."

"It was pretty hairy."

Kelly held up the holster and said to Rick, "I was wondering, could you take this for me, put it in your trunk? I don't think I'll be here long."

Rick looked back at Kelly a moment before he took the holster and said, "Sure," but Kelly could see he wanted to say something else.

"Yeah?" Ready for whatever shit was coming.

Rick looked down at the gun in the holster, then at Kelly, and said, "Listen, just so you know, there's a lot of us think what you did was justified."

"Justified?"

"We just want you to know that we're, you know, cool with what you did. That's all."

Kelly asked, "Who's we?"

"You know."

She watched as Rick from auto then turned and walked off with the holster. She remembered Dooley and saw that the guard was still standing there.

She said, "How 'bout you tell me what happened?"

He started moving again, shook his head and whistled. "Man," he said. "It was pretty fucking—"

"Outside of how hairy it was." She glanced up at the dark window above the security guard's head. "Start with what exactly your gig is."

"I work for Valley West Security. Senior patrol officer. I've got six buildings over on Hart, all of them damaged in the quake."

Kelly nodded. At least a dozen apartment buildings in the area had been condemned after the quake and now the owners were paying guys like Dooley to keep out the transients, drug dealers, and prostitutes while the owners either waited for or squandered their FEMA checks on other projects.

Kelly said, "What were you doing over here, you got buildings over on Hart?"

"I heard a gunshot."

"What time?"

The guard said, "About nine."

"You heard it from over on Hart?"

"It was quiet," he said. "I was just sitting in my cruiser, eating dinner when I hear the shot. So I start driving."

"You didn't call the police?"

"I wanted to check it out before I bothered you guys."

"So you drove from Hart over to here, passed by the alley . . ."

"I see these kids with guns out. I can't see what they're doing, so I shine my spot into the alley."

"You hear a gunshot," Kelly said. "Then you see kids with guns, and you still don't call us?"

"They were about to kill that guy." He nodded in the direction of the ambulance where Officer Fry was now climbing into the back with the wounded man. "They had him dead to rights and I could see the other guy was already down."

"So you hit them with your Q beam, then what?"

"They started shooting at me. Blew out my windshield and my rear window. It's raining glass, so I open the door, get into a crouch and return fire." He stopped moving long enough to add, "I don't think the little fuckers expected me to return fire."

"How many little fuckers were there?"

"There were four of them," he said. "All blacks." Then he added just in case she didn't get the hint, "No doubt bangers from some set around here."

"How many of them had guns?"

The guard said, "Two of them had firearms. One of them had a little machine gun of some kind. I know because it jammed and they took off running after the other two."

"What direction was that?"

He pointed down the alley. "That way."

The guard looked at the dead man. "I thought he looked familiar, too."

"Sergeant." It was Quintana. He jogged over to Kelly, pointed to the window and said, "Nobody was home, but I left a card."

Kelly looked up at the window. "Somebody's up there," she said. "I saw him."

"Well, nobody answered the door."

She looked across the street. Kelly wondered if the face she saw upstairs might be somewhere in the crowd of fifty people that now stood in front of the duplex. Three more patrol units had arrived and she could see the yellow tape stretched across the mouth of the alley.

Kelly said to Quintana, "Officer, would you take Mr. Dooley to the car, see if you can't get some description of the suspects beyond they're black and in gangs."

Kelly smiled at the security guard, put her hands behind her back, and started to walk the alley. She noted a half dozen more shell casings, at least two different calibers, as well as a brown grocery bag and a folded piece of paper. The paper looked newer than anything else around it, so she crouched down, unfolded it. It was a torn-off piece of a map. A name and address were written in what looked like a child's handwriting: *Martin Shine. 1322 Laurel Canyon. #12.*

"I've seen this guy before." She turned and saw Rudy Bell, a tall, rail-thin black detective and, up until six months ago, her partner, now holding the blanket back from the dead man's face. Across the street, Kelly saw three more homicides getting out of their cars, jogging her way.

Rudy said, "Sorry I'm late. We had another thing."

"I heard."

"He looks familiar, doesn't he?"

"Not really. But Rick what's-his-face in auto said the same thing."

Rudy Bell looked at her and smiled. "What's the matter, sunshine? You just wake up?"

"It's been a long night and I'd like to get the fuck out of here now that the men are here."

"Who's more of a man than you are?"

"According to my rep, I'm not anything anymore."

"How'd that go?"

"Seriously, Rudy. You guys need me?"

"No. Get out of here."

Rudy watched her pull off her gloves and said, "You're letting yourself go."

"I never had ahold of myself to begin with." She nodded to his suit and said, "What is that, Armani?"

He tugged at a lapel and said, "Hugo. You like it?"

"You always look good, fatso," Kelly said.

Rudy looked at her, started to say something when out in the street someone screamed. A high, shrill wail that split the crowd in two. Kelly saw a woman push through the center to where the uniform stood by the tape. Kelly couldn't hear all that she was saying, but caught one word: *husband.*

Kelly called to the cop standing near the yellow tape, "Keep her over there."

The woman, wrapped in a pale blue bathrobe, tried to push past the cop and yelled, "Frank!"

Kelly and Rudy walked forward, Rudy saying, "Ma'am, we can't let you back there."

"What's happened to my husband?"

Rudy looked at Kelly.

"My neighbor called, said he was lying in an alley. He was out doing his exercise, didn't come home. I was about to call the police when—My God, is that him?" She was staring at the body by the wall.

Kelly knew this woman from somewhere, but wasn't sure where. She asked, "What's your name, ma'am?"

From somewhere behind her, Kelly could hear Rick, the auto guy's, voice, "Wait a minute, I know who this guy is . . ."

"I'm Theresa Peres."

Rudy said, "Your husband is Frank Peres?"

She looked up at him. "He's dead, isn't he?"

Kelly looked at Rudy, who turned and muttered, "Oh, Christ."

Behind her, Rick was saying, "He's that guy, that city councilman running for mayor." Kelly turned around and Rick smiled at her. "I knew I recognized him."

Kelly looked at the woman, at Theresa Peres, who was trying to shove her way past Rudy, but was being held back by Rudy and another cop. Kelly turned and watched a news crew now headed this way. The reporter was fumbling with her earpiece when she looked up and saw Kelly.

"Sergeant Maguire?"

Kelly turned and started to walk away from the crime scene. Then she started to run. She got in her car and watched as two other patrolmen now helped restrain Mrs. Peres. She watched as Rudy Bell stepped away from the hysterical woman and tucked in his shirt, ducking his chin to see if the grieving woman had left a mark on the linen, and then looked off to where Kelly now sat.

Kelly started the car, made a U-turn, and drove off without looking back.

seven

Science put Roy Cooper's gun under his pillow and lay there in bed listening to the sounds just out the window on Agnes Street, picturing the neighborhood in his head. It was something he did every night to chill, help him fall asleep.

He could see the houses, all of them built in the early fifties and painted white, green, or blue; all of them the same design—one story, a living room, a kitchen, two bedrooms and a bathroom. Maybe a third of the houses had lawns. A few had rosebushes or crape myrtle trees out front. All of the backyards were cement.

Tonight, Science, whose real name was Noel Bennett, was having trouble calming down. The only sounds he could hear outside his window were the hum of the electrical wires that ran between the houses, and his older brother, Cole, standing out on the lawn talking to a friend in low tones.

The quiet felt good after the hour that Science and Truck had spent hiding in the weeds near the DWP right-of-way, a ten-mile-long corridor bordered by dirt berms and cement-block walls that ran along the Southern Pacific railroad tracks. The walls were supposed to keep people away from the overhead electrical towers that ran up the center, but Science and Truck made it in one jump to the top, their adrenaline carrying them up and over.

At one point, a five-o whirly flew over and they leaned their backs against the dirt, certain the spotlight would catch them and they'd have to run for it, but the white beam moved on to nearby Hart Street and then swept over Laurel Canyon Boulevard.

Science was cold and had pulled on the hoodie he took from the jogger. It was huge on him, two sizes too big. He looked down at himself, then turned to see Truck watching him with one eye.

That's when they started laughing. A full hour of it. They couldn't stop. They would try to get up and walk, maybe get a few steps, when they would look at each other and then fall down in hysterics.

Mothafucka shoulda kept on runnin'.

True that.

He ain't gonna run nowhere no more.

No doubt.

Science was relieved that Truck didn't bring up the slap. Glad to be just laughing. But he understood that, at some point, he would have to do something about it. He would have to rectify. And soon.

Science put his hand on the gun under the pillow, knew he should have tossed it, but he couldn't let it go. It was his now and it felt good to wrap his fingers around it. He wasn't about to lose it, let someone else down the line shoot him with it. It was old, but bigger than the little black .32 his brother carried with him. He knew that he'd go nowhere from now on, he wasn't strapped. And this funky old piece with the hair trigger was now all his. No one would take it away from him, ever.

He listened to a car pass by the house and tried to imagine who was driving, where they were going, what the people inside were talking about. He heard a plane overhead on its way out of Burbank and Science made up an itinerary in his head: Hawaii. Tahiti. Buenos Aires. And then maybe San Diego where his oldest brother, Guy, had been stationed for the last two years.

Guy had written letters to Noel, telling his baby brother how the Navy had saved his life. How if it weren't for his job as a radioman, he'd probably be dead on the streets like Noel was going to be in a few years, he wasn't smart. Guy, anticipating Noel's response, adding that there's a difference between being intelligent and being smart.

Smart people don't become gangsters, live lives measured in dog years, dead by the time they're eighteen.

He could hear Guy on the phone barely a week ago: *You use drugs, you drink, and top it off, you gangbang. How are you supposed to make it, bro?*

But Noel didn't want to join the service. This country didn't do anything for him, why should he fight for it? Worse, he didn't care to take orders from men he knew more than. And Noel knew more than everyone. He was the Science Man. He knew everything about everything. Fuck, he was smart *and* intelligent. For Science, school was easy and a waste of time. Knowing who discovered America wasn't going to help keep his ass from getting shot off. School was a place for hanging and checking it with females, and the distribution of a little product, not learning.

At fourteen, Science already knew all that he needed to know.

The dog next door started barking and he could hear Mrs. Montclair pull her old yellow Volvo into the driveway. She was a speech therapist and had helped him with his stuttering when he was six years old. She was the first to say that Science had brains, that he would go far.

Lying there in bed, with one hand on Roy Cooper's gun, Science wondered what Mrs. Montclair would think of his actions earlier tonight.

Listening to the comforting drone of his older brother's voice just out the window, he played the moment over and over again. The old man on the ground. Science pushing the gun into his cheek, making a mark there, a little red "O." Science staring at it and thinking yeah, that's the spot, that's where I'm gonna do it.

But then deciding not to.

Because of the other man. Mr. Freeze. He kept his eyes locked on Science the whole time. Those eyes. On the street, Science could look another dude in the eye and hiccup the motherfucker's heartbeat. But this man was different. Science looked into this man's eyes and felt his face burn. Even when he turned his back, he could still feel the man's eyes on him, making little red "O's" in the back of his head. He knew that if he wasn't careful, the man would have killed him. He wasn't afraid. He was *waiting*. Science couldn't think of another soul could step into that situation and act that way. Not in real life anyway.

No, he knew that if he didn't kill Mr. Freeze right there in that alley, Mr. Freeze would surely kill *him*. The problem was, Science didn't think he could kill the man.

He wasn't even sure that he could kill the old Herb. But then the fucking hammer fell on that empty chamber. He hadn't meant for that to happen. Science was barely touching the trigger, was really just resting his index finger there when, all of a sudden, it came back with the weight of nothing.

And then that click.

Science, you played yourself, son.

For true.

Science knew that he had to do it for real then. No way he could walk away having *almost* done it. He could see from the way Truck was looking at him that Truck thought he pulled the trigger on purpose. L and Shake didn't matter so much, but Truck . . .

Truck had killed before. Truck wanted to do it again. If he did it now, for Science, they'd all be looking to Truck for the answers, not the Science Man.

So Science decided to kill the man for real. If Mr. Freeze made a play, he'd let Truck have him. He could afford that, but only if he wasted the old Herb.

Funny thing was, in that split second that he made up his mind, Science could feel himself relax. This was his night to cross the line. For that split second, Truck was irrelevant.

He had thought about it many times, lying in this very same bed; fantasized about different scenarios where it might happen. It was almost always self-defense. Or to save someone. Maybe some shorty he met at a party. His friends. His brother. Someone else he went over the line for. But tonight, looking down at the man, bleeding, soaked in his own piss, Science knew that the first time would be selfish; just for Science and no one else. He would fulfill his name. Be a straight killer, devious, do anything; be bad to the fullest. He'd do this thing and be an instant ghetto star. And from there it was a short hop to OG and then they'd all be his. He could bring them back to where they were before the Mexicans took it all away.

But then that motherfucker slapped him.

Goddamn. Out of fucking *nowhere*. Like the man didn't give a shit. Like the man *wanted* to get his ass whacked. Now Science had to step up and do *both* motherfuckers, Mr. Freeze and the old Herb. He could feel them all watching, waiting like Mr. Freeze, to see what Science would do.

Cole had always said that there were two kinds of bangers: hustlers and warriors. Shake and L were more the former, but Truck was a real soldier. He and Science were road dogs since they were practically babies. Truck was always gonna be the one to take Science where he needed to go. But Science had to keep his respect. Science knew that respect was one of those nonnegotiable things: you get and you give. And that slap fucked with his getting.

Science heard Cole's wheelchair on the wooden ramp outside and knew his mother would be home soon from the Airport Radisson where she worked as a maid. He heard the front door open and then a moment later watched as the dark form of his brother wheeled into the bedroom. Cole hoisted himself onto his bed, and a few minutes later Science could hear his older brother's labored breathing.

Cole had been shot in the spine two years earlier after he accidentally stepped on the sneaker of a fifteen-year-old Tiara Street Loco named Smokey at a Clippers game.

A few days later, while Cole was lying in the hospital staring at his useless legs, his mother was telling Cole's friends that she wanted justice. She wanted action.

She wanted headlines.

That same evening, the gangster who shot Cole was himself shot while he sat in his living room watching television. One of the high-velocity bullets, fired from the street, went through the house and out into the backyard, where it struck the gangster's eleven-year-old sister in the back while she helped her mother hang clothes on a line.

The little girl and Cole Bennett lay in beds two rooms apart in the very same hospital and were treated by the very same doctors. A reporter named Harvey Longo wrote a story for the *Los Angeles Times Magazine* about the two paraplegics called "Poetic Injustice" and won a Pulitzer Prize. Science was mentioned in the article as "The genius younger brother" and "The hope of the family."

The Bennett boys' mother had gotten her headline.

Science reached once more under his pillow and gripped the oily gun, now warm from the bed, and thought about how, lately, he'd noticed a lot of wooden ramps in front of people's houses.

A half hour later, he was still awake, though he pretended to sleep when his mother came into the room, smelling of Lysol and dope.

He could sense her standing there between the beds, looking down at her two sons.

Science wanted to open his eyes, tell his mother that everything was cool, that he would take care of all of them, that he was still the hope of the family. That tonight was just the first step for him.

That this time, *he* would bring home the headlines.

eight

Roy Cooper thought he was dead.

He remembered the nice-looking lady cop with the dark hair pulled back tight, the deep green eyes watching him as she touched his hand.

He remembered her smiling at him.

He remembered the young cop getting in the back of the ambulance with him, wincing at the sight of all the blood as he sat down beside the gurney.

He remembered hearing the siren, the young cop's voice just underneath it . . . *Sir, you've been shot. Chances are you're not gonna live. Would you like to make a statement? . . . What's your name? . . . Where do you live? . . . Are you married? . . . Is there someone we can call? . . . Do you know who it was shot you?*

And then silence.

And for a minute Roy thought he was dead.

But can the dead dream?

If he was dead, how could he have dreamed that he spoke to Harvey on the phone?

In the dream, Roy asked the old man what he should do now that he had been shot by a bunch of little kids.

Harvey told him to get the fuck out of there.

Roy told Harvey that he couldn't move. He'd been shot three times. How was he supposed to go anywhere?

Roy could hear Rita breathing on the extension. She was furious with him for putting them all on the spot like this. She said if he didn't die in the hospital, someone would come out to L.A. and kill him, make sure he didn't give up anybody back east who didn't want to be given up.

Roy said he wouldn't do that.

Rita said it didn't matter. That he should just die, make it easier on everybody.

Harvey told her to hang up, leave the boy alone. He would think of something. The meantime, he told Roy to get some rest, get his head clear so that he can make sense, the time comes the cops wanna talk to him.

Roy said, yeah, he'd do that, get some rest. He was so tired. His body felt like it was barely held together, like it might fall apart he made one tiny move. The thing to do was sleep, maybe for a day or two . . .

Then he remembered, right before she hung up, that Rita had told him to turn on the TV.

nine

Kelly had the hiccups.

She hadn't expected to be asked to this meeting, so she was in bed when Rudy called a half hour before. She drove through an In-N-Out on her way over, wolfed down a Double Double and a Diet Coke in the car, and was now seriously paying for it.

She sat way in the back of the room trying to concentrate on what Mike Araki—Rudy Bell's new partner—was saying while trying to control the noise her body kept making.

The other detectives were all sitting on top of their desks except for Rudy, who sat in a chair with his suit coat draped neatly over the back.

"So far, from the brass at the scene, we know at least three weapons were involved. We know one was a MAC 10, the other was the Glock belonging to the security guard, Dooley. The third belonged to one of the bangers, and from Dooley's description sounds like a smaller automatic, most likely a .25. We should know more by tomorrow afternoon."

Dennis Lyles, a blond homicide Kelly had been in the academy with, said, "Are we sure the guard's clean?"

"We're not sure of anything yet."

"I say that only because I know a lot of rent-a-cops been dealing out of those quaked-out places, supplementing their twelve-fifty an hour." Lyles shrugged. "Who knows, maybe the whole thing was a buy went wrong."

Rudy Bell asked, "You saying the councilman was there to make a buy?"

Lyles said, "I'm saying maybe he came along, stepped in something."

Kelly hiccupped and they all turned and looked at her and she suddenly felt compelled to comment. "Personally, I think the guard was just dumb, rolled up on something he should've just called in."

Leo Manning, the division CO, was watching her as she tried to stifle another hiccup. "You spoke with him, did you, Kelly?"

"Yeah. Guy seemed more like a wannabe to me than any kind of drug dealer." She glanced at Lyles, saw him smiling at her, nothing sweet behind it.

Manning said, "That would be your read, would it?"

"Yes, sir."

Kelly hiccupped again and Manning kept looking at her, probably wondering if she was drunk.

Kelly was amazed at how clean and pressed Manning looked at two in the morning. The little black goatee was trimmed and the bald head shined. The suit was unwrinkled and perfect, with the tie all the way to the throat. Kelly thought the top cops were all starting to look more like haberdashers than police officers.

"Maybe the whole thing was a hit on Peres," Lyles was now saying. "I mean, the guy's been pretty outspoken about the gangs the past few weeks."

Kelly hadn't watched much television lately, but had some vague recollection of the guy at a news conference, standing in front of an apartment building on Lankershim going on about how he'd been living in North Hollywood his whole life and wasn't about to move now.

Rudy Bell said, "Then how do you explain the other guy, the John Doe got shot with him?"

Lyles said, "Just some guy, stepped in the same shit."

"Sounds like a lot of people stepping in shit."

Kelly hiccupped, said, "I think it was the Pacas or the Vineland Boyz."

Again they all turned and looked at her.

Araki said, "I thought the Mexicans claimed Dehougne, the 18th Streeters, those guys."

Kelly shrugged. "They do and they don't."

Manning said to her, "You have any thoughts as to who it might be?"

"There's a few names come to mind."

"Think you could put some intelligence cards together, show them to the John Doe?"

Before she could answer, Araki spoke up. "Rudy and I should be there for that."

Manning said, "I want you and Bell to take the guard back to Dehougne, have him walk it, get some measurements, find out exactly how it all went down."

"We've done that."

"Do it again," Manning said, "now that he's had some time to think about it."

"Why not have Maguire do that while we go to the hospital."

"Because I want to do it this way."

"There's probably gonna be press at the hospital, too, that's what you're worried about."

"I'm not worried about anything," Manning said. "Kelly knows the area and the people better than you do."

So that's why she was here.

"Fine," Araki said. "Then have her put the cards together, and we'll take them to Valley Pres."

"I want you and Bell at the crime scene." Manning gave Araki a look that said, we're done talking. So for a moment everyone was quiet. Kelly caught Rudy looking at her, making sure she was all right.

She smiled at him.

And then Leo Manning slid off the desk and shook his head. "Christ," he said. "It had to be Frank Peres."

ten

The end of Kelly Maguire's career began on an overcast afternoon in May when an eighteen-year-old Whitsett Avenue Gangster Crip named Ronnie "Streak" Rabidou climbed in the back window of a green, one-bedroom house at the end of Gault Street and found twenty-seven-year-old Martha Gutierrez, a night nurse at Pacifica Hospital, giving her retarded nine-year-old daughter, Carla, a bath.

Streak had come through the window looking for a nickel-plated *tre five seven* his sister—who frequently baby-sat Carla—had told him she knew for a fact was hidden somewhere in Martha's bedroom. Streak needed the gun to do a guy who had turned out a party he was at the week before, then took off with a girl Streak was dancing with. But Streak quickly forgot all about that when he saw Martha and her daughter sitting there in the bathtub.

Over the next few hours, Streak repeatedly raped Martha in front of the little girl, then killed them both with a screwdriver after tossing the house for a gun that wasn't there.

At the time of the events in the little house on Gault Street, Kelly Maguire was part of a newly formed gang unit, set up to get closer to the female gangsters in Hollywood. In her two years there, Kelly had gotten to know dozens of gang members of both sexes throughout Hollywood, and later, in the neighborhoods around USC. The mayor wanted to try the same thing in North Hollywood and Kelly transferred there to lead the unit.

She had never met Streak, however, until the night she and her then partner, Rudy Bell, knocked on the door of the house Ronnie shared with his aunt and his younger sister on Hart Street, two blocks away from where he had spent the previous afternoon with Martha and Carla Gutierrez.

In the days that followed Streak's arrest, the press would often refer to the swift investigative work on the parts of Detectives Bell and Maguire. The truth was that Bell and Maguire had little if any investigating to do at all thanks in large part to Ronnie Rabidou himself, who, in all his excitement, had left behind a pair of jockey shorts with his name printed in black felt pen across the seat—the way all of the inmates were required to do at the Kilpatrick juvenile detention camp out in Malibu—on the floor beside the Gutierrezes' bathtub.

Kelly Maguire's career as a police officer ended twenty minutes or so after Kelly and Rudy brought their suspect to North Hollywood Division for an interview. Streak calmly confessed to the killings at the time of his arrest, but there were still a few things that Bell and Maguire needed to clear up.

Kelly remembered Rudy telling her that he was going to the john and that he would be back in a moment. After that, however, all Kelly could remember was picking up the phone book off the edge of Dennis Lyles's desk as she walked into the interview room to ask Streak one more time where he had dumped the body of Carla Gutierrez.

Kelly wouldn't remember the rest of it until a month later when she was sitting in an interview room, not unlike the one in North Hollywood, except that this one was inside the Internal Affairs Division in Van Nuys, and Sergeant Paul Hancock of IA Division played it for her on tape after first reading her rights.

Hancock was a thick-necked man who Kelly knew had once played fullback for USC and now liked to chew tobacco in the division vehicles, spitting the juice more or less into a Styrofoam coffee cup as he drove.

Kelly had bought a new suit for the interview, a black Anne Taylor, and felt overdressed, like maybe she was trying too hard.

Looking around the room, she couldn't believe what a pigsty the place was. Candy wrappers and coffee cups littered the floor. At one point her bare knee scraped the underside of the table and she could feel a hardened wad of gum stuck there.

These were the guys supposed to be always on the make for dirty cops and they couldn't even keep their own fucking space clean.

Sergeant Bill Hoyt, Kelly's defense rep and a twenty-year veteran, stood near the door staring into his own coffee cup as Hancock played the tape.

Kelly heard the sound of a door opening, followed by a voice that was both her own and yet unfamiliar at the same time as it said, *Hey, rapo, whassup?*

And then the whole scene came back to her.

The kid, who called himself Streak on account of he was the only one who ran fast enough to get away from a narco raid on a crack house a couple years earlier, was leaning back in the chair, staring at one of the D.A.R.E. TO KEEP KIDS OFF DRUGS fliers taped to the wall when Kelly stepped into the interview room clutching the phone book.

A handsome kid, Streak looked her up and down as he sat forward, resting his elbows on the table, a big grin on his face as he said, "Hey, mamma. Whassup yoself?"

Kelly hit him across the face with the phone book, knocking that handsome face momentarily out of round as Streak flew sideways out of the metal chair and into the wall that had the flier taped to it.

As Streak mumbled, *motherfucka,* struggled up onto all fours, Kelly raised the phone book over her head and brought it down hard with both hands onto the kid's neck, splaying his legs, and sending his face crashing to the linoleum, hard enough she heard his nose break.

"Get up, rapo."

As he pushed himself up, turned his head and looked back at her, she could see one of his bottom front teeth sticking out through his lip.

"Where's Carla?"

"Who?"

"The little girl, rapo. Where'd you stash her at?"

Streak sat up against the wall, grabbed at the back of his head and said, "I don't feel so good . . ."

"I'm sorry."

"I want my lawyer."

Kelly kicked him in the chest and Streak suddenly found himself without any air in his lungs. She then picked up the metal chair and brought it down on his head and Streak bent over, blood running into his lap from a three-inch divot in his forehead.

Kelly stepped forward, pulling the gun she wasn't supposed to have in the room from the holster on her hip as she squatted. She grabbed Streak by the front of his shirt, shoved the muzzle in his ear and said, "Wanna know a secret?"

"I want my lawyer, bitch."

"I wanna die, Streak. Today, if possible."

Kelly remembered his face was covered with blood, his eyes staring back at her, not blinking now as she pulled the hammer back on the Beretta.

"What I'm thinking is, let's go together. You and me. Right now. Make everybody happy."

"You can't be doin' this . . ."

"What do you say, rapo? You up for dying?"

And then Rudy Bell's voice on the tape, *Kelly!*

Paul Hancock was saying, "There appears to be a slapping sound near the beginning of the tape."

"A slapping sound?" Kelly turned to look at Paul Hancock. "I hit him with the phone book. I slapped him right out of the fucking chair."

Her rep, Bill Hoyt, said, "Kelly, you don't have to say anything, you don't want to."

"I want this done," Kelly said. "So I can go back to work." Then she turned to Paul Hancock and said, "I was drunk, okay? I'd been drunk for twenty-four hours."

"You were drinking on the job?"

"On the job. In the car. At the fucking dry cleaner."

"Since when?"

"Since right after we went into the house on Gault."

"You were upset?"

"Clearly."

"Because of the nature of Mr. Rabidou's crimes?"

"I was upset, but not at Ronnie Rabidou."

"I don't understand."

"I was upset with my husband," Kelly said. "My ex-husband."

"You were upset with your ex-husband, so you assaulted your suspect?"

"Steven—my husband—had just moved out the day before. He did it while Rudy and I were bringing in Rabidou."

"You'd had a fight?"

Kelly looked at Hancock, but it was Bill Hoyt who spoke. "What has that got to do with anything? She's saying this was a unique thing—a onetime deal. You've seen her complaint history, it's a big fucking nada."

"It *was* anyway," Hancock said. "Now she's got three 181's against her. I mean, were you drunk when you talked to the asshole at *Los Angeles Magazine*?"

"Hammered out of my head."

"Her husband left her for another man, for Christ's sake."

Kelly gave her rep a look that said *Please stop helping me.*

Hancock looked at her. "Are you drinking now?"

"No, sir. I've been sober since . . . the incident."

Hancock nodded and said as he made a final note, "Is there any statement you'd like to make at this time before I shut off the tape?"

"Yes," she said. "You've been very nice."

Hancock glanced at Bill Hoyt, then sat back and said, "I'm going to recommend on the record that you call the medical liaison, get yourself enrolled in our Alcohol Abuse Program."

"I'm already enrolled."

Hancock's report went to Leo Manning. As Kelly's commanding officer, Manning had the power to recommend a penalty of up to twenty-two days suspension: one working month. Anything over that, however, required a Board of Rights hearing.

Although Leo Manning respected Kelly, even liked her personally, he felt that twenty-two days wasn't enough. Given the bad PR the LAPD had been suffering of late, it seemed wiser to send this to the Board of Rights. After all, Kelly had broken a prisoner's neck and then said a few choice things to the press that she shouldn't have.

So while Kelly awaited her hearing as well as a lawsuit brought on by Ronnie Rabidou's family, she was temporarily reassigned by Manning out of the gang unit and into domestic violence. As a result, she was also switched from working days to working the 4/10 plan: four days a week, ten-hour days from 1:30 to midnight.

Kelly knew this was how it would end. Knew she'd be stuck doing this until she finally cried uncle and put in to go home. They were politely showing her the way out.

For the time being, working the 4/10 was fine with her since she didn't particularly feel like being alone with her thoughts anymore, especially not at night.

eleven

Kelly was walking into Valley Presbyterian when a tech named Osman Youness called her to tell her what she already knew: the idiot security guard had shot the John Doe eyewit while the still unknown kid shot the councilman with something else.

He didn't have to brief Kelly, she wasn't anywhere near lead on the case, but Kelly figured that Rudy had told him to call her just to make her feel better. But then Osman began talking about the slug they took out of what was left of Frank Peres's skull, and she realized that Rudy wasn't just being nice.

"It's a modified Glaser," Osman was saying.

"That's some kind of hollowpoint, isn't it?"

"An old one."

"So?"

"And an old pistol. Walther P38 looks like."

"How old?"

"Probably built by Jews in a camp somewhere."

"I seem to remember counting maybe a dozen Black Talon casings at the scene."

"Yeah, I'm looking at them."

"You sure it wasn't a MAC 10? I know they had one, the rent-a-cop told me."

"What I'm sure of," Osman said, "is that it was a Glaser that came out the end of an old Walther and went into the councilman's brain."

Kelly thought about it a moment and then said, "Figure a gun that old had to have been stolen at some point, from a collector most likely."

"Probably stolen a few times."

"What I'm saying, at some point, this was a special piece to some-one. I'd like to know who."

"Not much chance that someone connects to a little banger in North Hollywood."

"Not much," Kelly said, "but I'd still like to know."

The John Doe was still asleep when Kelly stuck her head into room 416, so she went back out into the hall to chat with his doctor.

A Korean nurse informed Kelly that the man was under the care of a Dr. Ravi, who was currently somewhere in the hospital on rounds.

Kelly had him paged and fifteen minutes later a dark, skinny guy who, Kelly thought, looked more like the kid in *Slumdog Millionaire* than any doctor stepped off the elevator and introduced himself as Wali Ravi.

Dr. Ravi told Kelly that the John Doe had been shot once in the chest, once in the side—that one really just a burn more than anything—and once just above his left knee. The shot to the chest had been through-and-through, entering through the anterior chest wall, then went through the lung and came out the posterior chest wall right by the vertebrae. He said that it caused some minor lung damage but, fortunately, missed the great vessel walls.

Dr. Ravi was most concerned with the round still embedded in John Doe's left femur. The damage to the leg, he explained, would be far greater if he removed the round than if he left it where it was. But if the round should move or shift, they, or someone, would certainly have to go in and remove it. Either way, the John Doe would walk with a limp for the rest of his life.

While Dr. Ravi went off to continue his rounds, Kelly returned to room 416 where she found the John Doe still asleep, sat down in the green vinyl chair beside the bed, and studied him a moment.

The night before she had looked at his childlike features and thought him to be in his late twenties, but today, in the bright light of the hospital room, she could see some gray in the sandy brown hair and now figured him to be somewhere in his late thirties, pos-sibly older. It was hard to say for sure. He had one of those faces.

She opened her handbag and took out the stack of ten intelligence cards and laid them down on the rolling tray table. Each white 4x8 card contained a mug shot, physical description, and basic crime history on a particular gang member.

A turf battle over Dehougne Street had recently broken out between the Tiny Locos, a Mexican gang that had had the area for the past five years, and the Vineland Boyz, a black gang that wanted to take over. The Vineland Boyz didn't stand a chance. The Locos, like all the Hispanic gangs now, had money and support from Mexico. The VBoyz, on the other hand, had been too busy making shitty music videos for YouTube to bother paying attention to their turf.

As she waited for John Doe to wake up, she looked over the cards, some of the names and faces coming back to her, making her suddenly feel queasy. Kelly got up and opened the window. It was the smell, she told herself, all the disinfectant and sick people. The hospital was making her sick, not her past.

She sat back down and set the stack facedown on the table by the bed, but when she looked up, she could still see the kids in front of her.

If only Steven could have seen how she was with these kids. He would've understood; he would've known that she was doing something remarkable instead of just ruining their marriage. She was thinking that he should've come with her on the job a few times when she realized that John Doe was looking at her.

She smiled and said, "Good morning."

He blinked, looked around the room as if he was trying to figure out where he was. Kelly thought early forties for sure now. He had a nice face, not handsome, but sweet, set off by the mess of hair and light blue eyes. It was the eyes that now made her think he was older. There was some history there.

Kelly's first thought was that he was some kind of engineer or computer expert. He had that sort of look about him. Intelligent.

She badged him and said, "I'm Sergeant Maguire from North Hollywood Division. If you're up to it, I'd like to talk to you about last night."

He smiled at her and said, "They've got ESPN."

He then turned and stared up at the television mounted on the ceiling. Kelly saw now that a baseball game was on, the sound muted, why she hadn't noticed it before. She had no idea who was playing—baseball bored her to death—but whoever it was, he seemed riveted.

"If I could get you to focus for just a minute."

"I'm listening. I just really need to watch this."

"What's so important?"

"The Kid's pitching today."

"The kid?"

"Joe Mills. He's going to break the record soon and I need to see it." Her John Doe sounding a lot like a little kid.

"What record is that?"

"Consecutive innings without allowing a run."

"Yeah? What's the record?"

"Orel Hershiser went fifty-nine innings in 1988. That's over six straight games without anyone scoring."

"What's your guy at?"

"Right now, he's in the middle of game number three."

"You're waiting for him to break this record and he's still got over three games to go?"

"It's his time," he said. "I can feel it." He then smiled once more and added, "Right now, the Reds are doing everything they can to help him."

She looked at the set, confused. "So he's on the Reds?"

He gave her one of those chuckles, said clearly she didn't get it.

She smiled, playing along. "Which team is he on?"

"The Cards," he said.

She just looked back at him.

"St. Louis." He pointed at the TV. "That's him."

Kelly watched as the pitcher jogged to the mound and said, "That guy? He's gotta be at least thirty years old."

"Twenty-nine. His birthday is next month."

"Still," she said, "a little old to be called *kid*."

"He was a star at eighteen and the name just stuck."

"I bet he loves that."

He said, "Oh, no, he hates it," and smiled.

She sat back and watched the game. It seemed to calm the guy. After a minute or two, she took out her notebook and asked, "What's your name?"

He just looked at her.

"You didn't have any ID on you."

He thought for a moment. Then nodded. "The boy took it. The one called Science."

"We'll get to him. But right now, I need—"

"Roy," he said, back to watching the game.

"Roy what?"

"Cooper."

"Could you give me your address and phone number, Roy?" For some reason she didn't feel like calling this guy "Mister Cooper."

"I live at 41 Carlton Avenue. Apartment 4C." And then, before she could ask: "That's in College Point."

"College Point. Where is that?"

"In Queens," he said. "New York." Never taking his eyes off the set.

"You're a long way from home."

He just nodded.

"What're you doing in L.A.?"

She watched him stare at the television as he said, "I was looking for a friend." And then, "A girl."

Roy Cooper smiled and clasped his hands on his chest, wide awake now, and said, "He's gonna break the record, I can feel it."

"And this girl you were looking for, she lives on Dehougne Street?"

"I thought she did," he said, his eyes never leaving the set. "I think she gave me a fake address."

"Why would she—excuse me, what's this girl's name?"

"Rosa."

"Rosa what?"

"Rosa Garcia."

"Why would Rosa give you a phony address?"

"I think maybe she didn't want to hurt my feelings."

"I don't follow."

"She moved out here a few months ago. Told me she would call me when she got here, but she never did. So I got her phone number from her mother and called her. She said she was working a lot and didn't know if she had time to see me."

"Where does Rosa work?"

"She's a dancer. At a club. I don't know which one."

Kelly had trouble picturing this guy with a stripper, but one never knew. She sure as shit never pictured Steven with another dude.

"Anyway, I told her that I still wanted to come see her," Roy went on, "and she said I could do what I want."

"So you came out here when?"

"Last night. I rented a car and drove over to where she said she lived, but the address she gave me was for some place that made kitchen cabinets."

"What'd you do then?"

"I walked around the neighborhood, thinking maybe I got the street wrong and then I got lost. That's when I saw the kids shaking down the old guy in the sweat suit."

Kelly studied Roy Cooper a moment. One minute he sounded like a little boy, the next he was using phrases like *shaking down*.

"How many of them were there?"

"At first," he said, "just three. But then another one came later."

"You remember what they looked like?"

He described their clothing, the names printed on them.

"Then what?"

"Then the fourth kid came, stuck a gun in my neck, pushed me into the alley."

"Outside the one called Science, you hear any names?"

"The kid who put the gun on me was called Truck. He had a burn scar on one of his cheeks, the left one I think. And his eye was messed up, too."

"Messed up how?"

"It wasn't open all the way."

"You have a good memory."

He actually blushed at the compliment. Kelly could not, for the life of her, figure this guy out.

"You remember any of the guns?"

"One was a little machine gun thing I'd seen in movies. The other two were pistols."

"The one they shot the jogger with, it look old to you?"

"Maybe." He turned back to the game. "I don't know much about guns."

"Can I ask, Roy, what it is you do for a living?"

"I install security systems," he said. "For a company called Gold Shield."

She wrote that down and then asked, "Could you give me your Social Security number?"

"What for?"

"Routine," she said. "Make sure you're not wanted for anything anywhere."

She could see he was uneasy about this. She smiled at him. "You're not, are you?"

"No. It's just that I don't have one."

"Oh?"

"Both my parents died when I was a baby. I sort of bounced around for a while before I was picked up by an older couple. I took their last name."

"Which was Cooper?"

"Harvey and Rita Cooper."

"And they don't have your Social Security information, birth certificate, et cetera?"

"They never asked for one."

"They still alive?"

"Yes."

"You have their contact information?"

Roy gave it to her and then added, "They'll tell you that I'm very hardworking and helpful."

She considered his profile as he watched the game, his lips moving as he silently mouthed encouragement to the nearly thirty-year-old guy stupidly called "The Kid."

"Is Roy Cooper your real name?"

"It's the name they gave me."

"So they don't know your real one?"

"If they do, they never told me."

Kelly nodded and they sat there watching the game for another few minutes. She wondered what the hell was going through Roy Cooper's mind. He seemed so disconnected from what had happened to him. She didn't think it was shock. But could he be that simple? Did he just not understand?

"I'm going to make this case," she finally said. "You know why?"

Roy shook his head. "No, ma'am."

"For starters those tiny Gs left quite a bit of evidence. Hair, fiber, shell casings. But the real reason I'll make this case is I've got an eyewitness. A guy who tells me he's hardworking and helpful."

He smiled, eyes still locked on the damn TV.

"I know you want to help, Roy. I think that's why you got caught up in this in the first place. Trying to help."

"I was walking by," Roy said. "One of them put a gun to my head." He shrugged. "I didn't help anybody."

"But you tried."

She had been looking at him, the way people do, and made that bad read that always got Albert laughing when he was around to see it: "There's no reason for you to be afraid," she was now saying. "Those guys are all going away."

"That's a relief." She was right. They *were* going away. Because the minute he got out of here, Roy was going to find the one called Science and the one called Truck, get his gun back and then shoot them both with it before they got picked up and told the cops exactly where it came from.

"Let's get back to the alley. For the moment, they've got two guns now, one on you and one on the other guy."

"Both on me."

"Both on you?"

He wouldn't look at her. Kelly wanted to get up and shut off the TV, but she thought that he might stop talking if she did. She decided that this guy was a bug for sure. She just couldn't figure out what it was, made him so off.

"Why's that?"

"They weren't worried about the other guy."

"But they were worried about you?"

"He was an old man," was all he said.

She looked at him a moment, then rolled the table with the intelligence cards over to the bed.

"See anybody here you recognize?"

She watched as he took the cards and flipped through them. "Take your time."

"It's hard to tell them apart. They've all got shaved heads."

"That's why they do that."

He stopped flipping, studied a card a moment, then handed it to her and said, "Him."

Kelly looked at the card and smiled. "My boy, L."

"Who?"

Kelly said, "His real name's Delroy Kinney, but they call him L on account of all the dope he smokes."

"Why wouldn't they call him D? For 'Dope.'"

"'L' is old-school street for marijuana."

He looked at her.

"Smoke it," she said, "it takes you to La La Land. And Delroy likes to spend a lot of time there."

"They like names, too, don't they?"

"That they do," she said, "just like baseball players."

Roy asked, "Who was the old guy?"

"His name was Frank Peres. He was a city councilman."

That finally got his attention away from the game.

"He was running for mayor. Lived in that neighborhood for quite a while, thirty years or something."

"Now I know why he was so tough."

"Tough?"

"The way he talked to them. Telling them to knock it off, even though they took his clothes and hurt him every time he opened his mouth."

Kelly said, "Did any of them give any indication that they knew who he was?"

"I don't think so," Roy said. "They were just there because they were there."

Kelly's phone chimed and she reached into her purse and read the text.

From Rudy.

One sentence.

Get out of there.

She said, "Excuse me," and got up and moved to the window, stood there a moment looking down at the parking lot, tried to process what she was seeing.

A white van with Channel 7 markings was parked at the curb near the Emergency entrance. A guy was on the roof setting up the microwave tower. Another van, this one from Channel 13, pulled in right behind it. Kelly could hear a helicopter, off in the distance somewhere, though not for long.

She heard Roy Cooper clap his hands and turned away and looked up at the television, not really watching as The Kid struck out another batter, then jogged calmly back to the visitors' dugout. Kelly decided that she'd have to leave through the morgue. It had its own entrance and she'd be able to get to her car without being spotted.

She looked at Roy Cooper, who was now staring up at her, his face a confused mirror of her own.

She smiled and said, "We'll have to finish this later."

Roy Cooper said, "Is something wrong?"

But she was already out the door.

twelve

Albert had always said that the best way to lie was to tell some of the truth. But that wasn't the reason Roy knew that this cop wouldn't be any kind of problem. No, Roy knew that he was safe because she made the same mistake everyone made when they met Roy: she worried about him.

His whole life, most people talked to him like this. They underestimated him. Lowballed him every single time. It was his superpower. So he said nothing, let her go on, knowing that she still didn't have the faintest clue as to who he was. Who he really was. He could disappear without any problem the minute she walked out of the room.

And he would do just that.

As soon as this nurse left.

A moment after the cop split, a severely bunned Filipino woman with Popeye arms and a dark brown mole the size of a Milk Dud riding shotgun on her chin came into the room and, before Roy knew what was happening, gave him another shot of Demerol. Her nametag said G RODRIGUEZ, HEAD RN, and Roy thought he could smell peanut butter as she leaned over him, yanked back the sheet, and frowned at his empty bedpan.

"You need to urinate."

"I can't."

"You have to try."

"I feel like I'm wetting the bed."

She said, "It goes in the pan." She rapped a knuckle on the bottom. "See? Right in here."

She pulled the sheet back up and asked if he needed anything else, but left the room before he could answer.

Roy spent the next hour watching The Kid pitch another shut-out in a hazy painkiller stupor. Another couple of games like this one and he would break the record. Roy was beside himself. There he was, doped to the gills and with two gunshot wounds, grinning like an idiot as Joe Mills, aka The Kid, got hoisted onto his team-mates' shoulders. He felt tears welling up as, later, during a locker room interview, The Kid told an equally moved Erin Andrews that he wished his mother was still alive so that she could see him accomplish this great feat.

Lying there in his rheumy daze, Roy thought The Kid looked uncomfortable with all of the attention, his blue eyes never landing anywhere for very long. He wondered how the ballplayer would ultimately cope with such fame. Roy had recently seen him in an ad for Big Brothers of America. He was surrounded by kids and he seemed so earnest and innocent. Roy could see just from looking in the man's eyes that all of that goodness and incorruptibility would last.

Roy recalled how Joe Mills had begun his career as a superstar, the Royals calling him up from the minors and playing the same day against the Expos. He came into the game in the seventh inning and immediately retired the next three batters. And then he did the same in the eighth and ninth innings, the stadium announcer saying "How 'bout that kid?" over and over.

But two years later he injured his shoulder and struggled for another two years until Kansas City finally traded him to St. Louis. Up there, he was just another journeyman pitcher until a month ago, when he caught fire and pitched a shutout against the Giants, and all at once The Kid was back.

Roy shut off the set and thought about the lady cop. He hoped like hell he told his story the way Harvey had told him to tell it. Roy had an incredible memory. Albert had once said it was near photographic. But this lady, this Kelly Maguire, she kept making him forget. Maybe it was the way she smelled of cigarettes and baby shampoo. Same as his mother. That was it. That's what threw him off.

A few hours later, Roy was asleep, dreaming that he was watching himself on television. There he was on-screen, standing in the alley, his hands raised. The little gangbanger, the one called Science, had Roy's gun pointed at the councilman's cheek. Except that, in the dream, Roy was watching it from a high point of view, looking down on the whole thing.

He saw himself slap the kid.

And then there was a red explosion and the councilman was blown backward against the wall.

There was no sound and the picture was grainy. The Demerol, Roy thought, somehow blurring the dream.

Roy watched himself take a step toward Science, like he was going to grab him, saw the alley bathed in light, and then the one called Truck was shooting at somebody Roy couldn't see.

Roy watched himself turn, take another step, and fall down beside the dead man on the ground.

And then, bizarrely, the whole scene played over again.

Once more, Roy saw himself standing there with his hands up. Once more he saw himself slap the kid. Once more he saw Science put the gun on the councilman, the man in nothing but a jockstrap. And once more he saw the red explosion as the gun went off.

And then it started again . . .

Roy realized that he wasn't dreaming.

He was actually watching himself on television. But how could that be?

Roy remembered the movement in the dark window above the alley.

Someone in the window with a phone.

Someone caught the whole thing.

Roy started to piss. Staring at the television, he could feel the metal bedpan warming between his legs as he filled it with a steady stream that seemed to go on forever.

Roy heard excited voices out in the hallway, turned and looked at the door. He could see shadows shifting in the light that bled underneath.

Then the door burst open and he caught a glimpse of a uniformed cop standing guard just outside before the large head nurse marched in, this time with a grin on her face.

"You're awake."

Roy tried to look past her into the hall, but his view was obstructed by the immenseness of her as she leaned over to again check his bedpan.

"Oh, Mr. Cooper," she said. "I knew you could do it."

She proudly gathered up his piss in her arms, glanced at the television, then looked back down at Roy. "You're on every channel," she said, and then bent down, kissed him on the cheek, and whispered, "You're a very brave man."

Roy could see several other nurses smiling at him from the corridor.

She said, "Do you need anything?" And then stood there waiting.

"No. Thank you."

She let her meaty hand rest on Roy's shoulder, then walked out of the room. Roy saw the cop standing outside the door looking in at him. Another young kid, like the one who had told Roy the night before he was dying. He nodded to Roy, then reached for the handle and pulled the door shut.

On the television Roy now saw a shot of the lady cop as she left the hospital earlier that day, quickly ducking into her car, waving off a reporter. Well—more like shoving him away from her car. The sound was still down, so he couldn't hear anything. He reached a hand out and felt about the bed for the remote, but couldn't find it.

Now on the screen there was a mug shot of some black kid Roy didn't recognize at all from the other night. This was somebody new. Before he could get a better look, the screen changed to snapshots of a Latino woman and her somehow genetically fucked-up daughter at Disneyland.

The picture changed again, this time to show a green house on a street that looked familiar to Roy. But who were these people? Were they there last night? He was confused.

There was a date at the bottom of the screen from several months earlier. A sheet-covered body could be seen just inside the front door.

Who are these people?

The picture then cut to a drainage canal near a power station in North Hollywood. The body of a little girl Roy assumed to be the one at Disneyland was lying at the bottom, the upper half of her body submerged in the water. The lady cop stood among a dozen others, hard to miss the bitter expression on her face.

Then more shots of the lady cop, this time as she stopped to talk to reporters outside a police station. She looked different. Stringy hair and red eyes. Tired, Roy thought.

Roy lifted the blanket and looked alongside his legs for the remote. He couldn't find it, but was startled to see his left knee wrapped in tape, looking five times its normal size.

When he looked up again, the black kid Roy didn't know was now standing outside what Roy guessed was his house in a neck brace and flanked by his mother and a white guy in a suit who was making some kind of statement. Along with the brace, the kid had two black eyes and a bandage across his nose. His lips were swollen and Roy could see that he was missing a couple of teeth.

Someone had really worked him over. Though, from the looks of him, Roy thought, he had it coming.

Then, finally, came a shot of the alley from the night before, cops crawling all over it. A body covered with a sheet. Roy couldn't see himself anywhere in the shot until they once more replayed the video and there he was again with his hands up. Only this time Roy noticed that he was talking to the one called Science, the one with the gun, saying something to him. Science threw something in his face.

Cash. Roy remembered now.

And then the slap.

Roy sat up, felt the remote under the small of his back and reached behind the pillow and grabbed it. He turned the sound up just as the picture changed to a shot of an attractive brunette in a cream-colored suit standing in front of the hospital . . .

". . . now know his name is Roy Cooper from New York City. Earlier doctors told us that Mr. Cooper suffered two gunshot wounds in the attack, but is expected to recover fully."

Roy threw his covers off and sat all the way up. His chest felt like there was a knife blade jammed in between his ribs. He swung his legs off the bed, looked up as the reporter was saying, "Earlier I spoke with Alonzo Zarate, the man responsible for the incredible images you just saw, and Mr. Zarate's lawyer, Milton Shamberg."

Roy took a breath and stood up on his good leg. His left knee throbbed, felt like it was a bunch of loose pieces held together in a thin bag made out of skin, Roy thinking that it might fall apart at any moment.

He tried to hop to the window, but felt a sharp pull in his forearm where the IV was attached. He pulled the whole thing out of his arm, ignoring the searing pain in his leg and his chest as well as the blood that now leaked from the puncture in his side.

Holding on to the IV stand for support, Roy hopped to the window and looked down at the parking lot. He counted nine news vans and half a dozen squad cars now parked out front. Several helicopters were circling barely a thousand feet up.

"The guy's a hero."

Roy turned and looked at the television set and saw the reporter as she spoke to a little guy, looked Mexican, maybe thirty, with black, slicked-back hair and a goatee. He was wearing a white T-shirt and baggy black chinos. Next to him stood a man in a black suit, ten years older, with a round head of curly hair and black-rimmed glasses.

The Mexican was saying, "I hear this music, I come to the window, I see the kids doing drugs. I tell them to turn it down, go somewhere else, they give me this." The Mexican raised his middle finger for the camera.

"You didn't call the police?"

"These are brats. I'm not afraid of brats. I agree with what Councilman Peres been saying. They're all cowards. They call themselves gangbangers, I call them brats. I work for a living, but I see the way people look at me, like all Latinos are in gangs. Like I'm dangerous."

"But these were African Americans?"

"I'm talking generally," he said. "About gangs in general. Black, Latino, Vietnamese. They're all punks."

"Where was Councilman Peres at this point?"

"Mr. Peres goes running by and this punk comes up, points a gun at him—you know right here." The Mexican pointed to his balls.

As Alonzo Zarate went on to describe how they started to push the councilman around, Roy tried to move to the bathroom, see if they put his clothes in there. He hopped over to the door, grabbed hold of the knob, then fell on his ass as it opened backward.

He felt something rip in his chest.

"You called the police at this point?"

"I was about to, when the other guy showed up."

"Roy Cooper?"

"He was just walking by, stopped when he saw what was going down."

"He *stopped*?" the reporter said.

"Yeah. He was gonna help out when one of the gangbangers snuck up behind him, put a gun to his head."

"He was trying to help?"

"He stopped, yeah."

The reporter asked, "And that's when you called the police?"

"That's when I went, got my phone."

Roy grabbed the door handle and pulled himself up to his feet.

"I wanted to make sure it wasn't just my word against theirs, the way it usually is."

The pain in his knee was so great, it made Roy's eyes water. And now a big red stain was spreading across the front of his hospital gown above the wound in his chest.

"I come back to the window, I see they got a gun on this other guy . . ."

"Mr. Cooper."

"Yeah."

"He's telling the kid to take his money and go, leave Mr. Peres alone. And then . . ."

"And then?"

"He slapped the kid. Right in the face. It was awesome. That's balls, man. Bravest thing I ever saw."

"Why did you wait so long to call the police?"

Roy forced himself to get up and walk to the door. He had to get out of there. He would just push past the cop standing guard and make a run for it. The pain in his body was so great now that he felt numb all over anyway.

On the TV, Roy saw that the lawyer was now guiding the Mexican away from the reporter, saying, "Mr. Zarate has no further comment."

But the Mexican was saying over his shoulder, "That guy, Roy Cooper, he's a hero."

Roy stopped in the middle of the room and stared at the set. Beneath the gown, his body was slick with the blood that now flowed from his torn skin. He felt dizzy and was looking for something to steady himself with when the door opened and the big nurse reappeared carrying a huge arrangement of flowers.

She said, "These are from the mayor's office," before she saw Roy standing there, swaying in the center of the room, and screamed, "Mr. Cooper! What are you doing?"

Roy pitched forward, knocking the flowers from her arms and forcing her back against the wall. The young cop was in the room now, too, trying to keep Roy from falling on top of her.

The nurse screamed, "Get Dr. Ravi!"

Then all at once, Roy lost his breath. He swallowed and found himself looking up at the fluorescent lights, the nurse's planet-sized face hovering over him, leaning down like she was going to kiss him. Roy thought she *was* kissing him when all at once he felt his lungs expand with hot, peanut-butter-scented air.

As he stared stupidly into her brown eyes, he could hear Harvey's voice saying over and over, *They're gonna kill you now for sure.*

thirteen

Science could not believe his fucking eyes.

It was happening all over again, not in the alley, but in his fucking living room.

He had gotten up around ten, came out of his bedroom to find his mom asleep on the couch in her underwear and a Clippers T-shirt.

As he walked through the yellow living room to the kitchen, he saw that the *Today* show was on and some good-looking lady—even though she had to be close to forty—was showing the white guy with the buzz cut how to make his own ice cream.

The place was a fucking mess. His mother had come home, fixed herself a can of turkey chili, and left it cooking on the stove. Now, the shit was splattered all over the walls. Looked like someone got shot.

Science put the scorched pot in the sink and filled it with soapy water to soak. He then grabbed a box of Frosted Flakes and was carrying it back into the living room, pulling a handful of cereal out of the box, when he saw it.

They played the entire thing start to finish three times.

They showed pictures of the old Herb at some meeting.

The newsman saying now that he was the fucking mayor. Or was gonna be or some such bullshit.

Science didn't have time to think much about it as the next image was a replay of Mr. Freeze slapping him in the face. For the fourth time in five minutes, Science watched himself stumble back like he was just another street twink.

Then the image froze. It enlarged and someone drew a circle

around Science's head the way they do during football games, they wanna show you how the defense or whatever works.

Even so, you still couldn't recognize Science or any of them really. The camera was too high and in the dark to get any kind of read on anybody except maybe L, who sat closer to the light than the rest of them. Science knew he was cool—no way anyone could say that was him.

He could hear his brother, Cole, rolling up the ramp outside in his chair.

"Did you *see* that shit?" he said as he rolled into the room. "Me and Gene been laughing at it all morning."

Cole put himself right in front of the television, leaning forward on his dead legs as he watched the image of Mr. Freeze slapping Science and shook his head. "Fool got his ass *played*."

"Fo' sure," Science said. "You know who that is?"

"Gene says it's a Paca, li'l homie named Romeo."

Science nodded.

If his *own brother* didn't even recognize him . . .

Cole grabbed the remote and turned up the volume and pointed at the set. "Mothafucka supposed to be mayor."

Science watched a shot of Frank Peres from a week or so earlier, walking through the neighborhood shaking hands.

"Tell you one thing," Cole said. "They gonna be a lotta dead niggas behind that shit."

Science said, "Fuck the Locos."

"I ain't talkin' about the damn Locos, fool. It's the pigs—they gonna fuckin' *invade* this 'hood."

Science just nodded as Cole tossed him the remote and said, "Stay up, little brother."

"All day."

Cole rolled out of the room.

Science looked at his mom a minute, out cold through all of this, wondering what she'd think about this latest development. What will anyone think? Sooner or later, one of his boys, Shake or L for sure, will say something. Truck would wait for Science to make it right. But for how long?

And how does he make it right? That slap might as well have been a nuclear bomb for what it would do to Noel Bennett's life should the truth ever come out. The Science Man and all his plans obliterated in an instant.

Science stared at the set. Some lady with a microphone was now standing in front of the hospital, three blocks away. He thought about the strap with the hair trigger that was still under his pillow. He thought about the way the guy they were calling Roy Cooper looked at him. Whoever he was, Science could see him walking up the ramp out front and knocking on the door.

The dude wanting his gun back.

So this was the position he found himself in. If the truth didn't kill him, sooner or later Mr. Freeze would.

But if he killed the man who, according to the TV, was currently lying tubed up in bed a mere three blocks away, the truth wouldn't matter.

Science knew that the mere mention of this plan would instantly put him in a better light with Truck. Together, they would go over to Valley Presbyterian and take care of business. Science would rather be on death row than let somebody do him like that. Slap him in front of the whole fucking world.

But there was another, much simpler reason why the guy had to get got: self-defense. All morning long, Science had heard a voice inside his head repeat the same warning over and over:

Kill him before he kills you.

Part II

fourteen

"She's a beautiful woman," Mike Martin was saying. "Only natural for a man to be jealous of her now and again."

Roy looked at Mike from behind his soda and guessed his age at around thirty, same as Roy's mother, but maybe ten years younger than Roy's father and a lot bigger. Officer Mike—what he urged Roy to call him—went well over six feet with broad shoulders and weightlifter biceps that looked permanently flexed as he sat there with his arms crossed, resting on the table in front of him. He watched Roy with navy blue eyes that seemed to exactly match his uniform. Roy knew that his mother was a sucker for blue eyes. She had said that to Roy often enough, her hand on the back of Roy's neck, as she bent to kiss him on the forehead.

They were just about the only people inside the Denny's except for a man a few tables back, eating a plate of eggs and bacon at four o'clock in the afternoon.

Roy watched the man fold back a page of his newspaper, some ketchup smeared in a bottom corner, then took a sip of his Coke and said, "Being jealous isn't a crime."

"No. Nothing illegal about that." Officer Mike leaned back to adjust the dark Ray-Ban Aviators that sat atop his blond head. Roy thought he looked more like a male model or a famous quarterback than a Kansas City police officer.

"It's the other things he does I'm worried about." He gave Roy his best concerned friend look and waited for Roy to respond.

Roy let him wait.

"You know what I'm talking about, don't you?"

Roy looked out the window, two boys a couple of years older

stood across the street, both in hiking boots and flannel shirts. The bigger one had a faded filthy green JOHN DEERE baseball cap on his head. Roy watched as he covered one nostril with a finger, blew a load of snot out of the other one into the gutter.

"It's the burns on her arms. The broken blood vessels in her eye. The clumps of hair he tears out of her head."

Roy kept on looking out the window. He saw his own reflection and thought he looked scared, the brown and orange decor of the restaurant framing his startled face.

"It's the fact," Officer Mike went on, "that she's been to the emergency room in Raytown four times in the last seven months. Once with two broken ribs." He tapped the table three quick times with his index finger. "It's these things that worry me." And then, after a dramatic pause, "And they should worry you, too."

Officer Mike looked at Roy another moment, then smiled at a passing waitress and said, "Another Coke for my partner here."

Roy didn't like the way he said partner, something about the policeman's tone made him feel small. Smaller than he already felt. Roy was the smallest kid in the sixth grade. Dave Spicer was closest to him, and he had at least a full inch on Roy.

"Your next-door neighbor," Mike said. "Mrs. Talbott? She says one night last month she's looking out her window and she sees your mother in the backyard, in the rain, banging on the back door for your father to let her into the house." Mike sat back in his chair and crossed his big arms. Roy thought he might wiggle his biceps the way his dad did sometimes, make him laugh.

"She says your mother didn't have all her clothes on."

"I don't recall that."

"Huh. That's funny, because Mrs. Talbott also told me that you were the one let your mother back inside."

For a moment, Roy saw her from his bedroom window, standing down there on the porch in black panties, her bare breasts small and still, even as she hammered on the door with her fists. He felt ashamed by the memory. He knew that he might have stood there and watched her all night if she hadn't suddenly looked up and seen him in the window.

Roy sat back as the waitress set down another Coke and smiled at him. Roy smiled back, didn't want her to think that he was here with Officer Mike because he was in trouble.

"Thank you, ma'am."

"You're welcome, sweetie."

Mike winked at her, then leaned once more on the table, all serious again. "That took a lot of guts," he was now saying, "do something like that."

"Something like what?"

"Go downstairs when your dad's in a rage like that, let your mom back in the family home."

"He wasn't in a rage."

"What do you call it, then?"

"It's not his fault," Roy said. "It's the headaches that make him do it."

"The headaches?"

"He gets them right before he does something bad. All the other times he's fine."

"Your mother didn't say anything about any headaches."

"She thinks he gets them just because he forgets to wear his glasses, but the doctor says he gets them from working around the gas fumes all day."

"Maybe your father should quit his job."

"He could never do that."

"Why not? I mean, if it's making him sick."

"He loves being around the airplanes."

For some reason this made the policeman smile and nod like he really knew the man.

Roy leaned his head against the window. It felt cool against his skin. The two older boys were still over there in front of the gas station, but now they were sitting on the curb, eating from one bag of potato chips. They were both looking at Roy. The one in the hat licking his fingers. And now Roy could feel Mike looking at him, too. He was stuck. He didn't want to sit here anymore. But he didn't want to go outside either. Though he knew that sooner or later he'd have to.

"Your mother is suffering, Roy. She needs your help."

"What can I do?"

"You can call me the next time your father gets a headache."

Roy turned away from the window and watched as Mike took a card from his wallet and slid it across the table. He looked down at the card, but didn't pick it up. It had Mike's name and badge number on it as well as the phone number for the stationhouse. His home phone was written in ink just below it.

Roy thought Officer Mike's handwriting looked worse than his own. He was still staring at the card as he said, "I think he's suffering, too."

Mike just nodded like he understood, then tapped the card with his index finger. "Call me anytime, day or night. Okay?"

Roy picked up the card and quickly tucked it into his shirt pocket. He turned and looked back out the window. And now Mike looked, too.

After a moment, he said, "I know those two." He turned to Roy. "You need a lift home?"

Roy shook his head, slightly humiliated that Officer Mike had possibly seen how afraid he was.

"They don't bother me."

"All right, then."

Mike got up and left him there.

Outside, the two boys watched as the cop walked out of the restaurant and over to the handicapped spot where he'd parked his patrol car. Mike opened his door and then leaned on it a moment while he said something to them, something Roy couldn't make out. They called back to the young cop from across the street. Mike laughed and then got into the car.

Roy couldn't believe what he just saw. He laughed. Why would he do that? Now he knew for sure that the man wasn't on his side.

Not that he had any doubts before.

Roy sat in the booth for maybe five more minutes while he finished the soda. And then sat for another five while he chewed up all of the ice in the bottom of the glass. He was thinking about buying one more soda when he realized he didn't have any money.

He took a breath and slid out of the booth, careful not to look out the window.

fifteen

"Say, miss? Miss? Can we have a word with you?"

Roy didn't turn around, just kept walking at the same pace. The trouble was, his normal walk made him look scared. Everything Roy did made him look scared. He stumbled on the uneven sidewalk and found himself jogging the next few steps.

"Please. Don't run, miss!"

They were right behind him. His breath was short and his heart felt like it might tear from his chest. He was shaking, he told himself, from the caffeine in the soda. He knew that he couldn't outrun them. They'd never let him do that. So he simply stopped walking and faced the two of them. Whatever happened, happened. He had lived through it before.

The bigger one was sweating, out of breath. Roy could see some crusted jam in the corners of the kid's mouth. His name was Jim McDonald and he was a year older than Roy. The other one, the one in the hat, Brent Garland, was two years older. There were streaks of grease fixed into his jeans, a smear of it on his forehead. Angry red acne ran off his face and down his neck where it disappeared under a stained yellow tank top. Roy thought about the engine he was always rebuilding. The old car he would drive when he turned sixteen. A Nova. Light green with gray primer bruises all over it. As Roy pictured the car in their backyard, it got him thinking about the shed back there, and about Brent's sister. The stories he'd heard about the two of them.

Brent took a step closer and Roy could smell tobacco. "You narc on us to that cop, miss?"

"He already knew about you."

"So you talked about us?"

Jim McDonald spat on the sidewalk a few feet from Roy. He stared at the little puddle of foam and said to no one, "Missed."

With that, Roy turned and resumed walking.

"Hey, girl! I'm talking to you!"

Jim spit in his hair, Roy could feel it, but he kept on walking. Roy felt a hand on his shoulder and started running. He didn't bother to look back. He turned up the first street he came to, the little houses breezing by in a blur. Raytown now in the dead of fall, the yards and sidewalks blanketed in yellow paper birch leaves.

Roy could still hear the two of them panting behind him as he turned onto Amapola Street, crossed at a sprint in front of a car just starting to pull away from a stop sign, someone now yelling at the group to, Goddammit, be more careful as Roy ran along the sidewalk, tripped over a downed branch, hidden in the leaves, but somehow managed to keep himself upright.

Roy's house was a split-level wrapped in brick wainscot below and dark brown siding above. Not a friendly house. There were no longer any shrubs in the yard, just a brown lawn, a circle of dirt in the center where an elm once stood. Roy was running across that circle when he heard her voice.

"Hey, handsome."

She was sitting on the front step, in pale blue cotton shorts and one of his dad's white shirts, legs folded to one side, an open *Redbook* magazine across her lap. She rocked the white bassinet containing Roy's baby brother with one bare foot, and Roy saw she had recently done her toes in the same blue as her shorts. It wasn't cold out yet, but it wasn't warm either. Still, there she was, dressed for the Fourth of July. She looked past Roy and watched the other boys now, the two of them skidding to a stop on the sidewalk, practically running cartoonlike into each other when they saw her.

For a brief moment, nobody moved. Roy hoping the fear on his face wasn't too obvious when his mother put her brown eyes on him. Nobody talks about brown eyes the way they do blue or even green. But she had some kind of brown Roy had never seen before. There was black in there that under normal circumstances would have made them dead, but on his mother only made them deeper, like that suede leather coat she once bought and modeled for Roy until Roy's father came home and made her take it back.

"Easy, boys," she said barely above a whisper. She smiled and pointed at the bassinet. "His nibs is sleeping."

"Hello, ma'am," Jim McDonald whispered back. Only Jim McDonald could speak. Brent was staring at her. The way they all stared at her.

"What's with this ma'am stuff?" she said. "Evelyn. Please."

The two just nodded. Roy didn't know where to look.

"How's your dad feeling these days, Jim?"

"He's back at work."

"Glad to hear it."

"I'm still doing the cooking, though."

"No wonder you look so good."

Jim McDonald inflated as if he'd just been kissed. And, in a way, he had. The two of them watched stupidly as she stood then, carefully gathering the bassinet as she uncoiled from the step. She turned back, gave them another smile over her shoulder. Like she was posing for a picture.

"You boys coming in?"

"Okay," Brent blurted before he could stop himself. But Jim McDonald quickly came to his rescue.

"We gotta be somewhere." And then he looked at Roy. "We'll see you later, buddy."

And they turned and started back the way they came. Brent looking back at Roy's mother one last time. Roy watched them go, feeling worse now than he did before.

It was cool inside the house for so late in the afternoon. But then Roy saw that she still hadn't opened any of the drapes and had probably only just woken up a little while ago. When she wasn't working, she and the Captain always took their afternoon nap together.

"How was your day, sweetie?"

"Fine."

"You should go wash that out of your hair."

Roy reached back, felt Jim's tobacco juice. When he turned to her, she wasn't looking at him, too busy now carefully setting the bassinet on the coffee table where she could keep rocking it with her foot while she watched Phil Donahue.

"I'm just gonna say hi to the Captain first."

"Don't call him that."

Roy looked down at the baby, eight months now, smiling all the time. The only one in the house who did.

"He likes it."

"I don't."

"Was what Dad used to call me."

"Yes. I was there."

Roy turned and looked at her over his shoulder. She was lighting a cigarette. After the shorts, that would be the second major infraction of the day. She went back and stood in the doorway, looking out at the street. At least she didn't smoke near the baby.

She stood there a good while, having some conversation inside herself while she slowly drew on the cigarette.

Roy knew she hated it here. There was nothing here for someone like her. She just woke up one day from one of her naps and here she was.

Stuck.

They all were.

Her back still toward him, she said, "I'm thinking of working full-time for Dr. Toomey." She shifted so that she leaned with her back against the door frame. "Maybe you could help out some after school, with your brother."

"Is Dad okay with that?"

"I haven't asked him." She turned to him then. "I know it's not how you want to spend your after-school time, but we could use the extra money."

"I don't mind."

And he didn't. Now he had a real reason to stay home. He looked once more at his brother.

"I don't mind at all," he said. "Do I, Captain?" Low enough so that she couldn't hear him.

. . .

Roy was upstairs giving his brother a bath when he heard his father pull into the driveway. He could hear the El Camino a full block away. The muffler busted and making a racket that made the car sound more powerful than it was. Before his baby brother was born, Roy would run outside to meet his father as he got out of the car. Roy grabbing him around the waist and smelling the jet fuel on his coveralls. His father making a big deal of stumbling back against the car and saying every time, "Man oh man, Captain, you're getting strong!"

Roy's father would then haul Roy onto his shoulders as he headed up the walk, Roy holding on to the man's ears to "steer," careful not to knock off his thick glasses. He could see the tiny cuts from where Roy had nicked him with the razor a few days before. Roy couldn't understand why his father continued to ask him to cut his hair. His mother did it better. But his father thought it was something every man should know how to do. And he liked it short. The same length it was in the Air Force before he had to leave.

Once a month, on Sunday, his father would open a beer and sit down at the table and call out, "Hey, Doc! Ready for surgery!" Roy would climb up on a chair behind him and work the razor back and forth. His father laughing when he nicked him. Both of them laughing until Roy's mother came in and looked at the clumps of hair on the floor and then in horror at his father, wondered why the fuck they couldn't just go to a barber like regular people.

Because, his father explained, they weren't regular people.

The two of them would then sit in the kitchen for the rest of the afternoon. This was their church, his father would say, while Roy watched him design the airplane they'd eventually try to build in the garage. Roy would later learn that it wasn't really his father's design, but something he'd found in a magazine. Still his father would spend hours narrating every move of his mechanical pencil to Roy, sometimes using the blade of his hand to describe the shape of the wing.

It was still out there, covered in a black tarp. "The Wrong Brothers" is what Roy's mother called them whenever she stuck her head out the door to find out what all the damn noise was. It was better when it was just a blueprint. Just an idea they could talk about until his mother told them to talk about something else, for Christ's sake.

Roy loved sitting at that table, the one place he wasn't afraid. He felt as if he could do anything on those Sunday afternoons. He didn't want to be anywhere else but right next to his father, listening to the man talk about flying.

But that was all before the headaches.

The first time Roy witnessed one was late one night, out in the garage. They were working on *the ship* as Roy's father called it, a BD-5 Micro plane the size of a Datsun that came in a kit. Roy's father claimed that he'd had a company design the parts from his drawings. But the truth was, his father had bought the whole thing off a guy at work who had himself bought it through the mail in the mid-seventies, but never bothered taking it out of the crate. The company had gone out of business a few years later. The manual stated right at the top that it would only take a thousand hours to build, but Roy and his father were closing in on three thousand and nowhere near finished.

There was also the matter of the seventy-horsepower engine, no longer manufactured since the company went bust. But Roy's father heard about a group of BD-5 owners that had a fly-in once a year in Placerville, California, and told Roy they'd drive out there and get some hints as to where to find an engine along with any other pertinent information they currently lacked. Roy's job was to plan the trip, even though it was never actually said when they would go.

The plane was designed for one, but Roy's father came up with a "modification" so that Roy could sit in front of him, toboggan style, while he flew. The fact that Roy's father never finished his flight training and had never flown a plane like this didn't seem to bother him. So there they were one night, trying for hours without success to fit the prefab Plexiglas canopy from the kit onto the newly modified, and now slightly enlarged, cockpit, when Roy noticed that his father's head was shaking. Roy was sitting inside the plane at the time, holding the bubble in place and looking up through the plastic when he saw a drop of sweat fall from his father's face. It was then he noticed that behind his dark-framed glasses the man's eyes were closed and seemed to be vibrating on their own, like an old dog having a bad dream.

"Dad?"

He opened his eyes and stared at Roy for a moment, and then at the mallet in his hand, as if he'd just noticed it was there. He then bit down on the big rubber head.

Roy could see his father's teeth penetrating the rubber, could hear the man screaming as he suddenly began to beat on the Plexiglas with his other fist. Roy quickly bent over and covered up, but it didn't take long for him to feel the plastic shards on his neck as the canopy began to crack. He yelled for his father to stop, but was drowned out by the man's pathetic howling. It was only a matter of moments before the man broke through and, Roy assumed, stove his son's head in.

But it was over as suddenly as it began. The garage was suddenly silent. Roy took his hands away from his head, carefully looked up and realized that his father was gone. Roy sat up and saw through the crack-blossomed plastic that the man was sitting on his haunches, sobbing it looked like, Roy's mother crouched beside him, holding on to him, as both of them collapsed onto the greasy floor.

Roy's mother put her husband to bed. An hour later, she came out of the bedroom and found Roy standing in the hall, shaking. She kissed him on the top of the head, then led him into his own room, helped him undress, and then got into bed with him. Roy fell asleep to the rhythm of her heart hammering against his back.

The next morning he found his father calmly moving about the kitchen making waffles. His mother sat at the table watching him over a cup of coffee, both of them smiling.

"Hungry, Captain?"

Neither of them ever said a single word about the night before. Nor would they ever about the nights that followed.

Roy listened to the El Camino shut off and rattle for a moment. He pictured the man taking off his glasses and rubbing his temples for a moment or two before he got out. He heard the car door first, followed a few seconds later by the front door as his father came inside.

And then his voice, loud, as he called out to everyone and no one, "Smells great in here!"

He was always in a good mood. That's what was so disconcerting. He was never upset or angry. He would just turn. In a single instant, he would become another man. A shadow would pass over his face and he would do something or say something that his father only an instant earlier would never have done or said. But there he was, somebody who looked and sounded like his father sticking a fork into a pot of boiling water and smiling at Roy as he speared a potato and stuck the whole scalding thing into his mouth.

When Roy carried his brother downstairs, he found his father and mother with their arms around each other, their mouths locked together. His mother grabbing the back of his head, pulling him into her. This happened a lot. They would find themselves in a room and just crash into each other. She was always the first to break it, backing away, wiping her mouth with the back of her hand and smiling at him.

Roy sensed they had real desire for each other. But with his mother, it was desire fueled by something else, something he couldn't yet understand.

She winked at Roy, then headed into the kitchen as Roy placed his brother inside the playpen that sat in front of the TV and waved to his father, who now paused, his arms having not yet shed the light blue windbreaker from his coveralls.

"A wave," his father said. "That's it? That's all I get?"

Roy walked over and hugged him, the man tossing the coat and giving his son a hard squeeze that felt like it might break his spine, followed that up with a strong pat on the back before he walked into the kitchen and took a drippy pull from the beer his mother had just opened.

"What'd you learn in school today?"

"Nothing."

They played this one every night at the same time. His father smiling as he passed the beer to his mother so she could take her own sip, and then asking, "Then why'd you bother to go?"

And Roy would shrug and answer, "I don't know."

It was becoming less and less of a game for Roy. Why *did* he bother to go? He wasn't so sure anymore. He sat in the back of the classroom, day in and day out, in constant fear that someone might notice him. Look at him. Speak to him. It wasn't hard to pick up that he was afraid. Always afraid. And no wonder, given the asshole he had to live with. Probably got smacked on the head once too often. Best if they all gave him lots of room. If he wanted to eat his shitty little lunch in the parking lot by himself, who cares? Let him.

Once the headaches started, the only time he was ever truly relaxed was when he was alone with his baby brother. The Captain made him forget. Especially when the headaches got worse.

"Scusez moi," his mother now said as she reached into a cupboard for a stack of plates.

"No," his father said as he came off the counter, Roy catching the small flinch his mother gave as his father then held up his hands. "Excuse *moi*."

Smile. Kiss. All good.

Even though Roy never saw him hit her, she was hand shy, the phrase his father used on a stray Irish setter they once found in their front yard and kept for a few days before his father put the dog in the car one morning and took him to work. He came home alone that night, told Roy that another fueler lived on a few acres out in Iola and had given the dog a better home.

Roy thought she was right to be nervous around him. The man always seemed to be watching her. Ever since she started working for *that fucking dentist*, Dr. Toomey, answering his phones. She never used to wear much makeup, or spend much time on her hair. But now she was getting up a full hour before she had to catch the bus to Dr. Toomey's office downtown.

Dr. Toothy, his father called him. He didn't know him, didn't know a thing about him other than he hated him.

What would later be billed as the third worst windstorm in Missouri history happened to blow through Raytown the same week that Roy killed his father.

The near-tornado-like gale snatched the roofs off a dozen houses in Roy's neighborhood alone. Across the street, the forty-foot ash that had stood guard over the Fitzgeralds' house for over thirty years broke in two and came down on top of Annie Fitzgerald's new Rabbit convertible. Roy had watched from his window as the little white VW got creamed by a chunk of the tree, a giant foot crushing a German soda can.

It all seemed like a dream to Roy. But then everything that happened that week was like a dream.

A few days later, on the drive out to the airport, his father was still dodging the debris that had fallen onto the roads.

"Guess they're just gonna leave it all on the ground until some poor slob runs into it," he said.

A half hour from their house in Raytown along Route 435, no real traffic this early on Sunday morning, Roy stared out the window at the cement percolation ponds that ran along the highway. The blue squares of water dotting the even, brown landscape like one of his father's shirts. Normally, Roy found the drive comforting. This flat world was the only place he'd ever been. Missouri becoming Kansas at some invisible point along the way. And then before he knew it, the gray wheel-shaped terminals of the Kansas City International Airport.

Their other church.

"What we do," his father was saying, "is we walk around the aircraft, check that everything that should be there, is; that what should move, does; and what shouldn't move, doesn't." They were on the tarmac, looking up at the undersides of a USAir 737, his father explaining the art of the preflight.

"Try to develop a routine, and stick to it every time you check your aircraft, inside or outside."

He pointed up at a luggage door. "Is this compartment really latched?"

"Looks like it."

"Check it," he said as he hoisted Roy up to the door.

Roy jiggled the latch and said, "All good!"

His father then lowered him back down so fast that Roy felt it in his balls. The man now crouching down to say, "Sometimes we see things the way we expect them to be instead of the way they are."

"Morning, Roy."

They both turned and saw a tall, silver-haired man in uniform, captain's bars on his shoulder, ducking under the wing. He smiled at Roy's father, nodded to Roy.

"Now that good-looking kid couldn't possibly be yours."

"You bet he is."

"Teaching him the trade?"

"No way. He's gonna fly 'em. Not fuel 'em."

The pilot smiled at him, then began his own, actual preflight. He was then joined by another man, this one in coveralls. A walkie-talkie on his hip. Clipboard in hand. The pilot said something and the man now looked at Roy and his father, who waved.

"Morning, Mr. Haas."

"You on today, Roy?"

"No, sir. Just showing my boy around."

The man looked at Roy, then back at his father. Uncomfortable or annoyed, it was hard for Roy to tell which. "You sign in at Operations? Talk to the desk there?"

"Was just about to."

"The kid can't be out here without a badge."

"We're just leaving."

The man nodded, looked at Roy another moment, then turned back and followed the pilot on his rounds.

Roy and his father parked at the end of runway 19R in a patch of dirt outside the cyclone fence and watched the planes take off and land. The jets screaming overhead one after another while the two of them sat on the hood of the El Camino, their backs to the windshield, Roy's father naming each aircraft as they touched down in puffs of rubbery smoke a hundred yards away.

The man had wanted only to be a pilot. He spent his childhood hiding in his room making models and watching planes land at the airport. Flying was all he thought about. In high school, he built a working glider in his backyard. On his eighteenth birthday, he joined the Air Force only to be told that his eyesight wouldn't cut it, so he became a mechanic repairing helicopters.

He hated helicopters almost as much as he hated helicopter pilots. They were cocky and didn't respect their aircraft the way fixed wing pilots did. They were cowboys. His eyes got worse. Contacts bothered him, so he wore those thick glasses. Smudging them with oil and grease until he could barely see through them. Watching the pilots climb in and out of the fighters all day. There was something the same about them all. Even the pilots he saw today. They all had this thing that he didn't have. An easy way about them. It was a connection they had, all of them being able to do this thing that very few other people could do.

That he would never do.

"Lockheed L1011. Most advanced plane ever built."

They watched the plane touch down. "Can practically fly itself. They got an elevator in there, goes down to the galley. You imagine that? An elevator? In an airplane?"

Another jet taxied into position right in front of them, the tail nearly above them as it sat waiting to take off. His father had made sandwiches for today's visit, egg salad, and brought along a couple of Dr Peppers.

In the last year or two, his mother stopped letting Roy have soda. Said it was bad for his teeth. Like pouring acid on them. This, of course, pissed off his father, who thought that little pearl of wisdom came from the fucking dentist and should, therefore, be ignored. So whenever he was with his father, there was always soda.

Roy could taste the jet fuel with the egg salad as the plane in front of them started rolling down the runway. His father watched it, saying "Rotate" a split second before the nose lifted and the plane rose into the sky on its way far the fuck away from here.

An American Airlines 727 touched down, his father explaining yet again that with the flaps all the way down like that, they can fly slower. And then a USAir 737, his father waving at that one, prompting Roy to ask, "Do you know who's flying that plane?"

"They know me."

His father claimed to know all of the pilots. Roy knew this wasn't true, but let his father find his connection any way he could.

"You really think I could be a pilot?"

"Captain, I think you can be whatever you want to be."

They were silent for a few minutes then. His father letting a Delta DC-9 land without comment, until out of nowhere, he asked, "Are you afraid of me?"

Roy turned to see his father looking at him now.

"Because I don't want you to be."

Roy looked back at him. "Why do you hurt her?"

"I don't know. Your mother thought she was going to marry a pilot. Have this nice life. Travel all over the world. Instead, she has to live here, work for some dentist. All on account of I can't see.

Even though there's nothing I can do about that, it still makes me mad."

He turned back to the runway as he said, "I wish it didn't, but it does."

A small general aviation plane taxied into position in front of them. A sleek six-seater with a tail in the shape of a "V." It was the strangest thing Roy had ever seen.

"Beechcraft Bonanza." His father smiled. "The Doctor Killer."

"The what?"

"V-tailed Doctor Killer. That's what pilots used to call it."

"How come?"

"Bonanza will do a hundred and seventy-five miles an hour at ten thousand feet, and that's only using a hundred and fifteen horse-power. But with that tail, it's more stable in a pitch than a roll. You hand fly that airplane in the clouds, you better be on top of it, as that plane wants to spiral. *Down*."

He looked at Roy. "And what do we say about a VFR pilot in the clouds?"

"He's autodead."

His father nodded and turned back to the plane. "If you know what you're doing, it's an amazing plane. *If you know what you're doing*. But doctors, they think they can do anything. They have the money, they get their license and they go out and buy one of those. Only they can't fly it. And they end up crushed and burned inside of it."

Roy watched the plane take off now, rotating in half the time of the big jets, Roy wondering if the man at the controls was any kind of physician. Wanted to ask, what about dentists, but didn't. Plus his father had now sat up and was looking at him with a strange look on his face.

"Don't ever try to be something you're not."

"Okay."

"I'm serious. You are who you are. You have to live with that. If you fight it, if you try to be someone you can't ever be, you'll never be happy. The trick is in knowing who you are. And accepting it. You understand?"

"I think so."

"Good." He watched another 727 land without comment, then

planted his palms on the hood, swung his legs off the car, and said almost to himself, "Let's go home."

Roy recognized the change and kept quiet. His father had moved into that silent, focused place where you could not speak to him or reach him in any way. Usually, these trances happened at home where Roy could simply take his baby brother and go hide in his room. But there they were, doing close to eighty on Route 435 with the rapidly setting sun off to their right. It would be dark soon and Roy didn't want to be alone with his father at night. Not when he was like this. Roy knew that the man was in a lot of pain. That some invisible asshole was inside his head at this very moment pounding nails into the backs of his eyes.

During these times, his father would sometimes cry. Would sometimes speak nonsense words. Would hammer his fists or break something. At home, they'd developed a system: Roy's mother would quickly help the man up into the bedroom and lay him down on the bed, while Roy quickly pulled the heavy blackout drapes, trying not to look at his father writhing on the bed like a sick child. If he was at work, his father would go sit in one of the toilet stalls and bite down on a small rubber ball he carried with him, his face pressed against the cold metal partition, and wait for the cloudful of white-hot pins to finally pass through his skull.

But at this moment, they were in a moving car. And even in the gathering dark, Roy could see something was wrong. The man now leaning his head hard against the glass. His eyes wide open behind the thick glasses, the passing lights like little stars in the lenses.

Roy leaned over, careful not to move too suddenly, and watched the needle on the speedo wipe past ninety.

"Maybe we should pull over."

Nothing. Just a slight moan from the dark shape beside him.

"Dad."

"Fuck her."

"Who?"

His father sat up straight. The car slowed down. Roy felt relief that it was already over. His father took one hand from the wheel and rubbed one temple with a thumb and whispered, "She's killing me."

"Mom?"

He turned to Roy slightly. It was hard to say whether he was actually looking at Roy or looking at anything for that matter. There were tears in his eyes, and then he vomited.

Roy recoiled, pushed up against the door, and could feel the car leaving the road. His father threw his head back against the seat and the car lurched forward along the shoulder before Roy felt his side of the car dipping as the El Camino started sliding down the embankment. The car lost speed as it plowed through the soft dirt and Roy waited for it to stop altogether. But, somehow, the El Camino surged onward. There was a splash and before he knew what was happening, Roy's door opened and he fell out of the car.

He hit the forty-degree water and immediately sucked the icy green liquid into his lungs. Roy thought he was drowning, until his feet hit the muck and he stood up, the pond less than five feet deep, the surface hitting him just below his chin. Even so, he couldn't catch his breath, couldn't stop coughing, and thought he might drown anyway until he saw the El Camino fifty feet away and stopped panicking, finally took in a lungful of air.

The car was in the pond with him, its rear end toward Roy. It was leaning heavily to the driver's side, but had remained upright. The passenger door was slightly ajar, so the dome light was on and Roy could see the back of his father's head, the man leaning against the door.

"Dad!" he shouted. "Over here!"

His father didn't move.

Roy tried to walk toward the car, but with the first step his shoe caught in the muck on the bottom and came off. His other shoe came off with the second step. His third step, his foot slipped and he went under once more. He stayed under and swam a bit in the dark, until he hit the back of the car and he popped up and grabbed his now bleeding head. Dazed, he hung on to the bed of the El Camino, and pulled himself up over the back and into the bed.

"Dad?"

He could see that water had risen and that his father's head was

halfway underwater. The car shifted under his weight and Roy realized that it was sinking deeper into the mud. He jumped back into
the pond and tried to open the driver's door, but the list and the mud
prevented it from budging. He looked inside and watched as the
water rose up to his father's mouth. He saw the huge black slice in
his forehead, the blood roaring from it mixing with the water on his
face creating a runny mask. Roy pounded on the window.

"Dad! Wake up!"

But Roy looked at the red face and knew there was no answer
coming.

He climbed back into the bed of the El Camino, then jumped out
the other side and tried to get the passenger door to open wider. Roy
wasn't strong enough to fight against the mud and the weight of the
water. He tried to reach through the small opening, tried to grab his
father's windbreaker and pull his head up but he was too small, a
full foot shy of getting his hand on the blue nylon.

It was dark now and he could see the headlights of passing cars
up the dirt embankment, the drivers on Route 435 oblivious to what
was happening barely ten yards down the hill. Roy couldn't believe
it. Didn't anyone see them go off the road? He began shouting . . .

"Help! Down here! Somebody!"

But the cars up there kept moving.

He swam to the cement bank and pulled himself up. Exhausted,
he turned and looked back at the pond, the dome light still illuminating the man hunched over inside the car, his head still facedown
in the water.

Roy yelled up at the passing cars.

"PLEASE! SOMEBODY! HELP US!"

His voice was raw already, and he couldn't get enough air to be
loud enough. So he just started screaming.

His voice was about to go when he saw the beam of a flashlight at
the top of the embankment. A man stood there, his features lost to
the black. He shone the light down at the pond, then at Roy.

"My dad's drowning!" His voice hoarse, barely rising above the
traffic.

The man started down the hill. Slowly. Roy watched as he tested
the earth beneath each and every fucking step before putting his
whole weight on it. It was maddening.

"He's under the fucking water!"

But the man kept the same slow pace. As he got closer, Roy could see that he wore coveralls and heavy work boots, but his face remained hidden in the dark until he finally got to the pond and handed the light to Roy, and said in a voice only slightly above a whisper, "You stay right here, son."

Roy took the light and crouched down as the man then carefully slid down the bank into the water and looked back at him.

"Son, I can't see in this dark," he said, no panic in his voice. "You need to keep that light on me the whole way."

Roy raised the flashlight and for a split second the beam caught a face wrinkled from the sun, flesh hanging loosely around the man's chin, deep dark bags under the eyes. The man rescuing Roy's father had to be at least eighty years old.

He waded into the water, took long, strong steps toward the El Camino. He got the passenger door open wide enough to reach inside and drag his father from the seat. He shifted his weight, slipped in the mud, and went down in the water on his ass, got himself up again and reached his upper body into the car. He grabbed Roy's father by the hair and pulled his face out of the water. He then maneuvered the unconscious man into his arms. The old man got him free of the car, stood up slowly, and walked back with him to the bank, Roy tracking him the whole way with the light. He finally dropped Roy's unconscious father on the cement, leaned over him and immediately started blowing air into his bloody mouth.

Roy crouched down beside them and stared at his father's closed eyes. He found himself thinking that it looked as if the old man were kissing him. As soon as he thought it, he hated himself. He reached out and held his father's hand. It was cold and dead in his own and he wanted to let go as soon as he touched it, but he held on. Squeezed it tighter.

Another light hit them from above and Roy looked up the embankment and recognized in the silhouette the tall hat of a state trooper.

"Anybody hurt down there?"

And in that moment, Roy's father sputtered and then coughed. The old man quickly turned him onto his side and for the second time that day, Roy's father vomited all over him.

. . .

It was a stroke. Something, according to the doctor, that was already there inside his brain waiting to happen. It had nothing to do with his eyesight or kerosene fumes. The headaches were merely a sign that something had been long cross-wired, fucked up and ready to blow deep inside the man's head.

Roy's father came home from the hospital a week later. He couldn't speak, couldn't move, the doctor declaring him "basically a vegetable." Roy wondered about the necessity of the word "basically" as the two ambulance attendants carefully set him down on the hospital bed his mother had rented from a surgical supply house in Belton. His father looked like he had been stuffed inside a sack made out of his former self.

Too big to make it up the stairs, the big metal bed was placed in the middle of the living room. Roy held his brother in the kitchen doorway, out of the way while the men from the surgical supply house helped the ambulance attendants, all under the supervision of his mother, get his father settled in. She stood halfway up the stairs, in denim shorts and pale pink blouse, smoking a cigarette as four sweating men gingerly tucked her turnip of a husband into what could accurately be described as his final resting place.

And then they were gone. Just like that, the house was silent save for the machine that monitored Roy's father's vital signs. None of which at the moment appeared to be visible, let alone vital.

She stared at the man in the bed, exhaling smoke in his direction as she now started down the stairs. She moved to the side of the bed and reached down to move some hair out of his face. There was a row of stitches just below the hairline. A low moan came from his half-opened mouth and she stepped back. Walked back around the bed, giving the man a wide berth even now, in this condition. She noticed Roy and the baby in the doorway and just looked at the two of them, her expression empty of anything comforting or loving in any way, her voice flat as she said, "You should have let him die," and then walked back up the stairs.

. . .

Roy listened to her door close and then carried his baby brother over to the bed. He watched his father breathe in and out. When he'd come back to life beside the pond, he'd looked at Roy and said, "I found a nickel," and then his face seemed to freeze and he said nothing more.

Roy looked at the hospital bed and wondered how long it would remain in the living room.

As it happened, not long.

He had just put the Captain into his crib and was himself dozing fully clothed on the floor beside it when he heard a THUMP downstairs and sat up.

For a moment, all he heard was the baby snoring. Then again: THUMP. THUMP. THUMP.

Roy got up and opened the door. THUMP THUMP. A pause. Then THUMP THUMP THUMP. He started down the stairs, saw one of his father's bare feet, now uncovered by the sheet, half off the bed, kicking the wall: THUMP THUMP. Roy took another step down and saw his mother straddling his father's chest, holding a pillow over his face, her nightgown hiked up and Roy could see that she wore nothing underneath. Her arms strained and her face contorted as she fought to keep the pillow in place, Roy's father thrashing beneath her in some bizarre parody of sex. Strange, muffled sounds were coming from under the pillow as his hands flailed like a dying fish, his body bucking and twisting before all at once, like a switch had been flipped, the man went still.

She held that pillow in place for another five minutes. She didn't trust him even in death. When she finally pulled it away, the underside was wet and bloody. She considered his frozen face. His eyes were wide open and his mouth was full of blood from biting his tongue.

She sighed and shook her head.

"Goddammit."

She looked up and saw Roy on the staircase.

"He chewed his tongue off." She climbed off of him and tossed the pillow aside. "Fuck."

Roy came the rest of the way down the stairs, staring at his father's horrible, panicked face while his mother lit a Salem and sat down on the couch, folded her legs to one side, and considered the scene through a long exhale.

"He couldn't have died in his sleep. Not with his fucking tongue chewed off."

Roy turned to her. She had just smothered his father with a pillow and was talking to Roy like she was having trouble vacuuming up a stubborn footprint. She took a deep breath and looked at Roy a good long while before she spoke again.

"Go to bed."

"I feel sick."

"You'll be fine."

"I really don't feel good."

He ran into the kitchen and threw up in the sink. She stood in the doorway silently smoking, watching him rinse his mouth out and then wash out the sink. He stood there, bent over, trying to catch his breath.

She said, "You wanted him dead."

She came over, dropped her cigarette in the sink, and stood over him.

"Why else did you wait so long to try and save him?"

Roy looked up at her. "I couldn't get him out."

"It was four feet of water. All you had to do was pull his head up."

"I couldn't get into the car."

"You could've broken a window."

"With what?"

"So you did nothing?"

"I called for help."

"And then?"

"The man was there."

She smiled at him. Put her hand on the side of his face and said, "We got what we wanted, though, didn't we?"

It was a little after three a.m when Roy heard a familiar voice downstairs. His brother was quiet in the crib beside him as he climbed out of bed and walked to the door. Officer Mike was at the bottom of the stairs looking up at Roy standing there in the Kansas City Chiefs pajamas his mother had gotten him a couple of years ago. They were too small and Roy felt stupid all of a sudden in the presence of the young cop.

"It's okay, son. Come on down."

So it was "son" now. Roy wondered if he should still call him "Officer Mike" or if that was only for that half hour at the Denny's. He beckoned with his hand for Roy to keep moving. And as Roy descended the stairs, he could see Officer Mike's partner, a bigger, redder-faced version of Mike, looking up at him. Roy's mother sat on the edge of the hospital bed, watching Roy's every move, her eyes red from crying, a tissue clutched in her hand. Roy was young, and not that wise to anything, but in that moment, any idiot could see that he was fucked. How exactly, he wasn't sure. He just knew that once he got to the bottom of the stairs, there would be no going back up.

Roy didn't say a word when they handcuffed him, looked at his mother as they read him his rights. She told him through tears that as soon as she found someone to watch the baby, she'd be down there with a lawyer.

Down where? Roy wondered.

The Wyandotte County Juvenile Detention Center was a cement bunker on North 7th Street. Roy sat in the backseat looking at Officer Mike in the rearview mirror, the young cop now giving him a little preview of what was to come.

"This is where you're gonna spend some time thinking about what you've done and learn to correct your behavior," he was saying to Roy now. "No more friends, no more going to the movies, no more home-cooked meals."

Roy wanted to say that his mother hardly ever cooked, but he didn't.

They pulled into a sally port and Mike helped him out of the car. His partner nodded in the direction of a security camera and the door locked behind them while the one in front of them now opened. They walked down a short, bright hall to a room marked INTAKE

AND RISK ASSESSMENT. There were racks along the walls with uniforms. Another rack with strange gray garments resembling the heavy apron the dentist draped over Roy when he X-rayed his teeth.

"That's a suicide smock," Mike said, and went over to it and pulled it out for Roy to see it.

"If the staff thinks you're in danger of hurting yourself, they might put you in one of these." Mike tugged at the fabric.

"It's one piece and really thick, so you can't turn it into a noose and hang yourself."

Roy wet his pants. It just happened. One minute he was standing there listening to Officer Mike go on about killing himself, looking at that ribbed gray smock and thinking about the dentist that day he went in for X-rays, how the dentist smelled like licorice and how nice he was to Roy, how nice he was to Roy's mother, and then the next thing he knew, his shoes were soaked in piss.

They kept him in Isolation that night. His mother came to visit him the following afternoon. She was with an older man in a wrinkled black suit with a sprinkling of dandruff on each shoulder. His mother said he was their lawyer and introduced him as Mr. Solomon. The lawyer said that Roy could call him "Doc," that everyone did, and got out a pencil stub and a yellow pad of paper and asked Roy to tell him how his father died.

"I don't know," Roy said. "I was in bed."

Roy's mother exchanged a look with Mr. Solomon and said, "Would you give me a minute alone with my son?"

The lawyer nodded, already fishing a pack of Kools from his suit coat as he got to his feet. Roy's mother waited for the sound of the visiting room's outer door to close before turning back to Roy and studying him a minute.

"How are you doing?" she asked. Then immediately answered her own question, "You're okay, right?"

Roy wasn't sure how to answer that one.

"Sweetie, you understand that if I go away, it's to the penitentiary for life." She let that sit with him a moment, then went on. "If you go away, it's to the Honor Center at Boonville, for a couple years at the most."

"Is that what Doc says will happen?"

"Think about the Captain. What's best for him? Should he lose his mother? He's already lost his father."

"Because you killed his father."

"You and I both know that he lost him before that, in the pond."

"How is he? The Captain."

"Fine," she said. "For now." She grabbed her purse and fished around inside until she found her own cigarettes.

Roy watched her and said, "But he'll be okay, right?"

She looked up from her purse and said, "That's really up to you." She lit her smoke, sat back, and looked at Roy. "He's at home now. His home. Not some foster hell hole with a dozen other filthy kids. Which is where he'll go—where you'll both go—if I go to prison."

They sat there in silence a moment. Roy's mother smoking her cigarette and looking around the room. Roy thinking about his little brother. Thinking about how it wasn't fair. He was just born into this bullshit. Roy loved him, couldn't imagine being away from him for a day or two let alone a couple of years. He realized then that the Captain was his only friend. That little baby was all he had that was good. When the two of them were together, he wasn't so afraid. Why? he wondered. Then it came to him. It was because he was taking care of somebody. The Captain depended on him. There was no room to be afraid.

He looked up at his mother. She crossed her arms and returned the look, but with nothing on her face. She was waiting.

Roy finally asked, "What's Boonville like?"

sixteen

Miguel Santiago.

The mayor had begun saying his name to himself. He would do it all day long. *Miguel Santiago.* Never aloud, but quietly, inside his own head. *Miguel Santiago.* He couldn't remember the exact moment when this little habit—this little *tic*—had started, but it had been going on for a while now.

He'd first caught himself doing it in the middle of one night when he'd gotten up to take a leak. He'd been having some trouble in that department, sometimes standing there up to three minutes before anything happened. And not just when he was alone. For years he had avoided public restrooms at all costs. Airplanes had become a permanent no-go without at least two Xanax and/or getting stupidly drunk first.

On this particular night, the mayor had been swaying over the bowl for what seemed like forever when, out of nowhere, he realized that he'd been repeating his own name like some kind of mantra. *Miguel Santiago . . . Miguel Santiago . . .* The instant he made this odd discovery, his entire being relaxed and he emptied his bladder in a euphoric rush.

It wasn't long before he couldn't piss at all without first following this ritual. The words *Miguel Santiago* working like a urinary abracadabra every single time. Even in places like Dodger Stadium where the mayor—unlike the ex–chief of police and previous mayor—had always avoided the public johns because he didn't want to look like some bladder-shy pussy in front of his constituency. But now, he could suck down a quart of beer and a Dodger Dog, then stroll into the can and surprise the male fans in there by walking right up to the big public trough that had always so intimidated him before, and smile at the voters on either side of him, giving everybody a big "How y'all doing tonight?" as he hosed down the metal backsplash.

And all it took to get there was that quiet little incantation.

Miguel Santiago.

Later, the mayor discovered that his name had power well beyond merely helping him void his bladder.

Once upon a time, when he felt embarrassed at something he'd said, something he knew to be idiotic the minute it left his mouth, he would punish himself by surreptitiously flipping himself off under the table or behind his back or in his trouser pocket. It was a weird thing he'd been doing since he was a kid. His own chickenshit version of self-flagellation.

No, the mayor had discovered a much easier way to deal with his shame. Now when, say, at a press conference the mayor might have casually mentioned (lied) that he loved football, and some asshole journo asked him to shout out his favorite player and he couldn't, the mayor just repeated his own name a few times to himself and, wouldn't you know, felt better instantly. Shame forgotten.

So earlier that morning, the meeting had just barely begun when the word "execution" was tossed out, followed by the phrase "possible federal investigation," and the mayor just sat at his desk, still as a hat rack, serenely running the *Miguel Santiago* loop over and over in his head (though lately he'd been experimenting with variations such as *You are Miguel Santiago,* or his new favorite, *And now, I'd like to introduce Miguel Santiago!*).

Not that the mayor needed a distraction. For most of the meeting, for most of most meetings, the mayor thought about Savannah, his latest conquest. While the others watched footage on Evan's little Vaio of some dark-skinned middle school dropout putting a gun to poor Frank Peres's head, the mayor saw Savannah smiling at him in bed that morning before turning over and sticking her ass in the air.

"Jesus fuck." Gordy Savage, LAPD chief, shook his head and said, "Some asshole takes the time to go get his phone so he can tape the whole thing, but not once does he think to call 911?"

The mayor heard himself saying, "Guy was really lucky."

They all looked at him like he was some kind of mongoloid.

Ladies and gentlemen, the mayor of Los Angeles. Miguel Santiago!

The mayor cleared his throat and beamed back down into the meeting.

"I just meant," he said, "that the guy's window was in the perfect spot."

He flipped himself off under the desk.

Joy Levine, the mayor's PR chief, came to his rescue. "He sold the footage to CNN for half a mil," putting that kind of face on it. Joy, even at seventy-one, was the best-dressed member of the mayor's staff, turning up this morning in a violet suit with a cream-colored scarf to match high-heeled shoes the same color. The mayor was fascinated by the fact that Joy Levine was black, but married to a white bankruptcy lawyer named Mickey Levine. The two of them together, no doubt, since the sixties.

Gordy Savage, on the other hand, looked more like he had just come off the back nine at Annandale—which he probably had—than L.A.'s top cop.

Gordy said, "We've already got one of those kids pretty solidly ID'd. I think we'll have them all by the end of the week."

"Have them all, or know who they all are?" The question coming from Evan Crisp, the mayor's executive assistant.

Barely thirty and the youngest person on the mayor's staff, Crisp had an MA in public policy from NYU. His family owned several shopping malls in Glendale and Arcadia. All through college, Evan worked a host of shit jobs in New York City—everything from selling footwear at Shoegasm to working food service at Bellevue—in a futile effort to ward off the inevitable label of Entitled Shit.

"Hopefully both," Gordy answered, trying not to look like he wanted to put one of his FootJoys up Evan's ass. "We've got good people on it."

"Yes, we'll get to that in a minute." Gordy watched uncomfortably as Evan made a note in his leather-encased legal pad with an eight-hundred-dollar Mont Blanc fountain pen. Evan liked to write down everything everyone said. This naturally made everyone uncomfortable. People felt they couldn't be as off-the-cuff as they might like whenever Evan was around. Especially since Evan tended to use their own words against them down the line. He may not have acted entitled, but he was still, in most minds, a complete shit.

The mayor looked at his watch. Just after ten. Savannah was well on her way back to New York City by now, back to that little apartment in NoHo on Bond Street. Every room in the place stinking of sex. The minute the mayor walked in and took a whiff, he lost all hold of himself. Just thinking about those three little rooms . . . Jesus.

They'd met last summer at a dinner party, on Martha's Vineyard of all places, at the home of a movie producer named Paul Fine, né Finkelman. They were seated next to each other at a table that somehow sat thirty and, once they were introduced, didn't talk to another soul for the rest of the night. Except for a few brief moments when Paul Fine announced to the table that Miguel Santiago, the mayor of L.A. and the next governor of California, would like to say a few words to us all. Miguel got up, gave one of his speeches about growing up poor and Hispanic in rich, white, and Republican Orange County. The Vineyarders lapping it all up along with the beach plum sorbet. As they were saying their good nights, the drunk ex-wife of the guy who had once upon a time bought and sold some energy drink company for a few billion, asked the mayor if anyone had ever told him that he looked like Antonio Banderas.

Only every fucking day of his life.

"No, ma'am, that's the first time I heard that one. But I take it as a compliment."

"Well you should."

Then she leaned in close, nodded toward Savannah, and whispered, "That young lady wants to put her finger up your ass."

The comment turned out to be both prescient and an understatement.

Savannah had a degree in finance from . . . somewhere. The mayor made a mental note to have Evan find out exactly where. She currently worked for a big investment fund in Manhattan. Shit, he couldn't remember the name of that either. She had just turned thirty the night before and they'd celebrated downtown at Patina with a rack of lamb for two and a three-hundred-dollar bottle of Opus One. The whole thing billed to the city. Savannah now a "financial consultant" to the mayor's office.

Funny thing was, the mayor had always dated older women.

Actually much older. Not that long ago, he was in a relationship with a woman who had twenty years on him.

But Savannah, she was—

"All it takes is one match."

It was Leila, the gang advisor. She was upset. But then, she was always upset. What a fucking joke that had turned out to be. Joy had persuaded the mayor to hire her. Dr. Leila Graham was a sociology professor and provost at USC, but looked more like an ex–fashion model. She was easily six feet tall with long gray hair streaked with black. Leila had spent the last twenty-five years hanging out with gang members and considered them all her family. She had written a dozen books on the subject and actually lived in South Central. The mayor wondered if any of her neighbors knew that the leggy white lady down the block grew up in San Marino, was a onetime Rose Parade Princess, and the only daughter of an heir to the Chandler fortune and a prominent real estate developer.

"If we go too fast," Leila was saying, "we will almost certainly cause an explosion."

Evan asked, "How so?"

"This might not be anything other than a shakedown, turned bad. But . . ." She let her *but* hang in the air for a second or two, then raised a finger as she continued. "But if we start accusing particular gangs of executions—"

The mayor said, "Stop saying *execution*."

"Whatever the language, if we accuse them of something they're not responsible for, they'll retaliate."

"We know they're responsible for killing the guy," Gordy said. "It's all right there on-screen."

"I'm talking about ascribing some sort of political motive."

The mayor was getting annoyed. "There is no political motive! The fucking guy got mugged!"

Leila looked at him, suddenly calm. "Miguel, Frank Peres has accused you quite publicly and on several occasions of taking cartel money for your election."

"Because of that one dinner." He threw up his hands. "Guy grows strawberries! Okay? How was I supposed to know he was part of a fucking *drug cartel*? And what does that have to do with Frank Peres?"

"The African American gangs have all been put down," Leila explained in that faux patient way of hers. "They all work indirectly for the Latin gangs, who are all directly funded by the cartels now. They want nothing more than to get out from under that kind of oppression."

"Oppression?" The mayor was trying not to laugh. "Are you fucking kidding me?"

"You saying they're not oppressed, Mr. Mayor?"

"The blacks," Gordy said, "the ones in gangs anyway, are rappers now. They have their own record labels. They're making music, if you can call it that."

"So?"

"They're *playing* at being in gangs. There's nothing serious about them. Not anymore."

Leila said, "That's a generalization, don't you think?"

Gordy just shrugged. *Maybe. Maybe not.*

"You don't understand." Leila keeping her voice low for maximum effect. "This city—the whole damn country—is just one match strike away from burning down. Ferguson and Baltimore were just the beginning. We got off light out here." And then, "So far."

Evan asked, "You saying this could lead to riots?"

"We're due. You all want one?" She smiled at the mayor. "With your name on it this time?"

Miguel Santiago. Miguel Santiago. Miguel Santiago . . .

"I've lived with these young men." Leila got up now and started pacing. "These neighborhoods, they've all been marginalized by the cartels."

"Marginalized?" Gordy said. "They're criminals, for Christ's sake!"

"They have nothing," Leila said, looking like she might actually cry. "The cartels control the drugs coming in from Mexico, and they won't sell to the black gangs."

"I'm confused," the mayor said. "Am I supposed to feel sorry for them because they're not selling drugs anymore?"

Leila stood by the window, the morning light hitting her on one side, making her look more like a fashion model from *Town & Country* than an academic.

"I'm merely telling that there's anger in the black community. What you do or don't do with that information is up to you."

She then turned and looked out at the city, ten a.m. and the sky already the color of butter, and went on: "The pain, the heartbreak, and the true injustice in the black community are not gone simply because they've been forced into silence."

"They're not silent," Gordy said. "They're all of them rapping about it."

She ignored him. "If anything it's getting worse. With fewer jobs, more cuts to social services, more imbalance in the economy."

The mayor looked at Evan Crisp. The young advisor was busy writing down her every word, so it was hard for the mayor to tell whether or not he was buying any of this.

"There used to be food stamps, social workers, free after-school programs—these things were cut during the last budget crisis. None of them have been replaced."

Joy said, "The libraries are back up to seven days a week."

Leila looked at her and smiled. "Yes, Joy, that's true. And I'm sure the black community is jumping in the air about that and the new film incentives Miguel brought back to the city."

Joy refused to let sarcasm keep her from her appointed rounds. "I'm just saying that it's not all as bleak as you make it."

"It's worse," Leila said, then looked at the mayor. "Miguel, it's the same old story. The only way to break out of the cycle for young men like the ones in that video is to work as a drug dealer for the Mexicans. But everyone on the street knows that in the end, you'd just have a job with rules made by Mexicans."

The mayor couldn't decide how he felt about her use of the word "Mexican."

"It's depressing," Leila went on. "The opposite of righting the wrongs of slavery—the black dealers just have a new owner now, because the people are slaves to their addictions and to the dealers that feed them."

She sat back and crossed her long legs and looked at each of them, one at a time. Trying to get a read on her performance. One of those types, the mayor thought, who needs to feel loved by the people who hate her the most. Or at the very least, loved by the people who feel that she's full of shit.

Or was that him?

Fuck.

That was him.

When Leila looked at Evan Crisp, he made a big show of looking at his watch. The mayor could have kissed him.

"Except," Evan was now saying, "that gang crime has actually gone down since the black gangs lost the drug trade. The problem, yet again, solved by money. Just not ours." He smiled, not daring an outright laugh, though the irony was pretty fucking funny if you thought about it.

Leila didn't say a word. Just kept looking at Evan. Hoping, the mayor thought, that if she looked long enough, the guy might actually dissolve.

Evan kept smiling. "But I take your point. And that's certainly all worth discussing."

With Evan around, the mayor didn't have to speak much. Gave him time to think. And right now he was thinking that the fucking quake a week earlier wasn't bad enough. Now this had to happen. The election just a few months away and his opponent gets his head juiced by a street gang, and in North Hollywood of all fucking places.

The truth was, Mayor Miguel Santiago, the Hispanic mayor, was not well liked by the Hispanic community in L.A.

The Hispanic community hated the drug dealers back home in Mexico. They cut off their relatives' heads and used them as hood ornaments. And here was the guy running against Miguel Santiago, Frank Peres, a respected and well-known Hispanic businessman, accusing Santiago of taking money from those same decapitating assholes.

And then, a few short weeks later, Peres gets himself dead on the street. By a black street gang. The mayor had to admit that if he were a voting civilian, he'd be looking hard at the mayor, too.

"What concerns me," Joy was now saying, "is how this makes you look on crime."

The mayor sat up. "How is this my fault?"

"It's your city. And apparently you can't control it enough to prevent a mayoral candidate from getting executed."

"Jesus, Joy."

"That's not me talking, of course. That's what they're saying. That your opponent got executed on your watch."

"Please, for the love of God, stop using that word. The man was murdered."

"I think Joy's right," Evan Crisp said as he took what seemed like the better part of a week to carefully cap his pen and replace it in his pocket. "Frank Peres was running an anti-gang campaign."

"He was talking about his own neighborhood," Gordy said. "And those aren't black kids over there."

"They sure as shit looked black to me," Evan said.

"An anomaly. The problem in Peres's neighborhood is brown, not black."

"Try parsing that one for the public."

Even the mayor had to ask, "You really believe that the public is going to think a street gang assassinated a mayoral candidate?"

"They already do," Evan said. "Go online."

"I'd rather not."

"Frank Peres had the city's attention. He was tough. An ex-cop. He wanted to take out the cartels."

Joy asked, "So why wasn't it a Mexican gang that shot him?"

"Because the cartels are smarter than that."

"You don't really think that *that*," the mayor said pointing to the frozen image on the laptop, "is anything other than a straight-up street crime?"

"Of course, that's all it is," Evan said. "But all of us in this room have enough experience to know that if we don't do something, the public might be persuaded to believe it's something else."

"What do we do?"

"I'll tell you what you *don't* do," Leila said. "You don't make it political."

But no one was listening to her. They were all looking at Evan, who now sat back and crossed his legs.

"You have to be tough, too. Like Frank Peres."

Leila said, "Daryl Gates was tough."

Evan kept his focus on Miguel. "You have to show that you're not corrupt and that you'll stop at nothing to find those who did this. That you're tough on the gangs. That you will tolerate no one and no policy that isn't as tough as you are. You have to be That Guy."

Tough on the gangs. Jesus. No wonder Leila hated everyone in the room.

Joy had persuaded the mayor to hire Leila by telling him Leila would interface with DCFS, make it look like the mayor was taking a *new* approach to gangs, one that was more child-centered by pretending to work within the labyrinth that was Children and Family Services. Joy convinced the mayor that this would get people off his back so that he could go back to doing what L.A. mayors do—fighting to get more business back to L.A., giving handjobs to the big Democratic donors, and yeah, working for more film incentives. The truth was, and everyone in this room knew it, the mayor hadn't really paid all that much attention to gangs.

So it was all the more amazing when he said "I'm already That Guy" with any kind of straight face.

"You are," Evan said. "But she has to go."

Joy and Leila both looked at him.

It was Joy who asked first, "She?"

"Kelly Maguire," Evan said, knowing he'd just tortured the two women for no reason, but now looking at Gordy. "One of the *very good people* you have working on this."

"You want me to pull Kelly Maguire?"

"Yes. She's wrong for this one."

"Are you stoned? She's perfect for this one."

"She's a lightning rod. Especially for this one."

"Son, maybe you haven't noticed, but out that window we're dealing with a goatfuck of monumental proportions. With the quake and all the assorted and sundry bullshit that came with it, I can't afford to lose even one cop right now. I mean, Jesus Marvin Christ, do you have any idea how many homicides are already getting back-burnered because of it?"

"You don't have to fire her," Evan said. "Just pull her from this case, put her on something else."

The chief shook his head. "She knows the gangs. She knows the area. I say let her run."

"She's a racist."

"She told the truth."

That got Leila looking at him. "I beg your pardon, Chief?" she said. "That woman publicly stated that the only way to cure the gang cancer in L.A. was to eradicate it, to either lock them up or line them up."

"She didn't publicly say anything. Someone recorded her conversation and put it on YouTube."

"Still—"

"She said a lot of stupid shit. But Kelly Maguire's not a racist. Not by a long shot. Good God, she's fucking Nelson Mandela compared to some of the Aryan assholes we got badged up."

seventeen

A few minutes later, with everyone sufficiently pissed off at each other, the room cleared out, leaving the mayor alone with Evan.

They sat there silently for a moment, Evan scribbling on his pad, the mayor staring off into space, thinking about a drink he'd had with Kelly Maguire a million years ago. He thought they had gotten along pretty well. The mayor had really liked her, had meant to ask her out again, but, for some reason, never did. He'd forgotten all about her until a few months back when she blew up and her name was suddenly everywhere.

Talk about dodging a fucking bullet.

"What are you thinking about?" Evan asked, not bothering to look up from his scribbling.

"Gun control."

"What about it?"

The mayor shrugged. "Maybe this is a good time to bring it up."

"Gun control isn't the problem, not here anyway. Money is."

"Now you sound like Leila."

"She's not wrong. All of those services she mentioned were cut."

"So we talk about getting them back."

Evan didn't answer, kept scribbling. The mayor looked at the frozen image on the laptop, Frank Peres lying there in a puddle of himself, and took a deep breath and shook his head. "Jesus," he said. "What the fuck happened?"

"Your opponent was shot and killed for one thing."

"Are you trying to be funny?"

"I'm trying to be honest," he said, finally looking up from his notepad. "This is an opportunity."

"You're not going to give me one of those God-closes-a-door-somewhere-he-opens-a-window speeches, are you? Because that kind of liquid shit doesn't really work with me."

"This time, God knocked down every cell tower but three up on Mount Wilson. Let's start there."

"Okay."

"The only people with consistent cell service are people with satellite phones."

"So?"

"Rich people."

"And drug dealers."

"Let's talk about gas and electricity."

"Okay," the mayor said. "Let's."

"The power, almost a week later, is out all over, from Compton to Reseda. But I see lights on in Brentwood and Bel Air."

"They never lost power in those neighborhoods."

"Doesn't matter. If I see it, other people can see it."

"You're talking about perception."

"How about this," Evan said. "How about you be the guy who turns on the power in the shittiest neighborhoods."

"I thought I was the guy who was tough on crime, et cetera."

"You can be both guys."

"Warren Russ over at DWP tells me that we don't have the juice to light up those neighborhoods. Not right now."

"You do if you turn the power off in Brentwood and Bel Air."

"Are you out of your fucking mind?"

Evan just looked back at him.

"We're talking about pissing off some big donors."

"Yes, Eli Broad will be upset for sure, but he's not going to run screaming out of his house, drive down the hill, and light Neiman Marcus on fire."

"No. I don't suppose that he would."

"On their best days," Evan said, "the poor have their Internet and their TV to soothe them. Turn those things off and they get antsy, go outside, start breaking windows."

"God, I would have paid good money to have heard you say something like that to Leila a few minutes ago."

"Leila's right about something else." Evan tapped the computer screen with a fingernail. "All it's going to take is one incident to start a new fire." He then turned to the mayor and said, "That cannot happen."

The mayor thought about it a moment, then said, "So I turn on the power. I bounce Kelly Maguire from the case. What else?"

"Go visit this—" He went a few pages back in his notes. "Roy Cooper." Then looking up again. "Go visit him in the hospital. As soon as you can."

"What for?"

"Shake his hand. Tell him the city's picking up all his medical expenses. He's a hero. Guy tried to step in and do the right thing. As opposed to the selfish cretin in the window who stood up there in his underwear filming it."

Evan put down the notebook, leaned across the desk.

"This city, in the aftermath of the largest earthquake in its history, needs more Roy Coopers. No—we all need to *be* Roy Cooper. We all need to be there for the people we don't even know, but share our city with."

The mayor shook his head and smiled for the first time all morning. "Tell me again," he said. "Why the fuck do I need Joy Levine when I have you?"

"Why the fuck indeed."

eighteen

Kelly Maguire was pissed off. It had taken nearly an hour and a half on a buckled and clogged 405 to get from her apartment in Marina del Rey to Covenant House in Hollywood only to be told that Carmen Suarez wasn't there, hadn't been seen since the quake. It was then another forty-five minutes to go a mere eight blocks to My Friend's Place and still no Carmen.

The quake had fucked up an already fucked-up traffic system. Most of the major freeways had at least one lane closed, while some had full-on detours around sections that had collapsed or were in danger of collapsing. The surface streets were no better. Many, like Hollywood Boulevard, had sinkholes, some half a block wide, while still more were flooded from all of the broken water mains. A three-block stretch of Sunset Boulevard, from Argyle to Ivar, near the Cinerama Dome, was still, a week later, under four feet of water.

Not only the traffic, but the shit cell service was also pissing her off. During the drive, Kelly had a broken conversation with Rudy Bell that she was still trying to process.

She had answered her phone and Rudy jumped right in, knowing they wouldn't have long. "Let's talk about your guy at the hospital."

"What about him?"

"I ran him."

"What possessed you?"

"I was sitting here waiting for Mike to get out of the john, thought I'd pitch in and take that one off your to-do list."

"You don't like him."

"He doesn't fit with the neighborhood."

"You've always been a suspicious fuck."

"I know, it's weird for a cop. Especially being partnered with someone like you, sees only sunshine."

"We're not partners."

"Not at the moment."

"Now who's seeing sunshine?"

"Kelly, listen to me—"

Kelly was grateful they got cut off. Not in the mood for another Rudy play for love disguised as a pep talk. He called back and this time she was the one who jumped right in.

"So you ran my guy."

"He's not in the system."

"He doesn't have a record."

"He doesn't have anything. No fixed address. No Social. He's nowhere. Dude's fucking light as air."

"He gave me an address in Queens."

"It's a P.O. box."

"That new data center got pretty rattled in the quake. Maybe it's a computer thing."

"All that information's in the cloud now."

"What do you mean?"

"You think it's all stored in a building? You're adorable. Listen. Something's wrong. The guy has a name, a post office box, and that's it. It's like he doesn't exist."

"He exists."

"But he doesn't *live*, know what I mean? Or he lives off the grid."

"He lives in Queens."

"Well, he's left the footprint of a gnat."

Kelly thought about Roy Cooper lying there on the ground, holding her hand. The man lying in bed watching the baseball game, infatuated with some pitcher. She said, "I think something's wrong with him. Like he's simple or something. I was gonna call his employer."

"Gold Shield Security. I called them."

"And?"

"Got a machine. Leave your name and number and we'll get back to you for all your security needs."

"I'm assuming you left a message?"

"I did. Left your name and number."

"You don't think he's the model citizen he says he is?" Though she realized that, so far, Roy Cooper hadn't said much of anything outside of his obsession with baseball.

"I think the question is, what was a guy from College Point, Queens, doing in that particular neighborhood?"

She was about to tell him about Rosa, the girl Roy had come to visit, when she lost him again.

Kelly didn't miss the phone. Not right now anyway. It was the phone that got her in trouble in the first place. Everybody and their fucking phones. Some guy sees that Frank Peres is about to get shot, he gets his phone and records it, more worried about missing the money shot than saving the man's life. But even the everyday is now urgently passed around like it's breaking news. Kelly couldn't understand those assholes, for example, that have to take pictures of every fucking meal. Cannot wait to share every damn detail of their boring lives. Get some likes. Thumbs up. Followers. Whatever the fuck people think of as social currency these days.

Kelly wouldn't know. She was the opposite of social. She was an angry dog. Or so the department shrink had told her. What she had, goes way beyond anger issues. She's "violent." "Deadly." Dr. Berg told her that she'd be a sociopath if she didn't overempathize with everyone. He called her personality a "delicious irony" in that it was her empathy that caused her violent behavior. His report said, "Sergeant Maguire sees and experiences things that she can't process, horrible things, feels bad for the victims, then goes and exacts revenge on their behalf."

Bullshit. Kelly knew that her violent behavior stemmed from the fact that she had lost all patience with her fellow man.

Especially when she was behind the wheel.

Like right now. Behind this plate-head in the Honda Civic who just now put on his left blinker, a second after the motherfucking light had turned green. He's got, what, eight cars behind him now, including Kelly, all of them thinking that he was going to go straight, all of them making the now-in-hindsight bad choice to stay behind him instead of moving into the right lane, which was now breezing through the intersection while this selfish dickhead inched forward, waiting for the oncoming traffic to clear so that he could make his precious left turn. People were honking and he, of course, was ignoring them. Instead, the guy looked at Kelly in the rearview mirror, thinking it was she who was on the horn, and flipped her off.

Kelly got out of her car.

She unclipped her badge from her belt and banged on the window with it. When the guy looked up at her, Kelly could see that he was maybe fifty with a big mustache and a T-shirt with *I do my own stunts* stenciled across the front.

He rolled down his window, confused.

"Have I done something wrong, Officer?"

"You sure as shit have," she said, waving her badge at the cars behind her, all of them honking now. "You just flipped me off."

"That was you?"

"That was me," she said. "But that's not why I'm standing here." She smiled and patted the top of the roof. "You didn't turn on your blinker."

He looked at his dash. "It's on."

"It's on now," she said. "But it wasn't on before you stopped. Before all of these people—go ahead, turn around and look—"

He turned around and saw the angry line of cars.

"Before all of these people," she went on, "pulled up behind you thinking you were gonna go straight through. But instead, the light turns green, and *then* you turn on your fucking blinker. So now what's everybody all lined up behind you supposed to do?"

"Wait?"

Jesus.

She smacked the roof of his car. "A hundred feet." The guy nearly jumping out of his seatbelt as she said it. "A hundred feet *before* the intersection. That's what it says in the handbook. That's the rule. Especially when there's no left turn lane like right here. You fuck up the flow of traffic otherwise. Imagine if every asshole on the road was just like you."

He looked at her, still confused. "Am I getting a ticket?"

"No. You're not getting a ticket. But I am gonna write down your tag. And then I'm gonna put you in the computer. You ever get pulled over for anything—I'm talking a broken taillight, late registration, whatever—you're gonna be double fucked, you understand?"

"Thank you, Officer."

Kelly straightened up, saw that the light had turned red, glanced at the cars behind her, and said, "When the light turns green again, you go straight through."

"But I have to go left."

Kelly looked at the guy.

"I'll go straight."

"Have a nice day."

Kelly turned back up Las Palmas, the traffic still crawling, trying to navigate all the detours and the war zone that was Hollywood Boulevard. All this traffic giving her time to think about what might have happened to Councilman Frank Peres.

The man jogged through his neighborhood every night. Making the point that his neighborhood was safe. And Kelly, knowing that area, would have thought it was. Relatively speaking. So what happened?

Peres was an old-timer. He grew up in the same neighborhood. He ran his own auto parts business for thirty years. By the time he retired, he'd opened seven of them, one for each of his kids. All of them grown now.

He became a councilman after he retired, so he was never a career politician. Kelly had met him once at some LAPD function and liked him immediately. For one thing, he was the only person there not drunk. But Kelly also found him tough, no bullshit. He even called her after "the incident," as Steven liked to call it, but Kelly was hidden away by then at a borrowed cabin up in Big Bear and never spoke to him.

While liked and respected by many, Peres also pissed off a lot of people. He certainly had been going after the current mayor with a level of commitment not seen in city politics since the forties; Peres all but accusing Miguel Santiago of being in bed with the Mexican cartels, of taking their money for his campaign, the drug trade in L.A. now being almost exclusively cartel-sourced. The Latin gangs were running everything while the black gangs were all focused on being the next Jay Z, rapping on YouTube and starting their own record labels. As far as Kelly could tell, a guy like Peres was no threat to them. He was, however, a threat to the Mexican gangs that ran most of North Hollywood.

And what about Roy Cooper? The man having no Social Security number and being, according to Rudy, a nonperson in the system?

That's almost worse than actually being in the system. In Kelly's experience, the only people who left no wake were people who were either hiding or doing something illegal. She now wondered if the whole innocent little kid vibe was just a bug act, something to make him seem slightly *off*, get her thinking what he wanted her to think.

Whether Roy Cooper was faking it or not, he definitely didn't shoot Peres. But Kelly was having trouble believing that a bunch of twelve-year-old tiny Gs whacked a mayoral candidate. Unless they got paid by the cartels to do it. And if that was the case, then things were about to go to a whole other level. What would happen next would be a lot worse than a little underground shaker.

Maybe now was the perfect time to do what they wanted her to do and retire. Maybe the universe was telling her to get out now before things got any uglier, if that was even possible. But then . . . what? Go into the family business, grow avocados? Teach at the academy? Now that would be something. After what she said, no one would ever let her within a city block of a rookie cop. She could move to someplace rural, be one of those small-town cops she always saw on TV. Solve one murder a year up in Montana or someplace.

She was thinking that at least she wouldn't have to deal with the fucking traffic when Carmen Suarez crossed the street right in front of her.

nineteen

"I've seen that a million times already."

"Good, then you know it."

Kelly was showing Carmen stills from Alonzo Zarate's cell phone footage of "The Peres Execution," as the media now referred to it. The faces were all difficult to recognize in the dark, but one or two were clear enough, though not all that distinctive, unlike Carmen with her shaved head and the clown tattoos on either side of her neck. The right side of her face was marked with a dozen angry red dots. Not acne, but tiny scars. A former member of the Fruit Town Brims, a mixed race gang turfed around USC, she was home watching TV with her boyfriend, his aunt and uncle and his nephew, when an aspiring member of Eleven Deuce Hoover, a gang they weren't even beefing with, came through the door with a sawed-off shotgun and pasted everyone in the room.

The house he wanted was two doors down. An honest mistake given they were painted the same color, but the other one was a crack house that directly competed with the Hoovers' own little fruit stand two streets over.

Carmen was the only one in the house who made it. The buckshot hit her on the neck and side of her face. She was blind for two months following, which gave her a lot of time to think. For most of her recovery, she stayed with Kelly and her husband, Steven, Carmen listening to Steven all day and at one point saying to Kelly, "That dude's not what you think he is."

Out of the mouths of fucking babes.

Carmen was still marked and full-on blue lit by the Hoovers as the trial of the shooter, Marcus "Tangle Eye" Shrieve, hadn't yet happened. So six months back, Kelly got her settled in Hollywood where soldiers from Eleven Deuce were unlikely to show their faces.

Carmen played with the little gold revolver she had on a chain around her neck and half-assed studied the photos. She put a finger on a face.

"Fat dude right there's named Shake."

"Shake? Like an earthquake?"

"Like a Vanilla Shake on account of his light skin."

"You know him?"

"I knew his brother."

"Knew?"

"He got dead outside a Dodger game, was last year."

"That was him?" Kelly thinking about the Locos and the Vineland Boyz going at it a year or so ago after somebody spilled a soda on somebody an hour before the game started.

Carmen pointed to another face. "That's Truck."

"Truck?"

"Looks like he got hit by one."

"They all Vineland Boyz?"

"Yeah, but they all puppies, tiny Gs. Sons of sons."

"You think it's possible that someone paid a bunch of little homies to whack this guy?"

"They did, they pretty fuckin' stupid."

"Because?"

"Because they ain't gonna keep their mouth shut."

"That's what I'm hoping."

Carmen turned to Kelly and gave her a look that said, *Fuck, here it comes.*

"You know everybody."

"*Used to,*" Carmen said. "Same as you."

Kelly waited.

Carmen sighed, looked around at the wrecked boulevard. "Any of that buckshot in my brain moves the wrong way, I'm a retard, you know that, right?"

"I'm not asking you to go anywhere or do anything at all strenuous, and for sure nothing that would get you in trouble." Kelly looked at the image of young Shake. "But if I get one, I'll probably get 'em all."

"Yeah?" Carmen looked down the block as a bulldozer knocked down the rest of the Chinese Theatre. "So you can eradicate their ass?"

Kelly felt that hit, then said to Carmen's back, "You got something you wanna say?"

"You're the one said some shit."

"I sure did."

"Did you mean it?"

"I did then."

Carmen faced her and asked, "What about now?"

"Probably. Some of it anyway." She looked at Carmen. "That gonna be a problem for us?"

"I'm still deciding."

"Okay," Kelly said. "But while you're doing that, tell me why you left Covenant House."

"My room got all jacked. From the quake."

"They got other rooms."

"Not now they don't. They all full up."

"So where you staying at?"

She shrugged and said, "I hear it was an eight."

"What was an eight?"

"The earthquake."

"That sounds high to me."

"That's what everybody says."

"Well, if that's what everybody says."

"Don't they tell you what it is?"

Kelly wanted to ask her again where she was staying, but her phone began vibrating, and she saw it was Rudy again. She raised a finger to Carmen and answered.

Rudy said, "Before we get cut off, I need you to meet me on the corner of Laurel Canyon and Kittridge."

She said, "Kittridge? That's what, three blocks from Peres?"

"Two. We got a white male DB. Sixty-something. Shot in the head. Happened sometime last night."

"Oh, my."

"How soon can you get here?"

"Depends on the traffic."

"Try not to kill anyone."

Kelly hung up, saw that Carmen was already backing away.

"I'm almost done, then you can run away."

Carmen stopped, looked around like she was in a big hurry to be somewhere else.

"You go see that guy I told you about?"

"He hired me."

"Good."

"Didn't work out, though."

"What happened?"

"I'm just not a waitress."

"No? What are you?"

Carmen shrugged.

"Okay. This has been awesome. Call me if you get raped or murdered, otherwise I'm gonna leave you the fuck alone."

"You broke his neck."

Kelly turned back.

"That kid you smacked up."

"I know who you meant."

"They gonna sue your ass."

"What happened at the restaurant?"

"I wouldn't ever call Carrows a restaurant."

"What happened?"

"That guy you knew? The manager? Your good friend?"

"Joel Spaihts. He wasn't a friend. He owed me."

"Well now he owes me."

"How many times you gonna make me ask?"

"He wanted to take my picture."

"Your picture?"

"In the kitchen. At three a.m. With my nice brown uniform unzipped."

"He touch you?"

"Touch me? Gimme a break."

"You want me to go talk to him?"

"I already talked to him."

"No kidding."

"Yeah, we had a real nice talk, me and Joel."

"Then what?"

Another shrug. "I left him there."

Kelly shook her head and stepped out her smoke. "Go back to Covenant House. I'll call them, get you a room to yourself."

"I'm a big girl."

"That's what I'm afraid of."

Kelly walked back into the street, headed for her car, momentarily stopping to talk to a guy in cargo shorts and a Universal Studios T-shirt as he was getting into a Tercel, the driver's door open wide into the lane.

"You know, asshole, you get your door ripped off by a passing car, it's your fault."

"Who the fuck are you?"

She badged him and said, "Next time, how about looking behind you first, maybe not swinging the fucking door into traffic?"

"Don't you have anything better to do?"

Kelly was beginning to wonder.

twenty

Roy woke up to his cell phone buzzing on the table beside him. He sat up in a panic, not sure at first where he was, but then he felt the pull on his wrist from the IV, sharp stings in his side and shoulder from the stitches there, and came back. He had meant to walk out of here an hour ago, but had instead fallen asleep.

He reached for the phone.

"We got a problem, sweetie." Rita's voice calm, which meant she was angry. "I'm of course referring to the unfortunate incident the other night with this Councilman Peres and the four little jigaboos who popped him with, I'm guessing, *our* gun?"

For a split second, Roy wondered how she knew all the way back in Queens, but then realized he was all over the television. Rita and Harvey did little but watch TV most days.

"I was just in the wrong place at the wrong time."

"No, *he* was in the wrong place at the wrong time. You just fucked up is what happened."

"I already talked to Harvey."

"He said you were pretty out of it. So now you're talking to me."

"Please tell Harvey that I'm sorry."

"What do you know about this Kelly Maguire?"

Roy said nothing.

"She's the cop, right? The one I saw on TV trying to sneak out of the hospital they got you parked at? I've been reading about her on the Google all morning. Turns out she's got a rather colorful past. Might be looking for a way to dull it down some by catching some big-time button from the East."

The Google. Big-time button. Rita couldn't decide whether she wanted to talk like some old person or a character in one of the old crime novels she loved to read.

"I don't know anything about her," he heard himself saying, not wanting to keep Rita waiting too long on the other end, or else she'd think he was working something out.

"But what does she know about you?"

"Nothing."

"You've spoken to her?"

"Once."

Roy sat up as a black nurse with straightened, dyed blond hair came into the room waving a blood pressure cuff.

"Just need to check your vitals real quick, sweetie." She had to be ten years younger than he was, but here she was calling him sweetie. Everyone calling him sweetie. Everyone his whole life calling him sweetie. Roy held out his arm, kept the phone tight to his ear as the nurse began wrapping the cuff around his biceps.

"Where's Little Mac?" Rita was now asking.

Roy looked at the chair in the corner, the plastic bag containing his bloody clothing still there. But then he remembered the black kid, Science, had the gun in his hand the last time he saw it. But then what? Did he drop it?

"Roy?"

"It's safe."

"What's that mean?"

"Nobody has it."

"You got rid of it?"

The nurse whistled, "One forty-eight over ninety." She looked up at Roy. "Pressure's a bit high."

Roy could feel his heart hammering on his chest. He needed to get that gun.

"You okay, sweetie?"

Roy nodded at the nurse and mouthed, "I'm fine."

"Have you by chance turned on the television? You're all over it."

"I'm sorry, Rita."

"Quit apologizing."

The nurse peeled off the cuff. "I'm gonna come back in an hour, take it again. Okay?"

Roy smiled.

"You're famous."

Roy almost said, "They think I'm a hero," but thought better of it.

"And while fame is good for some, it's not so good for you, is it?"

"No."

"So what are we gonna do?"

"What does Harvey say?"

"He says what I say. That this is a problem."

"Should I come home?"

"Please don't."

"Is somebody coming to see me?"

"I wouldn't be surprised."

"What should I do?"

"For starters, I'd get your ass out of that hospital."

twenty-one

Kelly pulled up to 1332 Laurel Canyon and saw Rudy Bell sitting on the curb wiping off one of his Nunn Bush loafers with a fast food napkin.

She got out of her car and said, "Step in something there, fat boy?"

"The vic's fiancée threw up on me."

"Any splash on Araki?"

"No such luck."

He finished wiping off the tassel, tossed the napkin into the street, and stood up. "I'll take you up."

She followed Rudy up the stairs, noted that he was in a light wool suit today, this one charcoal with a pale blue shirt and a navy tie with a tiny red diamond pattern. Dressed more for fall in New York or Chicago than L.A. She didn't have the heart to tell him there was what appeared to be a splatter of puke on the back of his trouser leg.

The indoor crime scenes were always tricky for Kelly. She was never comfortable crossing a new threshold. It wasn't so much the dead bodies in all their myriad shapes, sizes, and arrangements, so much as it was seeing how people lived. Being inside somewhere intimate and personal. Somewhere she didn't belong. The strong and sometimes unfamiliar smells, the family photos, the faded furniture, laying people bare in a way that never felt quite right to her. But it was this sensation of being somewhere foreign that had also protected her. She needed to pretend that there was some kind of separation between her and them. She needed to believe that these worlds were all alien to her in order to be able to leave it all behind at the end of her shift. This was the very thing that ultimately ruined the lives/marriages/children—fill in the blank—of every cop she had ever known. The truth was, they could never leave any of it behind.

Kelly had a particularly bad moment when, one night, she walked into the bedroom of a woman who'd been stabbed a hundred and eighteen times by her estranged husband and saw that the dead woman had the same Wamsutta sheets that Kelly did.

That put her over.

But this place, she thought, was just sad. Sad wasn't even the right word. *Tired* was more like it. Everything felt almost secondhand; either broken or about to break. There were a few photos and a vase on the floor. Not from any struggle, she thought, from the quake.

"His name is Martin Shine," Mike Araki was saying. Reluctantly filling Kelly in on shit he wasn't convinced she needed to know. "Sixty-four-year-old Caucasian male. According to his ID. Mr. Shine resided in Brooklyn N-Y-C. Girlfriend found the body." He nodded down the hall where a paramedic knelt in front of a tiny woman in her thirties with short black hair who sat on the edge of a bed taking deep breaths. "Her name's Ani Nahapetian. Mr. Shine had apparently come out here to stay with her."

Rudy said, "Long-distance relationships can be a bitch."

"She says she was in Palm Springs with two friends, came back this morning to find Mr. Shine's head stuck to the carpet."

Kelly could see the paramedic slipping an oxygen mask over Ms. Nahapetian's head, the woman still having trouble keeping her shit together.

"We got here, the uniforms had her laid down in the bedroom. She seemed to be okay, came out, had a good look this time, and puked all over Rudy's shoes."

"How long was she away?" Kelly asked.

"Just the one night."

Rudy said, "Right now they're putting it at last night around midnight, but nothing yet bona fide."

Mike Araki asked Kelly, "You all good now? Anything else you need to know?"

Kelly looked at the man on the floor. "What's he do?"

"His girl said he's some kind of accountant, but that's all we've got for the moment."

Kelly waited for Araki to walk back down the hall, and then turned to Rudy. "I know this address."

"What do you mean, you know it?"

"Was written on a piece of paper in the alley. I saw it last night, bagged it myself."

Rudy thought about that for a moment, then nodded to the door. "Feel like getting some air?"

"After you."

They walked the two blocks to the alley, the ground around the mouth now covered with flowers and cards in honor of the late Councilman Peres.

Rudy looked at the display and said, "They liked the guy."

Kelly could still see blood in between the offerings. "So why is Martin Shine's address floating around our crime scene?"

"Technically, it's his girlfriend's address."

"Either way," Kelly said, "someone's looking for him. They find him. They clip him. Then they either walk over here and somehow lose or get rid of the slip of paper, or, even more bizarrely, they get mugged along with Councilman Peres."

"Unless the same gangsters who whacked Peres, whacked Shine."

"Whacked him, why?" She shook her head. "I'm having trouble seeing Peres as anything other than a straight-up shakedown."

"So we're looking at your Mr. Cooper."

"A man with no discernible background as you pointed out. And, not incidentally, also here from New York, same as your Mr. Shine."

"So let's say that Mr. Cooper is out here looking for Shine, why?"

"I'm guessing Shine comes back wrong in some way. A CPA for other wrong guys. Maybe pissed off someone back home in Brooklyn. Decides to hide out with the Armenian girlfriend he thinks no one knows about."

"Which makes our Mr. Cooper, our Good Samaritan, a hired hand for some assholes back east." Rudy shook his head. "Awesome."

She looked up at the window above the alley. "How much he get," she asked. "The guy who recorded it?"

"I heard a few hundred grand."

"Fucking guy doesn't open his window, doesn't shout, doesn't call the po-po, just sits up there smelling dough." She turned around. "Maybe his neighbors should know."

Rudy smiled at her. "You can be mean, you know that?"

But Kelly wasn't listening. She was already crossing the street, walking to where a white Ford was parked all by its lonesome, the driver's window shattered. She looked at the gap in the dash where a radio and/or a GPS might have been. Rudy walked around to the other side, used his coat to open the passenger door, and got in the car and poked around. Nothing but some glass on the front seat. He bent down and grabbed a rental agreement off the floor.

He opened it up. "Joe Mills."

Kelly thought a moment, then started laughing.

Rudy said, "What?"

"You don't follow baseball?"

"I prefer to stay awake at sporting events," he said. "I'm a hockey man."

"Really? The way you dress?"

"Who's Joe Mills?"

"Pitcher for the Cardinals. They call him The Kid and apparently he's close to breaking some record."

"All these years, I had no idea you were a baseball fan."

"I'm not," Kelly said. "Roy Cooper told me."

They were walking back to the apartment when they saw Leo Manning leaning against his car trying to figure out how to work his newly issued sat phone.

Rudy said, "Hey, boss."

Manning looked up at the two of them, slowly came off the car, and stood there on the sidewalk, unsure of what to do with his hands.

"Kelly," he said. "Can I talk to you a minute?"

twenty-two

Albert Budin watched Vanna White hang a vowel and then changed the channel to CNN. The room was dark, the shades pulled for the baby's nap, but he could still see the mess on the floor. The crib with the dirty blanket in the middle of it, the sticky toys, a lonely little sneaker.

It pissed him off. He'd worked all night. What the fuck did she do all day? On CNN, that silver-haired homo was interviewing some general. In no other universe, Albert thought, would these two ever talk to each other. He was about to change the channel when he heard her voice.

"Albert?"

He could see her shadow. Even that looked small and frightened. He half turned, didn't want to move or speak for fear of waking the baby in his lap. Took him nearly an hour to get her to fall asleep. *She* couldn't do it. She wasn't much of a mother. She was tiny and pretty, though, like a little girl, and Albert dug that.

"Some men are here to see you."

"Some men?"

"Police."

He could see that she was nervous, so he smiled and said in a quiet voice, "Tell them to come in."

She didn't move. Just stood there looking back at him.

"What?"

She glanced down at the sleeping baby. "Do you want me to take Isabelle?"

"What for?"

He turned back to the screen. The silver-haired dude was now commenting on guns. On how there are just too damn many. Albert understood then that the other guy wasn't a general, but a police chief somewhere. Why the fuck did he dress like that? All braids and brass? What kind of bullshit costume is that for a cop?

A voice said, "Albert Budin?" Mispronouncing his name the way people always did. Making it sound like "Albert Booden."

Albert didn't bother looking at them as he said, "Al-bare. Boo-*dan.*" Then, nodding to the couch. "Please," he said, "make yourselves at home."

And as they entered his vision he saw that one of them had no hair. His shiny head reminding Albert of a piece of broken china. The bald man's partner was particularly tall. Albert guessing that he went well over six-five. He made the bald one look small, even though he was probably six feet himself. They were both in suits. Albert noticed the bald one wore a silver cuff on one wrist. He thought they were too beefy to be Feds. Marshals maybe. No. Too well dressed. They weren't local law, he'd know them, so most likely Staties of some kind.

The taller one saw the infant in Albert's lap and lowered his voice as he sat down. "I'm Detective Brown and this is Detective Weston. We're with the Washington State Police."

Albert knew they were holding up their badge folders, but, once again, he didn't bother looking, just rubbed the baby's feet, staring at the little pink socks as if he'd never seen anything like them before.

Brown, the taller one, kicked it off. "We'd like to ask you a few questions, if we may."

"What about?"

"About a few murders," he said. "Actually, more than a few."

Albert kissed the baby on the top of the head. "I don't know anything about any murders."

"These killings have all taken place in the Washington State area during the past five years." Brown leaned forward, the movement getting Albert to look at him as the state cop then added, "Since you moved here."

"I imagine lots of things have happened since I moved here."

Brown opened a notebook and asked, "Did you know a man by the name of Walter Castle?"

"I did not."

"Jimmy Cullotta?"

"Never heard of him."

Albert smiled at Weston, the shorter cop, and gently bounced the baby. Weston just stared back at him as Brown continued. "What about Dominick Lucci?"

"Sorry."

Albert looked at the television. A shot of some alley somewhere. A body covered with a tarp. Lots of little flags marking shell casings. Cops milling about. Albert couldn't turn away, hoped that these two would be leaving soon so he could rewind it to watch it all again.

Brown kept at it. "His wife said he'd gone to meet a man about some guns and had a large amount of cash on him."

Albert nodded as if he was listening.

"His body was found by the Walla Walla sheriff in a storage locker a month later."

"That's too bad."

"Sure you didn't know this fella? Dominick Lucci? Sometimes called Lucky Dom?"

"Doesn't sound so lucky to me," Albert said to no one in particular. He was too busy looking at the scene on the television . . . some shitty cell phone video. A bunch of black kids held a guy at gunpoint. Some other asshole, an older guy, was down on all fours.

Never demean yourself like that, Albert thought. Ever. Take the fucking bullet.

"Mr. Budin." Mispronouncing it again.

"Boo-*dan*. And I don't know Mr. Lucci."

"What about Mason Toole? Freddy Alderisio? Sy Attwater?"

Albert shook his head after each name. "I wish I could help you."

"Attwater worked at the Hormel plant with you. Was into pornography. We hear the two of you were in business for a while."

Albert turned away from the TV and smiled. "From whom do you hear such things?"

This was when Weston leaned forward and tapped the coffee table. "Mr. Boo-dan," he said with a sleepy Southern drawl, "how 'bout we just cut the cute act? It's a fuckin' bore."

This was supposed to get Albert looking at him, but Albert couldn't take his eyes off of what was happening on the TV: one of the kids had just shot the old guy in the head. The news people blocked out the money shot with a big black dot so Albert couldn't see the brains and blood that he knew had to be everywhere. And then it played over again. And this time Albert noticed the other man, standing there off to the side.

"Truth is, you've been a wrong guy for a long time," Weston went on.

Albert couldn't believe what he was seeing.

Was that him?

"Since age twelve, you've had over forty-one arrests, six before the age of eighteen. You did three years at the Honor Center in Boonville, Missouri, when you were sixteen. You've done state time in Florida twice as well as a five-year federal bump in Leavenworth. And that's just what you got caught for."

Albert resisted the urge to stand up and move closer to the TV.

Harvey told me the fucker was dead.

Annoyingly, Weston was trying to regain his attention with ancient history.

"Since then, you've been arrested for breaking and entering, auto theft, assault and battery, possession of burglary tools, strong-arm robbery, sale of stolen food stamps, possession of narcotics, statutory rape, and murder."

Albert stared hard at the shadowy man on the cell phone video, the guy on CNN now calling him some kind of hero.

That's him.

"You're a real renaissance man, aren't you, Mr. Boo-dan?"

Albert watched as the little black kids all started running, firing their weapons at anything and everything as they scattered. He watched the man he recognized go down in the middle of it all.

No. He cannot be dead. Not yet.

Ah, wait. They were showing some hospital. Saying he's in there. In critical but stable condition whatever the fuck that meant. What city? How did Albert miss that?

Then he saw it.

Roy's in Los Angeles.

Albert sat there, unaware of the baby. Unaware of anything other than the man on the screen. The man he'd thought about every single fucking day for a dozen years. No. Longer than that.

"Mr. Budin?"

Albert looked at the two Staties a moment, both of them watching him, and brought himself back. He smiled.

"I have a family now," he said. "This isn't Miami or Kansas City. I moved here to get away from those things." He looked at Brown, and then Weston, all sincerity.

"I honestly haven't heard of any of those men you've mentioned."

He then carefully stood up with the baby still in his arms. "If you have no more questions," he said, nodding to the playpen, "I'd like to put my daughter down for her nap."

The two cops stared back at him. Weston wanted to say something but Brown touched the side of his partner's leg, stood up, and considered Albert a moment. Actually had to look down at him. Man, the fucker was tall. Albert thought Brown was going to leave him with some threat disguised as cheap cop wisdom. *If I were you, Mr. Boo-dan . . . blah blah blah.*

But all he said was, "Thanks for your time."

Albert may or may not have heard Justine say something in the other room to the two men as they left, may or may not have heard the front door open then close. Albert was too busy looking at the little black kid with the gun. Too busy looking at the gun itself. Too busy looking at his old friend standing there in the midst of it all.

So many questions. A lot to do before he hit the road. Albert's mind was reeling. He already had a dozen different ways he was going to kill Roy. One bloodier and more drawn out than the next. After all, he'd had a lot of time to think about it. Eventually, he'd also have to go see that old fuck, Harvey, and that dry cunt, Rita.

That, too, would have to be settled.

But he was getting ahead of himself.

First he had to call Bob Spetting and tell him that their old friend was alive, shot once or twice, but alive and currently tubed up in some hospital in Southern California, ready and ripe for a long and bloody peeling.

twenty-three

The second Leo Manning finished what he had to say, Kelly got in her car and drove to the first liquor store she saw and bought a bottle of cranberry-flavored vodka. Once she got home, she drank most of it inside an hour. A record even for Kelly. She had stopped drinking some three months earlier, seeing as that's what got her into trouble in the first place. But after her brief conversation with the lieutenant, she needed a drink.

No, she needed to be drunk.

It went like this, Leo getting right into it as he always did:

"They're pulling you."

"I'm only on the guy."

"Then what are you doing here?"

"My guy may be part of this."

"Even so."

"Come on, Leo."

"They don't want you on any of it."

"This is bullshit. You know that, right?"

"What I know is, I need you."

"Then say something."

"You don't think I did?"

"There's no way this comes from Parker Center. There's too few of us as is."

Leo said nothing.

She shook her head. "The fucking mayor."

"I'm sorry, Kelly."

"Maybe I should have let him feel me up that time."

"You got here all by yourself."

"This is total bullshit."

"On that we agree."

Kelly had never thought of herself as a racist, which, according to the department shrink, is pretty much what all racists say.

Still, Kelly was nothing compared to her family. The stuff she'd listened to growing up in Orange County. And not the nice part like where the mayor spent his early years. Because Kelly looked white, a lot of people talked freely around her about how much it pissed them off that the immigrants were taking over L.A.

Her father had been an avocado farmer in Oaxaca, but moved to Anaheim two years before Kelly was born, working for most of Kelly's life as a manager for an Armstrong's nursery. Kelly's mom did nails alongside the Filipinos at a salon in a minimall on Harbor Boulevard, near the border of Garden Grove. Financially speaking, they were one step above white trash. They barely made ends meet and nobody at home was particularly happy. Especially once the black families started moving into the neighborhood and the shootings started.

Kelly couldn't wait to get out. But she also didn't want to sit around and stew in her anger like her parents had. She got recruited by the LAPD while taking a court reporting class at Foothill Junior College. The teacher, Janet Regal, was an ex-cop who had to leave the department after getting in a near fatal car accident on the job. She immediately took to Kelly, liked how bright and how tough she was and thought she'd be excellent on the street.

For her part, Kelly loved the first couple of years out there, hanging with the girls from the Fruit Town Brims. Satchi and Marvilla and Nola and all the others. She knew all their secrets. They knew hers. They were family. Even now, Kelly believed that. They loved her. She went to weddings, christenings, and funerals. Lots of funerals.

Of course, at first, they didn't know what to make of this green-eyed, light-skinned, half-Mexican chick who looked more like a newscaster than a cop.

Kelly had been recruited to the new and as yet unnamed gang unit because she spoke fluent Spanish. Around the city, especially in places like Hollywood or down near USC, the girls were becoming nearly as big a problem as the boys.

The mayor had been told by his newly appointed gang liaison that one gang in particular, the Fruit Town Brims, was using the women in the gang to expand into the Hollywood area. So the mayor wanted to start a new unit of younger black and Latina cops who would just "hang out" in the neighborhoods, get to know the families. "Listen to them," he said to Kelly one night over drinks downtown; he'd asked her to join him at WP24 to "pick her brain." But once she got up to Wolfgang Puck's big lacquered Chinese restaurant on the twenty-fourth floor of the Ritz-Carlton, and was sitting there looking out at four different freeways, it was clear what he actually wanted. The mayor kept talking about playing to her strengths, her *fortes,* apparently his word of the evening, all the while reaching across the table to touch her hand, ostensibly making a point, but really making all sorts of them.

For her part, Kelly kept it all business. Said that she had lived in Compton for a few years when she was in high school. Knew some of the girls in the Brims. They were mostly centered around Vermont Avenue, from Jefferson Boulevard and 38th Street down by Exposition Park and USC. And while some of them might be hanging out in Hollywood, there were other gangs he should be more worried about, such as the Brims' longtime rivals, the Rollin' 30s Crips.

"I just love the names," the mayor said, giving her that smile. "Fruit Town, as in L.A. and the whole orange grove thing?"

"Fruit Town as in North Compton. The streets up there are all named Cherry, Peach, and Pear. Like that."

"Compton?"

"They started there in the seventies, as an offshoot of the Fruit Town Pirus."

"Another awesome name."

"Most of them went to John Muir High School. Where I went for a while. Before we moved to Anaheim."

"Anaheim, really?"

He showed her a few thousand dollars' worth of dental bleaching and asked, "And Brims, like hats?"

"Black Revolutionary Independent Mafia."

"You know so much."

"Wasted childhood."

He stared back at her with his pretty blue eyes for what seemed like a week before tossing out this gem: "I want to focus on the family aspects of gang life. On the females in particular."

The females. Like they were some kind of ape in the wild that needed further study. How did this fucking guy get elected? No, Kelly knew how he got elected. This was L.A. And look at him. He was young. He looked like an actor. Like a specific actor. What was that guy's name? The Spanish guy, married what's-her-face from that movie, *Working Girl.*

Her husband's favorite movie.

"Listen," Kelly said, "you should know going in that these kids don't respond the way other kids do."

"How do you mean?"

"I'm talking about ideas, ideas *we* throw at them, like working hard to get ahead, going to school, *just saying no,* peace and brotherhood and all of the bullshit people talk about when they talk about gangs."

"What's wrong with working hard or going to school?"

"Nothing," she said. "But you need to understand that those things have a different meaning out there. Especially the possibility of any kind of peace. That's one they just can't picture."

"Why not?"

"Because these kids have no fucking idea of peace and tranquility. For them life has always been full of violence and struggle, especially violence."

"They do tend to shoot each other."

She wanted to hit him, but kept on. "I'm not talking about what happens on the street. I'm talking about where they live. Inside their own homes. I'm talking about the poverty of their families and the domestic violence among the people supposed to be taking care of them. That's all outside of the gang wars and what they consider to be an occupational police force. The only peace these kids see is on TV in shit like *Modern Family* and *Parenthood.*"

"They watch those shows?"

"Think about waking up every morning stepping over people sleeping on your living room floor. Your father is your mother's latest boyfriend. You're told in a hundred different ways, every day of your fucking life, that being subliterate and without marketable skills is just the way it is, the best you can hope for."

The mayor looked like he had tears in his eyes, but all he said was "Wow."

They talked for another hour about how the mayor's little task force could work and Kelly felt that she'd gotten the conversation, the entire evening, for that matter, back on track.

That is, until the guy made a sloppy pass as she was getting into her car, the man reaching around to palm her ass as he leaned in for a quick one, saying something stupid like *You and I make a great team.*

Kelly gently pressed her fist into his chest to stop his advance. The mayor bumped into it, looked at the wedding band that she was now showing him. But the fucking tool was drunk and either didn't see it or didn't care. She remembered him smiling and trying to put her finger in his mouth. Kelly pulled her hand away and got into her car saying, "I voted for you, asshole."

Even though she hadn't.

Kelly figured that was probably the end of that shiny new assignment, but a week later, there she was, walking up and down Hollywood Boulevard, hanging out. And after three years of that, she went to North Hollywood to do the same thing along Laurel Canyon Boulevard.

From the beginning, she was known for her big mouth, but Kelly thought she just called things as she saw them. Her fellow officers sometimes couldn't believe some of the goodies she said in front of other human beings, but they, for whatever reason, understood her and laughed it off as one of her many tics.

Kelly got the joke, but it also pissed her off that anyone would think she was racist, given everything she was doing to help the kids on the street, black, brown, or otherwise. She loved them all. She saw firsthand what they went through. And in her way, she took them more seriously than any other cop she knew. She *got* them. Damned if she would shut up about what she saw on the street every day just because other people hid behind being PC when, in reality, at least in her mind anyway, they were all pussies and couldn't be honest about anything.

In the end, though, it was the word "eradicate" that fucked her.

The only way to deal with the so-called gang problem is to eradicate each and every one of them.

Then, like now, she was drunk. It was late at night at Hollywood Station and all she could think about was that little rapo, Ronnie Rabidou, smirking at her. Did he smirk? Or did she just think he did. It didn't matter: he raped and murdered a woman in front of her nine-year-old daughter, and then killed the little girl as well. Guy's lucky that he's a cripple, can still play video games and get stoned with his homies, buy his groceries at the liquor store in his jammies after he wins his lawsuit eight years from now. He's lucky that Kelly didn't walk into that room and shoot him.

Of course, it also didn't help that earlier that same morning her husband, Steven, told her he was done. Told Kelly that he was on his way out the door for someone who was actually around once in a while. Told her that he'd found someone who paid a little attention to him every now and then, someone whose hair didn't always smell like a fucking crime scene. Of course, what he didn't say was that this special someone was another man named Neddy Mars, star of some show on the WB about vampire crime fighters who Steven had been training, privately, at the dojo for the previous six months.

That might have contributed somewhat to her anger.

And if she had just tooled up the kid and then taken whatever punishment came her way, she might have survived.

But Kelly Maguire being Kelly Maguire had to open her mouth. So what if it was intended to be heard only by her partner, Rudy Bell, at the other end of a phone call, Kelly calling him from the Burgundy Room in Hollywood, the night she got hit with her suspension. Rudy always there for her, maybe just a little in love with her if she really thought about it, which Kelly never would. Whatever. She still should have shut the fuck up. But for days after she left the kid on the floor of the interview room, she couldn't stop moving. She had all this energy with no place to go. Plus she was drunk.

So she called Rudy, got his voicemail, and started talking.

Jesus, there's just too fucking many of them. Rollin 60. Eight Trays. Fo' Trays. Twenty Bloods. 5-Deuce Hoover. 11-Deuce Hoover. Shotgun Crips. Outlaw 20 Bloods. Grape Street Watts. PJ Watts. Park Village Compton Crips. Altadena Blocc Crips. Marvin

Gangsters. Playboy Gangsters. Harlem 30s and Rollin 40s. 5-Six Syndicate. 6-Deuce Brims. And that's only a few. Christ. Fuck each and every one of them. I give up. I'm done.

There's just no way to win a fight against what's now an entire population with an average lifespan of what, nineteen years? These people have no choice but to join a gang. If I were them, it's what I would do. I mean, is it really so hard to understand why young black kids are killing each other with such gusto? The truth is, we could, if we wanted to, just wait for them to do the job for us. The self-cleaning-oven theory of law enforcement. And why not? The only way to deal with the so-called gang problem is to eradicate each and every one of them, starting with that smirking little black fucker, Ronnie Rabbit.

She knew Rudy would get it. They talked like this all the time, in the car, in bars, at lunch. Okay, maybe it was just Kelly who talked like that, hard to say, now, looking back. But either way, she was talking to Rudy. Just Rudy.

Except that she wasn't talking to Rudy.

She had not called Rudy Bell. In her drunken state, Kelly had actually called a man named Oren Krueger, a blogger (#OKstreets.com) and sometimes contributor to *Los Angeles Magazine*. Recently, Krueger had done a series of vines as he walked around various parts of L.A. filming himself on his iPhone while he spit out seven seconds on the history/troubles/color of whatever neighborhood he was passing through. His idea was to string together all of these informative bits about his beloved L.A. and make a film or publish them or both. At the time Kelly mistakenly rang him up, O.K. had several hundred thousand followers. A day later, he would have several million.

Here's how Kelly fucked up:

A week earlier, Rudy Bell had changed his number and personal email address after a still unknown *gangsta* had somehow managed to steal his phone and tagged a wall on Van Nuys Boulevard with all of Rudy's contact info.

Krueger heard about it from one of his tipsters and recorded one of his vines in front of the wall. Assuming correctly that Rudy Bell would immediately change his phone number rather than spend his days deleting hundreds of "Fuck you, pig" messages, Krueger walked into a T-Mobile Store on Fairfax and secured the number for himself so that *he* could record those messages that might come in from any OGs out there who didn't read his blog or follow the news in general, i.e., pretty much all of them.

Of course, that was also the week following the shit with Steven and Ronnie Rabidou, the same week that Kelly went on the Vodka & Weed diet, so she was pretty well juiced when she picked up her phone to vent, dialed Rudy but got Krueger's new voicemail instead.

Coincidence? As Miles Sugar, her training officer at the academy, used to tell her, "There are no coincidences, only what happens."

Twenty-four hours later, Kelly's private rant went viral. Soon, no one in the department was laughing at her, or even listening to her. She was a nonperson. Worse, a nonofficer. She was done. Not wanting to fire her, they decided to wait her out. They put her on DV Follow-up. Visit the battered wives and girlfriends late at night when no one was around, when cops and vics could supposedly have a better, more honest conversation. Maybe have a word with the abuser, leave behind a pamphlet or two, and then go home and try not to get drunk or, worse, eat a bullet.

But then, Councilman Peres got his head pulped and, for a moment at least, they needed her again.

Finally, a way back.

Or so she thought.

Kelly was pouring the last bit of vodka into a mug when the apartment began to shake. Just an aftershock, she thought, but a big one. And it kept going. A picture came off the wall and she could hear glass breaking in the kitchen. Kelly got up and moved her ass to the front door and opened it. She then stood there in the alleged safety of the jamb while the building rattled all around her.

Two units down, a fluorescent tube fell out of a fixture and shattered on the floor. A moment later, Kelly saw a woman in her underwear wobbly step out of her apartment.

"Careful," Kelly said. "There's broken glass."

The woman looked up the hall at Kelly. She was maybe thirty-five with short brown hair and, though skinny and small breasted, Kelly had to admit she had a decent body. She also had what looked suspiciously like a joint in her mouth. It was hard for Kelly to say for sure as she now pinched the smoke and put it behind her back.

The shaking stopped and the woman cut a nervous glance into her apartment.

Kelly smiled at her. "Not so bad."

"No," the woman said. "Not as bad as some have been." Then, as if obligated now that Kelly had seen her in her underwear: "I'm Erin."

"Kelly."

"Yeah, I know. You're the cop."

Kelly shrugged. "I guess so."

"You guess so?"

"There seems to be some question as to my position at the moment."

"Oh."

The woman looked into her apartment again.

"Everything okay in there?"

"My son. He's five."

"Is he all right?"

"Completely conked. He can sleep through anything."

"I bet," Kelly said. "Especially after breathing in all that second-hand ganja smoke, kid must sleep like a log."

"Shit." Erin took the blunt from behind her back. Looked at Kelly. "Actually, I was out on the balcony."

"Yeah, I know," Kelly said.

"You catch it over there?"

"Every night."

"Sorry."

Kelly said, "Don't be." And then she asked, "Can I have a hit?"

twenty-four

By the time the mayor arrived at Valley Presbyterian, well over two hours late, the press was good and pissed. There was a Santa Ana condition that afternoon and it was nearly ninety degrees outside, higher in the asphalt parking lot where everybody was standing around drinking bottled water provided by the hospital, a few hard-cases drinking beer stashed in brown paper bags. These veteran men and women waiting for their early retirement offers from the *L.A. Times,* so they could take their pension, then go blog or write a novel, become the next Michael Connelly.

The truth was, the freeways were still a mess and it took twice the usual time to get into the Valley from downtown, even with the police escort. But Evan Crisp was loath to blame the traffic for fear it would reflect poorly on the mayor. It had only been ten days, but people in L.A. were used to things getting fixed right away. Especially their freeways. Back in '94, then mayor Dick Riordon got the 10 back on line after the Northridge quake a full three months ahead of schedule. He even issued curfews and no one gave a rat's ass. They loved him.

So Evan decided to blame the delay on their stop before the hospital, the visit to Frank Peres's widow.

It was unscheduled, Evan feeling that it would play more authentic if the press heard about it *after* it had already happened. They called Theresa Peres from the car and told her they would be there shortly. But by the time they arrived at the modest home on Blix Street, barely fifteen minutes later, the place was packed. All of the grown Peres children were there, along with *their* children, plus what appeared to be everyone from the neighborhood. All of them looking at the mayor like he had just poisoned their dogs.

Worse, Mrs. Peres couldn't stop weeping, haltingly telling the mayor through a fistful of wet tissues that he must "find it in your heart to make this right."

As if he was the one who'd made it wrong.

The mayor tried to hug Mrs. Peres, but the keening bitch actually stepped back and stuck out her hand instead. Saying once more to the mayor, "Make it right." All of it caught on cell phones by the family and friends stuffed into the living room. For the next week there would be *vines* and *pix* of the mayor standing there, his arms open, stranded in the middle of the room, surrounded by Peres family photos while this woman held out her tiny mitt, to *shake hands*.

Things only got worse at the hospital.

That visit started out okay, the mayor saying to the by now sweating and sunburnt press that "Roy Cooper was a real hero. Fighting for all of us. A great example for how we might help each other right now, during this crazy—difficult time."

The mayor was hoping for a break once they got on the elevator, but the doors opened and he saw that the car was huge, big enough for four gurneys side by side, so most of the press piled in along with Evan and his security detail. Then, just as the doors were closing, two young black boys, maybe thirteen or fourteen, squeezed inside.

Roland, the mayor's head bodyguard, was about to boot them when Evan glanced at the mayor, who, against all odds, actually understood the look, and said, "It's all right, Rollie. We can make room for these nice boys."

The mayor felt the press all looking at him now and smiled at the two youngsters. One of them seemed to have a scar that took up half the real estate on his face while the other one was handsome enough to be a young TV star.

"You guys visiting someone?"

The handsome one said, "My moms," and then added, "She has cancer."

"I'm very sorry to hear that."

"She gonna die," the kid went on. "Maybe today."

Now the mayor could really feel the eyes of the press on him.

"That's awful. Would you like me to come by and see her?"

That got him a look from Evan. *Too much. Abort!*

But the kid saved him. "No, thank you," he said. "She voted for the other dude." And everyone had themselves a good laugh.

The doors opened and the press were able to snap a quick picture of the mayor with the boys—who also took their own selfies—before heading off in one direction while the mayor and his entourage headed off in another, the mayor already having forgotten them.

At the nurses' station, the mayor noted with some annoyance that an older black nurse with dyed blond hair was in the middle of a shouting match with a younger Hispanic nurse, this one, the mayor noticed, with poorly dyed red hair. Must be a thing, he thought, for nurses to dye their hair. He didn't give it much more thought beyond that as, for some reason, both of them seemed oblivious to the advancing horde.

Jesus fuck, hadn't anyone prepared them?

They saw the mayor and the assembled press behind him and both froze.

"Good afternoon," Evan said. "We're here to see Mr. Cooper."

The black nurse stepped forward, clearly in charge, and said, "Mr. Cooper is no longer a patient."

"Excuse me?"

She shot an angry glance at the redhead and said, "Apparently, Mr. Cooper checked himself out."

"What do you mean, checked himself out?" the mayor asked, his smile already beginning to hurt.

"I mean, he's gone."

The mayor could feel the heat on his back coming off the group gathered behind him, all of them now photographing and taping the two nurses.

"You let him check out?"

"He snuck out."

Evan glanced at the uniformed cop standing a few feet behind them, looking like he wanted to die. "Wasn't there a guard at his door?"

"There was, but . . ." the black nurse again looked at her redheaded associate, "he got distracted for a moment or two."

The redhead said, "It was Jordie—Officer McMann's birthday. We got him a cupcake."

"A cupcake," the mayor said and then looked at the young cop, who may have just ruined both of their careers, and added, "Well, happy fucking birthday, Jordie," regretting it the minute the words came out of his mouth.

He felt the hubbub behind him and tried to focus.

Let's all give a warm welcome to Miguel Santiago! Mayor Miguel Santiago. Mayor Miguel Sannnnntiagooooooo!

Fuck.

As Evan began shouting at the nurses and the idiot cop, the mayor went momentarily inert, unable to move or think, ignoring the questions now being thrown at him, the name Roy Cooper the only thing that he could take in. He had, after all, just called the man a hero. Maybe he was. Maybe he was just shy and didn't want all this attention. Or maybe he was something else and didn't want the attention for another reason. Whatever it was, the mayor needed to do something, and he needed to do it right now, so that he didn't look like a raging dipshit.

He was just turning to face the group, had something witty all teed up and ready when the lights in the corridor began to flicker and the building began to shake. The mayor, aware of something heavy falling over nearby, realized it was an aftershock. A big one. Somehow, now out of body, the mayor saw himself, from above, vaulting over the counter at the nurses' station and, shoving a tiny nurse's aide aside, wedging himself under the desk on the other side, where he remained for the next seventeen seconds.

When the building finally stopped rocking and rolling, the mayor opened his eyes and looked up to see a dozen or so members of the press either leaning over the counter looking down at him or shoving those people aside so *they* could see, all of them holding up their phones and calling out his name.

Mayor Santiago! Mayor Santiago!

twenty-five

The last time Truck and Science had been to Valley Presbyterian hospital, it was to drop off Laura Klein, the girl who taught writing at Camp Kilpatrick. The girl with the red hair and the freckles.

The girl Science still thought about most every night.

Shake had been at Camp Kill out in Malibu for six months, having been sent there for vandalism and grand theft after he had stolen a deep fryer and some utensils from the Roy Romer Middle School cafeteria. Shake's plan was to give all that stuff to his auntie for Christmas. She liked to cook and had just lost a leg to diabetes and Shake thought it would make her feel better. But in the middle of his big heist, he got stoned, fell asleep, and somehow started a fire.

Science thought he was a fucking dumbass for capering like that on account of the lady couldn't even stand up, let alone cook.

Laura Klein was getting her master's in film production at UCLA and had come to Kilpatrick to teach screenwriting. She was working on a script about gangs and had wanted just to do some research, but then "fell in love with the young men out there" and volunteered to teach during the summer.

She read a story that Shake wrote about his pops—he'd gone into L.A. Men's for selling dope, but then unfortunately killed someone inside during a fight over the TV and ended up at Pelican Bay where he remained, twelve years later, making yoga mats. Laura said that Shake had a "real voice." That he should keep going with his writing. She gave Shake her number and told him to call her if he ever wanted help with his writing once he was home. She encouraged him to talk about his story with his friends and family in order to "flesh it out just a bit more."

But all Shake wanted to talk about when he got home was Laura Klein. He started calling her almost every night, telling Science that she was helping him with his story in return for him helping her with dialogue and stuff. She wanted to learn how to talk like Shake, though Shake thought he talked pretty much like everybody else.

Science, skeptical from the get-go, told Shake that nobody was helping nobody, that Shake just wanted to get at her. Pure and simple. All of them laughing at Shake for being all sprung on the white college girl. But Shake said they didn't know her. Not like he did.

"So call her up," Science said one day. "Invite her over. Let's get to know her."

"She ain't never gonna show up here."

"You saying she's never been here?"

"No, dude. We talk on Skype."

"That's cool," Science said. "Tell her you want help studying for your SAT. They can never say no to that shit."

So they all listened as Shake called Laura Klein and tried not to laugh as they caught him changing his voice when she picked up, adding more ghetto, trying to be someone else, someone Laura Klein wanted him to be. Shake said that he just wanted to holler at her some, tell her more about his life on the street, stuff he was too afraid to tell her during their time at Camp K.

They made plans to meet up at an IHOP on Vineland, Laura walking in, surprised to see Truck and Science sitting in the booth with Shake. Shake told her that they wanted to talk to her, too. That they had ideas for movies just like Shake, and they could help her out with making her movie more authentic, same as he was.

Science had not expected Laura Klein to be a redhead. In all of his Laura this and Laura that, Shake had failed to mention that this shorty had red hair and a shitload of freckles. Even on her arms. And big round titties. You could see that even under the sweater she wore. She had on a denim jacket, some Converse sneakers, probably thought a lot about what she was gonna wear down here to the 'hood. Wanted to make herself look "cool."

But what she looked was nervous. Especially when she took a gander at Truck, but then she sat down anyway. Right next to Science, who thought the girl smelled like apples. He stared at her profile as she talked to Shake about the SAT, about how he was going to nail the essay on account of he was such a good writer.

Science thought she had soft arms and kept finding ways to lean against her. She wasn't chubby, but she had meat on her. Her face was full, a pale peach color with all those freckles, and the deepest blue eyes Science had ever seen. He thought at first that maybe they were fake, some kind of contact lens like the ones his cousin wore for a while.

They all ordered pancakes, even Laura Klein, and Science found himself telling her about his brother getting shot in the spine, asking her if she thought that would make a good movie. Laura Klein said they were lucky in a way, they had so much to write about. Yeah, that was a sad, but awesome story. Science thought that maybe *she* wanted to write it. He wanted to know how much money a person could make if they sold a movie script. She said it depends. Could be a lot, though.

She liked to eat. Science liked that about her. This bitch wasn't dainty. She kept up with them, even as she scribbled nonstop in her pink notebook. And Laura Klein couldn't seem to write it all down fast enough.

Science knew what she wanted to hear and kept feeding her. So when she asked if any of them had ever shot anyone, did they do any drive-bys and were they afraid of getting shot, they all traded knowing looks, and Science said, "I don't care one way or the other about living or dying. And I care even less about killing someone."

Science watched her furiously scribble his every word, threw in some shit he used to hear his brother say. "We all at this table the same," he said. "Uncut. Straight out of the bush. We all shoot somebody, it come to that. We all do whatever we gotta do in whatever way we gotta do it." And then he added almost solemnly, "No doubt, one day pretty soon, all of us gonna die on the trigger."

Shake said, "Righteous," and hit the bump.

"That's a great phrase," Laura said. *"Die on the trigger."* She smiled at Science. "That could be the title of my piece."

Science leaned against her. "It's all yours."

Truck looked at Science, but said nothing. Let him run his mouth. For now.

Shake, not wanting to be left out, chimed in with "I don't really like drive-bys 'cause innocent people might get hit, you know?"

"So you do worry about that?" Laura Klein asked.

Shake nodded and said, "My homeboy one time shot a baby, it was still in the stroller. He felt bad about it, you know, but he was like, 'That's just how it happens sometimes.' What could he do about it?"

Shake let Laura Klein's scribbling catch up while Science wondered exactly which homeboy Shake was talking about. This being the first time he'd heard this story.

"See, me, I'm like this," Shake went on. "If I want some dude, I park in front of their house, camp out all night, maybe drink a little, smoke some weed, and just wait for 'em. Soon as they come out they house, I splash 'em and I leave."

Science and Truck both started laughing.

Laura Klein asked, "What's so funny?"

"Man, this dude ain't never camped out to get nobody in his life. Ain't put that much work in. Fuck, he still a tiny."

Shake looked at Laura Klein, but threw a piece of ice from his soda at Science and said, "You trippin', cuz! You don't know shit about me!"

Science said, "I know you oughta get stomped."

She asked Science, "What did you call him? A tiny?"

"Tiny G. What he is. What me an' him are. Li'l homies. We got outta baby homie when we were like thirteen."

Shake nodded.

"We ain't gonna reach OG for a couple years yet."

"And you're what, fourteen?"

"Yeah, but Truck, he's sixteen. He still a li'l homie but he got the rep."

"How does one get a rep?"

"In our set? By straight killin'."

Laura Klein looked at Truck. Something holding her back from asking him what she really wanted to ask him. If she was nervous, Science couldn't tell. It wasn't until he asked her where she lived that he caught the hitch, the slight hesitation.

"Westwood."

"Whereabouts?"

She told him a street. And he knew for sure she was lying. He asked, did she have a dude? She said she lived with someone. Guy in his second year at the medical school.

That felt like the truth, but something at the table was changing. There hadn't been much talk about SATs or college. And now every time she looked at Shake, he looked away, embarrassed. The dude was clearly miserable. Anybody could see that.

Laura Klein was starting to figure out that she was here for another reason.

Science asked about the dude she lived with. What's his name? Greg. Dr. Greg. They all got a big laugh over that. She started looking at her watch. Asked Shake about when his SAT was. Did he have a workbook. Laura told him that he could get one online. Already disconnecting from what she now understood was rapidly turning into something she couldn't control. This was a mistake. She was still trying to be cool, but Science could see that now she was afraid.

He didn't try to make her feel better. Didn't help her in any way. He dug it. It was as if he could see inside her brain, could see exactly what it was that she was so afraid they might do to her. And the more he saw, the more excited he became.

And he wasn't the only one.

Truck watched her, too. All through the pancakes and the hash browns and the Coca-Colas, Truck had that one wilted eye locked on Laura Klein. He hadn't stopped watching her since the moment she sat her ass down. At this point, Science didn't know how the day would end, hadn't made up his mind whether or not, if it came to it, he'd have to step in at some point, or if he would just let Truck do his thing.

All Science knew was that he needed to see more of Laura Klein than she was showing him.

A whole lot more.

The waitress, a woman Science recognized as his fifth grade teacher and a former crack addict, set the check down. The last time Science had seen her, she was on the pipe and doing everything and anything to get a blast. Now here she was, in this place, refilling the boysenberry syrup.

Laura picked up the check, saying a bit too loud, "Let me get this, guys." They all watched as she started to grab a credit card from her purse, then changed her mind and instead handed a couple twenties to the waitress, saying that she didn't need any change. Science figured there had to be at least a forty percent tip there. It was clear that Laura Klein just wanted to get the fuck out of there, and Science, knowing what he knew, didn't blame her.

She started to get up when Truck said, "I'm not done." The first words he had said since Laura Klein sat down.

Laura smiled at him. "You finish up," she said. "I just have to get back." And then, as if she needed to sell her exit more, "I have a class tonight."

As soon as she slipped out of the booth, Science looked at Truck and the three of them got up and followed.

A minute later, they were all standing in the parking lot, Laura saying that Shake should keep in touch, let her know how he does on the test, when Science asked if she could give them all a ride home. She was caught, not sure what to say. He used his superpower and smiled at her, said it wasn't far. On the way to Westwood for sure.

They all piled into her Honda Fit. Shake sat up front beside her while Truck and Science squeezed into the backseat, Truck looking around and saying, "Nice hoop," which set him and Science off laughing. Both of them in the backseat just losing it. Completely checking out.

Science could see Laura Klein's smiling but confused face in the rearview mirror. She looked hurt in a way that made his heart hammer.

She asked, "Where am I going?"

He told her to take the next left.

Truck looked at the back of Shake's head and said, "My nig, put on some tunes."

Shake looked at Laura Klein.

Truck hit him in the ear. "You hear me?"

"Motherfucker—"

"Just do it."

It was Laura Klein who turned on the radio, already tuned to some "urban" station, which made Science and Truck start laughing all over again.

Science, nodding to the beat, said, "Righteous."

He and Truck bumped fists and sat back as they all headed down Sherman Way, Laura glancing at Science in the mirror every so often. Stupidly looking for help there. Reading him wrong from the minute she sat down at the IHOP.

Well, she'll see soon enough.

Somewhere near the 118, they passed a block-long building that was once a Lowe's, but now sat empty, the folks out this way not so much do-it-yourselfers.

"Turn in there."

"What for?"

Truck's knife was at her neck. "Cuz I said so, a'ight?"

"What are you doing?"

"Research."

More laughter from the backseat.

Shake turned around now.

"This ain't cool," he said, his voice unsteady now. "You both gotta be trippin'. We could get—"

Science jabbed him hard, felt Shake's nose collapse under his own stinging knuckles. Shake cupped his face and fell back against the glove compartment as blood now roared through his fingers.

That got Laura Klein screaming.

Truck grabbed her hair. "Turn the motherfucking car," he said, his voice quiet as he rubbed the blade of the knife against her sweater.

"Please," Laura Klein was now saying. "You can take my money."

Science turned to Truck. "Why they all of them think we want their fuckin' money?"

They were parked behind the building, beneath a huge billboard advertising some personal injury lawyer, the sign situated so as to face the eastbound traffic on the 118. Science, standing beside the car after it was all over, Laura Klein's sweater wrapped around his waist, could see an identical billboard on the other side of the highway, facing the other way. He could hear Shake, inside the car, saying, "Dude, she gotta go to a hospital."

Science had just wanted to look at her. Wanted her to take off that sweater so that he could really see what she looked like.

"That's all?" she asked. "Just my sweater and then you'll let me go."

"That's all."

And so Laura Klein pulled the sweater over her head. Just like that, didn't look like she hardly even thought about it. She kept the pink bundle in her lap and stared out the window as they all gawked at her.

It wasn't just the freckles on her chest, but that peach-colored bra that was too much for Science and he lost control pretty much the second he saw it. He hoped Truck didn't know, was relieved to see that *Cuz* wasn't paying attention to him, was too busy leaning forward in the seat, literally breathing down Laura Klein's neck as he snapped the bra and said, "Take that shit off, too."

"No."

It didn't really matter what she said, *it was on,* they were all pawing at her before she could react. She tried to open her door but Truck held on to her. Even Shake, the lower half of his face covered in blood from his crushed nose, was turning and reaching across the seat for her.

"I'm sorry," he said as he cupped one of her breasts.

Laura struggled to get her door open but Truck put an arm around her neck, covered her mouth with one hand, and held her while he reached down and grabbed at her with his other hand. Laura Klein squirmed and kicked at the dash. She turned and Science saw her staring at him over the top of Truck's filthy hand, the panic right there in her eyes.

Science reached out and touched one of her pale, pink nipples and for the second time in less than five minutes lost control. She was breathing hard and he thought that maybe some part of her was down for all this. He knew that she could read what happened on his face and that only made him more excited. He was reaching down to shove a hand between her legs, Truck's other hand already there, when he felt her phone vibrate.

"Someone callin' her."

Truck reached into her pocket, took out her phone, and held it up for Science to see the screen that now contained Dr. Greg's name and picture. Science could not believe what he was seeing. He looked at Laura and said, "Dr. Greg's a *black dude*?"

They all pounded it out, laughing now, until Science held up his hand, said, "Shut the fuck up," and answered:

"Laura's phone," he said. "Can I help you?"

"Who is this?" Absolutely no light in the voice.

Science said, "We Laura's technical advisors."

Truck and Shake found this fucking hilarious. Laura tried to scream but Truck kept his hand there and pulled her head back against the seat.

The voice said, "I'd like to speak to Laura, please."

Science looked at Laura, her breathing becoming more and more rapid.

"I'm sorry, but she can't come to the phone right now. We playing a little game with her. But she'll call you back later."

He hung up the phone, put it in his own pocket, and then watched as Laura, her eyes wide, began to hyperventilate.

They all froze.

"What the fuck?"

"She fakin' it," Truck said, and slapped her on the side of the face. "Cut that shit."

But she only became more agitated.

Science knew something was wrong. His cousin, Keen, came back from Iraq and would have panic attacks all the time. He looked like Laura did now. Science had heard that the only way to help him was with oxygen tanks and some kind of special dope.

Laura was having trouble catching any air and Shake finally said they had to take her to the hospital. Truck looked at him like he might hit him again, but then bailed out of the car.

Science went after him, but he knew there was no getting him back. He stood there in the parking lot, watching Truck walk at a clip back to the street.

"C'mon, cuz," Shake said. "We gotta go."

Science saw Laura Klein's sweater lying on the ground where it must have fallen from Truck's lap when he bolted. Science picked it up and wrapped it around his damp jeans.

"Dude. She gotta go to a hospital."

So the two of them carefully laid her down in the backseat and drove to Valley Presbyterian, keeping to the speed limit, making sure to stop at all the red lights seeing as neither of them had a driver's license.

At one point along the way, Science looked in the rearview mirror to find Laura Klein still lying down, but now calm and watching him.

"You just stay down."

She didn't move, didn't respond. Just kept looking at him.

"You understand," he said. "You in bigger trouble than we are, right? You tell anybody about this, they gonna ask, do you know where the fuck you are? Why would you go off in a car fulla niggas? Whatever you say, nobody gonna believe you, right?"

She blinked, so he knew she was hearing him.

"But if pigs do come and knock on our door," he held up her wallet, open to show her ID, "me and Truck are gonna come to Westwood and knock on *your* door, feel me?"

Shake turned to look at her. If he apologized again, Science was going to push him out of the moving car. But Shake wisely kept his mouth shut.

"And just so you know," Science went on, "if you move to another place, we'll still find you. Be no thing at all on account of you got a head like fuckin' Roman candle. You best just consider this an experience for your movie, which I look forward to seeing in the near future."

And then, for whatever reason, he felt the need to add, "All that shit we gave you at the IHOP, you can have for free."

They parked at the far edge of the parking lot, then called the ER from a pay phone. Told them someone was dead inside a car parked in space number 44, thinking that would get their attention.

They then watched from across the street as a nurse finally came out of the ER a full fifteen minutes later and found the car. Shake and Science didn't see what happened next. They went to Wendy's with the money they took from Laura Klein's wallet and ate in silence, too tired to talk.

Shake got over Laura Klein pretty much right away, stopped working on his screenplay. Stopped talking about her altogether. "That bitch wasn't all that," he said the last time he brought her up. "Shit, she didn't even know I was too young to take the damn SAT."

twenty-six

Initially, the plan was to walk into the hospital, find Mr. Freeze, and shoot him with his own gun. But that idea had several obvious drawbacks. Numero uno being that shooting someone in a hospital would be a loud event and once they started shooting, they'd probably never make it back out the door.

Science didn't mind this outcome as turning off the dude everyone thought was a hero would make him a ghetto star, a real soldier for sure, which is where he wanted to be. He'd go to jail, but he'd ride the beef and continue his gang education there, come out when he was eighteen, most likely a full-on general. From there Science could take the Vineland Boyz from a bunch of wannabe Jay Zs, all of them posing, fake hitting blunts on their YouTube videos, and turn them once more into a real army, take back the trade the fucking Mexicans had grabbed when they weren't looking.

But Truck was closer to eighteen and not anywhere near down for getting caught on account of he'd most likely do life at San Quentin or Soledad, one of those places. Truck thought they should either strangle the dude with a cord from one of the machines they got in the room or cut his throat, play it by ear.

Things were weird from the get-go. First as they were walking into the hospital, some famous actor dude showed up with all this muscle. Science remembered the guy from the movie *Zorro* back when he was like three years old, assumed the man was here to visit Mr. Freeze, shake his hand or some bullshit. Science figured they follow *him,* they find their dude.

All the news guys with the movie star made Truck nervous, but Science thought their presence made it all that much easier. They walk in with the group, but then hide or hang back and wait for everyone to have their visit and leave—"Time for Mr. Freeze to rest"—and then they go in and make the man do just that.

It all began just fine. The movie star at first not so sure about them, but then inviting them onto the elevator with his boys. On the way up, Science heard someone call him "Mr. Mayor" and told him his moms had cancer. Just popped into his head, and the guy was like all of a sudden his boy. They even took a few pix together before they got off the elevator and their plan went to shit.

The instant they got off and started roaming around the corridor, a uniformed cop saw them, asked them what they were doing. Science fed him the cancer mom rap, but a nurse overheard and said the oncology ward was two floors up. This floor was all post-op. Then, as they were walking back to the elevator, they heard that Mr. Freeze had left.

Another cop was giving them a funny look, so they just took off and ran down the stairs, which, weirdly, started swaying the minute they hit them. They had to stop and hang on to the railing until the shaking passed. They then ran back through the lobby and out into the parking lot. And fuck it if in that very moment, they didn't see Mr. Freeze crossing Sepulveda.

"Is that him?" Truck asked. "He looks different."

"He's in different clothes."

He was walking slow, taking his time. Looked like he was limping. So it was easy to follow him from the other side of the street. He definitely had on different clothes. Science could see even from here that they didn't fit him right. Fucker must have stole them from somebody. Where was he going? More importantly, *who was he?*

He was slick, that's for sure. They followed him into a Big 5, watched as he walked around, putting on clothes from the racks. Watched as he bumped into and easily snaked a wallet from a young white dude waiting in line to pay for a snowboard. Thirty seconds later, they saw him pick up another wallet from a guy in a suit looking up at the mountain bikes hanging from the ceiling. He paid for a jacket and a duffel bag, no one noticing that the clothes he had on were all lifted, the security tags somehow, magically, gone.

He stayed on foot for a mile up Sepulveda, not ever running or trying to hide or ever once even looking back. He made his way east on Victory for another mile or so, before finally stopping in the middle of the parking lot of a Super 8 Motel on Laurel Canyon. He stood there staring at the building for what seemed like a full five minutes, and then went inside the office. They watched from across the street as he checked in, then went into a room on the second floor.

Science turned to Truck, could see that he was staring at the motel, thinking the same thing Science was.

Who the fuck was this guy?

twenty-seven

Roy had just walked right on out of the hospital.

He had spent an hour coming up with some elaborate plan of escape when he got up and looked out the door, saw that the cop assigned to "protect" him was standing over at the nurses' station, all of them singing *Happy Birthday.*

A few minutes earlier, Roy had pulled the curtain around his bed and checked the plastic bag on the chair containing his clothes. Between the holes and the blood, none of it was wearable. So he stepped out from behind the curtain, looked at the bed next to him. A guy who looked to be near eighty and probably weighed just about the same number was lying there watching television.

Roy hadn't even realized this guy was in the room with him. He was even more surprised, then, to find a third bed, this one occupied by a dark-skinned man around forty, sound asleep with his hands folded across his chest. Well, one hand anyway. Where the right one was supposed to be was a giant, bandaged stump the size of a football.

Roy found the man's clothing in a duffel bag in the bathroom and grabbed it, along with some pain meds he saw in a cup, and brought it all back to his bed.

The clothing smelled like gasoline and cut grass, was a little big, but worked well enough for now. The shirt was wet and bloody at the cuff. The undershirt was sweat-stained, but otherwise okay. The man's boots were at least a size too big, but Roy pulled them on anyway, quickly laced them up, and went out the door.

The first person he saw was the nurse, G. RODRIGUEZ (*call me Genie, sweetface*), maybe fifty feet down the hall. Roy turned and walked the other way. He made the stairs and started down. He could feel a few stitches ripping as he went, but kept going, reached deep into one of the pockets and found a wallet with some cash and a Discover card.

Enough to get started. By the end of the day he'd have whatever he needed. Clothes. Cash. A place to stay. This wasn't the first time he had to start from nothing.

He picked up the two bangers the minute he stepped out the door into the parking lot. They were on the other side of the street, no doubt thinking Roy hadn't seen them. It was the pretty one, Science, and the killer. What was his name? Truck. Roy would have to kill him first. Talk to Science about what he did with Roy's gun. Hopefully he hadn't tossed it. Roy was pretty sure that this kid would have kept it. He got the feeling he liked it.

Either way, Roy was astounded by this bit of luck. Clearly the two of them wanted to finish what they started the other night. Roy was a witness, after all. And, to be fair, it's what Roy would have done. To be more fair, it's what Roy was going to do. They were also witnesses. The little bangers were probably going to get caught. That lady cop would get them talking. And with Martin Shine rotting on the floor a few blocks away, one of the first things they'd talk about is where that old gun came from.

Roy made it in and out of the Big 5 in less than twenty minutes. He and Albert had once strafed a Sears in Kansas City in ten minutes and walked out with a half dozen wallets and two complete wardrobes. But they were both in their twenties at the time and Roy had slowed down some since.

He grabbed a room at the first motel he came to, knowing he wasn't going to stay anywhere long. He drank about a gallon of water from the tap, then took a shower, redressed the hole in his side, and put on his new clothes. He took the pain pills he'd lifted from the hospital, lay down on the bed, and felt good for the first time in days.

He turned on the TV, watched the news hoping for something on The Kid. He was pitching at home against the Brewers before the team came out to L.A. for a series with the Dodgers. If The Kid shut out Milwaukee, he'd be going for the record here. Roy planned on being at that game, the irony not lost on him that if he hadn't gotten into this little predicament, he would have already been back in New York and missed it.

But right now Roy was wondering why no one had kicked his door down or made any kind of move.

He got up and looked out the window. He saw the two bangers standing down in the parking lot, shifting from foot to foot, passing a joint back and forth. They knew what Roy was. Maybe not specifically, but they had an idea as to what he might do if given the chance. Roy had been careful to let them see that. Yet there they were, laughing and smoking, right out in the open. Not a care in the world.

Roy thought, *No wonder they don't live long.*

"I'm thinking this earthquake was like maybe a good thing."

Science was bent, which always set him *philosophizing*. Truck let him, content to be just budding out as the sun went down. Gave him time to think on this Mr. Freeze, what he might be up to. He knew Science wanted to lay him down all by himself, but Truck had some concerns. So he had himself a deep drag on the blunt and thought about that while Science went on.

"I'm thinking maybe we need something worse," he was saying. "Burn it all down. Start over."

Truck had to ask, "What happens we all burn down with it?"

"Nah, fool, we'd be the survivors." He took the blunt from Truck, had his own hit, then went on as he let out a huge cloud of smoke. "Sure, we'd have drought and starvation for a couple years. Prolly more than that. But pretty soon, new shit gonna grow. New people gonna have they shot."

"Why you wanna start over?"

" 'Cause what we got now is bullshit. Fuck all these drunk OGs think they all down rappin' about smokin' and drinkin'. The idea of working for your set, that all gone now. It all about being famous. Not like once upon a time. You were a ghetto star because you *worked*."

Truck wasn't so sure about that. He worked plenty and, yet, here he was.

"I been readin' this book by that dude Monster Kody," Science was now saying, "Eight Trey Crip from back in the day, you know who I'm talking about? Now that dude was the real truth. Fuckin' Eight Treys, man, they one time go to a Blood funeral and steal the fuckin' body right out of the box so they can kill it again. They stab it in the face a buncha times, then go dump it back in Blood Hood. That's *hard core*." He passed the blunt back to Truck and said, "Dude, you gotta read this book."

Truck said, "I don't read no history books," ignoring the offered smoke. The truth was Truck didn't read anything. He was illiterate. He'd spent the last six years sleeping on floors or in the backs of parked cars. In all that time, he never once set foot in a school. His mom died from an OD. He had a grandmother, but the last time he saw her, she was going the same way. He had a brother that got killed—stabbed in a movie theater over some long forgotten beef.

Truck never thought much about any of this. He didn't care about starting over or creating a new, more powerful set or any of the shit Science went on about. For him, shit just happened. A blade or a bullet didn't have any kind of higher purpose outside of killing whoever had the misfortune of getting in front of it. A bullet had no name on it, it hit whatever or whoever it hit. To Truck, everything was random. Chance. He shot someone, stole something, did whatever he did not so much to defend himself or take a life, but to see what would happen next. That's all. He couldn't read. Some said he couldn't even *learn*. But he could for sure make shit happen.

And right now what was happening was Mr. Freeze had just come out of his room and was coming down the steps, slowly, in no big hurry.

Science saw him, too, watched him cross the now dark parking lot and start walking up Laurel Canyon, and said what Truck already knew: "It's on."

They kept a full block behind him. They figured that he knew they were there, between the street lights and the traffic, the sidewalk was lit up like it was mid-afternoon. Both boys were strapped, Truck with a silver .45 he called his "Forty-five Homeboys" and Science with that Walther. He had Googled the gun that morning and learned that it was German and older than his mom. He decided from then on, he'd go nowhere, he wasn't strapped. And this funky old piece with the hair trigger would be his strap of choice. No one would take it from him. Not ever.

Mr. Freeze stayed on Laurel Canyon for a good half mile before turning right onto Sherman Way, but when they got to the corner, no more than twenty seconds later, the man was gone. Science looked across the street. He wasn't there either.

"Where he at?"

They reached under their shirts, put a hand on their guns and continued cautiously up the street, looking inside storefronts and doorways. They looked in between buildings and around parked cars until finally Truck said, "Cuz, you know why we can't find this fool?"

"Why?"

" 'Cause the mothafucka's right behind us."

Science turned and saw that it was true: somehow Mr. Freeze was now following *them*.

He kept on walking, but what Science really wanted to do was sit down on the curb and think. Or they could just run. No way this dude could catch them, not after being shot a bunch of times. Science was about to suggest this very option when Truck looked back and said, "No big thing." He kept looking back at the man following them and said, "Let him come along." He then turned to Science and smiled. "We'll take him to Radford," he said. "Be some niggas there fo' sure."

Roy waited for the two of them to figure out that he was now a half block behind them. He was certain that it would be the smart one, Science, who caught on first. But it was the killer, Truck, who turned and looked back. Roy should have known. Science had the brains, but Truck had the gut. He probably felt Roy before he saw him. Same as Roy would have felt him.

He figured they were now leading him to some nearby neighborhood where they would have an advantage. That was fine with Roy as there was a good chance that it would be somewhere close to home, so that, afterward, if he had to, Roy could stop by Science's house.

They turned off the main boulevard and the street suddenly

became darker. Roy looked up and saw that all of the streetlights on this block had been shot out. The two boys had stopped walking and Roy realized that they had led him into a cul-de-sac, faded two-story apartment buildings all around, but no houses on this street.

Some lights were on. The blue glow of TVs flickering in many of the windows. Here and there people were out on the street, but Roy couldn't make out any details at this hour. The two boys were now standing near the end of the street. A couple of bigger kids got out of a car and stood beside them.

Science waved.

"Hey, Mr. Freeze," he said. "Come here and let us holler at you real quick."

They watched him come. Science could feel Cisco and Taco, the two OGs standing on either side of him. Twin brothers, the only way to tell them apart was Taco shaved his head while Cisco favored long dreads. Both were over six feet tall and well over two hundred pounds. And right now both were also sky up and bent out of their fucking minds. Science had smelled the dope as soon as they got out of the car. When *he* ran the set, that shit would stop. A sober and disciplined set would be undeniable.

"You two shoulda come to me straight up," Cisco was saying. "Instead you run off and hide while you all over CNN."

Science said, "I ain't hidin' from shit." He watched Mr. Freeze and put a hand on his gun. "I been lookin' for this fool."

"What you doin' over on Dehougne anyway?"

Science said, "We claimin' Vineland now."

"Since when?"

"Since I claimed it."

Cisco looked at him.

Science shrugged and said, "Tiny Locos are weak."

The two giant brothers laughed hard at that one. Cisco smacked Science on the back of the head, all the while watching Mr. Freeze make his way up the block. "I remember yo' li'l ass use to ride skateboards and them BMX bikes, actin' crazy an' shit. Now you want to be a gangster, huh? You wanna hang with real mothafuckas and tear shit up?"

"I *am* a gangster."

"You trippin' is what you doin', bringin' a mothafucka like him down here."

"I'm on it."

"You better be, loc," Cisco said. "You better blow up this fool right now. 'Cause any homies come up dead behind this, me an' bro gonna fuckin' stomp yo' stupid ass, drop you naked in Blood Hood somewhere."

Science took out the Walther. "He's good as got."

Taco looked at the gun and laughed, "Where'd you get the antique, homie?"

Science looked off toward Roy. "From him."

Before he left, Roy had swallowed a couple more pain pills and was feeling pretty good right about now. Of course, he would feel better if he had a gun, but he was pretty sure there would be someone down there at the end of the block who would have one he could borrow. And wouldn't you know it, at that very moment, as Roy got within fifty feet of the group, one of the big homeboys reached into the back of a car and came out with a sawed-off, pistol-gripped pump.

Roy could make out people in clusters standing around the apartment buildings. Too dark to really see them, but Roy heard children's voices and saw a couple of strollers, a few people in lawn chairs, everyone outside enjoying the fresh air, free for a moment from rooms that wouldn't stop shaking.

Roy knew the wide spray from that chopped shotgun could easily hit a dozen of them in any direction.

As Roy got closer, the one holding it concentrated on his hardcore stare, but Roy could see, even in the dark, that, big and fat as he was, he was strictly a gunfighter and wouldn't have much skill with his hands. The other one had a black Glock at his side, was absently rubbing his leg with it while the two younger kids stood directly in front of them, each with a hand under his shirt trying to look bored.

Roy was surprised, now stepping right up to the group, that the two big boys were twins, identical in every way except for their hair, and both clearly stoned out of their minds, tiny red embers where their eyes were supposed to be.

Roy raised his hands to his shoulders and said, "I'm unarmed," and then rabbit-punched Truck in the face, the blow shocking everyone standing there, especially Truck, who jerked upright and grabbed his face with both hands, making it that much easier for Roy to take hold of his Forty-five Homeboys and shoot the fat one behind him holding the sawed-off, the guy looking down at the blooming red flower on his white T-shirt, before backing away a couple of steps and then collapsing.

Standing this close, Roy had everybody jammed up, so his twin brother couldn't get that Glock high enough before Roy shot him just above the lip, covering Science, who was standing right in front of him, with pieces of his cratered face.

Panicked, Science fired once into the sidewalk, the damned Walther going off early, and was raising it again when Roy reached out and grabbed it by the barrel with his free hand and took it away. Science froze, just stood there looking back at him, waiting for whatever was coming next. All of a sudden, Roy wasn't exactly sure himself, so he hit the kid in the head with Truck's .45 so he could think about it, the kid going down on the sidewalk. Roy tossed that pistol aside, quickly jacked the clip on his Walther, happy to have the old gun once again nestled in his hand, and saw that he had a few rounds left.

Did he kill these two? They knew what he was. But he now had the gun, so there was no way they could prove it had come from him. Maybe it was time to just go.

He looked up to see Truck stumbling through the dark to where Roy had tossed the .45 on the grass.

"Leave it."

But either the kid didn't hear or didn't care and picked up his gun and spun around when Roy shot him twice.

Roy turned and put his gun on Science, the kid now picking himself up off the sidewalk and facing Roy.

"Go ahead," he said. "Ain't nobody care about me and I don't care about nobody on this earth."

Roy pulled the trigger, but somehow knew before he heard it that there would be a click, but no gunshot.

Science didn't even blink at the sound. He just asked, "You wanna go again?"

Roy thought about it, but then looked at the apartment building behind the kid. Every window seemed to contain a little blue flame, all the same rectangular shape. He looked around at the other windows and down on the street, a hundred flaming rectangles all around him.

Tonight, it seemed, everybody had their phone out.

It didn't really matter what Roy did next. There was nowhere for him to go.

"Why you trippin', cuz?" Science said. "Ain't you a killer?"

Roy looked at the kid, but had no idea what to say.

Part III

twenty-eight

The county held Roy for less than six weeks at the Wyandotte Detention Center. There was no trial as the young ADA assigned to the case took one look at the shivering twelve-year-old and suddenly had no taste for a public fight, agreeing with the boy's flaky-scalped lawyer, Doc Solomon, that this was essentially a mercy killing and, so, made a quick deal for manslaughter—a two- or three-year jolt at the most for, as the ADA described him, "an otherwise decent kid like this one."

Upon entering his plea, sealed because of his age, Roy was transferred to the Missouri State Training School for Boys at Boonville, or the Honor Center as it was somewhat ironically called before it was shut down by the state barely a month after Roy's release, and almost one hundred years to the day after it had opened.

A nearly obese fifteen-year-old with thick sandy hair, and what Roy thought were the long lashes and round brown eyes of a woman, was the only other prisoner on the bus to Boonville. He introduced himself as Jerome ("call me Jerry") Wethers, and assured Roy that he himself would show Roy the ropes once they got "up the hill." This kind gesture would turn out to be hollow since Jerry would be dead within a month of Roy's arrival at Boonville.

Roy would come to wish for a similar end shortly thereafter.

In an effort to keep calm, Roy told himself that he was riding on a normal yellow school bus. This wasn't all that difficult as there were no markings or bars on the windows. The only hint that this particular bus was bound for someplace other than a Missouri middle school was the curly-haired, seriously muscle-bound gentleman with the twelve-gauge sitting behind the driver. Darryl Deems—or Smiley, as the guard was called, because he was always grinning, though he never looked particularly happy—faced the back and eyeballed Roy for the entire ninety-minute ride.

When the bus began making its way through gently rolling hills and lush orchards, Roy started to relax. He thought that maybe his mother was right, that maybe everything would be okay after all. But a few minutes later, as the bus rounded a corner and Roy saw the long row of stark white headstones at the bottom of the hill, and then his first glimpse of the main building at the top, he immediately had trouble breathing. He pressed his face to the glass and stared up at the gothic brick and stone pile, the place looking something like a cross between a Southern military college and an insane asylum, and knew in that instant that nothing would be okay ever again.

Boonville held "unsettled juveniles" convicted of everything from petty larceny to rape all the way up the felony ladder to murder. There was no segregation of any kind; inmates were mixed indiscriminately. The younger with the older, the dangerous mental cases with the normal delinquent, the first-time offender with the hardened hoodlum. This was the murky, blackwater pool that the perpetually frightened kid from Kansas City was chucked into.

"*You're* in for Man One?"

That's what the processing guards kept asking as Roy undressed, all of them laughing at his pinched face, bony arms, and the trembling pale sticks he stood on, none of them believing that he could kill anything, let alone his own father.

The rough strip search left him bleeding in a couple of embarrassing places and Roy nearly fainted twice. The small, windowless room heated up to near ninety degrees didn't help. Each time Roy felt himself going, he caught Deems smiling at him from the back of the room and something told him to stay awake at all costs.

For the next two years if he could.

He fought the urge to piss down his leg and stared straight ahead like a good soldier until one of the guards tossed him a gray uniform and told him to get dressed.

Deems marched Roy, now balancing a foam pillow atop a fitted sheet and folded wool blanket, past a group of a dozen boys weed-ing an acre of vegetables. The gardeners ranged in age from ten to seventeen and were covered in mud, the ground still soaked from a storm the day before. One of them, a six-foot-tall white blond, nearly albino, leaned on his hoe and smiled at Roy.

"Hey, fish," he said. "Welcome to Boonville."

"Shut the fuck up, Knott," Deems said without turning.

Roy kept his eyes forward, but could feel them all now pausing in their work to watch him pass. He had that old, familiar sensation that someone was about to hit him or spit on him. Only now, his skin was suddenly alive, like someone was breathing on him. One touch would launch him out of his shoes.

He would have to somehow hide. Become invisible. That would be the only way he would survive this place. Stay out of everyone's way. Don't piss anyone off. Find those places where everyone isn't and live there. He had done that in school, he would do that here.

Unfortunately, just as he arrived at this conclusion, the pillow he carried slid off the blanket and fell to the muddy ground. Roy hadn't been paying attention and had let the blanket dip and the pillow dropped right in front of him, causing him to then trip over it.

Roy kept his feet, but that didn't matter.

They all saw it.

One or two of the younger ones laughed, but the others, the older kids, leaning on their garden tools, just looked at him. And waited.

Roy froze, too afraid to do anything, was staring at the muddy footprint now stamped onto the pillow when Deems realized that Roy was no longer alongside him, turned around and saw the pillow lying in the dirt.

"You gonna pick that up?"

"Yes."

"Well, do it," Deems said. "Move."

Roy stepped on the pillow. He hadn't really meant to, his leg was just the first part of his body that moved.

He looked up at the guard, was all set to apologize when Deems slapped him across the face, slapped him so hard Roy now dropped the blanket and sheet as his legs folded up and he sat down in the mud.

"Pick it all up."

Roy's left ear was ringing and he didn't hear the instruction.

Deems kicked him in the arm and said, again, "Pick it all up."

Roy heard him that time and, his shoulder screaming in pain, gathered up the now muddy bedclothes and turned around just as Deems grabbed Roy's chin with one hand and squeezed his jaw. Roy smelled beets as the guard bent down to get in Roy's face and said, "For long as you're here, none of that shit ever goes to the laundry. You got me? You sleep on it, filthy, just like it is."

They served dinner at five. Roy watched as inmate servers dropped a mound of ground beef, carrots, a tiny boiled potato, and a slice of Wonder Bread onto his plate. He turned away from the line and stood there with his tray looking around the cavernous dining hall. The faded green and black linoleum looked about as cold and hard as the cement ceiling, the resulting echo giving such a sharp edge to the already loud din that it actually hurt Roy's ears to listen.

The kid from the bus, Jerry Wethers, waved him over to a nearly empty table, jumping right in as Roy awkwardly tried to swing his legs over the bench.

"Stay away from the older kids."

"You're older."

"I'm not *them.*"

Jerry nodded to a tableful of boys Roy recognized from the garden. The big blond, the one Deems called Knott, was looking his way. Out of his coat, Roy could see that the kid was pretty well cut, lean like an athlete. The boys on either side of him looked to be a year or two younger, somewhere around sixteen, but all just as stoved up as the big pale kid.

They were all waving at Jerry.

Knott patted the bench beside him.

Roy asked, "They your friends?"

Jerry looked down at his plate. "Yeah, we're best buddies."

A few minutes later, Roy could feel the atmosphere change, the volume in the room dropping all at once. Roy looked up and saw half a dozen boys in jeans and boots stride into the hall. They all wore filthy Stetsons which they now tossed onto a table, immediately clearing the benches, the previous squatters either sliding down or getting up altogether in order to make room for the hats that now held six places.

Jerry saw the question in Roy's face and said, "Boonville Cowboys."

"Who?"

"They help with the cattle."

"There's cows here?"

"Over a hundred head." Jerry looked down at his plate. "They're the only ones get to be late for meals."

Roy watched a tall boy, he looked older than the rest of the group—looked older than anyone in there for that matter—go to the front of the chow line and start pointing at food, the servers all thumbs now as he made his way down the line. As he got closer, Roy thought he wasn't even a kid. He looked too old to be in here, maybe nineteen or twenty with his black hair slicked back and eyes that Roy could see were pale blue, even from fifty feet away.

"That's Albert," Jerry was now saying. "See if you can get away with never saying a fucking word to him."

"How do I do that?"

"You see him coming, walk the other way. You walk into a room he's there, turn around and walk the fuck out."

Roy watched as Albert and the other Boonville Cowboys sat down and tucked into their food. Albert laughing at some joke and then, out of nowhere, looking up across the room at Roy. Those eyes cutting through everyone else in between to get to him. Roy found himself unable to look away and stared back until Albert finally nodded and went back to his dinner.

Jerry shook his head.

"You're dead now."

C Dorm was the biggest of the three dormitories at Boonville. Over eighty metal-framed beds were jammed into a brick-walled space made for fifty. There wasn't enough room to walk between the cots, so the boys just walked *over* them, indiscriminately stepping on the other beds as they went. There were no bunks as, through the years, too many boys had been hurt being thrown off of the upper beds in the middle of the night.

The real estate nearest the bathroom was the least desired as some poor, soundly sleeping soul would get their spleen crushed during the night anytime anyone needed to take a leak. So, naturally, the only vacant bed was right beside the door. After the fourth time someone stepped on him, Roy noticed another kid, small and younger like himself, point to the floor. Roy shook his head, confused. He then watched as the kid grabbed his pillow and blanket, slid to the floor, and crept under the bed.

Roy did the same. It was tight and he couldn't roll over, but he fell asleep and didn't wake up until Deems kicked him in the neck at morning bed check.

The first half of every day was spent in school, the three Rs taught by teachers who couldn't otherwise get a job doing anything, anywhere else. Roy noticed that while most of the boys slept right through classes, no one seemed to care. Least of all the teachers, many of whom looked like they might fall asleep themselves.

Inmates got a free half hour after lunch and before their afternoon jobs, so Roy headed up the three flights to C Dorm to take a nap. There were only a few other boys up here, all of them, like Roy, younger, more vulnerable types. Mounted around the room were several security cameras with, presumably, a guard or two on the other end, so it seemed like a safe place. Roy would find out soon enough that there were no safe places at Boonville.

He lay down, immediately heard something crunch under his pillow, and sat up again. He pulled the pillow aside and saw a small brown paper bag folded over. Roy looked around at the other boys in the room, all of them were lying on their beds, trying hard not to look anywhere.

It took Roy a good five minutes to get up the courage to open the bag. When he finally looked inside, he was more confused than anxious. He first pulled out a note written on a napkin in pencil that said, *Don't share!* And below that: *I got your back.*

Along with the note there were three Hershey bars, a box of Jujubes, and five packets of Beech-Nut gum.

Again, Roy looked around the room and found no help.

At dinner, Knott sat across from Roy while two of his buddies sat down on either side, blocking Jerry just as he was about to sit. Knott smiled at him. "Hey, Jerry," he said. "Mind if we join you?"

Jerry said nothing and Roy could see that he was shaking as he set his tray down at the far end of the table.

Knott then turned to Roy and asked, "How you like it here so far, fish?"

"How come you keep calling me that?"

"It's what you are," Knott said. "A new fish." He then leaned down close to Roy. "Something else I should call you?"

"Roy is good."

"How old are you, Roy?"

"Thirteen. Almost."

"You really kill your daddy?"

This got Jerry looking at Roy from the other end of the table, but Roy said nothing, kept his eyes down, like he was fascinated by the peas rolling around his plate.

"They say you shot him."

"Who's they?"

"You shoot him in the back or the front?"

Roy looked up, about to say that he didn't shoot him at all when he noticed Albert sitting with the other Boonville Cowboys a few tables over, his back to Roy.

Knott asked, "You get my present?"

Roy turned to the older kid. Close up, Roy saw that everything about him was white—his hair, his eyelashes, but especially his skin.

"I got you a good job, too," he was saying. "If you need anything else, you just let me know." And then he and the other two boys got up. Roy watched them dump their trays and walk out of the hall.

The next day after lunch Roy found a paper bag with some toothpaste, a pack of cigarettes, and twenty dollars cash under his pillow.

That same night, Roy and Jerry were sitting with some other inmates watching *Hill Street Blues* when Knott and a few of the other older kids came into the room. Knott walked up to the television and started changing channels.

Turn it back! What the fuck, asshole?

Knott ignored them, looked over their heads, right at Roy and asked, "What do *you* wanna watch, Roy?"

Of course, now they were all looking at him. Roy got up from the couch. "Nothing. I was just leaving." And he turned to walk out, pausing only as he saw Albert sitting in a chair at the back of the room, looking up from a book with what looked to Roy like a French title.

Later that evening, Roy discovered that his bed by the bathroom was already taken by another kid. The kid, older with a massive burn scar covering his entire right arm, barely glanced at Roy before asking, "What the fuck you want, fish?"

Not about to inform the kid of his mistake, Roy just stood there trying to figure out what to do next.

"Roy."

Roy turned around and saw Knott waving at him. "You're not there anymore." He motioned to an empty bed in a prime spot near a wall. "That's you now."

Roy didn't move.

Knott once more motioned to the bed. "Go on, buddy," he said. "It's all yours."

All eyes were on Roy as he made his way over to his new and improved spot. When he climbed in, he could feel the stash of gifts under the pillow. Someone had taken the trouble to transfer it all over. He looked at Knott, who was now busy in some important conversation. And then Deems and another guard were yelling at them all to shut the fuck up and rack it, and all at once the room went dark.

The gifts kept coming for the next few days.

Something told Roy to just hang on to them; to not eat the candy or spend the money or use the toothpaste. He just kept them piled up under his bed. In plain view for anyone who looked, hoping someone might take them off his hands, but no one touched them.

Roy's afternoon "job" consisted of sweeping the bakery. That was it. He just pushed the broom for a few hours. Jerry, who worked as a mixer and had to scrub all of the pots and utensils and was responsible for stacking the fifty-pound sacks of flour he carried up each afternoon from the cellar, asked Roy how he had secured such a cush job. Roy said he didn't know. Jerry asked if he'd been getting any gifts of any kind. Roy lied and told him he hadn't. Jerry said, "Good," and left it at that.

In the middle of one night, near the end of his third week at Boonville, Roy woke to voices in the bathroom. The spill from the light in that room was bright enough for Roy to see that several beds were empty. He crawled over those and stood on one so that he could peer into the arched, tiled cavern that was the lav and shower room.

Roy saw a group of boys, their backs to the door, standing in a half circle. Roy recognized the white hair on one of them and saw that Knott's pajama bottoms were down around his ankles exposing an ass so white it almost blended in with the tile. Knott was looking down at something in front of him, both of his hands holding on to whatever it was, his elbows rising and falling in a steady rhythm.

"Hurry up," Roy could hear someone say.

Knott's hands moved faster and faster and then stopped altogether as he arched his back and looked up at the ceiling. Roy could hear someone choking as Knott stepped aside and Roy saw a nude and kneeling Jerry Wethers vomit onto the tile floor. Roy watched as one of the other boys put a hand on Jerry's ass and began rubbing it with almost absurdly gentle strokes.

There was a scuffle between the group, one of the bigger ones winning and getting a fistful of Jerry's hair and yanking him closer while pulling his prick out with the other. Rubbing it against Jerry's lips he said, "Open your mouth, girl."

Jerry took the kid in his mouth, pausing only when he saw Roy standing on the empty bed. Knott turned and saw him, too.

And waved.

Roy started to climb back into his bed, noticing that many of the boys in the dorm were likewise awake, but had their backs turned to the bathroom. Roy climbed into bed, was pulling his blanket up when his heart nearly exploded. Darryl Deems stood in a far corner of the room, arms folded across his chest, calmly watching all of it, but now focused on Roy as he quickly pulled the blanket over his head.

The action in the bathroom would go on for another half hour. Deems stayed put for all of it until Knott and his boys finally left the bathroom for their beds, and then Deems went in there himself and dragged a catatonic Jerry into one of the showers. They didn't come out for another hour.

At their job the next afternoon, Jerry wouldn't look at Roy. He just stared out the windows at the row of white unmarked gravestones at the bottom of the hill. As bad as Roy felt for Jerry, he was terrified for himself. He knew it was only a matter of time before Knott and his friends came for him in the middle of the night; pulled him out of his bed, and laid him out on the cold bathroom floor.

He knew that when that happened, there would be nothing he could do. They would take everything from him, just as they had taken everything from Jerry, turned him into the shell that now leaned against the wall, looking less alive than those stacked bags of flour he had just carried up the stairs.

Roy grabbed a load of trash, walked outside, and was headed to the incinerator when he saw Albert standing a few feet to one side of the door smoking a cigarette. Without thinking, Roy turned around and started walking the other way.

"His name is Jeff Knott."

Roy stopped and looked back at Albert. The older kid standing there in a clean uniform. His hair slick and all in place. Everything about him right now neat and clean.

"I'm of course referring to the albino roid freak that seems to have taken a shine to your pinky fresh asshole." The accent was slight, but there.

"I know who you mean," Roy heard himself say.

Albert dropped his smoke and took a step toward Roy. "I bet you didn't know that Jeff was a varsity tight end. He might even have made All American if he didn't have such a bad temper."

Albert, already going for another cigarette, held out the pack to Roy, who shook his head.

"One night after a game," Albert went on, "Jeff took the homecoming queen second runner-up out for a drive. He parked high in the hills where they both got drunk and he did his best to ruin her. Except Jeff apparently had some . . . technical difficulties."

Albert smiled at Roy and lit his cigarette.

"The almost homecoming queen who, if you ask me, had already demonstrated rather poor judgment, went on to seal her fate by suggesting that perhaps Jeff's end wasn't so tight after all. Well . . ." Albert smiled at Roy. "Needless to say, Jeff became upset."

Albert considered Roy for a moment, then held out his hand and said, "My name is Albert Budin. And I'm here to tell you your future." Pronouncing it as he always would, Al-bare Boo-*dan*. Roy didn't move. He couldn't if he wanted to. His feet were bolted to the asphalt.

"You've been receiving gifts?" Albert asked. "From Jeff?"

"I don't know who they're from."

"Sure you do, but that's the past. Let's skip ahead."

Albert turned and looked out at the field where Jeff Knott and some other older kids were working out. "What's going to happen next is he's going to write you a letter."

"A letter?"

"These things are very formal."

Roy looked off at Knott, tried to imagine him writing anything.

"Anyway, this letter's going to say that you ought to be his boy because he'll look out for you. He'll protect you. He's going to tell you that, with him, you're in better hands than fucking Allstate."

Roy didn't quite understand, but he knew enough to keep his mouth shut.

"Then he's going to come see you. He's going to say you ate my Oreos. You smoked my cigarettes. You spent my cash."

"But I didn't—"

Albert put a finger to his lips. Shhh. "It doesn't matter. But . . ." And now he leaned back against the wall and looked Roy over. "You killed your old man. You got that in you."

Roy let Albert think what he wanted to think.

"So if I'm as good a fortune-teller as I think I am, you will then tell Jeff to please fuck off. Of course, Jeff won't like that."

Roy flinched as Albert reached out and took the trash from him, walked with it to the incinerator. "His plan will be to wait for you to go into the showers where he and his friends will throw a towel over your head, soap your stick, and fuck you in the ass until you can no longer stand. Then they'll beat you until you either die or turn into what they want you to turn into."

Albert opened the metal door and tossed the bag inside. He then stepped back and looked up at the smoke coming from the black chimney.

"What you have to do, as soon as you can, is go down to the gym and get yourself a dumbbell. Or better yet, you could unscrew a mop handle from the bakery. Or even better, you could take the ringer off the bucket and then beat Jeff Knott with it until he can't move. Be good if he lost an eye. Something he could carry with him forever. Anyway, then you have to stand there and scream at him, even though at this point he won't hear you, you have to scream loud and clear so that everyone *else* will hear . . ."

"What?"

Albert turned to Roy and lowered his voice to a whisper. "Motherfucker," he said, "I'm a man. And if anybody, and I mean anybody, tries to take my manhood, I'll fucking do to them what I just did to him."

Albert smiled. "The guards will then come and take you away and beat you," he said, his voice normal again. "They'll put you in one of the Adjustment Units. But you'll be able to handle that because you'll now know that when you come out, no one will fuck with you. Ever."

Roy watched Albert finish his cigarette and asked, "What about Jeff Knott?"

"He'll most likely want to kill you," Albert said and blew a perfect smoke ring before he turned to Roy. "But now," he said, "I'll have the right to protect you, because you've already stood up for yourself."

"Why?" Roy asked. "Why would you help me."

Albert was suddenly serious. The smile all gone. He studied Roy a long while, then said, "Because you and me, we're the same."

"What do you mean, the same?"

"Tell me, how did you feel when you smothered your papa?"

Roy just looked back at Albert. It wasn't so much the question that threw him as the feeling that Albert knew more about him than anyone else in here.

Roy asked, "You killed your father?"

"No. I'm in here for stealing my sister's car. Little cunt couldn't take a joke. But that's another matter. I'll go visit her when I'm out and clear things up."

Whatever *that* meant. Roy decided to just nod.

"No, you and I are alike in a different way. Do you know what the word 'empathy' means?"

Roy didn't move. Albert smiled.

"It's okay if you don't. I didn't expect you to. But maybe later you'll stroll over to our pathetic little library and look it up."

"Why?"

"Because you need to know what it means. And because I want you to."

Albert looked off, ready to go wherever it was he went during the day. Roy never saw him around.

"But you need to do this other thing soon," he said, his tone cold now. "You need to do it soon or people will start to wonder." He then looked at Roy a long moment and added, "I'll start to wonder."

Roy watched as Albert walked away, disappeared around the corner. He looked off at Jeff Knott and the others lifting weights out in the field. He then stared at the spot where Albert last stood. Stared at it until the dinner bell sounded and he jumped, his heart beating so hard he could feel the pulse in the back of his throat, his mind reeling at how someone who had always hid from force of any kind could have gotten himself into such a sorry situation.

He sat by himself at dinner and didn't dare look up from his food for fear of accidentally making eye contact with the wrong person.

While no one had yet to make any kind of physical move on him, Roy knew he was afforded this reprieve only because everyone thought he was a murderer. But he could feel them all watching him, trying to figure him out. And once they did, once they saw what he really was, Albert's nightmare prophecy would come true. Albert might even join in.

Roy could certainly never do what the weird, vaguely French kid had suggested. He had never hurt anyone. Whenever Roy imagined himself fighting back, his kicks and punches were all slowed down, as if he were underwater or in a dream. The blows always softening before they landed. If he were to strike someone like Jeff Knott, the first shot would have to put him down or Knott would surely come back at Roy, maybe even kill him.

Roy thought about those unmarked graves at the bottom of the hill and pushed his tray away.

He wondered where Jerry was. How had he missed the dinner count? There was no sign of Deems either. If something was wrong, the other guards didn't seem too concerned. And then the bell sounded and it was time for everyone to line up for another count. Roy kept his head down as he dumped his tray, started walking toward the back of the line when he bumped into Deems.

"Watch your little feet, sunshine," Deems said, and shoved Roy aside.

Roy noticed that the guard's khaki trousers were wet at the hem, but didn't think anything of it until they found Jerry dead in the showers two hours later.

By the time everyone filed in for evening rack, a thick cloud of steam had drifted from the lav into the dormitory. A guard went into the bathroom to shut off the showers, but came running right back out, yelling for them all to stay put.

An order they, of course, ignored. The instant the guard left the dormitory, barking into his walkie about "that fucking Wethers kid," everybody bolted for the shower room. Roy was at the rear of the pack, but he could see well enough.

A nude Jerry lay curled up on the shower floor, eyes bulging, his skin beet red from the hot water, a seemingly endless discharge of white foam surging from his mouth. They would hear later that Jerry had choked himself to death by eating several large bars of county soap. But as Roy watched Deems, in those wet trousers, now push his way through the crowd, he knew that someone had helped Jerry stuff all those bars down his throat.

In that moment Roy felt something that he'd never felt before. Rage. Real, true, white-hot rage. His entire body burned with it. He could feel the flush on his face as he thought about just how much he hated everyone standing outside the shower gaping at Jerry Wethers. He hated the guards and he hated himself for being so weak, for allowing himself to end up in this God-fucked place in the middle of hell.

In that moment Roy decided that he would not, ever, let himself become Jerry. He would not, ever, let anyone do to him what they had done to Jerry. He would be stuffed into one of those unmarked graves before he would ever let that happen.

On the way back to his bed, Roy grabbed a large bar of soap from one of the sinks and put it inside his sock.

The next day he got two more bars and put them in the sock along with the first. He then swung the heavy sling at his open palm and fought the urge to scream. For a moment, he thought he had broken his hand.

Roy thought, *This will do.*

For the next three nights, he lay awake clutching the weight close to him working up his nerve. On the fourth night, he rolled out of his sheets, slid to the floor and started the long crawl under the beds to where Jeff Knott slept. Twice, he had to stop and wait for the occupant in the bed directly above him to fall back asleep. Once, he was almost caught when a kid reached down to the floor in the middle of some bad dream, grabbed Roy by the hair, and then leaned down and stared under the bed wide-eyed, but still, thankfully, sound asleep.

Nearly an hour later, Roy found himself standing beside Knott's bed covered in dirt and sweat. The sock had snagged on several bed frames along the way and was already ripped. Roy cursed himself for not bringing a backup as the first swing might now be the only one he would get.

He studied Knott's face, so pale it seemed to glow on the pillow. He had thought that he would hit him in the chest first, knock the wind out of him before hitting him in the head a couple of times. But now he thought he might have to hit him in the face first and get it over with. He was debating these two options when Knott woke up and those pale blue eyes fixed on Roy. There was a question there to be sure, but luckily for Roy, Knott's instinct was to smile and then ask it. He got as far as "Hey, fish" when Roy hit him in the mouth with that sockful of county soap.

He knocked out most of Knott's front teeth with that first hit, was going for a second when the sock snagged on a broken molar in the back of Knott's mouth. Roy yanked the sling free and lost a bar of soap in the process. Rather than fight back, Knott covered his face and so Roy hit him again, this time nailing him on the Adam's apple. The sock shredded and lost the remaining bars, but Knott was now trying to sit up, too busy gagging for air to fight.

Roy was surprised how easy it was to shove the bigger kid off the bed. He then squeezed around between the other cots, a couple of kids waking up, but leaving him alone as Roy started to jump up and down on Knott's face.

He heard a strange voice somewhere far away, yelling.

I don't want your fucking candy bars! Or your fucking jobs! I'm a fucking man! So if you or your faggot friends come anywhere near me, I'll kill you! Do you fucking hear me? I will kill you, just like I killed my old man and just like I killed every other asshole who fucked with me!

Roy realized that there was a bedspring in his hand. He didn't know how it got there, but he turned and saw an unfamiliar face in the dark, acne-scarred and the tiniest eyes he'd ever seen now nodding at him and then at Jeff.

Roy looked at the spring and then crouched down, pulled one of Knott's hands away from his face and jammed the spring into the dark softness underneath. He then stood up and heard that strange voice say, *All of you, stay the fuck away from me, or I'll do the same to you!*

He could now hear other voices, adults, Deems among them. He was turning away when he felt something burning hot on the back of his head, and fell at once into a deep and, finally, peaceful sleep.

When Roy woke up two days later, he tasted blood and couldn't yet open his eyes all the way. His tongue worried a spot in the back of his mouth where he'd lost a tooth and his face hurt at the turn of his head. He had at least two bruised ribs and could feel a third that might have been cracked. His hand was wrapped with two of his fingers splinted. Roy figured this injury was either the result of repeatedly hitting Knott or from the guards stomping on it, or both.

Thankfully, he could remember none of his own beating and wondered if he had even been awake for it. He could only remember the first blow of his attack on Knott, and had no recollection whatsoever of his journey from the dorm to where he was now, what he assumed to be the Adjustment Unit.

He looked around at the cement walls, all chipped and stained, a clump of hair on one of them, seemingly growing out of a smear of dried blood.

There was no bed or any furniture of any kind. Just a thin wool blanket and a foam pillow without a case. There were no windows or vents, the only air coming through a narrow slit in the door through which meals were delivered. There was a commode in the corner, chipped and streaked in colors that Roy couldn't immediately identify.

He wrapped himself in the blanket and fell back asleep for what felt like an entire day. He remembered waking up in the dark and having to piss. It took him a while to find the commode in the pitch black cell, and then emptied half of his bladder before passing out again.

He woke up to a metal tray being pushed through the slot on the door. Roy grabbed it and stared at the gray-green brick that sat on the plastic plate. It was hard to the touch and smelled vaguely of macaroni and spinach. A key in the lock startled him out of his examination and he backed up against the wall and readied himself for whatever new hell was about to come through the door and hurt him.

But when the door swung open, it was Albert Budin who stood there with a towel draped over his shoulder, a bucket in one hand, and some clean clothes in the other.

"Oh, good," he said. "You're alive."

"What they do," Albert was saying, "is they take all the leftover food and press it into these blocks." Albert had sat on the floor, his back against the wall smoking a cigarette as Roy washed himself off with the water in the bucket, politely looking away when Roy changed into the clean clothes. Roy moved very slowly, discovering more and more bruises along the way. His skin was so sensitive that the simple act of cleaning up and getting dressed nearly brought tears to his eyes.

"It looks like shit, but it doesn't taste so bad. And you need the calories."

Roy wondered just how Albert was able to be in here. Albert said something vague about the guards owing him a small favor. Later, Roy would learn that the guards at Boonville owed Albert a lot more than any favor. For the truth was, as Roy discovered, that the peace at Boonville was kept by Albert, not the staff. And when the time came for Albert to leave, Roy would, for a little while at least, take over that role.

"They had to take him to a hospital in Springfield."

"Who?"

"Knott. Do you know what you did to him?"

"I can't remember."

"You should remember," Albert said. "You well and truly fucked that boy up."

"I remember hitting him in the face with a bar of soap."

"No, you hit him in the mouth and knocked out all of his front teeth on the top, another three on the bottom."

"I did?"

"You broke his jaw and both cheekbones."

"With a bar of soap?"

"With your heel."

Roy looked at the bruises on his bare feet. Both of his heels were black-and-blue, with deep cuts in one.

"You also tried to poke out his eye with a bedspring."

Roy could see the kid with the pocked-up face and the lizard eyes handing it to him.

"But as it happens, you missed by a sixteenth of an inch, and pierced his sinus canal." Albert shook his head. "His fucking sinus canal—that's a new one."

Roy asked, "Are you from France?"

Albert smiled, as if Roy had just passed some test he hadn't realized he was taking. "No, I'm originally from Canada, Montreal, but they speak French there and that's very perceptive of you. Most of the other dipshits in here are too stupid to know the difference between accents, but you picked it up. That's very good. You're not like the other mental cases in here. Bunch of fucking hillbillies, worse thing they ever did was take their daddy's tractor for a joyride."

"Mental cases?"

"Most of the people here are fucked up for sure, but they're not criminals."

"What about Jerry Wethers?"

Albert considered Roy a moment and said, "You feel bad for him."

Roy shrugged.

"He was in here the first time for putting a gun in someone's face for fifty dollars. *Fifty dollars.* That's like doing it for fifty cents. He was a fucking moron. He had no chance to survive this place. Quit wasting your time worrying about him. You're not like him."

Albert got up and sat down next to Roy. His eyes were clear, like he slept a full ten hours a night. Roy could smell aftershave. Unlike most everyone else at Boonville, the place seemed to make Albert stronger.

Roy asked, "How old are you?"

"Almost eighteen. They can keep you here until you're twenty if they want to."

Roy nodded, thinking Albert looked a lot older than eighteen. Roy also wasn't entirely convinced that Albert's "French Canadian" accent was genuine. During the brief time they'd spent together so far, Roy had already noticed it coming and going.

"Did you look up the word I told you to?"

Roy nodded. "Empathy."

He asked, "You know what it means?" Then answered his own question, "The ability to feel for our fellow man."

Roy nodded, not sure why Albert was so obsessed with this particular word.

"There anybody you feel for, Roy?"

"My little brother."

"Why?"

Roy just looked at him.

"What has he done for you?"

"Done? He's not even two."

"So you feel love for him just because he's your brother?"

"He's my family."

"And is everyone in your family so deserving of your unconditional love?"

Roy couldn't answer that one.

"The family you choose is the only family that matters."

"I love my brother."

"Love is a waste of time. Worse, it makes you weak. I know this because I was in love with a girl once."

Call it instinct, but Roy was pretty sure that he didn't want to hear about Albert and this girl he once *loved*. Maybe if he told Albert that he was tired . . .

"Her name was Betsy. She was half pit bull, half something else I can't remember. Beagle, maybe."

Roy said, "Oh."

Albert smiled and shook out another cigarette. "I was in our apartment in Montreal when I spotted her out the window, all the way from the fourth floor. She was trying to cross Boulevard Newman and fuck if anybody was stopping for the poor thing. I was sure she'd get hit by the time I got down there. She had made it halfway to the divider and was looking to step off the other side when I ran out into the street, waving my arms like a traffic cop, and scooped her up."

Albert lit his smoke and said, "The dog didn't have a tag, so I just brought it up to the apartment and let it fall asleep on the couch. My sister came home from work and told me to get rid of it, but I refused. I didn't blame her. It was just the two of us then, and she barely made enough as it was. I told her not to worry, that I would figure out how to feed it. She just shook her head and told me to keep it off the bed. I slept with it in the bathtub."

Albert offered the smoke to Roy, who shook his head.

"The next day I see a notice in the lobby by the elevator. *Missing Dog. Betsy. Pit bull mix. Trained.* I ripped the notice off the wall. But my fucking sister . . ." He shook his head. "She had already seen it and called the number. That afternoon, there's a knock at the door, it's Jorge Panadero, this teenage dealer liked to wear his hair in a ponytail, hang out, do his thing up on the roof. He said he got off the elevator one day and Betsy didn't follow him. A whole hour went by before the guy had any inkling she was gone."

"So you gave the dog back?"

"What else could I do?"

Roy knew there had to be something else. He didn't have to wait long to find out what it was.

"It wasn't the same without the dog. I missed her. So I go up to the roof a few days later. Jorge's up there like usual, sitting in a lawn chair getting high on his own weed, waiting for customers. Betsy's chained to a pipe, looks miserable. But I can tell she's glad to see me. I pet her, say to Jorge that I'll buy the dog off of him. He says she's not for sale. I tell him that she's clearly not happy. He tells me to get fucked, and so I throw the dog off the roof."

"You what?"

"She was chained, so she didn't go far, but then her collar broke."

"What did Jorge do?"

"I think he was in shock. He got up and made a move for me, but he was so stoned it wasn't all that difficult to throw him off, too."

Roy opened his mouth, but could not speak.

"The dog lived. Somehow. I don't know how. But it did. So after Jorge's funeral, I went and asked his mother if I could have it, but his mother said no. A week later, I left Canada."

Albert stood, picked up the towel and the bucket, and loudly knocked on the door. "Teddy!"

A moment later, Roy once more heard the key in the lock and the door swung open. Teddy, a tall, reedy guard with a flattop, looked at the two of them. If Albert was bothered or self-conscious he didn't show it. He nodded at the guard, started out, and then stopped.

"Love and hatred are both weaknesses," he said. "The most powerful thing a person can feel is indifference. You can't hurt a man who feels nothing. Don't forget that."

On Sunday, Roy stepped out of Building A and saw his mother—sunglasses, legs crossed, sitting by herself atop one of the redwood picnic tables. She'd cut her hair in a new way and wore a dress that Roy had never seen before. She smoked a cigarette and looked off at the graves at the bottom of the hill, ignoring the stares from the other families. Roy figured that, from the way they kept looking and whispering, they probably thought she was a movie star. He also figured that she was well aware of the attention.

Roy walked up to her and said, "Hey."

She turned to him, took him in for a good long while and said, "What happened to your face?"

"I got into a fight."

She gave him the briefest kiss on the cheek, and then moved over. He sat down on the tabletop beside her, put his feet on the bench alongside hers and couldn't help but notice that the shoes she wore were brand-new.

"I tried to come last week, but they said you were somewhere you couldn't have visitors."

"Where's the Captain?"

"You really think this is the kind of place for him?"

"There are lots of little kids here."

"You want him to see you like this?"

"I'm fine."

"And the other kid?"

"He's fine, too," Roy said.

"Everybody's fine. I'm so glad." She got out her cigarettes and lit up another.

"Who's with him?"

She paused mid-light and stared at him.

"The Captain."

"Oh," she said and lit her smoke. "Lucinda."

"Who?"

"The nanny."

"He has a nanny?"

"You poked that kid's eye out."

"I didn't," he said. "I missed."

She shifted on the table to face him now.

"They're tacking eleven months onto your sentence."

"What?" Roy couldn't believe what he was hearing.

"You nearly killed him. What were you thinking?"

"He was threatening me."

"Well," she said, "he's not threatening anybody anymore, that's for damn sure."

She studied him for what seemed like a minute and then said, "You're different."

"I am?"

"You can't let this place change you."

"You're just now worried about that?"

She leaned away from him, as if trying to get a better perspective, and looked at him over the top of her sunglasses. "You're not backing out of our deal, are you?"

"It's not easy here."

"I understand," she said. "But I think that maybe you're . . ." She gestured to the bruises. "Making it harder than it has to be."

"I don't think I can make it, period."

"You have to."

She looked at the cigarette, decided that she didn't want it after all, and dropped it in the grass. She said, "I have to go," and then slid off the table. "It's a long drive."

She turned back to Roy and opened her arms.

"C'mon," she said. "Give me a hug."

He did as he was told. She held on to him and whispered, "This is the right thing, for everyone."

"I'd really like to see him."

"I'll send you a picture."

She kissed him once on the top of the head and started across the grass for the parking lot, Roy keenly aware that every eye in the joint was on her back. A guard opened the gate and a second later a red Cadillac Seville pulled up alongside her. Roy couldn't see who was driving, but he had a pretty good idea. She opened the passenger door, paused to look back, waved, and then slipped inside the car.

It would be sixteen years before Roy would see her again.

The only legitimate rehabilitation effort at Boonville was the agricultural program where inmates were taught various farming techniques, including cattle ranching. In many ways, the cattle were treated better than the boys. They were well fed and housed in the winter in a huge barn built and paid for by Armour Meats.

Roy became a Boonville Cowboy and worked the pasture alongside Albert and another inmate, Bob Spetting. They would do everything from feed the horses to help the actual cowboys gather the herd and run it a few miles north to the meatpacking plant in Jonesburg, on a part of the Missouri River known as "Slaughterhouse Bend."

Once there, Albert would always have a smoke, strike up a conversation with any members of the Killing Gang who happened to be outside on break. Albert told Roy that he was going to get himself a job upon his release from Boonville the following year. Taking in the smell and the sounds coming from inside, Roy couldn't understand why anyone in his right mind would ever want to work in a place like that.

But then, Albert wasn't in his right mind.

Before Roy, Bob Spetting had been the closest thing Albert had to a friend in Boonville.

Roy first met Bob at dinner one night, shortly after his mother's visit.

After what had happened in the dormitory, Roy no longer had to prove himself, but there was always the occasional challenge. Thankfully for Roy, Albert would always magically appear ahead of any violence. Roy wasn't sure why Albert had taken him on in this way, but it was clear that, for whatever reason, he was always watching Roy.

On this particular night, Roy had just sat down for dinner, was preoccupied with thoughts about his brother and this nanny, *Lucinda*, when someone said, "He don't look that mean to me."

Roy looked across the table where a big redheaded farm kid now sat beside another, equally large inmate. He snatched a piece of bread from Roy's tray and asked, "How'd you kill your pop?"

Roy ignored him.

"You're kinda small, so I'm guessing it wasn't nothin' to do with your hands."

Roy surprised himself and snatched the bread back. He took a bite and looked the other kid in the eye. He'd reached the point where he didn't care. It wasn't so much bravery, as he was just done with this place. His mother had put him here, left him to his own devices, and then had taken his little brother away from him, all because he had become the very thing he'd been pretending to be in order to save the kid from a foster home. Roy was angry and just wanted out.

"Maybe one of these days," the redhead was now saying, "me and you'll go a round in the basement. How's that sound?"

Roy was about to get up and leave when, before he knew what was happening, Albert and another kid sat down on either side of Roy, Albert saying as he swung his legs over, "You go a *round* with this one," he said, patting Roy on the back, "he's going to tear those big ears off your deformed head and eat them in front of you and all your farm boy pals."

Albert looked at Roy and smiled. "He's not big, but you can see that he's scrappy and smart, and those are the ones you gotta look out for."

The redhead asked, "This guy your friend, Albert?"

"Al-bare, dipshit. And yes, he's my friend."

The other kids froze. Weren't sure what to do next.

"Go on, get out of here and go jiz all over pictures of sheep or whatever the fuck it is you farm boys like to do."

The guy on the other side of Roy started laughing. Roy remembered him the first time the Boonville Cowboys had come into the hall. He had a face covered with dark red acne, two black gnats where his eyes should have been. He was the one who handed Roy the bedspring that night in C Dorm.

Albert said, "Bob Spetting, say hello to Roy."

The creature called Spetting held out his hand, but when Roy turned and held out his own, Spetting grabbed hold of it and spit into Roy's palm. Roy jerked his hand away as Bob started laughing.

Albert shook his head and handed Roy a napkin. "You'll have to forgive Bob," he said. "He's mildly retarded. Not enough to really feel sorry for, but enough to annoy you now and then, and one of the few truly *mean* retards I've ever met." He then reached behind Roy and hit Bob on the back of the head. "Shake his fucking hand, Bob."

Bob turned and once more held out his hand. Roy hesitated, but then grabbed it. Bob squeezed hard enough to bring tears to Roy's eyes as Albert went on.

"Bob's mommy and daddy thought Bob was gonna die by the time he was twelve. Imagine how pissed off they must be."

Albert turned and pushed his chair back a bit, crowding the terrified kid at the table directly behind him. If Albert noticed or cared, Roy couldn't tell.

Roy then looked around the hall. He could see that the other boys were all watching him. Not openly, they were too afraid of Albert for that. But Roy could see that they were paying attention. It occurred to Roy in that moment that he'd been wrong. The way to survive this place wasn't to spend every day hiding. The way to survive was to simply not give a shit.

One day Roy woke up and found himself nearly as tall as Albert. He had grown six inches seemingly overnight. He couldn't get used to his new body. He no longer recognized himself in the mirror. He started lifting weights with Bob and was soon bigger and stronger than most of the other kids. One positive result of all this growth was that Bob would no longer randomly punch Roy in the arm, or pick him up and throw him in the manure pile. The bad news was, it once more made him a target. But this time, it wasn't the other inmates who came looking for him, but the guards.

They had begun goading the inmates into fighting with each other down in the basement so that they could bet on who would win. If you didn't fight, you lost privileges, would find rocks in your food, or could even lose a cush job. Like being a Boonville Cowboy.

"You want to end it quickly," Albert said. "You don't punch their face, you hit them in the throat."

He then *demonstrated* by hitting Roy in the throat. He went down to his knees gagging while Albert went on. "One jab, real quick, doesn't have to be all that hard, you just have to nail the right spot. Do that, and the fight's over."

Albert then crouched down and smiled at him. "I don't care how big you are."

Albert taught him how to fight. Or, more precisely, how to quickly end one once it started. It was helpful to Roy, who fought exactly one fight in the basement: the redheaded farm kid. Roy fucked him up so bad, the warden found out about it and the fights were halted, Roy earning himself another week in the AU and sixteen more months on his sentence.

Not long after that, Roy received a letter from his mother, imploring him to stop his violent ways. She'd heard about the fights and about the guard who'd been stabbed some fifty-four times in the showers. And while they didn't directly accuse Roy of being involved ("no actual proof"), his mother got the feeling that they certainly assumed he was. She wanted to know if that was true.

Of course, it was true, but she would never understand that Darryl Deems needed to pay, however delayed, for what had happened to Jerry Wethers two years earlier. Roy and Albert had spent months planning it so that there would be no witnesses or evidence of any kind. And while they made some mistakes here and there, they both learned a lot from that little experience. It was knowledge that would pay off once they got out.

There was a photograph along with the letter. His mother and the dentist, Dr. Toomey, sitting outside at a table in what Roy figured to be Hawaii. Both were tanned and lei'd, dressed in shorts and shirts covered with hibiscus, a couple of blue-colored drinks in front of them.

But what caught Roy's eye was the little boy at the table with them. He sat in a booster seat, in his own shorts and flowered shirt, sipping his own little blue drink through a straw. His face was turned so that Roy could only see part of it. One eye, the barest hint of a nose and a corner of his mouth. Was he smiling?

Roy kept turning the photograph this way and that in a hopeless attempt to get a better angle on the boy's face. He knew that this one photograph, inadequate as it was, would be the only one he would get. Her way of cutting him off, but it felt more like she was killing him.

The work in the pastures was hard, but it kept Roy outside in the fresh air, which was what kept him sane. Sitting in the saddle or cleaning out the stalls brought him a kind of peace. He remained quiet, never joined in any of the conversations, which were of only two varieties: Albert would talk about the various mobsters they'd meet and work for once they were all out of there, or Bob would talk about the famous women he was going to fuck the minute he was free.

One afternoon, they were on horseback guiding sixty head of cattle into the pen when Bob proclaimed Lisa Simpson his latest crush.

"I wrote her a letter," he said, "telling her that maybe someday, when she was older, we could meet."

Albert asked, "She answer you?"

"Not yet."

"You do know she's a cartoon."

"I know."

"You cannot fuck a cartoon."

Bob just looked at him.

"On top of that," Albert went on, "she's a child."

"Right now maybe. But in ten years she's gonna be like sixteen or seventeen."

"What's wrong with Betty and Veronica?" Albert asked. "They're all grown up."

"They're not real, they're just a comic."

Albert looked at Roy, who had only barely been paying attention. "Can you believe this guy?"

Roy just smiled and reached down and latched the gate behind the cattle. Their horses, as they did every night, automatically turning back to the barn at the sound, Bob now saying as they spurred them into a canter, "Plus, I said *when she was older.*"

And then, one day, Albert was gone. He never said a word to Roy or Bob about leaving, just up and left without so much as an *Au Revoir*. Roy heard that he had moved nearby and was working at the Armour plant. Once, Roy and Bob saw him there, outside on his break, in a bloody apron, smoking with the other men on the Killing Gang. They waved from their horses, but Albert never looked their way.

Roy served out the rest of his time without incident, quietly reading books when he wasn't working the pastures. Bob had been released six months after Albert and for his last eighteen months at Boonville, Roy ate by himself, slept in a room above the big dormitory with only three younger inmates, one of whom had Tourette's and would bark in his sleep or strike his head against the wall. All these boys were considered weak and so Roy looked after them, the old love he felt for his own little brother finally finding some purpose in this shithole.

That same dedication came out in Roy's job. He liked to be around the horses and took good care of all of them. On top of that, he had become a skilled rider and taught his dorm mates. All of them would become part of the next group of Boonville Cowboys.

The rest of the time, he lifted weights, walked the grounds, and didn't talk to a soul. The new kids thought he was simple. When Roy heard this from one of the guards, he liked the idea. It occurred to him near the very end of his time there that being underestimated was as safe a way to live as keeping out of the way. It somehow felt more than just comfortable. It felt exactly right.

So Roy did nothing to dissuade them.

At night, he would look at the photograph his mother had left behind. He would study it, sometimes for hours on end, trying to imagine his brother's face now that he was seven years old. Roy wondered whether or not he was happy, or if he ever thought about his older brother.

On the day of his release, there was no one outside the gate to pick him up, so Roy took the bus to Raytown. He found himself walking up the same street Jim McDonald and Brent Garland had chased him that day six years ago, the whole incident now seeming like it happened in a different life altogether.

When he reached his house, he knew immediately that it was no longer his. It had been painted a bright yellow; the drab wainscoting had been replaced with red brick. There were shutters on the front windows; a split-rail fence ran along the sidewalk. Red, white, and blue impatiens bordered a thirty-foot square of dark green sod. A Volvo station wagon was parked in the driveway, a pair of pink bicycles beside it. And while he hadn't really expected his mother and brother to still be living here, he had hoped for some sort of clue as to where they might have gone.

Roy stood on the sidewalk, was thinking about knocking on the door to ask about the previous owners when he heard a car round the corner. He turned to see a dark blue, mag-wheeled Malibu two-door rumble to a stop at the foot of the driveway. The driver's door opened and Roy knew before he saw him that it was Albert. He uncoiled from the car and smiled at Roy across the roof.

"You are nothing if not predictable."

Bob Spetting hung his elbows out the passenger window and said, "We just missed you at Boontown."

"Get in," Albert said. "And meet my good friend, Harvey Cooper."

Roy hadn't noticed the older man sitting in the backseat. He was about sixty, with his long gray hair pulled into a ponytail, revealing a face that looked like it had been baked too long in the sun. He stared straight ahead.

Roy looked once more at the house, then walked around to the other side of the car. Albert had his own look at the place and asked, "You go inside, say hello?"

"They're not here."

"They out somewhere?"

"They're gone."

"Where?"

Roy just looked back at him. Albert nodded and then tilted the front seat forward so Roy could get in.

"Fuck them," he said as Roy climbed into the back. "Fuck them all."

twenty-nine

The mayor thought he was watching an action movie. A younger Bruce Willis or maybe Tom Cruise taking on a bunch of well-armed bad guys with his bare hands. *BAM! He nails one guy in the throat and then BANG! He shoots another one. Wait—where did he get that gun? Oh, shit, he took it from one of them—nice! And now he's shooting the other big one. BANG! And the first guy is crawling for his gun, he grabs it, but gets blown off his fucking feet!*

"Jesus," the mayor said louder than he wanted to. "This guy is good."

Leila gave him a look cold enough to chill the entire room. She was *pissed*. She had barely looked at the screen since the little presentation began. Dressed in a white suit with a white, gold-trimmed Hermès scarf wrapped around her head like she had a million-dollar toothache, she kept her legs tightly crossed and stared out the window while everyone else watched the collected footage.

Twice in the past ten minutes, she referred to Roy Cooper as "another Zimmerman."

The mayor was just glad people had moved on from his own, not quite so heroic, video. It was bad enough that Savannah had stopped returning his calls, texts, or emails, her assistant claiming that she was either "unavailable" or "traveling." The worst part is that his name had suddenly become a punch line. All the power he once felt in its silent recitation vanished overnight.

It had taken less than twenty-four hours for the myriad musical GIFs and YouTube videos to go viral. The image of the mayor diving under the desk at the nurses' station had become the most popular wallpaper in America, second only to his peeking out from under said desk like an overgrown third grader. But come on, wasn't he doing exactly what every elementary school kid in the state had been taught to do in that situation? Except for the shoving-the-nurse-out-of-the-way part? Although, as Evan optimistically pointed out, one *could* watch the video and think that he was trying to *help* her, you know, pull her under there with him. But then, Joy Levine, in a rare moment of nerve, said, "No offense, Evan, but one would have to be a fucking idiot to think that."

Since *The Desking,* as it was now referred to, the mayor avoided the press like typhoid, the *L.A. Times* venting their impatience on the front page with the headline *Where in the World Is Miguel Santiago?*

Joy felt that no good could come from the mayor talking to anyone just now. She believed that it would all blow over eventually and then Miguel Santiago could show his face again. Somewhere the press wouldn't bother him. Like at, say, a ribbon cutting at a daycare center in Compton.

But the next thing anyone knew, the mysterious Roy Cooper went all Charles Bronson on the boyz in the hood and the mayor could no longer hide. So this morning, feeling more out of his depth than usual, he had summoned his inner circle to try to figure out how to deal with this latest development. The public, of course, loved what they saw. This was way better than the video Alonzo Zarate shot of Peres getting whacked. For one thing, this one was much clearer and, as the day wore on and more videos were posted, one could watch it from any number of different angles.

Gordy Savage, in uniform for that afternoon's press conference where he would stand alongside the mayor while he mumbled some shit Evan wrote about why vigilantism is bad, marveled at the sheer number of people who caught the action on their phones.

"This time, we'll certainly be able to ID everybody on the street that night."

Leila said, "Yet you still haven't been able to ID this Roy Cooper."

"We know who he is," Gordy said. "And we know where he lives."

"You know where he *says* he lives." Leila then looked right at the chief and added, "From what I'm hearing, you don't know the first thing about him."

The mayor stepped in, still fascinated by the footage he'd been watching, and said, "I'm sure all of these people are going to try to follow in Alonzo Zarate's footsteps and sell their footage?"

Joy said, "They're too late. If they wanted to sell any of it, they shouldn't have posted it all on Facebook."

"Forget selling it," Leila said. "I'm worried about how these images are going to stir up the community."

Gordy took the bait. "How so?"

"You don't think that people applauding this white man shooting and beating the shit out of these black youngsters will have some effect out there?"

"What *youngsters*? The twins are both in their fucking twenties. Their *late* twenties. And the other two look like teenagers to me."

Leila said, "Are you trying to fuck with me or are you really that stupid?"

The temperature in the room dropped another few degrees and for the moment Gordy seemed to have lost all power of speech.

"Let's not quibble," Leila said. "They're four young black men and one white asshole turned on by the fact that he has an excuse to kill them."

Gordy somehow found his voice and said, "In self-defense."

"What was he doing there in the first place?"

"What difference does it make?"

"Context is everything."

"Not to me, it isn't. Especially not if one or maybe two of those *young black men* had something to do with the Peres execu—" He looked at the mayor, who waved him on with an *I give up gesture.* "With the murder of Frank Peres."

Leila said, "We don't know that for sure. What we *do* know is that the media is now covering this Roy Cooper like he's our own, homegrown George Zimmerman. Like he got mugged once, so now he's out there on some kind of vendetta."

The mayor stared at the two younger boys on the screen. One particular angle was closer and brighter. He would even call it well composed, *pleasing.* Their faces were familiar. Especially the pretty one. Where had he seen him before? The mayor was certain he'd seen that kid recently, maybe even met him. But, again, *where*? The walk through Watts last week? He shook a lot of black hands. No.

Maybe that group of kids from South Central he spoke to in the lobby here at City Hall a few days ago. No, these two didn't look like they go on many school field trips.

He looked up and saw Evan staring at him. Evan gave him that subtle head shake, the way he did whenever he was trying to stop the mayor from saying something stupid.

And then it hit him.

Oh, fuck.

The hospital. The elevator.

Fuckity fuck fuck fuck FUCK.

The kid said his mom had cancer. He took a fucking picture with him!

The mayor looked at Joy. He had to tell *her*. They had to get in front of this. But, now, Evan was vigorously shaking his head. *Do not say a word.*

What could Evan be thinking? That maybe no one will catch it? Maybe they won't. Maybe no one will make the connection that these two thugs who quite possibly gunned down Frank Peres took a selfie with the mayor at Valley Presbyterian while they were there to . . . *what?* Clearly, the story about the kid's sick mother was just that, a story.

Roy Cooper was a witness to the murder of Frank Peres. That's why they were there.

But Roy Cooper split before they could get to him. And somehow ended up going after *them*. Why? Suddenly, the mayor didn't want to think this through any further. He worried that the answers would only lead to more humiliation.

While the mayor definitely had a problem, he wondered if maybe, just maybe, Roy Cooper would take care of it for him. After all, he already got one of them. Maybe the best thing is to leave him out there on the streets.

That's when Leila said to Gordy, "You need to get these kids into custody before they're gunned down on the streets by this Roy Cooper."

"We're working on it."

"I mean, God forbid, they get killed in any way that makes them look helpless."

"Except they're not helpless."

"Then God forbid," she said, "some vigilante does what the police couldn't do, and this Roy Cooper becomes an even bigger hero. First he tries to stop Peres's killing and then he goes after the killers himself."

The mayor heard himself say, "Wow."

She turned to him. "A white man hunting down and killing two young black men. Can you imagine that?"

The mayor certainly could. Even without the earthquake and the subsequent frustration in some of these neighborhoods, that would surely be the match Leila loved to talk about.

Gordy nodded. "Of course, I know that you're right."

"Thank you, Chief."

"So untie my hands."

"Excuse me?"

"You know what I'm talking about. You just said that the best thing for everyone is to get these young men in custody, so let me put a cop on it who can catch them."

Leila shook her head. "Not her."

"No one knows that neighborhood better."

"Were you not listening to what I just said?"

"Give Kelly Maguire this footage and I promise you that within twenty-four hours we'll have the kid in the video as well as the other two that are still out there somewhere."

Leila smiled and said, "I just need to be sure that I'm understanding you correctly. You want to put the most famously racist LAPD cop since the eighties on the case and set her loose?"

Joy jumped in. "Leila, you do know that Maguire is actually Hispanic herself? That her father was at one time an illegal immigrant?"

"Bless her heart."

Gordy said, "She made a shit terrible mistake. I'll be the first to say I was disgusted by her behavior. But she's too valuable to lose, not if you want to get these kids yesterday."

Encouraged that Leila was nodding, Gordy went on. "We could do it very quietly. She doesn't have to be the face of the investigation. She'd just be in the background. What would you think of a scenario like that?"

Leila stood and said, "I think that you might as well just go out and start the riot yourself."

The mayor jumped in, smiling as he said, "Leila, come on, there must be some way to make this work?"

Leila looked at him. "I'm very sorry, Miguel, but I can't be a part of this." She shook her heads at all of them, adjusted her silk scarf, and walked out of the office.

They all sat there in silence for a moment. Waiting for the mayor to say *something*.

But it was Evan who was the first one to speak. He said, "Leila's right."

He turned to the mayor. "Maguire's a problem. And it's not just about the media and how they play it. People on the street know what she looks like. So what happens if she makes another *mistake* in the middle of an *official* investigation? That comes back to us."

Bless his little dark heart, the mayor thought. He's more worried about everybody in the room keeping their jobs than what might happen out there on the streets. Well, not everybody in the room. Just the mayor and, of course, Evan.

"As I recall," Evan went on, "Maguire's ex-partner, Detective Bell, is African American. If memory serves, he caught a lot of grief for defending her. I suggest Detective Bell lead the investigation."

Gordy said, "He *is* leading it."

Evan held up his hand, "I suggest he *continue* to lead the investigation. But . . . that he very privately . . . *consult* with Sergeant Maguire."

"How's that any different than what I was suggesting?" Gordy asked.

"It's different," Evan said, "in that in my scenario, she's not actually on the case."

"Then how the hell does she help him?"

Evan looked at the mayor, who understood. But Evan couldn't say it aloud.

"What he's saying, Gordy," the mayor said, "is that you can do whatever the fuck you want. But we don't want to know about it."

thirty

After buzzing Kelly's condo from the security gate for ten minutes without any response, Rudy badged a mailman as he was getting out of his truck and had the guy let him in. She didn't answer the door either, so he went back outside, crossed the small courtyard with a fountain featuring what, to Rudy, looked like two angels pissing on each other, and climbed over the patio wall, shredding a wool blend pocket on the rough stucco in the process. There Rudy discovered that the sliding glass door had not only been left unlocked, it was ajar, a piece of the curtain blowing out through the small opening. Rudy pushed it aside and walked right on in.

"Kelly?"

He took in the bong and the empty wine bottles, the overstuffed ashtrays and the clothes strewn all over the floor and hoped to Christ that she hadn't OD'd. He called her name again, was starting down the hall when Kelly, in an open bathrobe, came out of the bedroom, her Beretta down at her side, and nearly ran into him.

"Rudy? What the fuck?"

He put up his hands. "Don't shoot."

"What are you doing here?"

"You don't answer your phone. You don't answer your door. I thought maybe you shot yourself."

She looked at the gun in her hand. "That how you think I'd do it?"

He said, "It's how I'd do it," and then, "We need to talk."

"I'm fine."

"Not about you."

To Rudy's mild surprise, a woman now came out of the bedroom.

She was petite, in her underwear and what Rudy was pretty sure was one of Kelly's shirts, now unbuttoned to the navel. The woman smiled at the two of them and said, "Party in the hallway."

Rudy said, "My lucky day."

"Okay, fatso," Kelly said, shoving Rudy toward the living room, "give us a minute."

He wandered back into the living room and started to pick up the mess, Kelly's house guest whispering something about her ex dropping her son off in an hour. He could hear the bedroom door close and went in search of a garbage bag.

Kelly came out twenty minutes later, showered, dressed in jeans and a UCSB sweatshirt, and caught him picking up the last of the trash.

"You don't have to do that, for Christ's sake."

"I'm almost done."

She grabbed a pack of cigarettes off the now spotless coffee table, fell back on the couch, and lit one.

Rudy asked, "Who's your friend?"

"That's Erin. She's down the hall."

"How convenient."

"Rudy. Seriously. Stop cleaning."

He stood up as Erin now came into the room, dressed in shorts, a T-shirt, and work boots. She smiled and said to Kelly, "I'll come by later on."

Kelly smiled back, a bit forced Rudy thought, and said, "Be great."

Erin then extended her hand to Rudy and said, "Nice meeting you," even though they hadn't actually met, and then she was gone.

"So," he said, "what's *Erin's* story?"

"She's a lactation consultant. Or a doula. Or both. Or she used to be. Now I think she runs, or maybe just works at some nursery in Ocean Park."

"She likes babies."

"Not that kind of nursery. She's into plants. You should see the lovely little felony garden she's got growing in her bathroom." Kelly blew out a long line of smoke and then added, "Little girl's got quite the green thumb."

"What about her other fingers?"

"Funny. Will you sit down already? You're making me nervous."

He grabbed a kitchen chair and sat down and gave her a long look.

"So, what, are you gay now?"

"Erin's just a friend."

"Since when?"

"Since the other night."

"This some way for you to get back at Steven?"

"I don't know what it is. I just wanted to feel good."

"And do you?"

She said, "Yeah," and then nodded. "I feel really good."

She saw that he was sulking and said, "Don't be jealous, it's gross."

"She's not the only one, you know, could make you feel good."

"You're married."

"At the moment."

"You're also an idiot," she said and got up from the couch. "You want some coffee?"

"No thanks, but I made you a pot."

"How thoughtful."

"I figured you could use it."

She went into the kitchen, poured herself a cup, and looked at him over the top of it. "Why are you bothering me?"

"Where's your laptop?"

Rudy showed Kelly enough of the footage of Roy Cooper making short work of the four members of the Vineland Boyz to know things were now officially upside down. The guy, despite the holes in his body, could move, that was for sure, he'd clearly been trained. But for what?

Rudy said, "Interesting that he let the other kid go."

"Looked like the kid said something to him."

"I was thinking that when you find him, maybe you can ask him what he said."

Kelly looked up from the computer.

"If you're not too busy being a lesbian."

"They cut me loose. You were there, remember?"

"They want you back."

Kelly wondered who *they* were.

"You'd have to behave, of course."

She sat back down and said, "I'm sure you got lots of people can help you."

"Not enough, as you well know."

"The kid in the video, not one of the Marcus twins, but the one he put down with the fucked-up face? Goes by Truck. I don't know his real name."

"Kenny Meadows." Rudy smiled at her. "See? You can't help yourself."

She sat back down on the couch with her coffee and folded her legs under her and said, "I'm quitting."

"Bullshit."

She looked out the window and said, "I don't give a shit anymore. And that's not a good place to be."

"No, it's not. But before you decide what you do or don't wanna do, let me tell you where we're at."

"You're nowhere. You got everybody in the wind."

"I've got a gun that did both Peres and Shine."

"You have ballistics, not the gun."

"You know what we found among the trash at Dehougne?"

"A signed confession."

"Something better," he said. "We got a map from Payless Car Rental with Martin Shine's address written on it."

"Map?"

"The little slip of paper you found was torn off one of those maps they give you."

"They still do that?"

"If you're old or you ask."

"You've got footage of him at the counter?"

"As well as a statement from the clerk who showed him the route. But that's not the best part." He gave her a big grin.

"Look at you, all aquiver."

"On the security footage, you can clearly see he's got a small duffel with him."

"So?"

"So it got me thinking, what happened to it?"

"Stolen out of the car along with the radio and the other shit."

"Probably, but it does make me wonder how he gets a gun on the plane. He can't carry it on, and they screen the checked bags. Or at least they're supposed to."

"He picked it up. Somebody gave it to him. What difference does it make?"

"I'm curious."

"Uh-oh."

"I spent a large chunk of my life yesterday looking at LAX security footage of Mr. Cooper. I got him coming off the plane carrying the duffel. I got him getting into a shuttle. Ten minutes later he shows up at the Payless counter. They got six cameras on the lot, two on the counter, four on the parking lot, and the exit booth. You can watch him as he writes down the directions, then follow him outside as he walks to the car and puts the duffel in the trunk. He sits there a minute, adjusts the seat, whatever, then he backs out . . . drives to the booth, hands over his agreement, and goes left out of the lot onto Century Boulevard."

Kelly shrugged. "Okay."

"Freeway's to the right."

Kelly remembered the chicken-scratch handwriting and thought of Roy Cooper lying in bed, talking about The Kid.

She said, "Maybe he got confused."

"He not two minutes earlier got directions on how to get to Martin Shine's place in North Hollywood. First thing the clerk tells him, would *have* to tell him, which he *writes down* is to go *right* out of the parking lot to the 405. The entrance is right there. You pull out of the lot and go left, you see right away you're heading back toward the airport."

"So what else is to the left?"

"Lots of things," he said, "but most notably a FedEx Office Center."

Kelly looked up at him.

"Like a block away."

"And you got him there."

"Picking up a package. Just the right size. From guess where?"

"Gold Shield Security. College Point, Queens."

"How 'bout that?"

Kelly shook her head. "Jesus," she said. "He really made it easy for you."

"In all fairness, he wasn't supposed to get mugged."

"Now all you gotta do is find him."

"And I will," he said. "While you go look for the other three tiny Gs."

She sipped her coffee for a moment and just looked back at him. He smiled. "What?"

"Why haven't you said anything to me about my little rant?"

He didn't move, just kept smiling at her.

"I would think that you might have had some reaction."

"Do you care what I think?"

"More than what anyone else thinks."

"That's funny."

"How's that?"

"If that were true, you would have said something to me. You would have told me what the fuck was going on inside you."

"So I hurt your feelings?"

He looked around the room.

"It's okay," she said. "I can take it, whatever it is you have to say."

He said, "All right," and then leaned forward, his elbows on his knees, and said, "I think you embarrassed yourself."

She laughed. "I'll say."

"I get that you were pissed off about Steven leaving you. I get that you went and got drunk and said some shit about shit that you weren't really mad at, but was easier to be mad at than deal with your own shit. And I don't even care about how racist it was because, to be honest, part of it was true, but most of it was just stupid. At first I thought it was just exactly what it sounded like: the ranting of a fuckin' drunk."

"Okay." That one hurt.

"But what it really was, was *suicide*. And I never saw you that way. I'm sitting next to you, day in, day out, and you never say a word to me."

"You said that."

"I'm saying it again."

"So you *are* hurt."

"I'm not through."

She shut up and waved him on.

"What *hurt* me, what broke my heart was realizing that you didn't take yourself seriously. That you figured that you were enough of a joke that you could actually say that shit and get away with it. That you didn't care if you were remembered as just another asshole."

She nodded, wondered why she opened this door. She didn't want to hear any of this. She already knew it.

"But," Rudy went on, "if what you say is true, that you don't care about the job anymore, then, by all means, stay here and get drunk and stoned and scissor your cute neighbor all day, I don't give a fuck. Just tell me now so I can stop taking you seriously and start forgetting about you."

"Jesus, fatso." Kelly realized that her hand was shaking and carefully put down the coffee cup. "Wow."

They sat in silence for a while. Well, not complete silence as the gardener was out in the courtyard with his leaf blower. Kelly caught a glimpse of him through the blowing curtain, had been wanting to go out there and tell him that all he was doing was blowing dust and shit particles into the air, making everyone's unit smell like diesel and dirt, when she realized that she'd just completely tuned out Rudy. Shit. How often had she done that before? She turned back to him and saw that he had been watching her the entire time.

He finally shook his head and got up.

"I have to go. I'm catching a plane to New York."

"What for?"

"Go see Mr. Cooper's place of residence. If it exists. And pay a visit to Gold Shield Security."

He started for the door.

Kelly said, "Hey."

He turned back to her.

"The other kid in the video, the pretty one, I don't know who he is, but he looks a lot like a kid I remember, got shot in the back a few years ago, at a basketball game downtown. Cole Bennett, I think his name was."

"You think that's him?"

"Cole's in a wheelchair," she said. "But I seem to recall he had a little brother."

"Okay."

"Maybe I'll start there."

She felt Rudy looking at her to see if she was for real and lit another cigarette and sat back. She could quit her job later. What she couldn't do was fuck over Rudy, the only person left in her life that actually cared about her.

Rudy knew better than to make a big deal and said, "Sounds good," and reached for the door, but then turned back and added, "I don't like it when you call me fatso."

She looked at him. "It's ironic."

"Well, I don't like it."

"You're skinnier than me, for fuck's sake."

"Whatever. I'm asking you to stop."

"Anything else?"

He thought about it. "No," he said. "I think we're good."

"Phew."

"But just so as you know—"

"Sweet Jesus."

"If I come back here and I find a bong or a bottle of anything stronger than breast milk, I'm going down the hall and busting your girlfriend."

thirty-one

When Science was eight or nine, he used to listen to his brother talk about "putting in work for the set." Cole would say something like "Banging ain't no part-time thing. It's all day every day. It's a *life*." At night, Cole would lie in the bed across the room from Science and tell him, "You need to be down even when ain't nobody else down with you. You get caught, you don't ever tell. You ride the beef like a good soldier." When Cole got his driver's license, he'd drive Science to the park and sit with him and tell him, "You gotta be ready to kill and not care. You gotta be ready to die and not care. Only thing you care about is your set. You love your set and you hate your enemy."

Then their older brother, Guy, joined the Navy and then Cole got shot in the back. And then Cole's best friend, Levon, got shot in the stomach and would have a bag strapped to his hip for the rest of his life. And while Cole kept up a good front, said that it was all just a test, he pretty much stopped talking about "banging as a career" after that.

Science felt like he was being tested right now. He was on his own, fully on his own, with nobody out there to help him. But that was how he wanted it. He had stood up to Mr. Freeze and come off like a real soldier. *Go ahead, shoot me, motherfucka.* Less than twenty-four hours later, it was all over YouTube and Science was an instant Ghetto Star. No way he was gonna wallbang his life away like all them other clowns. Run around tagging walls proclaiming *other* OGs or, worse, some lame-ass rhyme somebody thought up while smoking a bowlful of weed.

No, Science had *real* shit to do.

Those first few hours, he had to admit, he missed Truck. He felt scared, way out of his depth. So after a long night of hiding in the back of a car, he walked home, only to find a sedan parked out front of his house with city plates. He went around back and could see his mom talking to a lady cop, the same one he'd seen on TV, the one that fucked up that Whitsett Ave homie with a chair and a phone book.

So he kept on walking. And after two full days on the streets by himself, like Moses wandering the desert, he had a vision. All at once, he knew exactly how he would parlay his big play with Mr. Freeze into something way bigger.

The vision came to him at about three a.m. Science had been walking along Vanowen Street for the better part of an hour, was thinking about where he might get something to eat, when the side-walk began to rise and fall in long waves.

Science stood there riding the heaving cement as the few cars on the street at that hour all came to a dead stop. One woman got out of her Kia, took one look at the power lines overhead swaying forty-five degrees in either direction, and started screaming.

But Science stayed calm. Cool as Mr. Freeze, and for the first time all night, he realized that he wasn't afraid. Somehow, he knew, he just *knew* that he was fine, that this was actually the *beginning* of something, not the end. And when that feeling still hadn't left him another twenty-four hours later, Science knew that it never would.

This was his moment.

He would create his own set—the Vanowen Shakers, or the VShakes, he hadn't decided which—and take over all business in the 'hood. He would do it without any sanctions from Vineland, because, fuck it, now that the Marcus twins had been conveniently pushed off the planet, there really wasn't anyone left to get in his way. The twins were the real soldiers. Everyone else was rapping on YouTube.

The problem was, without Truck, he had no lieutenant. No road dog he could count on. He had L, but that dude spent most of every day baked. He wasn't so much scary as skyed up. Plus, Science heard through L's shorty, Keshawnda, that L was right now lamming with his cousins somewhere in Northridge. No doubt laying low. Science wasn't worried about him, though. Dude was straight up, he'd never say a word to anybody about that night in the alley.

But Shake? Science wouldn't steal a fuckin' hat with that fool. Not anymore. Not since last night, when he went by his house and saw him getting sweated by that same lady cop. Science peeping through the front window this time, Shake sitting there on the couch and looking like he was bawling. Science knew there was no way that fat-ass buster would ride any kind a beef. It came down to it, he would for sure give up everybody. So soon as he possibly could, Science was going to have to put that homie down, hopefully in front of a few people.

But right now, he needed a strap and a place to stay. He knew where his brother had stashed a little deuce-five back home, but after seeing the cop at his house and then again at Shake's place, there was no way he could ever go back there. But then, a few hours later, as the sun came up and he found himself walking along a now quiet Dehougne Street, he was suddenly visited with the most bugged out idea ever as to how he could maybe kill two birds with one stone.

Or one bullet.

thirty-two

Albert Budin's Alaska Airlines flight finally took off for Burbank Airport a full three hours late, after Albert had sat in a vinyl chair at SeaTac for almost as long as the trip itself. He hated flying, and, to make matters worse, had the misfortune of being assigned a center seat at the very back of the plane. So for two hours he sat wedged between a surly, headphoned kid in a U of W T-shirt who reeked of alcohol and garlic and slept through the entire flight with his body hanging over what should have been Albert's armrest, and a sixty-something nun whose vigorous needlepointing left him battered and bruised from the sharp elbow jabs he received every time the sister pulled her needle through the fabric. Albert was so miserable that, at one point, he thought about making himself vomit into the air sickness bag, just to see if that might motivate either of his seatmates to get up and seek comfort elsewhere. But, thankfully for all concerned, Albert nodded off before he could bring that idea to fruition.

Before he left Seattle, Albert called Bob Spetting, currently in residence at Pelican Bay State Prison for one offense or another, though Albert was pretty sure that whatever crime it had been, it had probably involved some sort of arson mixed with loss of life, ensuring that Bob would in all likelihood breathe his last demented breath inside steel-reinforced walls.

"He's alive," Albert said as soon as Bob fished his contraband cell phone out from behind the toilet and got on the line.

"Who?"

"My old friend," Albert said. "The one I wake up every morning thinking about."

"How do you know?"

"Same way I know everything. CNN."

"Harvey said he was dead."

"Yes, well, he looked pretty healthy to me. Before he got shot anyway."

"Someone shot him?"

"A little gangster, in L.A. somewhere."

"You positive?"

"There isn't a doubt in my mind."

"Fuckin' A." Almost a whisper.

Albert knew that Bob couldn't talk long so he quickly got to the real purpose of his call. "Listen," he said, "I need a couple of guns."

Bob laughed and said, "Yeah, you do."

"Something big and loud like a .45, will scare people away when they hear it, and something small like a .22, can hold a silencer, which I'll also need, and a car, something invisible."

"Who do we know in L.A.?"

"Jesus, Bob," Albert said. "Why the fuck do you think I'm calling *you*?"

Less than an hour after he landed, Albert took a Super Shuttle to an auto body shop in Lawndale where, for three thousand dollars, he secured the requested hardware and the use of a six-year-old beige Toyota Camry. His next stop was Valley Presbyterian Hospital, the place he'd seen on TV, but after chatting up a young Chinese nurse, Albert learned that Roy was no longer a patient there, and that no one had the faintest fucking clue as to where he was now.

Albert had to admit that he felt some mild sense of pride at Roy's disappearing act, as he drove the mile or so to LAPD's North Hollywood Division on Burbank Boulevard. He found a spot across the street from the station giving him a solid view of the building. Albert found the structure to be one of those modern pieces of shit that went up all over the country in the nineties, looking like something his kid would make with blocks as soon as she could sit up. A square shape here. A cylinder there. No windows. Every pod painted a different color. It agitated him just to look at it.

The goal here was to pick up the lady cop he'd seen on TV. He had been reading up on her and knew she worked out of this building, so it would only be a matter of time before she showed up. Albert would then sit her down and ask her what leads she might have on her now vanished star witness. Of course, this wouldn't be as simple as smiling and complimenting her lovely braid, as he had done with the nurse at Valley Pres. If he was to get this one to give up anything about Roy, things would have to get wet.

To be sure, this Kelly Maguire fascinated him. He had enjoyed reading online about her episode with the gang kid. She seemed broken and fucked up and Albert wondered if, like Danny Leone before her, Roy hadn't bared his soul to her, too. Perhaps he had mentioned Albert in one of their conversations. He might have even told her their whole story. In which case, she'd see Albert and think she was seeing a ghost. He knew that's how Roy would react. Roy had underestimated Albert, had forgotten the golden rule of killing: you point a gun at another man, you pull the trigger and you keep on pulling it until you're sure that the other man is dead. Albert had said it often enough. *You kill him, and then you kill him again.* You don't walk away until you're beyond a doubt certain that whoever caught your bullet or knife blade will never get up. Ever.

And yet Roy still made the mistake. Though Albert was fairly certain that he wouldn't make it again. But this time, Roy would be the one on his heels. Roy would be the one who didn't see it coming. And if, by chance, he somehow managed to get off a shot, he'd find that he was facing a very different man than the one he faced all those years ago. For if Albert had once merely been invulnerable, the years in the slaughterhouse had now made him invincible.

There was a golden rule in that place, too: *The chain will not stop.* No matter what happens, *the chain will not stop.* Nothing was to ever stand in the way of production; not mechanical failures or breakdowns or accidents, not forklift crashes or overheated saws or dropped knives. On more than one occasion, Albert had seen workers lying unconscious on the floor as the dripping carcasses overhead kept on swaying right on past.

The chain will not stop.

Over the past decade, Albert had, himself, suffered injuries that would have crippled or killed anyone else. He had been struck by a falling ninety-pound box of meat and pinned against the steel lip of a conveyor belt. He blew out a disc on that one and had back surgery that kept him from walking for six months. He once inhaled too much chlorine while cleaning out the blood tanks and spent a month in the hospital, his lungs scorched, his body covered in blisters. He damaged the rotator cuff in his left shoulder when a ten-thousand-pound hammer mill dropped too quickly and pulled his arm straight backward. He broke a leg when he put his foot in a hole in the slaughterhouse floor. He most recently got hit by a slow-moving train behind the plant and got knocked out of his boots. He spent a mere week in the hospital before coming back to work, his shattered ankle still held together with four steel pins.

But the most common little mishap was when workers accidentally stabbed themselves or, worse, stabbed the guy working next to them. The struggle to keep up with that chain was hard enough, but add power tools, saws, knives, slippery floors, and falling carcasses, and the chances of something going bloody wrong quintuples. Of course, when the company started bringing in Mexican labor in an effort to bust the union, Albert made sure that he was always stationed next to one of the newcomers. And, in the end, he alone among the white workers had lasted.

Nothing would ever stop Albert Budin. Driving through L.A., looking at all of the damage from the quake, he knew that he, like the city itself, would keep going and, in the end, out-survive them all, including Roy.

At this moment, though, Albert had to wonder about the well-being of Kelly Maguire, now two cars ahead of him on the 405. He'd been following her for only ten minutes and he had already witnessed her scream at two other drivers, badge a third, and was pretty sure she had just waved her gun at a gentleman in a black Aston Martin who had been dumb enough to glue himself to her rear bumper. The lady was a tiger, one that a curious Albert wanted to ride. It was going to be harder than he thought, he decided, to leave her here when he was all through.

He was definitely having trouble figuring out what she was up to. She had driven from the North Hollywood station to an area in the shadow of downtown. She parked at a high school just as it was letting out, the lot full of mostly colored kids, and went inside. Twenty minutes later she came out and walked down to the athletic field. Albert waited two hours while she sat in the empty bleachers watching football practice.

When the boys went into the locker room, she sat in her car and, again, waited. A half hour later, a lanky black kid came out and got into a minivan. Kelly followed them, and Albert followed her. He wondered if that kid was one of the ones who had put down the old man, but he didn't look like it. This one looked like a jock through and through, and they were too far from North Hollywood. Albert had no choice but to tag along in the hope that Sergeant Maguire would eventually lead him home.

Albert followed the little procession from the high school to another neighborhood full of well-kept houses, though the faces he saw were all black. The minivan pulled into the driveway of one of them and Albert saw a woman in a nurse's uniform get out, followed by the high school kid and what Albert assumed was a younger brother.

Who were these people? Were they connected to Roy? Neither kid looked much like a gangbanger. Albert was thinking that he may have to go into that house at some point when Kelly Maguire started her car and pulled out once more.

It was dark now, more difficult to keep her in sight with all the fucking traffic. But eventually Albert found himself parked across the street from what had to be her apartment. One look at the place and he knew that she lived here. The dark shingle siding, the sad palm trees, the stupid fountain. This was her.

He would wait an hour before going in. Let her get settled, maybe even have a drink or two. That was the plan anyway. But Albert was tired after the trip down and fell into a deep sleep. And so it was that he didn't enter her apartment until six hours later, a little after five a.m.

thirty-three

"Sometimes you get your ass kicked on your own block. The OGs get drunk and they look at you and be all like, 'Let's see if this nigger's down,' and next thing you know you gotta fight. Always happens when I hang with my cousin and all his homies. They always be drinking or smoking some shit. And you can't cry or punk out, 'cause then they just hit you harder or they bust you, be all like, 'Get the fuck outta here!'"

Kelly said, "That's gotta be rough."

Trevor Green nodded. Kelly could see that he was near tears just thinking about it. This kid didn't want to be in a gang. Not anymore. It would be a relief to find a way out, and Kelly was just about to give him one when his fucking lawyer walked in the door and ended the interview. Though not before handing her his card and saying, "Be good for someone in your situation to have a face with some color on your team."

Knowing the kid wasn't going to school, Kelly had been calling Trevor Green, aka Shake, at his home for the past twenty-four hours. She'd left messages with his aunt, his grandmother, his grandmother's boyfriend, and, finally, his little sister, Taya. Kelly left her number that time and said to tell Shake/Trevor to call her back if he wanted to get out of the deep shit he was currently up to his lips in. The little girl said she'd be sure and pass that on.

Of course, the kid never called, so Kelly finally showed up at the house unannounced and found him eating cereal in front of the TV. She was making good progress and was about to ask the kid where the gun that did Councilman Peres had come from—*tell me that and we can make a deal*—when Johnnie Cochran walked in and pissed all over everything.

As the lawyer correctly pointed out, Kelly couldn't arrest Trevor. Not yet. There was no way anyone could pick him out on the Zarate video and her only witness was AWOL. Did she, given her current *situation,* really want to risk a misstep like that? She got up, looked at Trevor, and said, "To be continued."

Meanwhile, Delroy Kinney, aka L, was in the wind. No one in his family had any idea where he'd gone to and Kelly actually believed them. She figured that the kid would eventually turn up, especially now that she'd released his mug shot—Delroy having been arrested twice for possession of narcotics with intent to sell, once for possession of an illegal firearm, and once for mayhem—to the press. He and the now deceased Truck, aka Kenny Meadows, were the only two faces that were clearly visible in the Alonzo Zarate cell phone footage. Although Zarate himself was turning out to be a terrible witness, picking out only Truck with any real degree of certainty the day after the shooting. He said he had been too busy staring at his phone, trying to get the framing just right, to notice any other details.

Kelly paid a visit to Cole Bennett's house and asked about his little brother, Noel. Cole appeared to be in genuine shock that Science had been involved with the shooting of Peres as well as the shooting of Truck and the Marcus twins. He had never thought of his little brother as a killer or much of a worker. But then the kid never said shit to him these days. Never spoke to anyone except their older brother, Guy, who had taken a leave from the Navy and was at this very moment on his way home from San Diego to go look for their baby brother, try and stop him from getting into any more trouble. Noble, but late, Kelly thought. Way fucking late.

Science's mother, Nicole, was another matter. She told Kelly that she hoped her boy was out there heading up with anybody who got in his way. He was doing what was right for his 'hood. Didn't matter that, as Kelly pointed out, it was a " 'hood" he didn't even live in, his house being two miles away from where the shit had been going down. Nicole just shrugged and said, "It's all one big 'hood now."

Carmen couldn't give Kelly any help with Science. While she'd heard much about Cole, she didn't know that his little brother banged until now. Carmen remembered hearing that Cole had a brother in some charter school for genius kids in Studio City around the same time that Cole got shot, but that was about it. Kelly found the school, and they told her that for a few years the kid was a model student, got straight As and behaved himself, but then something changed, and when he wasn't disappearing from school for hours at a time, he was skipping entire days until, about a year ago, he stopped showing up altogether.

Carmen knew a lot more about Delroy Kinney, and told Kelly that L had a baby with a shorty named Keshawnda who wasn't hard to find. She had been one of Kelly's girls before the "incident." She and Kelly had always gotten along and helped each other out. Carmen informed Kelly that Kesha, as just about everyone called her, currently worked stocking shelves at a Rite Aid on Lankershim. Kelly brought up the baby and quickly got the girl talking. According to her, L wasn't so down for his set now that he was a father and Kesha was hounding him all the time for help. Kelly found that the girls in the gangs were getting much tougher these days on their boys. So now if death didn't end your banging, fatherhood certainly put a damper on it. Even if you were only fifteen.

And so it was that Kesha proudly stated that L was indeed in Chatsworth with his cousins, and had started going to high school out there. She wasn't sure which one, but said that it was a better school than any he'd been to and she hoped he'd stay put this time. She planned on moving there with the baby in the next month or so.

Kelly wasn't surprised that Kesha hadn't the faintest clue that L had been involved with the shooting of Frank Peres. She just thought that Kelly had stopped by to holler about the baby. She was, as they all were, in her own, very small world. This was the thing that always broke Kelly's heart: they had no idea what was out there. But she also knew the girl was lying. It was all too chatty and pat, as if Kesha had been giving the same line to anyone who asked.

Kelly would call the two schools in Chatsworth on the off chance Kesha was dumb enough to be telling the truth. If so, she could always get some uniforms from Devonshire to pick up the kid. Cell service being what it was, or, in the current case, what it *wasn't*, Kelly decided to go back to the station and use a hard line.

Of course neither school had any record of any Delroy Kinney, or any new male student for the matter, in the past three months. Kelly had just hung up from the second school when Rudy rang through on her cell, not knowing she was in the office. They managed to have a conversation for a full minute and a half before the call dropped.

Rudy was in New York, but was about to get on a plane for Missouri. It turned out that Roy Cooper's prints matched a Juvenile beef for Murder Two out there. Spent eight years in JD before all trace of him disappeared. Rudy had been to both Roy Cooper's apartment in Queens and his place of business, Gold Shield Security. The latter, a two-story hoarders' paradise in College Point, the place jammed floor to ceiling with newspapers, magazines, and junk mail, was now a crime scene, the owners, Harvey and Rita Cooper, having recently been found in their basement shot to death. Rudy said that so far it was looking a lot like a murder-suicide, with the wife doing the honors, but that was NYPD's problem.

"And Cooper's apartment?"

"Cleanest place I've ever been in. Hardly a stick of furniture and get this: no prints."

"None?"

"The place was wiped. Every inch. Even the baseball shit."

"Baseball shit?"

"Souvenirs. Apparently the man likes his baseball. St. Louis in particular. Kansas City before that. He's got score sheets, pennants, shirts, a full fucking uniform hanging in the closet. It's like he's twelve."

"I know what you mean."

"And Cooper's not his last name. We got a birth certificate from—"

And, naturally, that's where he dropped. She texted him and told him to send her a screen shot of the birth certificate when he landed. Kelly had been scribbling her notes on an envelope and now flipped it over and saw that it was the envelope Ruth Ann Carver had left behind a few days ago, but now seemed like another lifetime. Kelly had forgotten all about it.

She opened it and slid out the photo of the young black man. The father of the boy Ruth Ann Carver had asked her to look for.

And now something about Roy Cooper got her thinking about

Ruth Ann Carver and her long lost son. If the woman was to be believed, her boy disappeared, then reappeared as someone else. A new kid in another part of town. And now Rudy was telling her that Roy Cooper, or whatever his real name was, disappeared some twenty years ago, and then reappeared as whatever kind of wrong guy he was today. Kelly was the last person to believe in signs, but, nonetheless, she found herself unable to turn away from the photo.

There was, of course, no connection between Ruth Ann Carver's missing son and Roy Cooper, but Kelly thought she could hear both of them calling to her, so she spent ten minutes on her computer and found the old case file. The officer who signed the report was a woman named Dana Russo. Personnel informed Kelly that Russo retired fourteen years ago and was now an immigration lawyer in Huntington Beach. Curious, Kelly got her on the phone, mentioned Ruth Ann Carver, and Russo immediately said yeah, she remembered that one.

"We worked it for maybe six months, but all we ever found was the kid's blanket in one of the train yards near Union Station. I tried to keep track of Ruth Ann after that. But it was tough. The woman's life just fell apart. How is she now?"

"She thinks she saw the kid in Koreatown."

Dana Russo said, "Huh. Be something if she did." Meaning she doubted it.

They went through it for a little while longer and then Kelly thanked Russo and hung up before they could get into any other shop talk. She sensed the lawyer would be one of those ex jobs who wanted to hear about this cop or that, what it was like in the department these days, all of it a slow spiral toward what most cops, ex and otherwise, really wanted to know: was Kelly Maguire going to quit anytime soon?

She shoved the photo in her purse, would return it to Ruth Ann Carver at the shelter tomorrow, tell her there was really nothing she could do. If she thought her son was living somewhere near Koreatown, she should go to Rampart and Wilshire divisions and talk to them.

Right now, Kelly needed to find L. If Kesha was saying that he was in the Valley, then the chances were pretty good that he was somewhere in the opposite direction. There was one thing Kelly didn't think she was lying about: the best way for a kid in a gang to disappear was to get off the street and go to school. Nobody would look for him there. And with the new baby, Kesha would be pushing for L to better his ass.

Kelly knew from his previous arrests that Delroy had an older sister who was a Scientologist, did some kind of labor for the church, and lived in an apartment with a few other slaves on Fountain, several blocks west of Vermont. He could easily be crashing there. She didn't want to talk to the sister, set off any kind of alarm, so Kelly decided she would see if maybe she could get lucky and take a walk through nearby Dorsey and Crenshaw high schools. She knew that Delroy wasn't dumb enough to enroll under his real name, might not have enrolled at all, might just be there. Classes had become so overcrowded that he could probably pull that off for a week or two before he got caught.

Dorsey was a bust. No one there had seen Delroy. If he wasn't enrolled, the security guard told her with apparent sincerity, and he came on campus, someone would know. Kelly left a photo with the guard and did her own lap around the school. A few of the girls recognized her and gave her dark looks or threw their signs, but kept them low and close, as it was cause for suspension to fly anything for your set on campus.

Kelly gave them all waves and big smiles and then got back into her car and headed for Crenshaw High School.

The traffic was hell, not so much quake repair work as the usual L.A. fuckwits. There was the woman in the Nissan Leaf, for example, who ignored the dozen or so lane-ending signs on Fountain and drove right up to the back of a parked car and stopped *and then* decided to actually look over her damn shoulder and signal that she needed to move over. Pissed off, of course, that no one would now let her merge. She gave Kelly a dirty look as Kelly passed, and Kelly flipped her off and shouted, "Is that a *look*? You had two fucking blocks to get over!"

She looked in her rearview and saw that the guy behind her was laughing and said, "Fuck you, too."

Barely ten minutes later, on Slauson, Kelly got into a drag race with some asshole who sped up just as Kelly tried to move into his lane. She sped up to get ahead of him and then he sped up to block her move. So she pulled her badge from her belt and waved it at him.

"Back it off, asshole!"

The guy saw the badge, panicked and locked his brakes, the car behind him barely swerving around him in time. Kelly thought she recognized the driver as the guy who was laughing back on Fountain.

The teeny-tiny vice principal at Crenshaw High School was a little too chatty for Kelly's taste. Inviting her into his office while they discussed Delroy Kinney. Dr. Towns—he informed Kelly that he had a PhD in education within the first two minutes of meeting him—was a short black man, maybe five-two in his socks, fiftyish with this pencil mustache that Kelly had to believe every kid in the school made fun of. The man started nodding the minute she took the photograph out of her purse and passed it to him.

"Yes, of course he's here," Dr. Towns said. "But he didn't *just* enroll, he's been with us nearly four years." He looked up at her and added, "Someone's clearly given you bad information as his name is *not* Delroy, but Jamal. Jamal Allen Wilson."

"You sure?"

"Very. The kids used to call him 'Jaws' on account of his initials and the rather serious braces he had on his teeth back in his freshman and sophomore years." He passed the photo back to her and said, "It's an unusual picture. He doesn't really dress like that."

Kelly took it from him and realized that Dr. Towns had not been looking at Delroy Kinney, but at the photo of Ruth Ann Carver's late husband. She had apparently reached into her bag and come up with the wrong photo.

Kelly could not seem to escape Ruth Ann Carver.

Maybe she should quit trying.

She held up the picture once more and said, "This kid goes to Crenshaw?"

"One of our best students."

"Can I talk to him?"

Dr. Towns narrowed his eyes at her like she was here for smoking in the bathroom. "May I ask why?"

"You can ask."

"I'm just wondering, he's not in any trouble, is he? Because if he is, and you want to talk to him, his parents should be notified. And, to be honest, I should probably also be present for any interview."

"He's eighteen, so if I want him, I got him. But I promise," she smiled, "he's not in any trouble." She then stood up. "Where is he?"

"Where he always is at this time of day." He nodded out the window. "On the football field."

They were running a scrimmage when Kelly walked down to the field, the turf a typical L.A. mix of green and brown. In their practice uniforms, it was hard to tell one player from another. She saw a kid on the bench, obese with high curly hair, his helmet on the seat beside him, eating a power bar. She walked over and put a foot on the bench, leaned on her thigh.

He looked up and asked, "You the nurse?"

"No."

"My blood sugar's all jacked again."

"I just said I'm not the nurse."

"You look like her."

Kelly said, "That can't be true," and nodded to the players on the field. "Which one's Jamal Wilson?"

The kid said, "Number four." And then, as she scanned the uniforms, "The quarterback."

Of course, he was.

Kelly watched as number four, a tall lanky kid, rolled back and threw what looked to her untrained eye like a million-yard pass, the other players cheering when it was caught by another kid who trotted into the end zone with it. As they all lined up for another go at the play, Kelly climbed the stairs into the empty bleachers and sat down to watch.

She wondered what she was doing here. With everything going down, her life in disarray, why was she sitting here watching the Crenshaw Cougars practice? The truth was, she hadn't felt much like a cop in a long time. That was a place she never thought she'd get to. Be just like the rest of them after ten years. Angry and drunk. Numb to pretty much everything. That wasn't supposed to be her. But she now knew what they all knew: that the very thing you need to stay strong and keep your head, that daily and deliberate apathy you practice like meditation, is the very thing that, in the end, robs you of your desire to get in the car and catch bad guys. Nobody tells you that, once you put on the armor, you can never take it off.

Kelly looked across the field and watched a familiar-looking Camry loop around the parking lot in front of the gymnasium. She thought this could be one of those things, like how it seemed like every time Kelly looked at a digital clock, it was always when it happened to read 11:11. Maybe she looked at the clock a lot of times and those were just the numbers she remembered. Maybe it's just a coincidence that every time Kelly noticed a car today, it was a beige Camry.

Or maybe somebody was following her.

She was giving some serious thought to walking over there and knocking on the window when she heard the entire team yell *Go Cougars!* Practice over, they all began heading for the gym. Kelly watched number four as he unsnapped his chin strap and pulled his helmet off. She had to admit to a slight catch in her breath when she saw the kid. He was a dead ringer for the man in the photograph. A younger, cleaner-cut version to be sure. But still, there he was.

No wonder Ruth Ann first thought she saw a ghost.

Kelly watched him go into the gym, then looked off at the parking lot. The Camry was gone.

She sat in her car for nearly thirty minutes before she saw the first players leave the gym, hair wet, clothes hanging loose. All of them with that easy, confident walk of young men in complete control of their bodies, if only on the outside. She saw Jamal, a heavy book pack over his shoulder, come out with a couple of other kids. They stood and talked for several minutes before a navy blue minivan pulled up and Jamal bumped it out with his buds and got in. As the van drove past, Kelly caught sight of a woman in some kind of white uniform behind the wheel, and another, younger kid in the backseat.

She pulled out and followed them for a couple of miles to View Park, an upper-middle-class black neighborhood in South L.A. Kelly drove past as the van pulled into the driveway of a well-kept single-story home sitting on a corner knoll. She pulled to the curb and watched in her mirror as the woman in the white uniform got out. Jamal got out the other side and was now playfully shoving who Kelly figured had to be his younger brother, the kid looking to be about twelve. She waited for them all to go inside and then moved her car across the street. She wouldn't be able to stay here very long, as neighbors would surely clock a white woman parked in what looked a lot like an unmarked police car. She watched them in the kitchen window, still talking and playing around, and took a couple of pictures of the house with her phone. When the woman looked out the window at her, Kelly took one more picture and drove away.

If that was Ruth Ann Carver's son, it looked like he had a pretty nice life. From a distance anyway. *If* that was her son. No matter what, Kelly needed to be careful how she played this. Eighteen years later, there would be a lot of other people in the mix now, and sensitivity was never Kelly's strong suit. She wished that Rudy was here to advise her, instead of in Missouri doing God knows what.

Albert woke up stiff and pissed off. He had meant to take only a quick nap and here it was now ten minutes after five, the sun just coming up. He got out of the car and stretched, wanting to be limber for what was coming. It had been a while and he hoped that the muscle memory was still there. Killing, after all, contained its own very specific form of physical exertion and small motor skills. He took a series of deep breaths, knowing that he'd have to find some time to meditate later in the day, and crossed the street to Kelly Maguire's apartment.

Albert didn't have to wait long for someone—in this case, a guy in a little black BMW—to pull up from the garage. The man at the wheel, looking ahead, not behind, as he pulled out onto the street, never seeing Albert stroll down the ramp and duck under the metal gate as it slowly rolled back down.

He quickly found Kelly's unit and considered simply knocking on the door, but thought better of it and picked the lock. This took him close to twenty minutes as he was out of practice and had brought the wrong tools, locks having become more sophisticated during his dozen-year hiatus. Surprisingly, no one came out of the other units and no one inside this one had heard either his scratching at the door or the soft curses he kept muttering as he worked.

Once inside, Albert stood in the near dark for a good five minutes just listening and getting used to the feel of the place. It was clean, but she was a smoker. Had been smoking recently. There was an open wine bottle and half a glass of red on the coffee table. He pulled the silenced .22 from his coat and started down the hall.

Having already missed one opportunity to speak with Sergeant Maguire, Albert figured this time he'd be inside waiting when she returned home. Once he made a quick check to make sure that no one else was here, he'd look around and see if she by chance brought any of her work home.

The first bedroom was set up as an office. The computer on the desk was awake, someone having used it recently. A fresh butt in the ashtray. The computer would be his first stop in just a moment . . .

While blackout curtains in the bedroom made it nearly impossible to see, Albert sensed the bed was empty. The duvet lay piled on the floor as if it had been thrown aside. The bathroom was cold and the shower was dry. Where was she? He didn't think the smoker went for a morning jog. There was a chest against one wall and he looked through the drawers and quickly found a gun, a cop Glock, but no badge. Was she at work? This early?

He had just sat down on the bed to figure out his next move when he heard a key in the front door.

She was back.

He could hear her moving around the living room. She opened a cabinet, lifted the cushions on the sofa, then went into the kitchen and started to open drawers in there. She was looking for something. Albert crossed his legs and waited quietly on the bed. He could see her now go into the home office across the hall and heard her going through the desk. Heard her say, "Fuckin' A," and then she was in the bedroom.

She started going through the drawers Albert had just gone through. She didn't see him sitting there in the dark, moved to the closet and turned on the light. She rooted around for a moment or two, finally coming out with a box. She was about to set it down on the bed when she saw Albert and shrieked, let go of the box, which hit the floor.

She tried to bolt for the door, but Albert was up in an instant, blocking the way.

He turned on the light and looked down at the jewelry, cash, and another pistol that lay on the floor. She sure liked her guns. He then looked up at her. She was in jeans and a T-shirt. No shoes. Her hair was short and palmed back on her head.

"You're not Sergeant Maguire."

She was breathing hard and could barely speak.

"No."

"What's your name?"

"Erin."

"Well, Erin, right up top, let me say that I'm not here to hurt you or otherwise harm you in any way. I'm not a rapist nor am I, like you, a thief."

She saw the silenced pistol in his hand.

"You're not a cop either."

Albert said, "No," and then nodded to the box on the floor. "Did you find what you were looking for?"

"I was picking up some of my things."

"So that's your gun and jewelry, then?"

"Yes."

"And your cash?"

He pointed with the gun to where she'd tucked a wad of it into her pocket, some of it sticking out.

She said nothing.

He smiled and asked, "Can you tell me where Sergeant Maguire has run off to?"

"I have no idea. I haven't seen her since the night before."

"Yet you knew she wouldn't be here."

"I heard her leave."

He could see that she instantly regretted saying that.

"So you live nearby?"

He kept looking at her, knew that he probably shouldn't let her walk out the door.

Erin said, "Is Kelly in trouble?"

"Yes, I think she is. And I think it would be best if you stayed away from her for a little while. Maybe resisted the urge to come over and rob her until after this particular trouble has passed."

She was clearly relieved that he was giving her a future. Albert had always loved that little tease. Subtly imply that they have tomorrow, all the while planning where the body would fall. Roy had never been that way, and in the end, that's what blew them apart.

Albert was raising the pistol when he heard someone else come through the front door.

"Mommy."

And now Erin looked at Albert, even more frightened than she had been just a moment ago.

Albert took a step back through the door and looked down the hall. A little boy, no older than three, in *Toy Story* pajamas was coming this way.

"Hi, buddy," he said. "Your mom's just in here." And then the smile. "Come join us."

Erin looked at Albert and said, "Please . . ."

Albert hid the gun along his leg and stepped aside as the boy padded into the room and froze. He looked at his mother, wasn't sure how to feel.

"I woke up," he said.

She grabbed him. Tears in her eyes now.

"I'm sorry, sweetie."

"He's handsome." Albert looked at Erin. "Is his father that handsome?"

"Yes."

"Is he around?"

"More or less."

"Which is it?"

She glanced at the boy, clearly didn't want to answer in front of him.

Albert understood and said, "So he'd miss his mother then, should anything happen to her."

She clung to the kid. "Yes," she said. "He would."

Albert looked at the two of them while he ran the math on the situation.

She said, "I'm not going to say anything."

"Won't you?"

"No," she said. "I mean, what would I say?"

"I can think of a few things."

"I wouldn't. I won't."

Albert looked at the boy.

She got the message, took her son by the hand, and faced Albert.

"If you'll excuse us," she said. "I have to fix his breakfast."

Albert finally smiled and stepped aside.

"Nice meeting you, Erin."

Albert spent the next hour on Kelly's computer. There was some research on the house he'd followed her to the day before. But it was the email with the photo of Roy's birth certificate attached that got his attention. He stared at it for a good long while.

He went into Kelly's history and found that, along with an Alcoholics Anonymous website, she'd that morning spent some time on the Dodgers website. Albert studied the schedule of upcoming Dodgers home games and smiled.

A real smile, not the kind he used to flip people the fuck out. For Albert now realized that he didn't need Kelly Maguire at all to find his old friend. In fact, he knew why she had been taking her sweet time. There was no need to go out and hunt for him. Not when she, like Albert, now knew exactly where he was going to be.

thirty-four

Kelly woke up at four in the morning unable to sleep or stop thinking about anything other than Jamal Allen Wilson. She was convinced that there was a move here that would somehow redeem herself in her own eyes and maybe, just maybe, accomplish something good. But, being Kelly Maguire, she could also see the trap. She was no soft touch and, with her involvement, there were at least a dozen ways somebody or everybody gets hurt.

But she couldn't do *nothing*.

So she found herself parked once more in front of Jamal Wilson's house, this time at five in the morning and with Ruth Ann Carver now in the seat beside her. Kelly offered her one of the Egg McMuffins she picked up on her way to the shelter, but the woman waved it away, kept her eyes glued on the front door.

Kelly shrugged, took her own healthy bite, sipped from a watery Diet Coke, and noted another car in the driveway now parked alongside the minivan. A beige Lexus sedan that no doubt belonged to Karl Wilson, the man of the house and sole proprietor of a State Farm agency in nearby Baldwin Hills.

Kelly had at first planned on talking to the mother but then decided that she would first give Ruth Ann Carver another look at the kid. Mr. Wilson went for a run at around five-thirty. Lights went on in the house while he was out; for the last half hour, she had been watching the entire family eating breakfast. Who does that anymore? But there they were, all at the same table. The mother, Victoria Wilson, a dietitian at Children's Hospital on Vermont Avenue, came out of the house a half hour later and Kelly and Ruth Ann followed her and the two boys to Crenshaw High.

They were heading to Children's Hospital when Kelly's phone rang. After a brief chat with Rudy, Kelly let Ruth Ann Carver off at a salon in Koreatown called Loubelle and went to meet Rudy at the home of Trevor Green, aka Shake, where they served the warrant Rudy had secured based on a positive ID off the Zarate video made by not Alonzo Zarate, but a former UCLA student who had come forward just that morning. She had known Shake at Camp Kilpatrick where, according to Rudy, she had once taught some kind of writing workshop. Kelly was never big on the white women who thought they could parachute into the jungle for a month or two and "change lives." She had no patience for anybody who went to war as an "experience." Worse thing that probably ever happened to this UCLA girl, Kelly thought, was she got a C+ on some term paper.

Trevor/Shake, handcuffed straight out of bed in jockey shorts and Oakland Raiders T-shirt, gave up everybody in the alley before the cops had led him out the front door. By the time his lawyer showed up at North Hollywood, the only offer the pretty young ADA had for him was coffee. The kid would slam for sure, the only question was for how long.

While they were processing Trevor in North Hollywood, a radio unit from Hollywood Station over the hill spotted Delroy Kinney, aka L, going into an army surplus store on Vine. Upon the arrival of two more units, the officers went inside and somehow got into a "brief shootout" with Delroy, who, at the insistence of Kesha, had come to the store to purchase an earthquake kit for an apartment she neglected to tell Kelly they had been renting in Echo Park. Delroy took twenty-eight shots to the head and chest and was pronounced dead at the scene.

It wasn't yet ten a.m.

By three-thirty that afternoon, Kelly was back in the bleachers at Crenshaw High sitting beside a silent Ruth Ann Carver watching the Cougars run through the last half hour of practice, Ruth Ann's eyes following number four wherever he went on the field. When the coach finally blew three short blasts through his whistle and called it a day, Ruth Ann leaned forward and watched as Jamal pulled off his helmet. And just as Kelly had two days before, Ruth Ann let out a gasp when she at last saw his face.

Twenty minutes later, Kelly and Ruth Ann sat in the car as the boys began to emerge from the locker room. Ruth Ann sat up when Jamal came out in a group of three others, then craned her neck to better see Victoria Wilson behind the wheel of the navy blue van when it pulled to the curb and Jamal slid inside.

Ruth Ann Carver still had not uttered a single word when they pulled to the curb just down the street from the house in View Park. She watched as the two boys piled out of the van and went inside. Kelly rolled the car forward so they could see better into the house, and Ruth Ann watched the same scene Kelly had a couple of days before: the boys horsing around in the kitchen while Victoria Wilson worked on dinner.

It was nearly dark when Karl Wilson pulled into the driveway and Kelly turned to Ruth Ann and asked her, "What would you like me to do?"

Ruth Ann kept silent and watched Karl go inside and greet his family.

"Ruth Ann?"

The woman finally turned away from the house and stared out through the windshield at something only she could see.

Kelly asked again. "What would you like me to do?"

"That's not my son."

"Excuse me?"

"That boy in there. He's not mine."

Kelly considered Ruth Ann's profile a moment, the woman rigid in her seat, and asked, "Are you sure?"

"Yes, I'm sure." And then she turned to Kelly and said, "I'm damn sure."

Kelly nodded. "Okay."

"And how dare you drag me down here and waste my time with this bullshit."

"I'm very sorry."

"You damn well oughta be."

Kelly started the car.

"Let me give you a ride back to the shelter."

"Never you mind," Ruth Ann said and opened her door. "I'll walk."

She got out and slammed the door. For the next few minutes Kelly sat there and watched Ruth Ann Carver walk past the Wilson house and up the street until she finally disappeared over the hill. Kelly gave the house one last look, and said, "Fuck this," and began the twenty-minute drive to Dodger Stadium.

thirty-five

Science watched as Alonzo Zarate finally left his apartment a few minutes after two p.m. and got into a yellow Mini Cooper. Science waited for him to drive off, then went around to the front of the building, a two-story four-plex, and climbed the outside stairs to Zarate's unit on the second floor. There was a window beside the door and it took Science all of a minute to get it open and haul himself through it.

The apartment was a dim affair with that single grimy window in the front room for light. The beige couch and the green bean bag chair looked like they had been there since the early eighties, the new fifty-inch Samsung flat screen leaning against the wall standing out like a sore thumb. No doubt, Science assumed, purchased with the green the man got off selling his eyewitness video to CNN.

Science moved to the back bedroom and looked out the window at the alley below, every inch of it now crammed with flowers and balloons. Science pulled out his phone and took a few pictures. They had cleaned up the blood and the brain matter from the wall, but Science thought he could still see a dark stain there and took a few pics of that, too. Zarate, the lucky fucker, certainly had the choice view that night.

Science wondered how long the man had been up here watching, and if he'd seen them playing Russian Roulette?

That's how it got started. All of them just sitting in the alley budding out, listening to music. They'd each brought a gun with them that night and were anxious to shoot something. They were thinking about turning out a party down the block—they'd gotten word there were enemy Mara Salvatruchas over there—when L, bent off his nut, emptied his gun, save one slug, and put it to his head.

None of them thought he'd pull the trigger, so when he did, and they heard what would be the first *click!* of the night, they all went apeshit. Zarate might very well have heard them laughing as they couldn't stop for about ten minutes.

Shake was all like, "Righteous," but Science knew that he as *The Science Man* had to do better than that. He held his hand out for the gun and said, "Give it up, Loc."

L passed the strap to him and Science put it to his head and without hesitating pulled the trigger.

Another *click*.

More laughter.

Science said, "You're up, dude," and placed the gun in Shake's hand.

The fat kid tried to pass it back and said, "You're all sprung. No fucking way."

"You ain't punkin' out, are you, faggot?"

Shake said, "Fuck you, cuz. Two empties been tapped already."

"So spin it," L said. "And maybe it lands on an empty and maybe it doesn't. Or maybe it's on one right now and you fuckin' play yourself."

Shake stared at the gun, did whatever math would steel him up, and put the gun to his head, but then at the last second pointed it up at the sky and pulled the trigger.

Zarate for sure heard that gunshot. It was loud in the alley, so close that Science's ears were ringing. Shake stared at the smoking gun, doing a new kind of math now. Something had just passed through him. A new feeling. Science could see it. The boy would be wired for the rest of the night for sure.

"Ain't no thing."

They all turned and watched Truck come off the wall across the alley and take the gun from Shake. "You think you lucky, cuz?" He dumped the spent shell, picked up one of the bullets by L's feet, and loaded it into the gun. Thought for a moment, then loaded another. And then another. He spun it and put the muzzle in his mouth and bit down. They all flinched when he pulled the trigger.

Truck pulled the muzzle free and smiled. "Clickety click click."

He then pointed the gun upward and pulled the trigger twice, Science's ears ringing out once more at the two loud shots that now smoked up the alley. No doubt Zarate heard *that*.

Truck tossed the gun back to L, picked up his MAC 10 where he'd left it. They sat there in silence as Truck left the alley and disappeared into the dark to go take a piss or smoke or do whatever it was he did when he wandered off. Science traded looks with the other two, and they all once more burst out laughing. L turned up the music.

"What's going on here?"

And there was the old guy, shifting from one foot to another in his little jogging outfit, huffing and puffing at the mouth of the alley, looking pissed *off*.

"I heard a gunshot," he said. "What are you boys getting up to?"

They laughed at him, waved him on. *Get the fuck outta here.*

But he wouldn't leave. Instead he squinted at them and said, "I don't recognize any of you. You don't live in this neighborhood, do you?"

Shake said, "Move the fuck on, Herb. This ain't your shit."

Not about to be blown off by them or anyone, the old man didn't move, so they just shrugged and ignored him. Played their music and hit the blunt. Laughing about Truck and the fuckin' *meat* that boy had, put a gat in his mouth like that.

"You know what your problem is?"

They turned and fuck if that fucking Herb wasn't still there. Only now he started walking at them, pointing a long finger like he was Uncle fucking Sam.

"You have no incentive. You know what that is? *Incentive?* It means that you have no *drive*. You're always looking for someone to put something in your hand."

What the fuck? None of them knew what to say to that. None of them even knew what he was talking about.

A pumped-up Shake finally said, "I got something in my hand," and held up his gun and pointed it at the man. "And it's fuckin hot and hard and it's gonna blow your fuckin' head off."

And that was that.

. . .

Science spent the next hour rummaging around Zarate's shitty little apartment, his efforts rewarded with a Raven MP .25 automatic in a drawer beside the bed, as well as a new hunting knife, still in the box it came in. He put them both in his pockets and sat down at Zarate's laptop.

The world's most famous Witness of the Week had a file on his computer labeled "Scrap Book" that linked to all of his interviews both in print and on TV. There was a draft of a Wiki page that mentioned, among other things, Zarate's associate's degree in accounting from DeVry University and a blue belt in Tae Kwon Do. But Science was more interested in the dozen or so pictures of a girl who looked Filipino in her underwear posing all around the apartment.

Science's stomach started growling, so he went into the crappy little kitchen and ate a couple bowls of Golden Grahams and washed them down with a Mountain Dew. He then kicked back on what turned out to be the greasiest couch he'd ever sat on and turned on the new flat screen, passing the time watching a couple episodes of *SpongeBob SquarePants* and the last hour of *The Wrestler* before finally nodding off.

He woke up sometime later to Alonzo Zarate kicking at his Timbos and screaming at him.

"What the fuck are you doing in my house?"

Science yawned and sat up. "It's not a house, cuz. It's an apartment."

"Get the fuck out of here!"

"Ain't you gonna call the po-po first," Science asked. "Tell 'em you got an intruder?"

That stopped the dude.

"What?"

Science leaned back on the couch. "Go on, hit 911," he said. "I'll wait."

Zarate looked at him, cut a quick look at the bedroom, no doubt thinking about that jammy in the nightstand. So Science put his arm up on the back of the couch, opening his jacket so that Zarate could see the gun in his waist.

"You little fucker—is that mine?"

"Make the call, cuz."

Zarate looked at him and said, "You are so fucked," and then took out his phone and dialed 911. Waiting for them to pick up, he asked, "Do you know who I am?"

"No, but now that you mention it, I thought you looked kinda familiar? You famous?"

Zarate shook his head and put the phone to his ear. "You are *really* fucked." He stared at Science while he continued to wait for an operator to pick up. Eleven, twelve fucking rings. It was maddening. Someone finally answered and Zarate said, "Some asshole's in my apartment and he won't leave."

Science said, "I'm famous, too," and pulled the Raven out, waved it at Zarate. "Be sure and tell 'em I got a gun."

Zarate stared at him as he said to the operator, "I don't know—he was here when I got here."

"Tell 'em."

Zarate said, "He's got a gun," and seemed to finally see Science for the first time, recognition freezing his face.

"I know who you are—"

Science shot him three quick times, the gun jerking in his hand, sending each shot higher than the one before, the last .25 caliber slug hitting Zarate in the left eye.

If Science had missed the irony a few hours earlier when he had taken his own cell phone shots of the alley, he got it now when he stood up over the wheezing Zarate and said, "Witness *that*, mothafucka" and shot him in the other eye.

It was dark when Science came out of the apartment, but he still didn't run so as not to get anybody looking his way. He found Zarate's Mini Cooper parked around the corner and was unlocking the door when fuck it if he didn't see Mr. Freeze standing across the street.

Science didn't move. He was pretty sure that the man hadn't seen him, because he didn't move either. He was just standing there, still as an oak, staring at the alley. After about ten minutes of this, he finally turned and started walking away from Science up the street.

Science worried that the way things were going, if he didn't do something about it right now, he would continue to bump into this dude every day for the rest of his life.

He watched Mr. Freeze get into a car and pull out. Science jumped into Zarate's Mini and, after a minute of figuring out how to start it, took off after him. Science wasn't much of a driver to begin with, and the Mini had a manual transmission, so it took some doing to keep up with the other car. Science's older brother Guy had given him a lesson one afternoon in his Nissan, but that was a while ago and Science was rusty. The little Mini stalled out every time they reached a red light. Science was sure the drivers honking their horns behind him would get him made, but Mr. Freeze kept right on going.

It wasn't much easier when they got on the 101 and headed east toward downtown. Twice Science stalled when the traffic stopped, but soon he got the hang of it and discovered that if he just kept the car in second gear the whole way, he'd be fine.

Zarate had the radio tuned to some talk radio station and Science was about to change it when the topic of Frank Peres's murder came up. There was a lot of speculation as to what happened that night. Even more about the *deviants* who shot him and just what they were up to that night. There was mention of some shit that had happened in New York's Central Park a million years ago and another caller brought up a similar incident in Long Beach. The consensus was that these uneducated little thugs in North Hollywood had no idea that they were beating and then murdering the next mayor of L.A. That maybe Kelly Maguire had been crude and insensitive, but she wasn't wrong.

Oddly enough, Science wasn't upset. He felt that same sense of certainty he had the other night. This was just like the rest of it. Where he was, in this car, right now. It was fate.

A few cars ahead, Mr. Freeze suddenly got off onto the 110 toward Pasadena and Dodger Stadium. Science veered into the exit lane after him and dug into his pocket for his phone.

thirty-six

Roy spent a couple of nights in a couple of different shitty motels in North Hollywood and Reseda before stealing a white Honda Civic from the car wash on Cahuenga Boulevard and driving from there to Martin Shine's apartment. He would keep the car for an hour and then steal another off the street near Shine's place. But when Roy pulled up to the boatlike building and saw the yellow tape crisscrossing Shine's front door, he knew it didn't matter whether he got picked up in this car or another one just like it.

For all of his experience and caution the past twenty years, he had made a careless mistake and would now almost certainly go down for it.

He had hoped to come pick up the body and dump it somewhere on the way out of the city, but clearly that option was no longer available. The only reason he'd left Shine there to begin with was because there was no DNA, no witness, and, therefore, no way to connect Roy Cooper to Martin Shine in any way.

But by now Kelly Maguire would surely have figured out that the bullets in Martin Shine and Frank Peres came from the same gun, the bodies falling a mere two blocks away from each other. And while Roy had that gun once more in his possession, he knew that it didn't matter. Science or, more likely, one of the other little gangsters would certainly get picked up and eventually talk about where it had come from.

For the first time, Roy, the invisible man, had been made.

He drove around the corner and found the alley without any trouble. How had he gotten so lost that night? Even in the dark, it made no sense. He parked in the same spot he had left his rental car and got out. He looked at all of the flowers and balloons that had been left in the alley across the street.

Where would he go? Where *could* he go? He could hide, he knew how to hide. But when he thought about it, it was probably too late for that as well. He couldn't leave just yet anyway. The only thing he really cared about was the game at Dodger Stadium later that night. Once he saw The Kid break the record, and Roy knew that he would, he didn't much care what happened after that. Bust him, kill him—it was all the same to Roy.

But then he thought about the last call he had with Rita and Harvey two days earlier. He was sound asleep in a place called the Star Light Inn in Reseda when his phone rang.

"Good-bye, son."

"Harvey?"

"Rita and me are going away."

"When?"

"Right now. Today. But I wanted you to know that you're on your own. Don't come back here."

Roy could hear Rita in the background telling Harvey to hang the fuck up, they gotta go.

"You'll be fine, Roy. You always have been."

And then Rita's voice, *He's not gonna be fucking fine. Quit telling him that. Gimme the fucking phone.* And then she was on.

"Albert's coming."

Roy took that in.

"Did you hear me?"

"I heard you."

"He just called here," she said. "He knows you're still breathing and he's coming for you. And then, of course, he'll come for us."

Roy said, "I didn't know that he was alive."

"Sure, you did. A part of you had to."

"You never said anything."

"What would have been the point?"

"I can think of a few."

"You fucked us, Roy, like I always knew you would."

"Good-bye, Rita."

"Good-bye to you, too. I hope that psychotic French cunt finds you and turns you the fuck off forever."

"Albert's Canadian."

"Fuck you, Roy."

And she was gone.

As if the ground in L.A. hadn't been shaking enough, now Albert had to show up. Roy knew that no one who had come into contact with Roy would be safe now. That's how Albert worked. It was, after all, what Albert had taught him: When in doubt, kill everybody.

Roy got back in the car, took out his phone, and Googled Dodger Stadium. It took him a few minutes, but he managed to start the active map and pulled out, ignoring Science in the yellow Mini Cooper behind him. Science was no longer his problem. If Albert knew that Roy was alive and well, his first move would surely be to wipe out everything Roy cared about, regardless of who else might get blown away in the process. It was the "who else" Roy worried about most. And for that reason alone, he had to get to Dodger Stadium before Albert did.

Part IV

thirty-seven

For nearly twelve years, Roy, Albert, and Bob Spetting lived on Harvey Cooper's farm in Higginsville several miles north of Slaughterhouse Bend, not far from where the Armour plant had been. The three of them would often drive to nearby Concordia or Sedalia to get drunk, or, less often, head east to Kansas City for a job.

When Roy first met Harvey, his wife, Rita, had just begun a four-year sentence for embezzlement at the Kansas Prison for Women in Topeka. Harvey was lonely and depressed and, for a few years at least, glad to have them all there. But twelve years later he was ready to chase them all out at gunpoint. And if "the Danny Leone thing" hadn't gone down the way it had in Waterloo, he probably would have.

Harvey Cooper was an old-school B&E man who at sixty-two had gotten into guns as a way to fill the time between jobs. He customized weapons for an assortment of "made assholes" in Kansas City and Chicago, specializing in everything from shotguns to World War II–era German Lugers. At some point, he started making his own ammo that, along with his carefully reconditioned firearms, made him a favorite at gun shows throughout the Midwest.

But Harvey's first love was stealing shit. And soon he and the boys were making a good deal of money breaking into jewelry stores, pawnshops, and other establishments that kept a lot of cash overnight.

Harvey, not Albert, was the leader of the Hole in the Wall Gang as they started calling themselves. So named not for Butch Cassidy, whom Albert and Bob had never heard of, but for Harvey's penchant for finding the blind spots in alarm systems, blowing or cutting a hole in the wall, and simply walking right on through. Harvey's particular stylistic hallmark also prompted his underworld handle, "Harvey Wallbanger."

Albert, of course, wanted to do more than rob pawnshops. As far back as Boonville, Albert had talked about getting into business with the mob in Kansas City. He had always felt that the real money was working for those guys, not for themselves. Harvey was reluctant. Right now they were in control of their own destiny. But that would go away the minute they became part of some "family." He argued that no mobster would ever really trust them. They couldn't get made. They would never see a fair share of anything.

And for a long time, Albert went along with Harvey. Not so much out of any kind of loyalty, as that he hadn't yet figured out how to actually meet anybody in the mob. To that end, Albert and Bob started to spend more and more time in Kansas City, hanging out in various mob bars, particularly one spot called Dewey's. They would sometimes stay there until four a.m. closing, then sleep in the car for a few hours before driving home.

Roy preferred to stay at home with Harvey rather than go out and get shitfaced with Albert and Bob. The man had a lot to teach and Roy enjoyed learning it. Everything from guns to the various ways death could be dealt. Harvey knew it all. He had been a demo specialist in the early days of Vietnam and had a lot of stories that Roy loved to hear. Harvey wasn't like Roy's father. He was steady and, more importantly, stable.

Roy kept waiting for them all to get caught, but they never once had so much as a close call. They felt as if no one would ever catch them and this bulletproof feeling made them all even closer.

They all ate together and drank together and, like some kind of demented family unit, celebrated holidays and birthdays together. Every Wednesday night, Harvey insisted they all stay home. He would make dinner, usually spaghetti or some kind of Shake 'n Bake, and then the four of them would watch a movie they had rented in town. Their favorites were *Casino* and *Field of Dreams,* both of which they'd watched more than a dozen times each. Albert would often quote lines from the two movies and, for a while, started to dress the way he thought De Niro probably did in real life. All slacks and leather coats. Though, Roy once saw a photo in a magazine of the actor on the street in New York and he was wearing corduroy pants, a shitty windbreaker, and what looked like Velcro sneakers. Roy never had the heart to share the photo with Albert.

Along with his guns, Harvey had begun working with copper, making weathervanes in particular. The garage was full of them— roosters, pigs, sheep, animals of all kinds. Harvey said that the pounding of the copper calmed him, and was good for his arthritis. Roy watched him work and would often help with the cutting and the welding.

Roy was twenty-eight then. Rita's sentence had been extended twice, once for beating the shit out of a guard who shut down some business she had, and another time for beating her cellmate over something Harvey wouldn't talk about. The old man had become sad most of the time and Roy didn't like leaving him alone. Harvey was sixty-two and already frail. At nearly six-six, he had joint problems and suffered from chronic vertigo. He had to walk with two canes in order to keep his balance.

One day, they were out in the workshop, listening to the A's-Royals game when Harvey handed Roy a small pistol. Roy weighed it in his hand and said, "It's heavier than it looks."

"It's the nickel," Harvey said. "I knew this hitter, Rollie Sanchez. Half black, half Cuban. Out of Florida. Rollie used to carry fourshot derringers, one in each sleeve. Then a larger piece, like a .38, on his ankle for backup. What he'd do, he'd flick his wrist and the guns would be there. I used to make him these special loads, blue hollowpoints, blow a hole in a man big as a hubcap. Anyway, that's his piece you're holding."

Roy checked out the gun a bit more carefully now. He liked the feel of the smooth bone handle and oily barrel.

"Where's the other one?" he asked. "You said he had two."

"It's with Rollie," he said. "Inside a barrel, at the bottom of Biscayne Bay." And then he smiled. "Or so I'm told."

He then nodded to the gun and said, "Keep it. It's yours."

"Really?"

"I want you to have it."

"It's a lady's gun, Harvey."

Roy turned to see Albert and Bob come in with another guy following them. The newcomer was blond, tall, and dressed like a surfer in a tank top, shorts, and flip-flops. He was one of those antsy guys who never stopped moving, was always looking this way and that, touching and tapping his fingers on everything in sight.

Roy noticed that Albert's face was bruised, there was dried blood on his lip. All three of them were drunk.

Albert snatched up the gun.

"Look at this, it's a toy. Ken shoots Barbie with a gun like this. What are you giving my boy such toys for?"

My boy. Roy not sure how he felt about that. Albert talking about him like he was a little kid. Roy could see the blond guy looking at him funny, wondering the same thing. Wondering what people always wonder: What's wrong with him?

Albert pointed the gun at Bob, who grinned back up the barrel at him.

Harvey said, "Careful."

Albert ignored him, said, "To shoot someone with one of these, you have to be very very close. No accuracy from anything more than twenty feet."

Harvey said, "You don't know what the fuck you're talking about," and then looked at the surfer and asked, "Who's your friend?"

Albert ignored the question and pulled the trigger, sending the creases of Bob's delighted moron-smile to the outer reaches of his cheeks.

Harvey grabbed his canes and stood up and asked the blond guy directly, "What's your name?"

"Yeah," Albert said. "What's your name again?"

The man smiled warmly and extended his hand to Harvey. "I'm Danny. Danny Leone," he said. "I've heard a lot about you, Mr. Cooper."

"From who?"

"Teddy Bruno. Jim Pyle. I was in Lansing with those two assholes." Another smile.

Harvey ignored the proffered hand and the smile and said to Albert, "I wanna talk to you. You, too, Bob." He started hobbling into the other room.

Albert looked at Roy and winked. "Uh-oh. Dad's pissed."

They went into the kitchen as Danny walked over and watched Roy try to put the gun up his sleeve. Roy didn't look up at him, lost in childlike concentration until he dropped the piece on the floor. Roy turned red, refused to look at Danny as he bent down and retrieved it.

They could hear Harvey in the other room. "Where'd you meet him?"

"Dewey's."

"You meet a guy in a bar and you bring him out *here*? Are you out of your fucking mind?"

Roy looked into the kitchen and could see Harvey swing one of his canes at Albert. Albert made a move to hit back when a six-inch blade came out of the bottom of the cane. Albert stayed put and started laughing.

"Very nice, Harvey."

Danny asked, "This happen a lot?"

Roy wiped off the gun and said, "Yep."

"That's a nice piece."

"Thanks." Roy still wouldn't look at him. He was trying again to figure out how to get the gun into his sleeve.

Danny sat down at the table, bounced his leg up and down, and listened to the ball game a moment. "I saw The Kid play in Anaheim. One of his first games. He was cool as a cuke, rare for someone's just twenty."

"He's nineteen."

"Lot of power for someone so small."

"Weighs one fifty-five."

"If he takes care of himself, he'll be around for a long time."

From the kitchen: "Danny's good people, Harvey, wants to work with us."

"So what?"

"People vouch for him."

"What people? A couple of stick-up morons I haven't talked to in ten years."

Bob said, "He punched Albert," and then let out one of his sharp laughs. "Then he kicked him in the fucking head. Just spun around like Bruce Lee and tagged him."

Roy looked up at Danny Leone now.

"Albert said some shit about his shirt and why was he barefoot and Danny clocked him."

Danny Leone smiled at Roy, nodded to the gun and said, "If you want, I'll show you how to do that."

Harvey would never completely trust Danny and it was six months before he let him come out on his first job. But Danny quickly proved himself a skilled thief, one who could handle any tool or piece of equipment and he never lost his cool. He had experience with acids as well as explosives and Harvey, though he would never admit it, came to depend on him. Harvey did, however, forbid him to chew any gum on the job as the guy was so fucking intense with his nonstop bubble blowing and energetic chomping it drove all of them crazy. They eventually found that the best way to mellow out all that energy was to let him take a monster bong hit right before they got out of the car.

While it was Albert who had brought him in, it was Danny and Roy who became close. It wasn't long before Danny began hanging out with him in Harvey's workshop. At night, if there was ever a disagreement over where to eat or which movie to rent, Danny almost always sided with Roy. He was protective of Roy and, having grown up with three sisters, liked to call him the little bro he never had.

Although never in front of Albert.

Danny told Roy stories about growing up in the Huntington Beach surf culture, about being eleven years old and getting punched in the face while sitting on his board after stealing a wave from an older rider. He told Roy about the thirty-foot day he nearly killed himself at the Wedge in Newport and bagged the water for the next four years.

Danny loved everything about California and was desperate to go back. He had stupidly come to Missouri following some girl, got into trouble because of her, and ended up in Lansing for eighteen months. He was trying to save up enough money, get back to Huntington where he and some buddies from high school had plans to start a surf shop. Danny wanted Roy to come with him, promising that his friends would be Roy's friends. He said Roy could start all over in a place like California. It was the reason people went there. He was sure that Roy would love it.

Roy never saw Danny with a woman. He never showed any interest in anyone in particular, though they all showed a lot of interest in Danny. It wasn't as if Roy had anyone either. The only women he'd been with were prostitutes and that was fine with him. He didn't need anybody. But in the bars, Danny would draw all of the women, then go home with none of them.

This fascinated Albert, who would pick up women most nights of the week, but never bring them back to the farm. He would always find some place in the back of the bar, or a car or an alleyway, to complete whatever transaction Albert was in the mood for. He had no particular taste that Roy could see. Albert's women came in all shapes and sizes, and were of all ages and races. One or two were missing a limb. Roy could recall one particular paramour named Shauna whose face and arms were covered with burn scars. She was actually the closest thing Albert had to a girlfriend, that one lasting a couple of months before Shauna disappeared.

Albert had all along felt that the real money was in murder for hire. Harvey said that he would need to be sanctioned for something like that and Leo Bianchi, the man who, at the time, ran Kansas City, would never endorse an outsider like Albert. Albert argued that once the man got to know him, Albert would be embraced like a long lost member of the family.

Harvey said that he would more likely be garroted in a dark parking lot, then sawed into chunks and distributed to various dumpsters throughout the city.

"You get mired or dragged down into some family bullshit," Harvey warned, "you drag all of us down with you. Remember that."

"Or I lift you all up," Albert said. "Look at it that way."

"How do you even get in a room with Leo Bianchi?"

"Getting in a room with him is the easy part. It's getting him to look my way that's the trick."

One afternoon, Roy and Danny were watching the Royals lose to the Brewers. The Kid, still a rookie, was having a rare off day, when

Albert got a phone call. He listened for a few seconds, then hung up and announced they all were going to a bar downtown.

Roy didn't want to go, he was happy right where he was, in Harvey's living room. Danny, as usual, agreed. Albert said that he could watch the game at the bar. Roy thought about pushing it, but Albert gave him a look that said, *Get the fuck up and get in the fucking car.*

"Are you going to be antisocial?"

They were all sitting at a table in an old topless place called the Play Room on Hunter Avenue. Albert had kicked out three gentlemen who had been sitting there, explaining to Roy that he'd have the best view of the TV from here. Roy thought the best place to sit would have been the bar, but today wasn't the day to argue about anything. Everyone and everything seemed to annoy Albert. At the moment, he was pissed off that Roy hadn't said a word since they got there.

Roy said, "The game's almost over" without looking at Albert, who had chosen a red beret and a denim jacket with the sleeves cut off to wear in public. The place was crowded and they were all jammed around the tiny table.

"Roy loves his baseball," Albert said to no one. "Especially that itty-bitty pitcher, The Boy."

"The Kid."

"Whatever."

Albert's chair jumped and he turned around and looked at some pumped-up roid freak in jeans and an Izod shirt sitting at another table with an old dude in a black suit and two women in furs. The old guy had the look of somebody of note while the women were clearly both on the clock. The muscle went with the old man. He was watching the game and absently bouncing his leg, unaware that he was kicking Albert's chair.

"The Kid did a Right Guard commercial," Danny was now saying. The man's head hadn't stopped swiveling since they sat down. He kept turning it this way and that. He finally looked at Roy. "You catch that, Roy?"

Roy nodded. "I thought he was good."

Bob laughed and said, "Roy's his biggest fan," when the bodyguard once more kicked Albert's chair. This time Albert leaned back and twisted his upper body toward the other table. He smiled at the two hookers, then craned his neck to look at the old guy.

"Pardon me," he said. "But is there some reason your boy keeps kicking my chair?"

The old guy looked at him, annoyed, and said, "What?"

"Your muscle," Albert said. "He keeps kicking my chair. It's distracting."

The old guy looked at Albert, then at the bodyguard, and said, "Larry, quit kicking this asshole's chair."

The bodyguard shrugged and said, "I didn't know that I was doing it." And then he smiled at Albert and whispered, "Excusez moi, amigo."

Bob said, "Did you know that fan is short for fanatic?"

Albert sat forward and said, "I did know that, Bob, as I was the one who told *you*."

They sat there for another ten minutes until Roy caught Albert watching the bodyguard get up and head for the john in the back. Albert waited a three count and then stood up and said to Danny Leone, "Order us another round." Roy understood the look on Albert's face and automatically got up and followed him back. Danny stopped his bouncing and started to follow, but Bob put a hand on his leg and said, "Let's watch the game, so we can tell Roy what he missed."

Albert and Roy walked into the bathroom, Roy locking the door behind them, just as the big bodyguard was turning away from one of the urinals. He saw Albert and smiled. "Hey, it's *Pepe Le Pew*."

Albert said, "That's funny," and reached out and gently touched the man on the side of the neck.

The bodyguard recoiled and said, "What the fuck?" then sank to his knees and began pawing at himself where Albert had made contact.

He stared straight ahead, confused, and said, "Oh, God," his head lolling to one side as blood began roaring through his fingers. He felt the warmth and removed one hand and stared stupidly at the sticky liquid, somehow not understanding where it had come from. "Jesus Christ."

"No, no," Albert said. "Keep your hand there." He then crouched down in front of him, helped him put his hand back on his neck, and said, "Keep pressure on it. I don't want you to pass out just yet."

The bodyguard looked up as Albert held up a miniature knife for him to see, nestled in the palm of his hand.

"I call this one *Stuart Little* on account of how small it is. But then, as you can now see, size doesn't matter, does it?"

"I feel sick."

Albert helped the man sit all the way down on the floor and looked him over.

"Tell me—Larry is it?"

"Uh-huh—"

"Tell me, Larry, do you work out a lot?"

"Every day." For some people, it apparently takes a lot more than pain and looming death to keep vanity at bay.

"I can see that." Albert nodded and sat back. "But not me. I hate exercise. In fact, I'm in terrible shape. But I do know the names of all the muscles. For example, the one I just severed in your neck is called the sternocleidomastoid. It's a tendon that runs from the back of your big ears down and around to your sternum. That's why you can't keep your head up. Stay awake please."

The bodyguard started to fall over, but Roy helped Albert steady him.

"Now you were very disrespectful to me in there," Albert went on. "What I'm thinking is that maybe you don't know who I am."

"Who are you?"

"That's what I thought," Albert said and then stood up and loomed over the man like some kind of terrible shadow. "I'm Albert Budin."

"Albert—"

"Al-bare Boo-dan."

"Okay. I'm sorry, Mr. Boudan."

"That's all right, Larry. It's not like I'm some big movie star like Mickey Rourke and you'd be stupid not to recognize me. I'm just a working man, like you."

"I'm sorry, Mr. Boudan, I didn't know it was you."

Someone knocked on the door. Roy banged on it with the bottom of his fist and shouted, "Occupied!"

Albert said, "That's my point. You didn't know who I was. So you didn't know what I could do to you. You didn't know that I carry this small knife in my sleeve that can cut you ear to ear, just like you didn't know about this piece I have in my belt."

He lifted his shirt so that Larry the bodyguard could see a .32 nestled there.

"You didn't know these things, which is why you shouldn't have mouthed off to me like I'm just another low-level finger-breaker like you. You should have shown me some respect, just in case. Don't pass out yet, Larry. *Do not pass out.*"

"I'm sorry . . ." Barely above a whisper now.

"In French, we say *Mille fois pardons.* A thousand apologies."

"What?"

And then he tipped forward, his chin all the way to his chest, the blood from his neck dumping into his lap.

Albert kicked him over and said, "Apology accepted." He stared at him another minute, then turned to Roy and said, "Have you got a pen?"

Albert walked back out into the bar, sat down in what had been Larry's chair across from the old man, and said, "Hello, Mr. Bianchi. My name and number are written on your boy's forehead."

The old man started looking around for his muscle. Albert jerked a thumb toward the back and said, "He's in the john."

Albert smiled and leaned forward.

"At some point, I'd love to sit down and talk business with you. Talk about how I can make you safer and richer at the same time." He then kissed the hand of one of the hookers, smiled, and said, "*Au revoir,* ladies."

Naturally, Harvey was furious when he found out about Albert's dumbass move. "You killed the man's muscle?"

"He knows I have balls."

"What he knows is that you're out of fucking control."

"On the contrary, I was completely *in* control. Ask them." He nodded to where Roy, Bob, and Danny all sat on the couch like scolded teenagers, trying to look anywhere but at Harvey.

The old man shook his head, began to hobble out of the room, and said, "We're all dead."

Two days later the call came. Bianchi wanted to meet. Harvey was certain that Albert wouldn't leave the meeting alive. Albert insisted that the meeting be with his whole crew and, to everyone's surprise, Bianchi agreed.

Harvey refused to come along. He again stressed that this was good for Bianchi, bad for them. They don't need to do this. Albert said, "Do what you want," then spent the better part of an hour in the shower, another half hour shaving, and then asked Roy to cut his hair. He insisted that Bob wear clean clothes and spent some time alone with Bob, presumably going over how to behave, what to say, and most importantly in Bob's case, what not to say.

Danny was nervous, bouncing off the walls even more than usual. He confided in Roy that this would be an entirely different league for him. He didn't want to be a part of something like this, especially if he ever wanted to get back to California. He said to Roy, "You shouldn't do this."

"Why not?"

"You should split," Danny said. "Right now."

"Where would I go?"

The meeting was at a steakhouse. It was three o'clock in the afternoon and Leo Bianchi, the only customer, sat at a booth in the back reading a newspaper. A waiter set down an espresso and disappeared while two ape-shapes in slacks and tight polo shirts got up from an adjacent table and began frisking everyone.

Albert smiled at them. "Leo's new muscle."

They looked like they wanted to spit in his face.

One of them looked at Roy and said, "Your daddy know you're here?"

Albert said, "He's twenty-eight. Probably older than you are. And he killed his daddy. When he was eleven."

Leo Bianchi didn't look up from his paper as he motioned them all to sit, went back to stirring his coffee.

"Mr. Bianchi," Albert began, "I've brought you a tribute."

Albert then dropped a handful of diamonds onto the tablecloth in front of him. Bianchi ignored them and said, "Albert Budin." He then looked up at Albert over the top of the paper and said, "Your mama disowned you."

Albert just smiled.

Bianchi carefully folded the newspaper and reached for a black cigarette case as he continued. "There's a story I heard not too long ago, that you fucked the wife of a dead friend before the man's body even got cold. That was *after* you cheated the same friend out of fourteen grand, and then lost twenty pounds so that you could fit into the dead man's clothes. You then got the wife pregnant, beat her so that she lost the kid, and then you split." Bianchi then picked up his coffee and said, "Have I left anything out, Monsieur Budin?"

"Yes, you have. You neglected to mention that I was the one who killed this man in the first place."

Leo B stared at Albert, not so much studying him as deciding what he wanted to do with him and how he wanted to do it. For the first time in a long time, Roy felt the desire to run.

"And so," Bianchi said, "today, you come to me asking for my sanction, but only after you kill my bodyguard and only after you and your so-called crew," he waved a dismissive hand at Roy and the others, "have already robbed in my territory."

"That's all true."

"So tell me, Mr. Budin, why should I bother talking to you at all? Why shouldn't I have Theo and Chris throw your frog ass out a fucking window?"

Albert leaned forward. "First of all, Mr. Bianchi, I'm not French. I'm Canadian." Then he smiled at the old man and said, "It's an easy mistake to make, I know, because of my accent."

Bianchi cut a look at the two bodyguards. *Can you believe this guy?*

Roy thought that he might be able to get a gun away from one and shoot the other one with it. But only if Danny and Bob got up when he did. And even then, Roy made their chance of getting out in one piece less than even.

"Second of all," Albert went on, "my mother, God rest her soul, was a drug addict and a prostitute who OD'd a week after I was born on a speedball that, from all accounts, was so hot that her loving generous heart exploded."

Albert then leaned forward, clasped his hands, and rested his arms on the table.

"Finally," he said. "We both know that the man you referred to earlier, the one I killed, was Kolby Beck. Your personal chef and a snitch about to give you up to the FBI in return for a new zip code. Had Kolby lived to do this, you and I would not be sitting here having this nice conversation. You'd be in Leavenworth with the rest of your *familia* cooking your orechetta on a fucking hotplate."

After hearing the story, Harvey couldn't believe that they were all still breathing. Bob and Danny were laughing and drinking one beer after another just to calm down. Albert was laughing, too, like it was all no big thing, but Roy could see there was something else there. This was important to Albert, a long fermented ambition. For the first time, he cared about something, and wanted to make it work.

Bianchi had offered them a job right there in the room. He gave them a grand up front to shoot a man named Gale Collins, recent resident of the federal prison in Joliet and now living in Kansas City. The man's sudden parole was suspiciously coincidental to the capture of an Italian American fugitive who, until recently, had been living under an assumed name in Legion, Nebraska, for the past eighteen years.

The job was important to him, so Albert wanted to get every detail right. They would watch Collins's house, follow him everywhere for a week, and then once they knew his schedule, they would grab him up, take him to an isolated spot that Albert had long ago scouted along the Republican River, and shoot him. They would then put him in a barrel, fill it with acid, seal it, and sink it.

But from the minute they started their surveillance of the house, Roy knew that something was wrong.

The four of them were parked out front of the little house in the mostly industrial area of the West Bottoms. Bob and Albert up front. Danny and Roy in the back. They had enough food, dope, and beer to last a week.

For the first two days they watched the house and never once saw Gale Collins. They didn't see *anyone* until the third day when a woman showed up and went inside with her own key. The woman was Hispanic, looked to be about thirty, and dressed in some kind of domestic uniform. She would turn out to be the only person they saw going in or going out. The curtains were pulled on all of the windows, so there was no way to look inside and see if the man was actually there or not.

But they could *hear* him.

On several occasions, during the night, the lights would come on and they'd hear the man yelling at someone. Twenty minutes later the woman would show up. There would be some more yelling, before the house would go quiet for the night.

Finally, on the fifth night, they were sitting out there in the rain, watching the house, when Albert said, "Fuck this," and got out of the car. They watched as he went around the back and disappeared. A light went on inside, then off. Ten minutes later he came jogging back to the car and sat there staring straight ahead for a minute before Bob, sitting behind the wheel, finally spoke.

"You do him?"

"Nope."

"Is the guy even in there?"

"Yep."

"So—"

"Shut up, Bob."

Albert then turned around and looked at Roy.

"You go."

"Me?"

"No sense in all of us going in and marking the place up."

Albert opened the glove box and then turned back to Roy holding a .22 target pistol with a silencer attached.

He said, "One to the ear. One to the back of the head. One under the chin. Put the other three wherever you want, I don't care as long as you come back with an empty gun."

Danny reached for the gun and said, "I'll do it."

Albert pulled it away, said, "Roy's going to do it," and put the piece in Roy's hand.

Albert then turned back around and faced front. "The back door is unlocked."

Roy got out of the car and crossed the street, too distracted to feel the rain. The house was one of only three left in a neighborhood otherwise full of warehouses and manufacturers. Roy found the back door, paused to look up at a tall dark building that hovered over the house, the name KC BOLT & SCREW stenciled eighty years ago, but still visible on the rotting wood.

Everything about this neighborhood seemed wrong.

Roy took a breath, opened the door, went inside, and was immediately hit with the twin odors of fried fish and VapoRub. He felt his eyes water and pulled the neck of his shirt up over his mouth and nose. He was standing in a small kitchen, and even in the dark could see that nearly every inch of counter space was covered with dirty dishes or trash of some kind. He heard the TV in the living room, local news it sounded like, and put his hand on the gun in his pocket and started moving.

It was even darker in the front room with just a tiny square of light coming from the portable TV sitting on top of a card table. Roy stood for a moment behind a couch that split the room. There didn't seem to be anyone in here. Roy tried to pull the gun, but it caught in his coat pocket and he dropped it on the floor with a loud clunk.

There was a groan from the couch and Roy froze as an old man sat up on the couch right in front of him.

"Who's there?"

He fumbled about and turned on a light.

The guy had to be ninety. Beneath a few wisps of gray hair were a pair of watery yellow eyes set into a face the color of faded cardboard. Whatever the man was sick with, it was eating him from the inside out.

"Claudia?"

Roy retrieved the gun, came around, and asked, "Are you Gale Collins?"

The man squinted at him. "Jacob?" He then stood up and said, "C'mon, help me, I gotta piss."

The man grabbed a walker and started down a short hall. Roy saw a light go on and the old man turned and looked back.

"You just gonna stand there?"

Roy didn't know what to do, so he put the gun back in his pocket and started down the hall to the bathroom.

The old guy turned around and said, "I can't do the buttons."

Roy looked at his pants, stained in the front, and then up at the guy, who waited.

Fuck.

Roy unbuttoned the man's pants. Then helped him get them and his reeking boxer shorts down around his ankles.

"I gotta sit," the man said. And fell back onto the john. "Like a girl."

Roy turned away as the man began to urinate and fell back asleep on the toilet.

Now Roy understood why Albert was upset. Leo Bianchi had fucked with him. This was no job. This was an insult. Payback for Albert's disrespect. Of course, Albert wouldn't play along, so he sent Roy into the house. Roy was the only choice. Bob and Danny would forever question him if they saw what the job was. Harvey, if he were to find out, would certainly never let Albert forget it.

But Albert knew that, of all of them, Roy would say nothing. Roy would always protect him, because Roy would always owe him that much.

"I'm hungry."

Roy saw that the old man was once more awake and struggling to stand. Roy pulled him off the john and helped him get his pants up.

"I want some Jell-O."

And so Roy led him into the filthy kitchen and sat him down at a table covered with pill vials and old magazines. He found a bowl of green Jell-O in the refrigerator and brought it along with a spoon he fished out of the muddy sink to the table.

"I need my medicine." The old man nodded to the vials on the table. "She puts it in the Jell-O."

"Which one?"

"I don't know."

Roy looked at the man and for a moment saw the old guy who had pulled his father out of the sinking car and saved his life. Gale Collins looked like a man at that advanced age where the animal part of him starts to take over the human part. Roy looked at the table and realized that he had just been given a way out.

He grabbed several of the vials and went to the sink and dumped the pills onto the counter. The old man fell asleep in the chair while Roy crushed up the pills from three different vials. He couldn't identify the medicines, but was reasonably certain that, whatever they were, the amount would be enough to kill Gale Collins.

That task done, Roy sat down at the table and shook him by the shoulder.

"Hey."

He pushed the bowl of Jell-O in front of him.

The man took a bite and winced. He looked up at Roy. His eyes seemed to clear as he studied Roy for a good long while. He then dipped his spoon back in the Jell-O and said, "You're a good boy, Jacob."

Albert was standing in the backyard getting soaked by the rain when Roy finally slipped out the door.

"What the fuck took so long?"

Roy just stood there. Albert held out his hand.

"Give me the gun."

He passed it to Albert, who checked it and looked up at him, his face a question.

"I gave him some pills."

"Pills?"

"He's sick. He's gonna go anyway."

Albert shook his head and started for the house. Roy called after him. "Bianchi's fucking with us, Al."

Albert ignored him and went into the house. Roy stood there a moment, then went in after him.

Roy had helped the old man back onto the couch and he was out cold when Albert found him and slapped his face, "Gale. Wake up."

The old man opened his eyes and Albert shot him in the head.

The following day, Albert, Roy, Danny, and Bob—each armed with a shotgun sawed off by Harvey the night before and full of his custom loads, walked into Leo Bianchi's restaurant and quickly cut down both of his bodyguards before spreading a screaming Leo B all over the wall behind his favorite booth.

And while it all went without a hitch or a witness (the staff stayed hidden in the kitchen), Roy wondered why Danny's shots all went wide. Albert may have wondered the same thing, for it would be a long time before he brought him along on any hits, letting him work the robberies only.

And there were a lot of hits. Albert became a kind of folk hero and for a time that led to all kinds of work. So much work they couldn't keep up with it. Leo Bianchi's death set up a long-brewing war for control in Kansas City, one that would end with pretty much everybody losing and K.C. becoming a wide-open city.

Rita, freshly paroled and anxious to do something beyond cook for and clean up after Harvey and his crew of assholes, took over managing the money and running the murder for hire side of things. She knew a lot of people, had been with all of the old guys at one time or another and was still trusted by them. Albert would jokingly refer to her as their "agent."

Rita said to Harvey that if they could just sock away enough money, put enough "nuts in their cheeks for a long winter," they could get the fuck out of Missouri. Something Rita had been urging since before her trip to Topeka. She just had to finish out her parole.

Within a year, Harvey and the boys had garnered a near legendary reputation as fixers, killers, and thieves. Drinks were bought wherever they went. Girls followed. They earned approving nods from men who would have scared the shit out of most anyone else. Even Bob landed himself a steady lady. Though "lady" was somewhat of a loose description given she was at least twenty years Bob's senior, outweighed him by a good fifty pounds, and had previously worked in such varied fields as roller derby and the rodeo.

Harvey didn't trust any of it and kept saying to Roy, whenever they were alone in the workshop, that it was all too easy. Why hadn't they even had a single conversation with anyone in law enforcement? They had to be on some agency's radar. Furthermore, Roy noticed that Albert was starting to become cocky and careless. The very qualities that his father said would kill pilots. Worse, Albert's behavior "in the field" as they called it, was becoming increasingly sadistic. He enjoyed torturing people. He would stand over a "client," announce that they had violated some code or another and, therefore, needed to suffer a long, drawn out death.

What finally ended their run wasn't so much Roy's growing distaste for Albert's behavior, or the law—though the FBI certainly played their part. In the end, the person who brought them down, who blew them apart, was the same person who, in a way, had brought them all together: Roy's mother.

One day in Kansas City, Roy and Danny had been in a bar watching the Royals lose when Danny asked Roy to show him his old neighborhood. They drove over in Danny's old Saab and Roy told him the story of his father, the plane they tried to build together and how he had really died. Danny asked a lot of questions, particularly about Roy's mother and little brother. Where were they? Why didn't Roy try to find them? Roy didn't see the point. He remembered the way his mother had looked at him during her one and only visit to Boonville. He was certain that she would never let him speak to his brother again.

It took Danny less than a week to find her.

While it wasn't much of a shock to learn that she had long ago divorced Dr. Toomey, Roy was somewhat surprised that his mother had remained in Kansas City, living for the past three years in a two-bedroom apartment in Quality Hill. She had hated Kansas City, all of the Midwest, for that matter. Roy had always assumed that the minute she could, she would have fled.

Danny wanted to drive over right away, but Roy argued that showing up unannounced would likely upset her, make her defensive, and ultimately hurt his cause. The best thing to do, he thought, was to call first, give her time to think about a meeting. She might hang up on him, might not give him any chance to say what he needed to say, but at least she would know that he had found her, and could find her again. If she still resisted, he would go see her and make his plea in person. The bottom line remained, if Roy wanted to see his brother, there was no choice but to go through his mother.

Nearly twenty years had passed since Roy had last seen The Captain: eight years in Boonville and another twelve on the farm with Harvey. And though his brother would be twenty-one now, Roy was no longer sure of his own age. It didn't matter; Roy had died and was also born again in Boonville. Raytown, whenever that was, had been another lifetime. That wasn't him. It seemed impossible now to see himself then, running away from Jim McDonald, or cowering in the halls of middle school. The image of the boy afraid of everything around him had long since faded away.

Roy wondered if his little brother even knew of Roy's existence. He doubted it. He doubted his mother would ever tell him, or anyone, about his older brother. She, too, was born again when Roy went off to Boonville.

To Roy's surprise, she sounded genuinely excited to hear from him. Though Roy got the feeling he had woken her up in the middle of a nap, there was eagerness in the gasp and hitch of her voice, and as soon as he explained who he was, she said, "Sweetie, of course I know who you are! I'm so happy you called!"

She pushed for him to come see her as soon as he could. *Please, sweetie. Right away. Tomorrow maybe?*

Roy asked about his younger brother, could he see him, too? She said yes, of course, Roy *had* to see him and she would do what she could to make that happen. *Just please come as soon as you can!*

Danny suggested that Roy keep this visit to himself. He needn't have bothered. Roy knew full well that Albert would never understand and would, in fact, actively try to prevent this meeting from happening. He had always maintained a *They're all dead to you* position and would argue that any effort to make contact with his family would be a disloyal step backward and only lead to disappointment.

Harvey and Rita would certainly feel the same way, but then Harvey considered himself Roy's father now and would see any contact with his mother as some sort of threat to his own standing. He was right to worry about losing Roy. For once Roy saw his brother, he would explain to him what had happened and why he had disappeared, that it was for *him,* and then the two of them would start over. Roy would get a regular job somewhere far from this place and look after his brother for the rest of his life. He would keep the promise he had made twenty years ago. And nowhere in that plan was there room for Harvey or Albert or anyone else.

His mother's apartment was on the second floor of a recently redone brick five-floor on the corner of Broadway Boulevard and West 10th Street, across from the Quaff Bar & Grill, where Roy sat with Danny nursing a single beer and waiting for his hands to stop shaking. He was still tight in the chest an hour later when he stood alone in the hall outside her apartment, as a small Asian man in blue scrubs answered the door.

"You must be Roy," he said, extending his hand. "I'm Paul."

Roy followed Paul into the cheerful living room. The curtains were open, and the place was all bright colors and sunshine. The opposite of the house Roy had grown up in. A line of silver-framed photographs of his mother and little brother over the years ran along a green marble mantel and on the trestle table that sat behind the peach-colored sofa. There were no pictures of Roy or his father.

Paul led him down a short hall and said over his shoulder, "She's very excited to see you. It's all she's been talking about."

Roy peered into the first bedroom. A brown leather jacket was draped over the back of a chair. On a desk were more photos. Roy knew that his brother stayed here. He might not be here now, but he definitely stayed in this very room. Roy relaxed and felt overcome with good feeling, until Paul led him into the *other* room.

She couldn't have weighed more than ninety pounds. She sat upright in her bed with her hair, clearly a wig, fanned across the pillow behind her. Roy noticed that she had made the effort to apply some makeup—pale blue eye shadow and pink lipstick—but her face still looked hollow, like it was somehow slowly being sucked back into her skull.

She reached out with shriveled hands attached to a pair of fleshy sticks and said, "Come here, sweetie."

Roy bent down to hug her and felt sharp bones cutting into his chest and caught the smell of a strong perfume mixed with Listerine, all of it making him dizzy.

"Sit down," she said. "Let me look at you."

Roy took the chair beside the bed and she gave him a long once-over.

"I never thought you would ever be so tall. Or so handsome."

Roy found it hard to recognize his mother inside this emaciated old child lying in a bed that reeked of looming death. She could see him working it out and smiled.

"It's everywhere," she said. "All over my body."

"I'm sorry."

"It came on so sudden. I can only imagine what I must look like to you."

"You look fine."

Roy's eyes stung and he fought the urge to break down in front of her. After all he'd been through, all she'd put him through, he was still somehow so moved to see her. In that room, at that moment, he was once more ten years old. It wasn't so much that he forgave her for anything, he didn't, as it was a recognition that, absurdly enough, he still needed her. And so he sat, momentarily unable to speak, confused and determined at the same time.

She looked down her starveling hands and said, "I know that you're not here to see me."

Roy sat up and cleared his throat. "Where is he?"

"He travels so much these days."

"He lives here?"

"He stays here sometimes, to be with me. But he has his own place. A condo he bought with his own money. Can you imagine that? Someone his age being able to do that?"

"I'd like to see him."

"And you will."

"When?"

She closed her eyes. "I'm in so much pain, sweetie. You have no idea. A drink of water, I can feel it all the way down, like a thousand icy pins in my throat."

"Can't they give you anything for it?"

"They do. But it's no way to live. Waiting to die. That's as unbearable as the pain. More so."

"It's just you and Paul here?"

She nodded.

"What happened to Dr. Toomey?"

"That only lasted a few years."

She seemed genuinely upset about it.

"I had a beau," she said, "but he disappeared the minute I got sick."

"I'm sorry."

"I don't blame him."

She smoothed out the sheet in front of her and said, "The doctors can't really do anything for me." And then she looked at Roy. "But you can."

"Me? What can I do?"

"If you help me, I'll help *you.*"

"Help you how?"

"The same way you helped your father."

He just looked at her.

"Do you understand?"

"I didn't do anything to my father."

She said, "Of course you did," and then leaned closer to him. "You put a pillow over his face and saved him from that awful bed."

Roy opened his mouth, but found that he couldn't speak.

"Please," she said, and then leaned forward, grimacing from the pain as she reached back and grabbed one of the pillows from behind her and held it out for Roy. "I'm in so much pain."

Roy looked down the hall.

"Paul's leaving to do the shopping."

Roy just looked at the pillow and said, "Why don't you ask my brother to *help* you?"

"He's not like you. He couldn't do it." She held out the pillow for him. "Please, Roy."

"If you're gone," he said, "you can't do anything for me."

"Paul will make the arrangements for you to see your brother."

"Paul?"

"He knows all about it."

"You talked about it?"

"Of course. He just wants me at peace."

Roy considered her a moment, and then asked, "How much are you giving him?"

"There's not much left to give."

"You don't want to say good-bye to the Captain?"

She smiled. "The Captain. I haven't heard that one in so long." She then looked at Roy and said, "I can't let him see me like this."

Roy looked once more into the other room where Paul was now quickly putting on his coat. Roy then stood up and took the pillow from his mother. He held it a foot or two above her face and said, "I forgive you, Mom."

She smiled that smile Roy remembered, the one that made Jim McDonald and the other kid whose name he'd long forgotten trip over themselves. She said, "I love you, too, Roy," and lay back and closed her eyes.

He looked down at her another moment, then started out of the room.

He could hear her behind him. "Roy?" And then: "Where are you going?"

He didn't look back.

She began screaming. *You'll never see him again! He's too good for you! You leave him be! You hear me! He has a good life now, don't you fucking dare ruin it!*

Roy handed the pillow to a confused Paul, said, "She's all yours," and walked out of there.

She died a month later *in the arms of her loving son Joseph,* or so Paul had informed Roy when he called, though how he had gotten Roy's number was a mystery. He wanted Roy to know that his younger brother would be at the funeral in case Roy wanted to pay his respects. But by then, Roy was on the run a good thousand miles away, and worried about his own funeral.

Danny was sitting in the car, his leg bouncing against the dash, getting stoned, when Roy came out of his mother's building and got in the car.

"How'd it go?"

Roy looked up at her window and said, "Great."

"She gonna set you up with your little bro?"

"You know what, Danny? Just drive us home."

"You okay?"

"I'm fine. Start the car."

Roy made him stop at a liquor store and bought a fifth of Jim Beam, most of which he drank before they were even out of the city limits.

It was dark when they turned down the dirt road to the Cooper farm. Roy sat in the car when Danny got out, stared at Bob in the window, helping Rita set out a couple boxes of pizza, which Albert was now opening. There was Harvey in his chair smoking a pipe.

One big happy family.

He watched as Danny walked inside and Albert asked him something, then came to the window and looked out. He waved a hand and mouthed *Get the fuck in here.* If he hadn't been so drunk, Roy would have slid over, started the car, and backed all the way up that dirt road.

Instead he stumbled out of the car and threw up. He took another minute to get himself together and then went inside for what would be the last time they would all be together.

Albert was hyped up and running on some chemical. He was talking a mile a minute and going on about how they had been summoned to a place in Waterloo, an hour drive from there. From what Roy could make out in his fucked-up state, apparently some asshole had been running an unsanctioned poker game in the city and was currently in some hideaway counting his money, or something like that. The current Number One in Kansas City—Roy couldn't remember his name—wanted the man turned off and any recovered cash brought to him. Same old bullshit.

What was new was how Albert asked Danny to come along. There was a strong likelihood that the guy in Waterloo had muscle around him, so they would need all hands for this one. Had he been sober, Roy might have been just a bit wary of the invite, given that Albert and Harvey had never trusted Danny with any wet work before this. But Roy, still reeling from the five minutes with his mother and the fifth of bourbon after that, had no such clarity. He was simply too drunk and too angry to know that Waterloo would turn out to be an apt name for the town where all of their good fortune would finally end.

Three hours later, they were parked some fifty yards away from the dark house. Albert had gotten out of the car and went ahead on foot to have a look around. This was farm country and the nearest neighbor was several miles away. A fact not lost on an increasingly nervous Danny.

"There's no one out here."

Roy could see that Danny was anxious. His hands were shaking, but, for the first time Roy could remember, the rest of him was stock-still. He turned and caught Roy staring at him.

"How long are you gonna stay pissed off at me?"

Bob looked at them in the rearview mirror. This wasn't the time to have this conversation.

"I'm not pissed."

"I was just trying to do something good, you know?"

"I know."

Bob said, "What are you two lovers fighting about?"

But before Danny could tell him to fuck off, the front door whipped open and Albert leaned in.

"We own the place."

Albert got back in the car while Danny pulled a .45 from his coat and checked it. Albert leaned over the seat and put a hand on the gun.

"No need for that," he said. "Turns out our guy's solo."

He smiled and opened up a couple of beers, turned and handed a can each to Danny and Roy. Opened two more for Bob and himself. Danny drank his in nearly one go. Roy didn't feel so good after all that bourbon, took a single sip, and set the can on the floor. Albert opened another and passed it back to a grateful Danny.

"*Merci.*"

Danny, relaxed now, looked at the house and asked, "What are we waiting for?"

"He's getting ready for bed. Might as well let him settle in. What's Harvey say, Roy?"

"No sense making it harder than it has to be."

"So very true."

Roy then got out of the car and threw up again. Albert rolled down his window. "You all right there?"

"I am now."

Albert looked at the house and said, "Fuck it, let's go."

The other three got out, Danny swaying from inhaling the beer or from nerves. As they started up the gravel drive, he asked, "What's the plan?"

Albert said, "The plan is we go in, we kill the guy, and then we leave."

"He's gotta be expecting us, or someone like us."

Albert put his arm around Danny and said, "I guarantee you, he's going to be very surprised."

It was getting colder by the minute and the night air smelled of snow, yet Roy was sweating. If he hadn't sobered up on the drive over, walking up to this black-shingled house definitely woke him up. Everything about the place was wrong. Roy could see through a grimy window that there was a dim light on inside, but no movement of any kind. He hung back as Albert opened the door and walked right on in as if he lived there. He stepped aside for Danny and Bob to follow and then turned back to Roy and smiled.

"You coming?"

The entire place seemed to sag in one direction. The floor was warped with boards missing here and there, and wallpaper peeled from bowed walls. The only furniture in the front room was a couch minus a cushion and a couple of lawn chairs with frayed webbing. A lamp with no shade sat on the floor throwing off light that seemed to end before it reached the walls, giving the room a weak, yellow-ish cast.

A woodshop was set up in the corner of the room. There was a wall of tools along with a table saw and a workbench. Beer cans and candy wrappers were strewn among scrap pieces of lumber and sawdust. The entire house smelled of mold and was, if possible, colder inside than out. The bones of the place chilled well past the point of ever warming up.

Danny took it all in and said with a nervous laugh, "Cozy."

Roy took a look down a short hall and peered into an empty bedroom. He took in the missing window and the torn-up floor and said, "There's nobody here."

When he turned back, Albert had Danny's .45 pointed at Danny's head.

"Al?" Roy said. "What are you doing?"

Bob stepped up beside Roy and put his gun to Roy. "I'll need whatever you brought."

Roy looked at Bob.

Albert said, "It's all right, Roy. We'll give it back when we're done. I just can't have you interfering. I know this asshole made you think he was a friend."

"What the fuck are you talking about?"

Danny looked at Albert, laughed without any heart. "Yeah, Albert, what the fuck are you talking about?"

Roy noticed now that Danny could barely keep his eyes open and asked, "You hit the beer with something?"

"Rita's Valium."

Bob reached behind Roy, into his waistband, and pulled the old Walther Harvey had handed him as they were leaving.

Albert considered Danny for a moment and said, "I've been trying to figure out why they picked you for this job."

"Why who picked me? For what job?" Danny looked like he might fall asleep standing up.

Albert snapped his fingers, startling him. "You're brave. That must be it."

Roy said, "You gonna tell me what's going on?"

"No, brave wouldn't be enough," Albert went on. "I wouldn't trust you, wouldn't take you in just because you were brave. There had to be another reason they liked you for this little gig."

Roy asked, "Who's *they*?"

Danny forced himself to stand up tall and look at Albert. "Seriously, what the fuck are you talking about?"

The calm, confident surfer Roy had confided in was becoming someone else, even while stoned on Rita's pills, even while trying to hold on to whatever it was he had been playing at the past year.

Albert smiled. "I'm just asking, what it is about you they thought I would . . . respond to?" Danny flinched slightly as Albert gently touched his chest and said, "I mean, exactly what kind of man do they think I am, Danny?"

Roy asked again, "Albert, who the fuck is *they*?"

Before Roy knew what was happening, Albert ripped open Danny's shirt and pointed to the microcassette taped to his chest. "Them," he said. "Them is they. They is them."

And while Bob started laughing, Roy couldn't accept what he was seeing.

"Danny?"

But now Danny was gone and some new person stood there staring back at Albert, fighting the Valium. "There are two agents parked just down the road from here. Four more in a chopper five thousand feet above your head."

Bob looked up at the ceiling.

"You and Bob need to put down your guns and step away."

Albert didn't move.

"Albert, listen to me," Danny said. "You need to do what I say, and you need to do it now."

Albert said, "Uh-oh."

"In another thirty seconds this place is gonna be full of agents."

"You wouldn't by chance be referring to the agents that have been watching Harvey's farm for the past three months, would you? Are those the agents you mean?"

Albert then leaned down and spoke into the wire, "Hello? Special Agent Keefer? Special Agent Goetz? Are you there?"

Bob reached into his coat and pulled two badge folders from his coat and tossed them at Danny's feet, the leather on both caked with blood.

All at once, Danny seemed to sag like the room.

"Apparently," Albert said, "they've been transferred to a better assignment."

Albert then removed two pairs of handcuffs from his own coat and held them up.

"I believe you know how to use these." He handed a pair to Danny. "Behind your back, please."

Roy watched as Danny did as he was told. There was no point in fighting. If Albert didn't shoot him, Bob would. Hell, if what Albert was saying was true, Roy was certainly thinking about it. He wondered about all those times he had spoken to Danny, who else had he been talking to?

Roy shoved Bob aside and walked over to him. "You're FBI?"

"DEA," Albert said. "On loan for this very special assignment."

Roy said, "What have you been waiting for?"

"He likes you, Roy. I'm sure he was hoping you'd get out before they made their move."

Danny said, "We never wanted any of you."

"Maybe not these two," Albert said. "But I made your partners following me a month ago."

"Don't flatter yourself. You're nothing compared to the Coopers."

"The Coopers are fucking geriatric."

"So they've made you think. They're smart, and they stay out of it, mostly by using you or others like you to keep clear and clean."

"Bullshit. Harvey *is* out of it."

"You put him in it the minute you took out Leo Bianchi for him."

"I didn't do that for *him*."

"Didn't you?"

Albert looked at Bob and the two of them started laughing at the thought of the old couple pulling strings. But Roy could see that Danny was telling the truth; that Danny's instinct to protect Roy had been as genuine as Harvey's was calculated. But there was still no escaping that the man was the law and had come to put them all down.

"Will you look at the size of that vise."

Roy slipped out of his daydream and watched as Albert dragged a rheumy-eyed Danny over to the workbench and began to winch open the big iron vise mounted there. Roy realized now that it was the only thing in the place that was brand-new.

Roy asked, "What are you doing, Al?"

Albert smiled at Roy and said, "When you love someone, you

gotta trust them. There's no other way. You've got to give them the key to everything that's yours. Otherwise, what's the point?" He then looked at Danny and said, "And for a while, I believed, that's the kind of love I had."

"What is that? *Casino?*" Roy said. "You quoting a fucking movie now?"

"And then, boom! The fucking car blows up. You remember that? Right at the beginning? Was my second favorite scene."

Danny struggled as Albert now tried to bend him over and put Danny's head in between the iron jaws.

"Help me hold him."

Roy stayed put as Bob hurried over and leaned on Danny while Albert started to crank the vise tight around Danny's head. Danny opened his eyes and looked at Roy.

"Albert, just shoot him."

"When I'm ready." Albert looked at Bob, who opened his coat to show that he had Roy's gun. "Hold him, he's gonna buck." And then Albert slowly started to crank the vise shut. Danny screamed and thrashed, but Bob held on to him. Roy could see blood running down his cheeks and heard what sounded like a floorboard creak when one of his eyes seemed to collapse in the socket sending a threadlike stream of blood into Bob's face.

"Motherfucker—"

Roy heard a sound like nothing he'd ever heard before. The mewling of an infant mixed with the panicked cries of a trapped and wounded animal. Danny was screaming.

Albert was only cranking the handle a fraction of an inch at a time, but the pain it delivered increased a thousandfold with every push. Through it all Bob was laughing at the way Danny squirmed and fought. It was that laugh that finally pierced the new skin Roy had long ago created for himself.

He felt the cold night air, felt himself wake up after a twenty-year sleep. He felt the pistol in his sleeve slide into his palm, raised his arm, and fired twice. Not used to the little gun, his shots went low and he hit Albert in the chest with both pulls.

Bob backed away from Roy, looked at Albert lying on the floor, wheezing through the two small punctures.

Roy pointed the gun at him and said, "Do me a favor, Bob. Laugh."

"What the fuck did you just do?"

"You've got my gun along with one of yours. Put them both on the floor."

"There's only two shots in that thing."

"Wanna bet?"

Bob thought about it, then did as he was told.

There was a groan from the vise.

Roy motioned with the pistol. "Open it."

Bob opened the vise and Danny slid to the floor beside Albert. Roy grabbed Albert's gun and crouched down. Danny's head looked like it had been dipped in a bucket of blood. He was almost drowning in it. He looked at Roy with one white eye as Roy handed him Albert's gun.

"That's all the help you get from me."

Behind him, Roy heard Bob run out the door. Roy gathered up the remaining guns and walked out after him. Bob stumbled in the dark as he ran for the car, once going down face-first in the gravel.

"What's the matter, Bob?" Roy called out as Bob struggled to his feet ahead of him. "Isn't this funny?"

Roy raised his gun to tag him when there was a gunshot from inside the house, and Roy paused and looked back. There was no other sound until the car started and spit gravel as Bob drove away down the dark road.

It was an hour hike in the dark to a gas station along Route 14. Harvey told him he would call him back in fifteen minutes from another phone. He had known about Danny, and he and Rita had been operating for the past few months under the assumption that all of their phones were tapped.

When he called back, Roy could hear the sounds of a restaurant or bar in the background while he told his story. Harvey listened quietly and said to stay put, that Rita was already making calls to have it cleaned up. Later Roy would learn that "cleaned up" meant burned to the ground and the bodies all disappeared. Bob had not come home as yet, and Harvey didn't expect him to. Bob would run. He would eventually get picked up for something, but he'd never talk.

Harvey was more concerned about Roy. Where was he going to go?

Roy told him that he didn't know, but that he was done with all of them.

He heard Rita say, "Let me talk to him." And then she got on and said, "We'll kill your brother."

"What?"

"You run anywhere and he's dead."

"I'm already gone, Rita."

"We've got too much invested in you. You're gonna come with us."

"Where?"

"We'll let you know. East most likely. New York or Boston."

"Fuck you."

"Okay. But your brother is dead. Wherever he is. We'll get him. And the little baby his new wife is about to have. It's dead, too."

"Rita—"

But Harvey was back on the phone, and said in a cheerful voice, "She's letting me start my own business this time. We can all slowly move into something legit."

Like with Leo Bianchi before, Roy realized that he had just done the two of them a huge favor. They wanted Albert shut down and Roy just did that for them. They probably knew about Danny from the beginning. They probably told Albert about him.

"I won't live with you and Rita anymore."

"We'll find you a nice place."

"I'll find my own place."

"Sure."

"And I get a say in what errands I run and how the money breaks."

"We can talk about that."

"We just did."

"Okay, Roy."

"What's this business you're gonna open?"

"I'm hoping you come work for me. *With* me."

"What is it? The weathervanes?"

"Better," Harvey said. "Home security."

"And my brother?" Roy said. "How secure is he?"

"That all depends on you."

thirty-eight

The mayor sat in the back of the SUV, crawling along the 110 toward Dodger Stadium, and fumed. Evan Crisp was in his usual Zegna get-up, while this afternoon the mayor had on full Dodger regalia. Hat, jersey, jacket, the whole shebang. It was the first game since the quake and he was to throw out the first pitch. Joy Levine thought it might help erase the memory of him diving under the desk. Joy saying that even the people of L.A. couldn't accept a pussy as their mayor. The mayor had spent all morning in the City Hall garage throwing pitches to Marco, his driver, and was now pretty sure that he'd injured his rotator cuff. But all he needed was one good throw, and he had been feeling confident enough when they got word that "Science," one of the kids who whacked Peres, had supposedly called into Tim Conway Jr.'s show on KFI and bragged about starting a new gang called the Vineland Quakers.

"Quakers," the mayor asked. "Like in Pennsylvania?"

Evan said, "I think he's referencing the earthquake."

"Oh, for fuck's sake."

If that wasn't bad enough, someone had already in the last hour tagged the inside of one of the freeway tunnels leading to the stadium with THE SCIENCE MAN! According to Gordy Savage, the LAPD graffiti unit was reporting that similar tags had been popping up all around the city.

The fucking Science Man was on his way to becoming some kind of folk hero.

Why hadn't they picked him up? Gordy had promised him that Kelly Maguire would be able to find him in twenty-four hours and yet here the little shit was calling into KFI. Gordy reminded him that they had picked up one of them—the kid's lawyer already suing the city for violating his civil rights—and another had been shot and killed just that morning. The only one still out there was Science.

Yes, but Science, the mayor wanted to tell him, was the only one he gave a fuck about.

thirty-nine

Science was parked in the C lot three cars down from Mr. Freeze. The game was another hour away and Mr. Freeze had been sitting in his car for the past fifteen minutes. Science was strapped, but knew he couldn't get the gun past security. He thought about the various ways to get around that problem, and finally texted his brother Cole and then a tiny G named Zack Combs.

Zack had moved from North Hollywood to Mount Washington, five minutes from the stadium. Zack beat Cole by ten minutes, and was sitting with Science when Mr. Freeze, St. Louis hat on, got out of his car and headed for Gate 4. Zack opened the door to follow and Science grabbed hold of the kid's jacket and pulled him back.

"Just find out where he's sitting," Science said, "and then hit me back. Don't talk to him. Don't look at him."

Science had purchased from a scalper three tickets up in the nosebleeds. He didn't care about the crap location as the tickets were just to get his ass in the gate. Outside of Mr. Freeze having a VIP box or Dugout Club seats, Science would be pretty much able to follow him most anywhere he went. And if Science still got bumped or bounced, he'd come back outside and wait for the man in his car, do it then.

But that wouldn't be nearly the same as doing it in front of fifty thousand people.

Science would finally be the ghetto star he deserved to be.

Cole texted him from a spot in the K lot, a five-minute walk around half the stadium, then down to the outer rim of parking lots. As soon as Science got in the car, his brother, sitting up front with his lifelong road dog, Mickey, said, "Dude, you in a mothafuckin' shitload of ice."

"Not for long."

"Why didn't you tell me none a this?"

"Keep you clear, bro."

"Who says I wanna be?"

"Well, you in it now."

They got out of the car, helped Cole into his chair, and started for the gate. Security was a breeze. Science and Mickey went through the detector while they ran a wand over the chair-bound Cole. They found nothing on him, gave back his wallet and phone, and waved them all through. The whole thing took maybe forty seconds, the little Raven .32 making the trip undetected, duct-taped to the underside of Cole's wheelchair.

As soon as they were away from the gate, Cole asked, "Now what?"

Science looked at his phone and said, "Dude's Lower Reserve, first base side."

Kelly and Rudy stood at the back of the room, their eyes flicking between several dozen monitors. Looking at the images, it struck Kelly that no part of the stadium had been damaged in the quake or the subsequent aftershocks. Whereas the Memorial Coliseum, six miles away in Exposition Park, had been deemed totally unsafe due to several columns that had either cracked or collapsed completely.

Sketches of Roy Cooper were taped to the walls all around the security office. Kelly assumed that he would disguise himself somehow, so they were all scanning any male face that looked over thirty. After an hour of this, Kelly was starting to get a headache. The stadium was nearly full and she still hadn't seen anyone who even resembled what Rudy was calling *The Button Man from Kansas City*.

It was just about game time and Kelly could hear the announcer say, *Here to sing our national anthem, please rise and give a warm Dodger welcome to international singing sensation, Mr. Justin Beeeeeeeber!*

Rudy said, "He's fucking Canadian."

Kelly could hear people booing.

She watched the kid start to sing the first line, stop, and then start over.

"Awesome."

As the kid murdered the tune, Kelly caught a commotion on one of the middle decks, saw that it was the mayor and his entourage making their way down to the field.

And now to throw out the first pitch, the mayor of Los Angeles, Miguel Santiaaaaaaagooooh!

The applause, if possible, was even more tepid than what had greeted Bieber.

Kelly watched Miguel Santiago start down the steps toward the field, waving to the crowd. At the club level, he stopped to greet a kid in a wheelchair. A made-for-the-cameras moment, the kid was black, pushed by another black kid, both wearing Dodger jerseys. As the kid pushing the chair turned to scan the crowd, Kelly came off the wall and put her face close to the monitor.

"Fuck me," she said. "That's Noel Bennett."

The mayor came down the steps, could hear people shouting his name and immediately felt better.

Miguel! Hey, Miguel!

He waved at the sound of the voices, and saw people ducking and covering their heads with their hands.

Hey, Miguel, where's your desk?

The mayor just smiled through it all. Kept heading down the steps. There was a young black man in a wheelchair at the bottom, parked right in front of the stairs that led down to the field.

"How are you?" the mayor said, and held out his hand, then panicked that the kid might be paralyzed and not able to shake. But the kid grinned and held out his hand and said, "I'm just fine, Mr. Mayor, how are you?"

"Wow. Quite a grip you've got there. You're a damn good shaker."

He saw the camera and instantly regretted whatever had just come out of his mouth. He looked at Evan, who had a smile that said, *Damn good shaker? What a fucking idiot.*

The young man in the chair was saying, "This is my brother Noel." And the mayor instinctively held out his hand to the kid who stood behind the chair.

"Pleasure, Noel."

And the kid smiled and pounded it out with the mayor, who stared back at him, a horrified look on his face, having realized a second too late who he was.

The kid said, "Good to see you, cuz," then turned and saw himself on the Jumbotron and waved to the crowd.

The mayor looked out at the sea of raised cell phones, and then at the giant screen where the image of the kid standing beside him waving to the crowd was sixty feet tall. He moved away as gracefully as he could, turned to Marco, his guard and driver, and started to say something, but Evan had him by the arm and led him down the steps to the field.

Magically a mitt appeared on his left hand. The mayor jogged out to the mound and waved with it to the crowd, the baseball he hadn't realized was there falling from the mitt to the ground in front of him. He snatched it up and looked up to see if he could see Science, but he and the other one in the wheelchair were both gone.

He tried to say his own name, but was drowned out by the crowd saying it for him. So instead he just said over and over, *Throw it straight. Just throw it straight.*

The catcher squatted down and punched his mitt. All set. The mayor put his glove to his chest, then wound up as he had practiced with Marco and threw a slow, high-arcing lob that dropped straight down into the dirt a full ten feet in front of the plate. The mayor could hear the laughter in the stands as the catcher made what the mayor thought was way too big a deal of standing up, stretching, and then walking several long paces toward the mound to retrieve the ball.

At least it went straight.

Kelly was heading down the steps toward where she'd last seen Science and his brother when her cell rang. She saw that it was an unknown number and was about to let it go when it occurred to her that it might be one of the stadium security guys down on the field— they had all been given her and Rudy's numbers—so she picked up.

"Maguire."

A slightly accented voice (*French?*) said, "Did you know that your boy, Roy, one time spent eleven months at Two Rivers? You know what that is, Two Rivers?"

"Who is this?" The crowd was clearing some and she could see Cole Bennett in his wheelchair at the bottom of the stairs, in a row of other disabled souls.

"I'll give you a hint," the man on her phone said. "We used to visit him there sometimes. He said he was hearing voices. His dead daddy was talking to him in the middle of the night."

"You gonna tell me who you are?"

"He even got headaches like the old man used to. But then he got better and came back to work, good as new."

"I'm hanging up now." She saw that Cole was by himself and started looking around, scanning the crowd.

"You won't find him."

Was this guy watching her?

"No matter how hard you look."

"How'd you get this number?"

"It's what we used to do together, Roy and me, get people's numbers. If you know what I mean."

"And now you're a model citizen, offering up your assistance to the police?"

"I'm a baseball fan who happens to know where my old friend is at right now."

"I know where he's at."

"But like I said, you won't find him."

"How do you know?"

"Because he's good."

"I'm pretty good myself."

He laughed. "But I never taught you."

"And in return for this information?"

"Ten thousand will do."

"A bargain."

Another laugh.

She looked around the stadium. "Where are you?"

"Outside Gate 2."

"A skinny black gentleman is going to meet you there in five minutes."

"I'm a skinny white gentleman in a leather coat and sunglasses. I'll be waving a St. Louis pennant."

Kelly said, "Way to blend in," hung up, and texted Rudy. She would have loved to go meet this asshole, but had to find Science. Rudy could sort out this character and get back to her, if there was anything there.

"What's up, Cole?"

Cole turned in his wheelchair and squinted up at her.

"Where's the little ghetto star at?"

"You hollerin' at *me*?"

"Jesus, you really gonna play dumb? Right now? After I just watched the two of you practically dry hump the mayor on the fucking Jumbotron?"

Cole just stared at the field.

"Or maybe you are dumb. Maybe it's no wonder you got shot, you stepped on some Blood's Air J?"

Cole raised his middle finger without looking at her.

A kid came down with a couple of beers and passed one to Cole. She recognized him. "Hey, Mickey. When'd you get out?"

"Month or so ago."

"Good for you. Your PO know you're drinking?"

Neither of them looked at her.

She pointed a finger at Mickey. "You stay put."

She then got up and rolled Cole away.

"Hey, what the fuck, bitch?"

"It's Sergeant Bitch to you." She rolled him into the tunnel, empty now as the game was about to begin, and leaned down and put her mouth to his ear.

"Little bro's gonna get his ass killed, you know that, right?"

"Comes with it."

"That what you told him? That the big brotherly advice you gave him? *Shit happens when you bang?* That what you tell yourself, you roll down your fuckin' ramp every morning?"

"I didn't tell him shit, he's on his own."

"Where'd he go?"

Cole just looked at her.

"You don't tell me, I'm gonna get on the phone, get Mickey violated back to Soledad or wherever the fuck he was, you feel me?"

Cole shrugged. "I don't know where he is."

"Then what are you doing here?"

"Same as all these other folks. Watchin' the game."

"Who's playing?"

He turned and smiled. "Dodgers."

She smiled back. "And?"

He just looked at her. Something in his face, a kind of smug defiance that Kelly had seen so many times on the street, almost always immediately following some bloody bad shit that had gone down. She didn't have time for this. She walked around the chair, grabbed the handles, lifted it straight up, and dumped Cole face-first onto the tunnel floor.

"Motherfuck—"

She kicked him in the ribs, knocking the wind out of him, and flipped the chair all the way over. Two pieces of duct tape dangled from the underside of the seat. She tore one off and stuck it to his forehead. "Tell me, Cole," she said. "What'd you bring him?"

Albert realized that getting into the game wouldn't be a problem; he had passed at least a dozen scalpers already, and had yet to reach the parking kiosks. No, the tricky part would be getting any kind of weapon inside. He thought about it as he inched the Camry forward, the line of cars behind him stretching all the way down to the exit off the 110 freeway.

What was it he used to tell Roy and Bob? If you need a gun, just take one from the person who's trying to shoot you. No one was trying to shoot him, but he knew who might be armed and already inside the stadium. Twenty minutes on her computer, and he had all of her contact information. So why not give her a shout?

The call turned out to be just as fun as he expected. Kelly Maguire was truly someone he wanted to get to know. If only there was some way to do what needed to be done, and then spend a few extra days in Los Angeles with Kelly at her place. Maybe her friend, Erin, could join them. He wasn't sure, though, how all that could work given the little idea he was currently chewing on.

He hadn't been waiting five minutes when he saw a tall African American man, put together in a nice suit, come out of the gate.

Albert watched as the cop's eyes scanned the immediate crowd, finally landed on him. Albert smiled and waved the pennant he'd bought a few minutes earlier.

The cop, looking impatient, made his way over and said, "Turn around." He frisked Albert, took out his wallet, inspected his ID and said, "What can I do for you, Mr. Budin?"

"Boo-dan. It's French."

The cop said, "Really," and then fuck it if he didn't rattle off in perfect French, *I don't give a shit what you are. If you've got something for me, say it now or fuck off. We're kinda busy here.*

"I only talk to the lady cop. What I have to say only gets said to her."

The cop kept looking at him.

Albert said, "Another time then," and turned to go.

"Hang on."

The cop led him through the metal detector. It went off and they frisked him again, and again found nothing.

Albert said, "It's my hip," and then smiled. "Two tours in Iraq."

The security guard ran a wand over Albert, pausing when it chirped over his hip, then sent him through.

Some kid was singing "The Star-Spangled Banner." Albert had always thought it a ridiculous national anthem. It was hard to sing and it was, in the end, about a fucking flag. He much preferred "America the Beautiful." He could sing that one and figured little kids could, too. Even the one down on the field butchering it right now could probably get through it okay.

Albert saw that the tier was relatively empty and figured that now was as good a time as any. He said, "You mind we make a quick pit stop?" and nodded to the men's room they were just now passing.

The cop looked at his watch, and headed for the door.

"Make it quick."

There were only a few fans in here when Albert sidled up to the metal trough and unzipped himself, while the cop went to the sink and ran a pick through his hair. Albert reached in and pulled out the tiny knife taped to the inside of his leg, palmed it in one hand as he then took a leak, careful not to cut off his own cock with it. As the cop came away from the sinks, Albert came away from the trough and bumped into him.

"Excuse me."

The cop stood there, confused, and Albert put his arm around him and led him over to the stalls and sat him down on the commode, reacting to the looks he got with a smile and "Think we got here a little too early."

If anyone had bothered to look down, they would have seen the line of blood running from the cop's trousers to the tile floor. Albert closed the stall door and crammed inside with the cop, who was now shaking and white as the wall behind him. His left leg was soaked with blood.

"The femoral artery," Albert said. "The big one." He then took the cop's gun, badge, and cell phone and put them all in his coat pocket. The cop looked up at him, his face now more gray than anything else, and said, "Don't kill her."

"You just relax," Albert said. "Close your eyes."

Roy watched The Kid warm up. He had picked this seat because of its great sightline straight across the field into the visitor dugout and bullpen. When they introduced the team, The Kid kept his head down. Roy wondered if he wasn't a bit preoccupied, or just focused on breaking the record today. The Dodgers were tough and shutting them out for the needed innings would be nearly impossible. But the Giants and the Brewers were even tougher and The Kid had put both teams to bed without much trouble.

Roy had spent twenty minutes in the car working on his disguise. Not much more than a mustache, a blond wig, and wire-rimmed glasses. The Dodger cap probably would have been enough. He was sitting amongst a group of women in suits "playing hooky" from the office to come see The Kid. They all got up and whistled when the announcer called his name and now had their phones up, trying to get a few shots of him loosening up.

Roy clocked the various security people in his section and hoped he could make it through the game, long enough to see The Kid break the record. What happened after that, Roy had no feelings about one way or the other. Though he had a pretty good idea he would never leave the stadium alive. Looking around it now, breathing in the warm afternoon air as the Dodgers held the Cards to one hit at the top of the first, he thought that he should have moved to L.A. a long time ago.

Roy watched The Kid walk to the mound and kick at the rubber with the toe of his cleat. Roy sensed a slight hush in the crowd. The hometown fans thinking, if their Dodgers were going to lose, better to go down in the record books, even on the other side. The Kid stretched his neck left then right, spit into the dirt, and stood up straight. He stared at the catcher a moment, and then leaned into his windup.

A fastball. Roy could barely see it, but he heard the crack in the catcher's glove all the way up in his seat. He thought he felt the stands reverberate with the sound when he realized it was something else: an aftershock.

A big one. Nearly as big as the initial quake. For a moment, the crowd was silent as together they processed what was happening. Roy watched the pitcher's mound rise up like a new volcano and knock The Kid off his feet. Then the home dugout collapsed, the bench just dropped into a hole, taking the first row of the club section with it. Roy got to his feet as, all at once, fifty thousand people started screaming and running for the exits.

forty

The mayor felt Marco grab him by the back of the shirt and usher him down the steps and onto the field. He turned to see Evan some ways behind them fighting to keep up.

Marco screamed, "Don't worry about him," and shoved the mayor forward toward the first base line. He looked back once more and watched as Evan, struggling down the same steps, suddenly pitched forward onto his face and disappeared beneath the relentless swarm of panicked fans. The mayor lost all sight of him, save a brief glimpse of his soon to be late executive assistant when, during a brief break in the rush—a member of Stadium Security had fired a gun into the air to turn everybody around—Evan somehow managed to sit up, the whites of his eyes visible in a now otherwise red and misshapen face, and reached out with a bloody and broken arm, the gold Rolex Daytona the mayor had bought him after the election the only recognizable thing about him, before the crowd once more trampled him back into the ground.

The mayor felt his arm nearly wrenched from its socket as Marco yanked him further onto the field, relatively safe from any part of the structure that might fall or topple.

He was vaguely aware that Marco was yelling at him. *We need to wait here for the crowd to chill some before we find a way out!*

But the crowd out here was growing, filling the entire field. The mayor could feel Marco being pulled away, but the man held on, and now a sharp bruise was rising on the mayor's biceps where he squeezed to keep him close. There was a violent tug as the crowd surged their way and the mayor was suddenly free of the man's grip.

He watched as his bodyguard and driver of three years fought to get back to him.

Strangely enough, the mayor wasn't panicked. In fact, if anything, he felt a kind of peace and began to wonder if maybe this wasn't the real *way out*. He could vanish. Right now. Like Evan. Well, not exactly like Evan. But he could get eaten up by the crowd and disappear. The Vanishing Mayor. It would be a mystery for the ages.

But surely he would be recognized out there in the world.

Someone in uniform barked into his face, "Keep moving, asshole!"

Maybe not.

The mayor had the sensation of riding a wave as a gate opened at the far end of the field and the crowd surged toward it, carrying him along. He could no longer see Marco and pulled off the Dodger jersey he had on over a black T-shirt as he shuffled forward through the gate. Once free of the stadium, he dropped the jersey on the ground and stayed with the crowd as they fanned out into the parking lots. The mayor kept on walking until he hit Solano Road and followed it all the way into Elysian Park. He paused and looked back toward the stadium, feeling calm for the first time in years.

The mayor stood there a moment, breathing in the night air, and then headed into the park. He had walked maybe a dozen paces when he felt someone's strong grip on his arm.

"Gotcha."

The mayor turned and immediately wanted to cry.

"Jesus, boss," Marco said, the man completely winded from running. "Didn't you hear me yelling?"

Kelly didn't think the kid was half bad. He sang a lot better than Roseanne did, that was for sure. She was there that day at what was then Jack Murphy Stadium, spending the summer with her cousins in San Diego while her parents, in the middle of their divorce, fought over the money from the sale of the avocado farm in Fallbrook. Probably the last time she was at a baseball game.

Cole had finally given Kelly Roy Cooper's section and she was now trying to find his seat when her phone rang.

It was Stadium Security. "Somebody got knifed in the A tier men's room."

"Who?"

"We just got the call, but I wanted to let you know we had to pull some people to secure it."

"Okay."

"Once LAPD gets here, I'll send them back out."

She hung up and located Roy Cooper a few rows down. He was pretty much the lone guy in a sea of women, all of them in suits. Clearly some kind of office *outing*. Cole had warned her about the disguise, but seeing it for herself, Kelly had to admit that she was impressed. She never would have spotted him in the crowd.

It didn't take her long, however, to spot Science, the kid leaning against a cement wall at the top of the tier steps, one row over. Kelly knew Roy wasn't going anywhere, so she decided to go up and grab Science first. She would then hand him off to someone in security, if she could find them.

And where was Rudy?

She would text him as soon as she had Science cuffed and stuffed.

Kelly jogged back up the steps to the tier and walked around to the adjacent row. Science was too busy watching the man Kelly now knew he had come to put down to see her coming. She had to admit she was curious to find out how he planned to pull this off in a stadium full of people. It would be the first question she asked when she had him in the back of her car.

It was either dumb luck or Science had somehow sensed her approach; whatever it was, the kid turned just as Kelly was reaching for him. There was no hesitation as he reached into his coat for what Kelly knew was the little Raven.

She said, "Don't be stupid," and grabbed his wrist and pulled it from his coat, while at the same time twisting it back so that Science winced and went down to his knees in order to keep her from bending it back any further.

She crouched down and smiled at him. "Hi, Science. I've been looking forward to meeting you for a while now."

She pulled the Raven from his coat and held it low.

"Fuckin' Shake," the boy said. "He oughta be stomped for being a general coward."

"Shake didn't give you up. Your brother did."

She watched to see how that would go down. Science wasn't sure what to say. So she smiled and kept on.

"Yeah, just now," she said. "Told me how you snuck the little gat in here on the underside of his wheelchair."

She watched him look away in a feeble attempt at hiding his anger, then leaned close.

"I'm just bummed you're not eighteen, so I could watch them gas your black ass."

He glared back at her a moment and she laughed.

"What, you gonna wolf me now? That the best you can do? You look like someone just took away your Popsicle. But you keep working on it."

He started shouting. "Help me! This lady is hurting me! It's that crazy pig who beats up nigger kids!"

She cranked on his wrist, said, "Shut up, Noel," and started to haul him to his feet.

But he wasn't about to stop now. "Ow! Man, she's hurting me! Please! Somebody help me!"

Kelly looked around and saw that at least a dozen people now had their cell phones out and were recording the struggle. Some were shouting at her to let the kid go. She turned away from the crowd, put Science up against the wall, and reached for her handcuffs. The next thing she knew, the wall wasn't there anymore and she was lying flat on her back. And now people were stepping on her. She sat up and got knocked back down again. After a few seconds of this, she finally managed to grab ahold of someone's foot and pull herself upright. It seemed as if everyone in the stadium was now running.

She no longer had the Raven and looked around for Science. She saw him fighting through the crowd to get down the steps to where Roy had been. Half the crowd was going up the stairs to the exits up on the tier and half were trying to get down onto the field. Roy, she saw, was among the latter.

Kelly started to fight her way down, walking directly down over the seats against the tide of people walking up. She could see Roy already on the field fighting his way toward the visitors' dugout. She saw Science go over the rail and drop.

It took her another few minutes before she fell up against the same rail, felt the bruises on her ribs and cheek—where she'd just taken a wild elbow—as she leaned out to look for either Science or Roy Cooper.

She saw Science first and watched as he slowly made his way to within a few feet of Roy Cooper. His hat was now off and so was the wig, both presumably lost in the chaos. There was a muzzle flash, but no sound, the high-pitched shouts and cries of the panicked fans drowning out anything else. Roy Cooper spun around, rocked, seemed to see Science, but then, somehow, turned back and continued on his way. Kelly watched Science move to follow him when another kid, this one a beefy Hispanic, someone she didn't recognize, grabbed him by the hair and then she lost sight of all of them. She then did as Science had, climbed over the rail and jumped down to the field.

Science wasn't afraid. This was *supposed* to happen. He knew that now. Like the aftershock that hit during his long walk two nights before. This was a sign: it was all his. He just had to pay attention, he had to watch. And right now he was watching Mr. Freeze make his way down to the field.

Fuck that lady pig. She distracted him. But Mother Nature came through and distracted *her*. Now once more in possession of the Raven, Science shoved his way through the crowd. Nobody knew where to go, so people just ran in every direction. Science saw a guy in a suit, his head crushed to a bloody pulp, blocking the stairs down to the field, so he leaped over the rail and dropped the fifteen feet to the ground. No way he was gonna get *his* head fuckin' stoved in and stepped on by any mob.

Mr. Freeze was making his way over to the crushed visitors' dugout. Science could see St. Louis players stumbling out of the rubble. Some of the other players and coaches were now helping to pull out those who were trapped. People who had been sitting in the club seats above lay on the ground waiting for medical attention, some bleeding, some crawling, some still as stone. Science clocked one dude still sitting in his seat, staring straight ahead.

All of the security people were busy trying to keep some kind of perimeter, shoving back against the shocked people who ran at them, forcing them to find another way out. Mr. Freeze was one of those turned around, but he didn't leave. Instead, he was trying to see into the rubble. He was looking for somebody.

Science started to make his way over, the Raven now pointing at the back of Mr. Freeze, but down at his side. He was going to poke him in the spine with the gun, say, "Remember me?" and then shoot him, put him in a fucking chair for the rest of his life. If he lived. This was an idea he had come up with while he was pushing Cole into the stadium.

But he was barely a dozen feet away from his target when he felt someone grab him by the hair.

"Hey, mothafuck—"

That was as far as he got when the damn gun went off.

It was hard to hear the shot over the panicked clamor, but he could see Mr. Freeze spin around and paw at his leg. The second time in a fucking week that he had shot someone by accident.

Science lost sight of the man as his head was yanked down toward the ground behind him. He reached up to grab at the person holding him, when a brown face got right up close to his.

"Hey, *vatos,* it's the Science Man!"

Science couldn't recognize the upside-down face, or the other two that were now on either side of it looking down at him, but he knew from their ink that all three were members of the Alley Locos.

They were pumped up and broad in the shoulder, and as they hauled him upright, Science could feel something sharp jammed up against his ribs. One of them got right up to his ear and hissed, "You feel my little *filero* there, homes?"

Science nodded, the pain from the knifepoint making his eyes water.

"We gonna get the fuck out, go for a ride."

Science was having trouble accepting this latest development. It couldn't be happening. He was too close. He was *there*. He felt himself fall into a kind of shock, as for the first time since he had shot Frank Peres, Science realized that he might actually get dead. For some reason, this possibility had never occurred to him before now. He was too busy imagining his future to pay attention to trivial matters such as who he may or may not have pissed off. A real leader doesn't concern himself with those things. It's not about being liked, it's about being respected. Isn't that what Cole had always said?

He wasn't feeling much respect as the three Locos now dragged his ass through the crowd, everyone too lost in their own panic to pay any attention to them.

There was no fighting them. First of all, they had the Raven. They took it from his hand the second he fired the shot. Second, there was no softness in the arms that held him. These were three bodies made of lumber, all built in some prison out in Lancaster. Science couldn't move. They were, he realized, not dragging him, but *carrying* him.

Within minutes they were at a maintenance gate that security had just unlocked at the end of the field, and then they were moving through the chaotic parking lot.

"You claiming Vineland now?" one of them asked as they dodged moving cars. This one had the number 13 inked on his forehead and on each cheek. Years ago, Science's oldest brother, Guy, had once told him 13 stood for the letter "M," which meant that this one was Mexican Mafia. They each had several 13s and Ms on their faces. One of them had a black hand on each cheek. The letter "M" inside one, the letters "AL" inside the other. The third was covered head to toe with ink, but the eagle and the snake on his neck were what Science kept staring at. What that eagle was doing to that snake was pretty much what Science expected to be his own fate in a few short minutes.

They carried him to the outer reaches of the lot. Horns were honking all around them and the three of them laughed at the sound of drivers backing into one another in an effort to get the fuck out of there.

When Science saw that they were leading him toward a black van, he struggled comically against the inked-up girders that held him. They laughed as they put him up against the side while they checked each other for the fucking key.

I gave it to you.

No, homes, you have it.

It's not there.

While they went on like this, one of them, the one with the Raven, put the muzzle of the gun behind Science's ear.

"You shoot Frank Peres, Negro? That's some balls. Shoot an unstrapped old man like a dog."

He could hear them laugh.

"And now you want Vineland and what else? What else can we give you?"

Science couldn't stop shaking. Just feeling this one's breath on his neck made Science's heart beat so fast, it was vibrating.

"You ever been to Mexico?" the third one went on. "We think maybe we should send you down there, meet some people. You can tell them all about how you want to take away their business. Tell them how badass you are."

More laughter.

Science felt his bladder go and the dude backed away, shouted *Fucking panocha!* and backhanded Science across the face. Science's legs went out from under him. He tried to sit down, but the strong hands held him up.

One of them stood on the hood of a Nissan parked beside them and looked at the line of cars.

It was clear they were going to be there awhile.

So the question became "Walk him down to the park or put him in the back?"

They decided on the latter and lifted him into the back of the van. Shoved him on top of a damp mattress that smelled of blood and smoke and were climbing in after him when Science saw one of them pause and go stiff.

He could hear her say in Spanish, *"Te pego un tiro en la cabeza."* *I will shoot you in the head.*

They all turned around and he saw her standing there, badge around her neck, gun pointed their way. She nodded to the one holding the Raven. "Put that on the ground."

He just looked at her like he didn't understand.

She said, "*Now's* good."

He then looked at the gun like he was thinking about what it was used for when she shot him in the knee and he dropped the pistol and fell to the asphalt screaming.

She said *"Gracias"* and then, as one of the other two went to help the one on the ground, "Leave him."

She gestured with her gun. "Look around. It's Armageddon. I can shoot you both and say you were trying to steal that Maxima. In this situation, that's looting and I'm good as gold."

She wasn't positive that was even correct and could see that they were both figuring out what move to make, so she said, "I'm gonna assume you're both armed, I really don't give a shit. The three of us, I'm sure, will meet some other time over some other beef and we can shoot it out then. Right now I just want the kid."

"So do we."

"And I don't blame you. But the fact is, if you wanna kill him, you'll have to get him in jail. He'll be there soon enough."

"Not if homes can't hold his mud and they wrap him up, send him to Nebraska or someplace."

"They do that," she said, "I'll personally send you his new name and address."

Kelly waited with Science while the two of them hauled their wounded *compadre* into the van and joined the endless line of cars. She could feel the stadium calm down now that people understood that they were alive, and the atmosphere shifted from panic to anger when those same people found themselves once more stuck in horrendous L.A. traffic.

Cops and EMTs were crawling all over the now otherwise empty stadium. The place had cleared out that fast, and like a receding tidal wave, only the mess was left behind. So far eight dead and several dozen injured according to the security radio she had clipped to her belt.

She looked down at Science sitting at her feet, hands cuffed at his back, head ducked, crying.

Kelly, overcome with a feeling that she couldn't quite define, sat down beside the kid and put her arm around him. She took a deep breath as he then leaned into her and began to sob loudly. Not so much sob as howl. She could feel him shaking and wrapped her other arm around him as well. They sat like this for a full ten minutes before her phone rang.

. . .

"Somebody knew right where to poke. Got him in the big trunk. That alone would have bled him out, but they cut his throat just to be sure."

Rudy was sitting on the toilet, but he had tipped to the side, one cheek was against the stall, his mouth open wide in some kind of grotesque frozen laugh.

Kelly felt sick.

"Do we have to leave him there?"

"We're waiting on the Homicides."

"Where are they?"

"Stuck in the same shit everyone else is."

"At least cover him up."

She walked to the security office and tried to hold it together. The aftershock had scared her, but seeing Rudy in that stall had put her into a trance. She couldn't feel a thing, yet she knew that she felt everything. Rudy was the closest thing Kelly Maguire had to family. What was she supposed to do now?

Find whoever did that to him. That's what.

For the next hour, she watched footage from eight different cameras. There was Rudy out front of Gate 4 talking to someone. Kelly got a better look at the guy as they went through security. Tall. Dark glasses. The face. She knew that face. There they are again going into the men's room. *Jesus, Rudy, how could you be so stupid?* Now the guy was coming out of the john by himself. He put a hand to his back—probably checking to make sure the gun he'd just taken off Rudy was snug—then looked up at the camera and . . . *Did he just smile?*

The Camry. He'd been driving behind her. He had laughed at her when she gave that stupid bitch shit for not merging. Then there he was again at the high school. How long had he been following her? *Who the fuck is he?* Somebody they busted? No. She kept a file on the hot ones. Who was this guy?

Whoever he was, he was now running around with Rudy's gun and badge.

Kelly's phone rang. Erin. She let it go. Wanted to think about what this guy's next move might be. With the aftershock, the guy could have gotten out of here without any kind of problem. It would take at least a day or two to go through all of the parking lot footage. And even then, he would have to be in a car they could read the make and model, if not the tag. And the car was probably stolen anyway. No way this guy would be in his own car, he was a pro.

Not unlike another pro who had recently come to town.

Was this guy working with Roy? Helping him get clear and clean up his mess? That made no sense. Why go after the cops? That only makes things hotter, unless Rudy found something he shouldn't have on his little field trip to Missouri. Kelly had to wonder, though, if this guy had been following her for the past two days, why was she still breathing?

Why Rudy and not her?

She stood and looked out at the empty stadium. Trash and abandoned clothing and chair backs were everywhere. The place already felt haunted. She shivered, not from the cold, but from the certainty that the person who slit open her closest friend was still here.

Just outside the players' entrance, at the far end of the now empty VIP lot, Joe Mills, aka The Kid, was losing his shit. His fellow players had already split and were at that moment onboard their luxury coach back to LAX. Joe refused to go with them and was now arguing with—per his latest contract—his personal bodyguard. Joe couldn't accept that the game was over and that he, with his freshly injured right shoulder, was done pitching for the season. He couldn't leave the stadium. Not yet. He couldn't face the interviews, or listen to Mike Lupica's wry take on his misfortune. The fact that he was a historical *almost* was just too much to bear.

The bodyguard, a tall, blond ex–Special Forces type dressed—improbably, given the circumstances—in an immaculate and still perfectly pressed suit, gently tried to lead Joe Mills by his good elbow to a black Escalade parked a few feet away from the locker room door.

Mills said, "Just give me another minute," and pulled free. He turned back for the building and nearly ran right into Roy, who, now standing directly in front of the door to the building, seemed to have appeared out of nowhere.

"Sorry, buddy," Joe Mills said, "I'd give you an autograph, but as you can see . . ." and turned so that Roy could better see his wrapped right arm in the sling.

The bodyguard saw that Roy was a bit unsteady, caught the blood on his pants, and said, "Sir, the medics are all on the other side."

Roy had waited a long time for this moment. He had thought about exactly what he would say should he ever find himself in the presence of The Kid. But, instead, he just froze.

Joe Mills said, "Could you please move? I really need to get inside."

Roy stepped aside and anxiously watched as Joe Mills reached for the door. He could feel the bodyguard's hand on his own shoulder.

"You need to go now, sir."

Joe Mills tried the door and said, "Fuck me, it's locked."

Roy said, "You'll get another shot at the record."

Joe Mills said, "Yeah. I'm sure I will," then nodded to the bodyguard. "Lance," he said, "you got a key?"

The bodyguard shook his head and Joe Mills started hammering the side of his fist on the metal door. "Can somebody open this door please?"

Joe Mills saw that Roy was still standing there and said, "Buddy, I don't wanna be rude," and then gave the bodyguard a look: *Will you please deal with this guy?*

"Sir, please, step away." The bodyguard was now pulling Roy away from his client.

Roy reached out, grabbed Joe Mills by the good arm, and said, "I'm so proud of you, Captain."

Joe Mills looked at him in disgust and said, "Fucking hell, Lance."

The bodyguard reached out and barred Roy around the neck with his forearm, but then turned as the metal door opened behind him.

Joe Mills said, "About fucking time," and started forward, but abruptly stopped when he saw the gun come up, and instinctively turned to his bodyguard just in time to see half the man's head disappear in a red mist.

Roy stepped away, now covered in the man's blood, and stared at Albert, not believing that he was now seeing him standing there, right in front of him. Even when Albert smiled and said, "The ghost of Christmas Past."

Joe Mills, like most people unaccustomed to such close and immediate violence, was shaking, rooted to the spot. His expression was
more confused than horrified. Roy wanted to reach out and steady
him, but Albert had already grabbed Joe by the bad arm and now
had the gun pointed at the pitcher's stupefied face.

"Let's all go inside and talk, shall we?"

The empty locker room looked much like the empty stadium. Dis-
carded clothing and trash were everywhere. There was a foot-wide
crack in the shower room wall. The lights were still on as were the
three televisions mounted in the ceiling. Albert and The Kid followed behind Roy as he stepped over a pile of towels that seemed
to be soaked in blood, and sat down heavily on a bench. He looked
again and saw that the towels were covering the body of a stadium
security guard. Another guard lay dead beside the door that led to
another corridor and then the field. Both had their throats cut.

While this part of the stadium seemed to have been abandoned,
Roy knew it wouldn't be long before they had company. Cops and
other first responders had probably already begun a sweep in search
of the injured and the criminally opportunistic. The minute Albert
heard them coming, he would certainly kill both Roy and The Kid.

Roy had no gun, and there wasn't much chance he could take
Albert's away. He was already feeling weak from the new bullet in
the back of his leg and didn't think that he could even stand up now
that he had sat down. He wasn't sure that he could stay awake long
enough to keep Albert talking. And Albert would certainly have a
lot to talk about, but there was also a good chance that he would
shoot The Kid right away to kick off the conversation.

Roy watched him shove Joe Mills down onto the opposite bench.

"You're not to move or speak unless I give you permission."

The Kid stared at the body at Roy's feet, looked up at Roy with a
face as white as the towels once were.

Albert moved aside a dirty uniform tossed haphazardly into one
of the open wooden cubbies and then leaned against the built-in
drawers below it. For several moments, he looked back and forth
from Roy to Joe Mills, studying the two of them.

"I don't see it," Albert finally said to Roy. "He looks nothing like you."

Joe Mills sat there, clutching his bad arm trying to make sense of what was happening.

"What is he talking about?"

Albert came off the locker and grabbed Joe Mills by the hair, pulled his head back and put the gun under his chin.

"Once again," Albert said. "You're not to move or speak unless I give you permission. Is that clear?"

"I don't understand. Who are—"

Albert pulled harder. "Is that clear?"

Joe nodded. Roy could see tears in his eyes.

"Leave him alone, Al. You want me. I'm right here."

Albert turned to Roy.

Roy said, "I'm sure you've thought about how you're gonna do it."

"It's all I've thought about."

"Well," Roy said and spread his hands. "Here I am."

Albert looked down at Joe Mills and Roy knew that he was thinking about pulling the trigger.

"What are you doing," Albert said, "wasting your time with this one?" He let go of The Kid and said, "You think your baby brother will want to hang out with you, wave to you in the stands, talk about you with Diane Sawyer?"

Joe said, "I'm an only child."

Albert slapped him in the face. "Shut the fuck up."

"Go ahead, guy," Joe Mills said. "Shoot me. Shoot Joe Mills and see what happens to you." For an instant, Roy could see his mother's defiant face and gesture.

Albert looked at him and began to laugh. In the old days, that would have been the moment Albert shot him and said something like "*That's* what happens."

Roy said quickly, "Let him go, Al, he's got nothing to do with any of this."

But Albert wouldn't turn away from Joe Mills.

"Seriously, why save this cunt's life? Why do you even care about him anymore?" Albert poked Joe Mills with the gun. "He's a spoiled prick. All these people, some of them trampled to death. All he's worried about is his fucking *record*." Albert then put the gun to his injured arm, and said, "I should shoot it off, and then beat him to death with it."

"Al."

"I was all you had, Roy."

"You saw to that."

"I was certainly more of a brother to you than him."

Roy said, "You were."

That got Albert looking at him.

"For a long time."

Albert released Joe and stepped back. He looked as if he was about to say something, but then turned away, stared off, and slipped into some kind of daydream.

It was quiet while Albert thought about whatever it was had just caught hold of him; the only sound, the whir of jets in the whirlpool tub, which, in all of the commotion, had been left running.

Roy caught Joe looking at the door, thinking about whether or not he could make it. Joe's eyes met Roy's and Roy shook his head. *You won't.*

Out of nowhere, Albert said, "Did I tell you about the time this fox got into the slaughterhouse?"

"No," Roy said, "but I'd rather you just shot me and got it over with than have to listen to another second of your bullshit."

"It was just a baby," Albert continued. "A *kit* they call them. The mothers are *vixens,* I love that."

Roy felt himself slipping and forced himself to sit up straight. No matter what, he had to keep upright.

"Anyway, this little fox somehow gets into the slaughterhouse and runs onto the cutting floor. Everyone starts chasing it, trying to kill it with their knives. But this one butcher, a Guatemalan—Modesto was his name, but we all called him Stu—he wants to *save* it. He starts yelling at everyone to stop trying to kill it. So we all back off and watch as Stu starts to chase after it with a burlap bag. It was quite a thing to see a man in a bloody butcher's apron trying to *save* this animal, in a fucking *slaughterhouse*. Needless to say the irony was lost on him. He starts shouting for everyone to stand still, but of course no one in a slaughterhouse is allowed to ever stand still. So we all had to keep working while Stu chased the fox, until finally the poor man slips and falls against the Hide Puller and the chain cuts him in half." Albert ran the muzzle of the gun across his chest. "Right through here." He then shook his head and said, "Was the strangest thing I ever saw."

They sat there a moment, Albert and Roy looking at one another until Joe couldn't take it anymore and said, "What happened to the fox?"

Albert shrugged. "I can't remember," and then smiled at Roy. "And that's the point."

Roy said, "Whatever you say, Al."

"I tried to save you," Albert went on, "and look what happened to me. Danny Leone tried to save you, and look what happened to him. Or the other way, you try to save your daddy and look what happened to him. You try to save the old man in the alley and look what happened to a lot of fucking people. And now you're gonna save *this* asshole." Albert laughed. "I'd say that your baby brother's a lot safer with anyone but you."

Roy saw that Joe Mills was staring at him and Roy wondered if maybe he somehow understood. Even so, it was so late in the day that it no longer mattered. Joe had become something, just as Roy had, that Roy could no longer recognize. Roy knew, had probably always known, that they had stopped being brothers the night Roy left the house in that squad car. His mother had been right about one thing: that should have been, for everybody's sake, the last time they saw each other.

Roy pushed off the bench, shakily stood up straight, and faced Albert. "What do you wanna do now?"

Albert said, "It's not what I *want* to do, Roy."

"What's your plan?"

"We all die together. One big happy family."

"Okay. Let's do it."

The Kid said, "Please, I'm not a part of whatever this is."

Albert shot him twice. Both bullets hit him high, in what had been his good shoulder, and spun him into the locker behind him. The Kid slipped to the floor, his legs still draped over the bench. He struggled to sit up, but then gave up and stared at Roy. His eyes already heavy.

Roy said to him, "Keep your eyes open. Stay awake."

Albert poked Roy with the gun. The silencer was hot and burned his chest.

"We were brothers."

"Yes."

"Say it."

"We were."

"And if you knew I was alive?"

"I would have done the same thing you have," Roy said. "I would have come for you."

Albert nodded.

"I don't feel anything for anyone," Roy said. "That way no one can hurt me, isn't that right?"

"I'm pretty sure I taught you that one."

Roy said, "You taught me everything," and felt his legs buckle. Albert reached out with both hands to catch him. Roy could feel the silencer under his arm, burning his ribs.

Albert put his mouth to his ear.

"You're already done," he said, "so I'm going to shoot you in the heart now, but then I'm going to take your little brother out of here, and play with him somewhere else."

Albert pushed Roy away and once more put the gun to Roy's chest but then froze. His expression changed as he looked down and saw his little knife was now in Roy's hand.

"The gastric artery," Roy said.

Albert ducked his chin and saw the blood that poured out of a deep wound in his stomach.

Albert looked up at Roy, started to say something when Roy's hand reached out and brushed past Albert's neck, left to right.

"You were a great teacher, Al."

Albert's head leaned to one side in a mist of blood and he fell back into the open cubby. Roy stepped forward then, pulled the gun from Albert's hand and shot him in the heart.

Roy considered Albert, making sure he was done before he turned to see Joe Mills staring at him with the disgusted look of someone who had just seen one animal take down another.

He flinched as Roy moved to him and sat him up.

"I'm not going to hurt you."

Roy grabbed a couple of towels and wrapped them around his shoulder.

"Hold on to these."

Joe just looked at him.

"You're gonna be okay, but you have to stay awake."

Joe Mills grabbed hold of the towels and stared up at Roy. "Who the fuck are you?"

Roy could hear a door open somewhere and now voices somewhere down the corridor that led to the stadium. He stood up and listened. Someone with a radio. And another voice he recognized.

He would tell her everything, another time.

He looked down at Joe Mills, said, "I'm Roy Cooper," and went out the other door.

forty-one

After an hour of walking, Roy still had no idea where he was. He kept stumbling in the dark and even fell down a couple of times. For a while he could hear the freeway up above him somewhere and followed that. He crossed the L.A. River on a footbridge. He watched a mattress and a bicycle float down the shallow cement waterway. He wasn't sure how much longer he would remain conscious, but he kept going.

He crossed a wide boulevard that had no structures or business of any kind along it, and soon found himself in tall weeds. He walked for another half mile until he was finally confronted by a barbed wire fence.

It seemed impossible to go around, slightly less so to climb over, so he began to pull himself up the chain link, one painful step at a time. Was twenty minutes to get to the top, another fifteen to get through the barbed wire. He cut himself on both arms before he was able to half climb, half fall to the dry dirt on the other side. He lay on his back awhile, then once more got up and resumed walking.

Soon, he felt large rectangular shapes all around him. Giant iron boxes. It took a few moments to realize that he was walking through a field of trains. Hundreds of them. Rows upon rows of empty freight cars. Roy could see the glass towers of downtown L.A. all lit up ahead of him. He followed a set of tracks for another half hour. Every now and then, he thought he saw the movement of another man out here—a vagrant or the like, he figured, sleeping in the cars. But when one of the men played a flashlight into the cab of an engine, Roy caught the tin badge and uniform of a security guard, so he kept his distance.

At a certain point, his injured leg just gave out and he sat down right where he was on the track. He wanted to curl up and go to sleep, but a figure was walking toward him. He first thought it was the guard, but after a moment, he realized it was a woman.

As she got closer, he saw that it was his mother.

He watched her approach, and wondered why she had become so small. Maybe it was the cancer. Roy certainly felt a lot smaller this past year. And then he saw that she was black.

Now Roy was confused. Was he dreaming?

She stopped in front of him and asked, "Are you all right?"

Roy reached up to her. She took his hand and sat down on the tracks beside him. Roy tried to speak, but he no longer had any voice. She put her arms around his chest and pulled him close to her.

"It's all right," she said. "What's your name?"

"You know," he whispered.

She started to gently rock him and said, "Mine's Ruth Ann."

Roy felt the ground rumble once more, thought it was another aftershock and started to panic. He reached for the rails and tried to push himself up, but she held on to him.

"It's okay, sweetie, it's just a train, on the other side."

Roy saw it then, outside the yard, sounding its horn and moving away from Union Station. Somehow, even with the distance, Roy could still feel its power in the rails beneath him. And for the first time in a long time, Roy felt afraid and began to shake.

She must have sensed this and pulled his head back to her chest, rested her chin on top.

"It's all right, sweetie."

Roy could feel her breath in his hair. He closed his eyes and allowed her to resume rocking him back and forth.

"I got you," she said. "I got you."

Acknowledgments

I've had three great teachers in my life, and Cathy Colman was one of them. It was in the early nineties, while sitting with a dozen other creative souls in Cathy's warm bungalow in Pacific Palisades, that I began first working on this novel. I had been writing screenplays for ten years and was already bored out of my skull. I had written ninety or so pages when I woke up one morning and realized that somehow my wife and I had had three kids seemingly overnight. I set the book aside to focus once more on my day job.

In 2000, I was looking for someone to help me do research on oil workers in Mongolia, for a film that needs no mention, when I met the legendary researcher Mimi Munson. At the time, Mimi had been, among other things, triple-checking the buttons on the uniforms for accuracy on the film *Master and Commander*. Somehow during our first meeting we got to talking about street gangs in L.A., and the book was born again.

I'm forever grateful to Mimi for her meticulous research here, as well as for her invaluable contributions to everything I've written since our collaboration began, fifteen years ago. She truly is my secret weapon.

Further gratitude is extended to my old friend Jamal Joseph for his insights into the worlds of gangs, juvenile prison camps, and the young kids caught up in both. His own experience and history were invaluable to me and, as such, can be found all over the pages you've just read.

My editor, Peter Gethers, has read these pages more times than I can count. His gentle nudges and spot-on suggestions have not only made the book significantly better but have also no doubt saved me greater embarrassment. All I can say is that I'm lucky to have sat down next to him at dinner all those years ago. Luckier still to have him as a friend.

There are many others, including Sonny Mehta, whose faith in me continues to baffle, as well as my literary agent, Andrew Wylie, who has far more important clients, yet still somehow manages the patience to answer what I'm sure are the dumbest questions he hears on any given day. Bless you both.

Speaking of agents, I cannot go a foot further without mentioning the cool and classy Beth Swofford, who has helped me fashion a film career that is somehow now going on thirty-one years. While Beth occasionally protects me from the bad guys, she far more often protects me from myself, a nearly impossible gig, as you have probably gathered.

I sincerely hope that my father, Barry Frank, who unlike Roy's father was a real pilot for Pan-American Airlines, will read this tale and see that I was actually listening when he shared his knowledge of all things winged, particularly his words of wisdom regarding the art of the preflight. He was a rock star in that uniform. Thanks, Dad and Mom, for all of your love and patience, and for not being psychopaths.

Finally, my three kids, Sophia, Lukas, and Stella, along with my wife, Jennifer, have for many years put up with a level of madness, mania, and interference on my part that no one should ever have to deal with. I can only hope that your certain knowledge that my love for all of you is constant and unbounded is somehow mitigating. It's been a lot of fun so far. For me, anyway.

October 18, 2015
New York City